SOME FARAWAY PLACE

ALSO BY LAUREN SHIPPEN

The Infinite Noise
A Neon Darkness

THE BRIGHT SESSIONS

SOME FARAWAY PLACE

Lauren Shippen

TOR TEEN
A TOM DOHERTY ASSOCIATES BOOK
NEW YORK

SOME FARAWAY PLACE

A Tor Teen Book
Published by Tom Doherty Associates
120 Broadway
New York, NY 10271

www.tor-forge.com

Tor® is a registered trademark of Macmillan Publishing Group, LLC.

The Library of Congress Cataloging-in-Publication Data
is available upon request.

ISBN 978-1-250-29757-0 (hardcover)
ISBN 978-1-250-29758-7 (ebook)

First Edition: September 2021

Printed in the United States of America

0 9 8 7 6 5 4 3 2 1

For Mom and Dad—

For trusting in my dreams and teaching me to follow them

You have always been superheroes to me

December ??, 2016 (I assume)

Dear Mark,

I've been here, in this place, this prison, for god knows how long. A month? Maybe more? They kept me unconscious—in a coma—for a few weeks and I've been awake now for . . . well, at least a week, I think. And, according to her, to Director Wadsworth, they're going to keep me here. To make sure I heal. What a crock of shit.

Wadsworth also said you brought me here. I know that's not true. I know you wouldn't do that.

But the whole thing's . . . hazy. Is this what you felt like, when you were here? Like time was slipping through your fingers, like you were existing outside of it all? Existing outside yourself?

Everything hurts and I'm fucking handcuffed. That's how I know you didn't bring me here. It had to have been them—Dr. B. and Sam, the people who love you so much and hate me more. You would have known what this place would do to me and you wouldn't subject anyone to that. Not even your worst enemy. Not even me.

I should have listened better when you talked about it.

I don't know why I'm even writing this like the AM will let me have a pen pal—even though they're the ones that gave me the marker and paper, like they're waiting for a confession to appear. I know that they'll probably read anything I write down. So I'll keep my escape plans in my head, just in case.

For you AM lackeys who read this when the drugs kick back in . . . that was a joke.

I know I'm not getting out of here alive.

I

EMPTINESS

AUGUST 24TH, 2016

There's something in the corner. Something enormous and *breathing*. Air rattling through its lungs, claws scraping the floor of this deep and dark void. Something hides. Something waits.

Every night is exactly the same and also totally unpredictable. I fall asleep suddenly and get dropped into an empty, endless space and then . . . nothing. I stand in that void, changeless and infinite, never knowing when I'm going to wake up again. *If* I'm going to ever wake up again. I always do, obviously, but when I'm in that space, it feels real. Like that's where I live now and I'm no longer in control of waking up and going back to my *actual* life. Which, you can imagine, is pretty anxiety inducing!!

I don't know why the doctors thought keeping a dream journal would help me. "Doctors." Who am I trying to impress here? It was a high school nurse. Despite the fact that my *own mother* is a nurse, I went to the nurse at a school I don't even go to anymore to talk about the fact that I'm sleeping so much—too much—but never feeling rested, my head full of strange, as-real-as-life dreams, and he suggested keeping a journal.

"It's most likely anxiety," he said, as I sat on the sticky plastic chair in his un-air-conditioned office.

"What?" I said, "I'm getting so anxious I'm passing out?"

This seems like a dubious diagnosis to me, but then again, my idea of medical intervention is holding up my bleeding hand until it stops and julienning single-handed so that the sous chef doesn't yell at me.

"You're in the workforce now," the nurse went on. "That's a very stressful transition."

"High school was stressful." I snorted. "A restaurant kitchen is spa-like compared to this place. I don't *feel* more anxious than I was before."

He just smiled at that sadly and patted my knees. A little patronizing, but I'm the nineteen-year-old who went to her old high school because I'm . . . taking too many unplanned naps? So . . .

Wasn't as bad as it would have been if I had gone straight to my parents. My mom would have a million things to say about my lifestyle and "those restaurant hours aren't good for you, why can't you just *consider* going to college" but that wouldn't even be the worst part. No, if I tell my mom and dad that I'm having an unusually difficult time staying awake, they'll make me go see *their* doctors. Their special doctors. And I just don't want a bunch of people poking and prodding at me to see if I burst into flames. I'm nearly twenty—if I were Atypical, we'd know by now. Or my mom would have had a vision about it. *Something* would have happened. But no, instead I have to be the ONE person in my family with a normal human ailment. And I just couldn't stand the disappointed looks when the Atypical doctors tell my parents I just have extreme anxiety or narcolepsy or whatever other boring non-superpowered thing I might have.

So we'll give this dream journal thing a shot.

There's a door in the middle of the void. It isn't shaped like a door, doesn't have a handle or a frame, but I know that's what it is. Light seeps through the cracks around its curved edges and I can feel a breeze, crisp and clean, flowing through from the other side. I walk toward it, my feet tracking over something solid, even if there's no floor beneath my feet, wanting to see what's on the other side.

The light fades and I wake up.

AUGUST 27TH, 2016

Describing dreams is . . . hard. Not to mention, usually mind-numbingly boring, even if the only person you're describing them to is yourself. The edges of that void are getting clearer with each sleep. But trying to picture it—the look of the place, the way it makes me feel—is like trying to catch light in my hands.

Writing has never exactly been my strength. Neither has talking, if I'm honest. I'm at my best in the kitchen, moving silently through my routine, or having orders barked at me by Chef and frantically prepping the mise en place. Restaurant communication is the kind of talking I can get behind—efficient, straightforward, with no expectations around "politeness" or "socializing."

It's not that I'm an antisocial person, it's just that I'd much rather spend my time laser-focused on mastering a brunoise or getting the perfect rise on dinner rolls than trading stories with a bunch of people I'm squeezed into a kitchen with day after day. I meant it when I told the nurse that a high-paced restaurant environment was more relaxing than high school. I was never into the "school" part of school very much—too active and impatient to sit and focus on a lecture or a test—and I barely talked to the other students, too afraid of being made fun of for being chubby and gay or, even worse, somehow revealing my family's secret. To my classmates' credit, I never was teased for anything. I mostly wasn't noticed at all.

Sometimes it feels like that in my family—I skate by unnoticed except on the rare days, like today, when my mom takes TOO much notice of my life choices.

"I just wish you would save *some* of that hyper-focused energy for things unrelated to food," she'd said as I was cooking dinner tonight (last night? it's 3 a.m., so whatever).

"But I like food," I said, hoping that'd be enough to end this conversation. It wasn't.

"You don't only like food," she said and I braced myself for a list. "You like rollerblading and Lord of the Rings and girls."

"Oh my god, Mom, you're making me sound like an eleven-year-old boy." I had to speak up to be heard over the sizzle of the metric ton of wet spinach I'd just dumped into the hot pan in front of me, dampening the delicious smell of garlic already in the pan.

"There's nothing wrong with your interests." She sniffed.

"I know that." I rolled my eyes. "But none of those things translate to a career. I'm not going to be a professional rollerblader or *Silmarillion* scholar or . . . well, I guess I *could* translate liking girls into a career . . ." I mumbled.

"Rose!" she gasped, trying her best to sound scandalized, even though my mom loves a saucy joke. "You're spending too much time with those edgy restaurant people."

"Mom, no one has *ever* called Milton *edgy*," I said. Milton, despite the vaguely pretentious one-word name and gold lettering on the windows, was less Michelin-star and more "old man Boston supper club." The menu hasn't changed in a thousand years and we don't get a lot of foodies in, so it isn't exactly cutthroat. The fact that I'm allowed to do meal prep at all, as a teenager with no formal training, is proof of that.

"Inappropriate jokes aside," she said, "when was the last time you went on a date?"

"Whenever it was, I distinctly remember it prompting a conversation about you staying out of my love life," I muttered. The memory of looking my mom straight in the eye and asking her to back off still makes my skin crawl. Usually evasion and deflection are the best modes of escape with my family, but some things require a stronger hand. And BOY do I hate that.

"Oh, are we sticking to that?" she asked innocently. I turned my back on her again, facing the stove in the hopes that giving my full attention to dinner would be a sign that she could leave me alone for the time being. A hollow wish.

"I just think it might do you some good. You never hang out with your high school friends anymore—"

"Because they're all away at college . . ." I explained calmly, the air around me filling with steam and making this already oppressive conversation even more claustrophobic. I didn't mention that plenty of them ended up at college in the city because then I would be forced to admit that we weren't really all that good friends to begin with.

"—and I know that Aaron has invited you to go see a movie with him a few times this summer." Her voice was moving into dangerous "you're making me sad, Rose" territory, and I really hated wading in those particular waters.

"Pity invites from my brother aren't exactly the height of social life." I wiped my forehead with the back of my wrist—I can normally handle the heat of the kitchen, but I had started to feel distinctly sweaty and woozy.

"I wouldn't know *what* your ideal social life *would* be, Rose," she continued, like a dog with a bone. "That's part of the problem."

I sighed. I avoided confrontation with my mother at all costs but she's so unrelenting about this stuff. I turned toward her, keeping my voice steady, trying to explain this as rationally as possible.

"Just because I want to live my life a little differently from you doesn't mean—"

And that's when I passed out.

I know! This journal just got interesting.

I don't know where I went—if I did go anywhere at all. I remember everything going black, a quick flash of light, and then I woke up on my back to see my mom's face above me, pulled tight in worry, her hands gripping my shoulders to shake me awake.

"'M fine," I mumbled, though I wasn't sure that I was. She made a fuss over me all the same, making me sit down at the kitchen counter while she attempted to finish dinner for me. "Attempted" is maybe harsh—she actually did a pretty good job even if I did have to add a lot more salt at the last second.

And I *do* feel fine! I mean, as fine as I've *been* feeling, which is a lot more run-down than I would have expected to feel at nineteen. Despite the fact that I keep sleeping in longer and longer and, apparently, now just passing out randomly, I'm still inexplicably *exhausted*. Maybe writing down all my thoughts in the middle of the night *isn't* all that helpful.

Enormous trees stretched their branches over me like a loving canopy, their roots floating above pristine, glittering, blue-green water. The smell of salt and pine filled the air, even though there wasn't an evergreen in sight. I glided over the water, watching it ripple underneath me, and I felt like I was barely touching the air, skimming weightless and free.

Flowers blossomed up from the tree roots, sending sweet perfume up to me as I flew along. I've rarely felt such peace, such calm understanding. I was contented but still curious, moving forward to something exciting and glorious. A light shone bright in the distance, reflecting off the water of the horizon, and I felt as if the water must be cascading down the side of the earth, falling into the sun, mixing with its beams to create warm, swimmable light. I moved swiftly through the trees, out onto the open water, closer and closer to the light, ready to touch it, knowing it wouldn't burn me and knowing that, when I did make contact, I would finally understand.

But before I got there I suddenly did understand—I was dreaming, I was somewhere deep inside my mind, or somewhere else entirely . . . but that light . . . if I just kept soaring toward that distant horizon, everything would come into sharp focus, the dream would be mine again and then—

I woke up.

I don't remember ever . . . waking up inside a dream before. Is this what lucid dreaming is?

I know I should go downstairs, eat breakfast, start the day. I slept right through my alarm, again, wanting to stay forever in that breathtaking beauty of water and trees. But I could feel consciousness encroaching back on me, the water underneath me starting to ripple away, the horizon growing dim. I feel tired and heavy, and like if I just stayed in that place, flying through that world, I'd figure out how to finally get some rest.

AUGUST 29TH, 2016

"Skate to work today," she said. "You'll be glad you did," she said.

I wonder, did she have a vision of me sitting in urgent care with what feels like a broken wrist? Because that's exactly what I'm doing right now. Sitting in a cold plastic chair in an overly air-conditioned waiting room, writing with my one remaining good hand (thank GOD I'm a leftie), trying to keep my mind off the heinous amount of pain shooting through my right wrist at the moment.

Having a psychic for a mom is usually . . . well, it's FINE. Mostly because she never tells us anything, for fear of steering her children's lives TOO much, which, I'm realizing as I'm writing this, is actually pretty ironic considering she's always trying to steer our lives in every other way?? Like, I *rarely* get the benefit of "study hard for that math test because it's going to have this question on it about this type of equation that you do NOT understand currently" but I DO get the constant pestering about my love life, my career choices, "are you *sure* you don't want to at least apply to some colleges?"

Despite this, this infuriating hypocrisy, the fact that my mom has visions of the future, which should be unbelievably cool and useful, except she chooses NOT to share them more often than she does . . . despite allll that, I still listen to her every. Single. Time. Even when she sends me falling ass over head into asphalt. I don't get to be special like the rest of my family and I don't even get to interact with *their* specialness in a good way. I'm always on the outside, face-planting into the ground.

LATER

Oh my god, oh my *god*, okayokayokay—

Maybe my mom isn't totally cracked after all.

All right, so, yes, my wrist is a little messed up, but it's more bruised than anything else (thankfully, not broken), and I'll have to get new skates because my front wheel is cracked from when I went careening into the curb, *but*.

There was a girl.

At the urgent care, there was the most beautiful girl I have ever seen.

Firstly, she came in because she wiped out on her skateboard, so, like, BIG mood. Normally, I find skateboarders a little annoying, but she rides a longboard so that's a whole other thing.

She also came in with a broken wrist—*really* broken—and we sat next to each other and got to talking about rollerblading versus skateboarding and it made me entirely forget about the pain in my arm.

"Are you a writer?" she asked, once we had gotten past the initial "broken wrist? broken wrist! same hat!" stuff. She gestured with her good arm (the right one, which immediately made me think how it felt like fate that we hurt opposite wrists, leaving our good arms still perfectly equipped to hold hands) at my notebook and ink-covered hand.

"Oh," I said, "um, no, not really. I mean, yes, I am literally writing"—I continued when she lifted up one perfect eyebrow—"but I'm not, like, a *writer*. I'm just . . . journaling."

The moment it came out of my mouth I wanted to sink into the cold plastic and die. I couldn't tell how old the girl (woman? are we women now?) was—she seemed about my age but so much more effortlessly cool. Her dark brown hair was cropped short on one side, her curls chin-length and bouncy on the other, the ends of them kissing her jawline, making *me* want to reach out and touch. She was wearing a tank top with a graphic of the Iron Man helmet on it and jorts cut off at the knee and her legs were all scuffed up from where she'd crashed. She had a pierced eyebrow and bright brown eyes that were filled with such incredible warmth, I could feel my face getting red.

Or maybe that was just because I told this hot girl that I was *journaling*. Like a thirteen-year-old. But she just smiled and gave a little nod and said, "Cool, cool. That's cool."

I don't know that I believed her that it's cool, but I found myself smiling in return.

"What about you?" I asked. "Are *you* a writer?"

"Trying to be," she said, grinning. "Poet, more specifically."

A *poet*. This cute girl with the longboard and the warm brown eyes is a *poet*. *Kill me.*

"Oh wow," I said, the blush on my cheeks getting to a truly lava-like degree. "That's amazing."

"I don't know about that." She laughed. "It's not exactly the most lucrative career, but there are worse ways to spend your time in college than reading Márquez and going to spoken-word nights."

She smiled at me like we were in on a private joke, like I would immediately understand what she was getting at. My stomach dropped—this *always* happens. Anytime I meet someone new my age, they just assume I'm in college. That's all anyone can talk about. College college college. But I'm not *in* college because a) who can afford that level of debt and b) why would a chef need a liberal arts degree?

"Oh, I'm not—" I started, before promptly falling unconscious.

THE GODDAMNED TIMING OF THIS THING I SWEAR.

So, on the plus side, I guess, passing out in an urgent care usually leads to someone, you know, checking on you and wondering why the hell a girl with a broken wrist went off to dreamland. *I'm* wondering that still. I can barely remember the dream—it was fuzzy even while it was happening, blurred and cracked around the edges, like I was watching a broken TV—but there were two men in snowy woods, blood . . . a helmet. I swear I'd seen the men before, somewhere, but it slips away if I think about it too hard.

Anyway, after a long chat with the doctor, she was pretty certain that I have narcolepsy. Which, okay, yeah, I should have seen coming, given how much I'm randomly falling asleep, but I don't know that I believed that it was a thing people really had. I live in a family full of superhumans and somehow the medical condition I have is a totally normal, but still really rare one. What are the odds?

She wants to run a bunch of tests, so I guess I now have to do some weird sleep study things. Guess I'll keep writing in here. Seems like something that should be documented.

Anyway, all of that hardly matters when I didn't even get the girl's name! That's right. I passed out, she, I guess, went in to get her cast put on or something, and we totally missed each other. My mom might have been right about skating to work today but I wish her vision had been a *little* more specific. Meeting the girl of my dreams doesn't count if I never see her again.

08-29-2016, morningwafffles, text post

Oh, Mumblr, do I have a story for you. Today went from bad to worse to . . . maybe really great?

I was boarding to class—*suuuuuuper* late—when a stupid Ultimate Frisbee team ran into the middle of the street. Cut to: me, in the emergency room, cradling my broken and useless wrist. I think I can probably still skate, but my balance is going to be way off. *And* I missed my seminar, and it was my turn to read my work today, so that sucks. Not that I love reading my own poetry out loud in front of a bunch of strangers, but I was pretty proud of what I came up with this week and *no, dear readers, I will not be sharing it, so don't even ask.* You are very sweet to want to read my original work, but I would literally rather die. Fanfic is one thing, my embarrassing poetry is another. Besides, if I read something aloud in class and then someone read this blog and realized who I was I WOULD DIE. I have actual nightmares about the anonymity being destroyed. It's not that writing fanfic is shameful or anything, it's that I know some people in my life who are not Stucky shippers and I have too many ship wars in my internet life to want to tempt them IRL too.

(Ooh, speaking of Stucky, I'm thinking of maybe finally writing a post-fall fic, but one where Steve actually finds Bucky after he falls from the train and takes care of him, so please send me all of your Hurt/Comfort fics plssssss. And before you all start piling into my asks, don't worry: I'm committed to finishing *somewhere a place for us* first.)

"Get to the good stuff, Waffles!" you say as I ramble on about nothing. Okay, okay, disclaimer over, anyway, yeah, my day started terribly!! I have to wear a cast for eight weeks, but whatever, I can live with that. Put in the replies what stickers I should put on this thing.

It was ALL worth it because, at urgent care, there was another girl there who had a broken wrist. And, reader, SHE WAS CUTE AS HELL. She rollerblades, which is *completely adorable,* and she was just sitting in the waiting room, journaling!! Like, old-school, in a notebook, with a pen, journaling. Le swoon.

So, like, great start, right? Total meet-cute. I started telling her about how I write poetry, which is something I *never* do but her perfect dimpled smile made me feel like I could tell her anything and everything. And I was going to but then . . . she passed out!! I'm not even kidding, she was totally fine, talking completely normally and then: bam, unconscious. I'll be honest, it was *terrifying.* I immediately went to the nurse's station of course, to try and get help and they checked her out and it turns out she was just sleeping? They asked me if I knew if she had a history of sleeping disorders and I had to be like, "uh, I have no idea, I just met this girl and was trying to get my flirt on when she went all slack in these super uncomfortable plastic chairs." They said they'd check her out for a concussion, but then the doctor called me in to put my cast on and by the time I came back out, she was gone.

Now, this is the moment in a fic where'd I'd bite my nails and stay up until two in the morning reading to see how the writer is going to get the two characters together again. Except, that's not how life works! Other than the fact she journals and her passing out gave me some good inspo for aforementioned Hurt/Comfort, I know nothing about her. I don't even know her name. I don't know how I would even *begin* to find her again.

My life is a *t r a g e d y.*

AUGUST 30TH, 2016

I woke up in my house. The same house I've lived in for my whole life. And I knew I was dreaming. I was at the front door, facing it like I was about to go out. Except the door was shut and I knew—somehow I *knew*—that I shouldn't open it. So I turned around and I walked past the small mirror in our front hall, expecting to see my own face. But nothing was there.

There was something wrong—*really wrong*—with that. It wasn't just that I wasn't seeing myself in the mirror, it's that I knew, deep in my bones, that I wasn't looking at a mirror at all. But a window. I was peering into something, through glass, into the other side, where unknown things lurk.

I looked down at my hands and they were unrecognizable, shrivelled and veiny, a heavy flannel shirt that I don't own creeping its way down my arms. I looked back up at the mirror and saw a thick, black fog deep in the distance, moving closer, closer, closer. I took a step toward it, now just a foot from the glass, wanting to reach out and touch, wanting to walk through and sink into the fog, understand it, except I couldn't, I knew it would swallow me whole. I didn't even know what the fog is, but I knew it was coming for me.

As I stepped closer to the mirror, the fog did too and then I saw my own face. My own face but not mine at all—my cheeks were sunken, my eyes all whites, my hair short, my jaw sharp—I was me in the dream, but *not* me, not Rose, someone else, some other me. The other me brought his hands up in front of him, palms facing me, and then pushed, reaching through the glass of the mirror and outward, stretching his long fingers toward the fog.

Just as my fingers touched the smooth surface of the mirror, the glass shattered into a million pieces, a loud blaring noise rattling my teeth, the fractured mirror bits pushing out toward me, slicing my face, the fog rushing forward, overwhelming me and then—

I woke up.

AUGUST 31ST, 2016

Every morning, I wake up more and more exhausted. It feels like the fog from my dream followed me out and is weighing me down, clouding everything around me. I feel completely off-kilter, my frustration over sleeping so much and not feeling rested the only emotion I can access.

I passed my dad in the hallway this morning, thinking that I *needed* to talk to him. But I don't know what about. That fog was still gathered around me like a heavy coat, my frustration mounting when I couldn't figure out *why* I wanted to talk to him. I still haven't told my family anything about the dreams or the falling asleep or what really happened at urgent care. Which brings me to . . .

Yesterday, when I was writing in the kitchen and Aaron was lurking around, he eventually started looking over my shoulder, nosing his way into my business like usual.

"Writing about how cool and accomplished I am and how you've always felt inferior to your older brother?" he said, crunching on a carrot loudly next to my ear.

"Oh yeah, that's exactly what I'm writing about." I rolled my eyes but snapped the journal shut all the same.

"What do you care anyway?" I asked, swiveling in my seat to look up into his dumb, smug face. "You know everything I'm thinking and feeling—you don't need to read my diary for that."

"Diary?" He took a step back, leaning against the counter. "What are you, twelve?"

I stuck my tongue out at him for lack of a witty retort.

"Besides," he continued, "I don't know what you're feeling. I'm not an empath, I'm a mind reader."

"Thank god for that," I muttered.

"I don't know, I wouldn't mind trading one for the other," he said, taking another large chunk out of the carrot, like he was freaking Bugs Bunny or something.

"Really?" I asked, genuinely surprised. Aaron and I never talk about his ability in depth. Mostly because I'm too afraid and nervous to ask and he seems to have people to talk to about it, between our parents, his psychologist, his doctors, his group therapy. I don't really know what little old me, non-Atypical Atkinson, could really contribute to the conversation. Even thinking stuff like that puts me on edge because I know that Aaron could hear it and maybe feel weird or pressured to say something or pity me for being the one person in the family without abilities but he's not here now, so I'm going to think whatever I want to think.

It's like this: two years ago, Aaron started acting really weird. Like, *really* weird. He was getting really distracted all the time, kept having these random outbursts, these really intense headaches . . . it caused a lot of family drama. I really don't like thinking about it, honestly, whether he's in the room or not. It was a really awful time. I was a rising senior, and I was already stressed enough as it was. We were all pretty on-edge at first, not really understanding what was going on with him. We couldn't tell if it was some kind of mental break or the appearance of his ability. Both my parents first showed signs of being Atypical when they were around fourteen, so when Aaron and I skated by that deadline, they kind of just assumed we were normies. All that said, my mom started to suspect that Aaron was a precognate like her—that he was getting visions of the future and didn't know what they were yet so it was totally bugging him out. Long story short (too late) and a few trips to the good old Atypical Monitors later, and the truth came out: Aaron *is* Atypical. He's a mind reader.

Can you imagine? I have no powers—ZERO—and on top of that, I get stuck with an older brother who can HEAR MY THOUGHTS.

My life is one big cosmic joke.

Which is what I was thinking when Aaron, unprompted, slid into the chair across from me. He took another big crunch of the carrot and leaned his arms across the table, stretching out like a floppy dog, his bangs falling in front of his face and giving him that effortlessly cool look that I can literally never achieve.

GOD, I hate him sometimes.

"Listen to me, Rosie," he said with a world-weary sigh.

He does this constantly. Despite the fact that he is exactly sixteen months older than me, he always acts like he's the wise old brother who knows absolutely everything about the world and I'm his silly little sister "Rosie" (which NO ONE else calls me, by the way).

"I get that it's weird to be in this family and not have an ability—"

"Aaron, *stop* listening to my thoughts—" I said, knowing he didn't actually *want* to invade my privacy (or at least, so he CONSTANTLY TALKS ABOUT, always so smug about his ethical code).

"You know I can't help it, sometimes," he said, eyes big and puppy-doggish. "Stuff just jumps out."

I wanted to jump out of that conversation. But he kept going.

"I'm just saying, I understand."

"No, you don't," I mumbled. "You *have* one."

"Yeah, but I didn't," he said.

I wanted to say that it wasn't the same. That when he thought he was a normal human, he also had *me*, Rosie, normal human number two. He didn't have to do this *alone*. But Aaron and I have never really talked like that before. We've always gotten along decently—I complain about him being a know-it-all and he complains about my Switzerland-like neutrality when he gets into arguments with Mom and Dad, but we've never been, like, genuinely mad at each other for a long period of time. It's just sibling fighting. Normal brother-sister stuff.

Except it *isn't* really normal, is it? Not when we were inseparable as kids, before coming out on the other side of middle school as complete strangers. We never really talk to each other about the big stuff, like how we were both unmoored when our grandmother died or how we can both hear when our parents argue about my mom's visions and we pretend it doesn't bother us. Maybe ignoring all that stuff *is* normal, I don't know, but what's definitely, completely *not* normal is that now it doesn't matter if I want to talk to Aaron about that stuff or not, because he knows. All his insistence that he has it under control, that he feels strongly about respecting our privacy doesn't change the fact that he *could* be listening, at any time.

"Rosie," he started, and I tensed, wondering what he'd heard. He was squinting, like something was hurting his eyes—I didn't know what *that* meant, but I really did not want his pity or a placating speech about how it's okay to be normal, so I pulled the emergency switch.

I started to think about kissing mysterious urgent care girl.

"Aw, come on, Rosie!" He flinched back, shaking his head like he could shake the thoughts out. "Blech."

“Oh, I’m sorry, did you hear something?” I asked innocently.

“*No*, I didn’t,” he insisted. “You know I’m actually pretty good at the whole ‘controlling my ability’ thing. All I know is that you were thinking thoughts I don’t want to hear or see.”

“Aha! So you *were* listening,” I said.

“It’s hard to avoid seeing the beginnings of the tracks,” he explained and I rolled my eyes, having heard this lecture before. “But that’s all they are—the start of a train of thought. I don’t actually know the contents of the thought. Just the . . . brand.”

“So, when I’m thinking about making out with a cute girl . . .”

Aaron made a throwing-up noise.

“It’s just a big neon sign saying ‘Sexy Thoughts, Stay Out’?”

“Kind of,” he said, wincing. “And then the whole system automatically shuts down.”

“Like how you cover your eyes and scream like a little kid whenever a snake shows up in a movie?” I teased. Aaron glared.

It worked every time. And thank *god* I figured out a method of getting Aaron out of my head. Things had been okay for the past year, but in those early days, when he couldn’t help it, I always worried he would say all the brutally honest things I think about myself, about our family, out loud and destroy the peaceful balance I had created.

“For the record,” he went on, “I wasn’t listening to you before. I don’t know what *you* thought I was going to say, but I was just gonna point out that it’s weird. Seeing you do something day after day that isn’t cooking.”

“What?” I asked, trying to catch up.

“Come on, Rosie,” he said, gesturing at my journal. “You’re not exactly the ‘commit to a hobby’ type.”

Another wince, except this time it was me. He pulled his arms back, leaning back in the chair and gazing down his nose at me. As if putting some degree of physical distance between us could fix the fact that he knew he was hurting me.

“I commit to things,” I said, fiddling with the edge of my notebook.

“Like what?”

“Cooking.” I barely resisted the urge to stick out my tongue at him.

"*Besides* cooking."

He had me there. I became obsessed with cooking at age eight and never really looked back. I was never very good at focusing in school or extracurriculars that weren't food based and I've never had an enormous bevy of friends. I've never really had a serious girlfriend either. I came out sophomore year and then endured about nine months of nonstop questions from my family about my love life. I think they worried that I'd been bottling up my sexuality and now that I was finally out, I was going to peel back the curtain on my exciting life of romance.

The reality is much less thrilling. It's more that I didn't think about *anyone* that way for a long time. While every girl in my class was going boy crazy in middle school, I was finding everyone my age completely ridiculous. That's still mostly true, but I did just wake up one day when I was fourteen and realize that I thought girls were very, *very* cute. I still think that but: thinking girls my age are cute + thinking most people my age are ridiculous = my mother calling me "too picky" and saying "let me just introduce you to the Lowenthal girl, she's an LGBT too" and me turning up the food processor as fast as it goes until I drown her out and ruin the pesto.

So, yeah. Commitment. Not so much.

"Rollerblading!" I blurted, finally. Aaron rolled his eyes but I could see a tiny smile on his face.

"What are you doing with *your* time anyway?" I asked.

"I've got stuff," he said, shrugging.

"Oh yeah? What stuff?"

I wasn't being combative—I really did want to know. Aaron's been jumping from job to job since taking a leave from college. Mind reading and a packed classroom don't mix, I guess. He's been taking online classes, but that doesn't really fix the "doesn't know what he wants to do with his life" problem. HE'S allowed to flounder and go a nontraditional route because HE'S Atypical.

"I think I could be good at tech stuff," he said.

"Tech stuff?"

"Yeah, like, computer science, IT, that kind of stuff."

"Where is this coming from?" I asked. Aaron spent a lot of his time on his computer, but it's 2016, *everyone* spends a lot of time on their computer. I just assumed he was watching YouTube and, I don't know, getting into podcasts like everybody else. I didn't realize he actually *liked* computers.

"I've just been learning coding and stuff," he said and, shockingly, I saw some red rise in his cheeks. Aaron *never* gets embarrassed or shy or anything that remotely resembles seeming uncool, so watching him blush talking about something he cares about was sweet, sweet victory.

"Where are you learning coding?" I scoffed, wondering how much shit I could give him for turning red and if the lecture I would get from my dad would be worth it. He hates when his kids fight.

"Online," he said, like it was obvious. "There's tons of free classes."

"And this is something that you think you'd actually want to do? For, like, a living?"

"I think I could be really good at it," he said softly, like he was trying to convince himself that was true. I've never seen Aaron uncertain about anything and suddenly my impulse to tease him into the ground was dampened.

"That's . . ." I searched for the right word. Aaron and I don't really . . . encourage each other? We're not *mean* to one another, we just . . . Aaron and I exist in our separate corners of the world, sometimes waving at each other from our individual castles, but never going into one another's kingdoms.

"That's . . . really cool, Aaron," I said eventually, unable to come up with anything more profound. He smiled a tiny bit, but I think I disappointed him by not asking more. I wouldn't have known what to ask.

I never know what to ask.

community/TheUnusuals post by n/thatsahumanperson

Hey folks, I know it's been a while since I've posted in this sub—I've actually been making a stab at real life stuff lately and it's taking up a lot of my time. But, you know, I can still read minds, so that's something I'm dealing with.

A little update on that end: I've been better. I think last time I posted on here, I'd just made *the* breakthrough: the one a few of us have experienced when the thoughts start to separate themselves like trains on parallel tracks and you can choose which cars to get on. I've been doing well, I think, able to change the volume, the speed of the tracks. I've been feeling pretty proud of myself, if I'm honest, but then something . . . weird happened.

I was talking to my sister—trying to have an actual conversation with her, focus on what she was saying, and nothing else—but she kept accusing me of listening in, which I absolutely wasn't, so don't get on my case, n/chuckxavier. I've been doing really well at not eavesdropping on people's thoughts.

I could still sense all the different tracks, but instead of her thoughts being a stream, a linear track like they usually are, they were *all over the place*. Shooting off in disparate streams, totally unconnected. So I tried to hold onto one but wasn't able to get a foothold and follow any of them (and then she booted me out by thinking about a girl she likes, a tactic she's discovered that is deeply annoying). Nothing like this has *ever* happened to me before. There have been people with confusing and scattered thoughts, of course, but never to this degree, especially not with her. She's a really ordered person in her thinking and each train of thought always has a really distinct feel (which is what makes nope-ing out of there any time she's thinking about anything remotely romantic very easy thank GOD), but other than a few clear tracks, it felt like some of the thoughts weren't even . . . tangible? Like there was no train to grab onto.

Has that ever happened to anyone before? Any telepaths experience a non-drug-induced block?

tldr: Something has shifted in my sister's head that's making it hard to read her thoughts. She also got hurt recently and has been kind of squirrelly around us, telling us she had a Rollerblading accident but sidestepping giving any more details. She wasn't seriously hurt at the time, or so I thought, but could she have a head injury? Is it something I should talk to my parents about (both "Unusuals") or should I just let it go?

iwannabelieve
damn, dude, your posts are always my favorite—do you sell any of your original writing? I would totally buy a kindle book of yours. With all the mind reader fiction I've read, I never would have thought about when it *doesn't* work.

> **lokilover**
> is anyone gonna kick this guy off this sub? he clearly isn't one of us.
>
> **iwannabelieve**
> first of all, why do you assume I'm a guy? second of all, I'm still learning, just chill. not everyone is good at fully immersing themselves right away.
>
> **onmyown**
> n/iwannabelieve I think you might be looking for the community/scifirpg or community/fantasyrpg pages. This forum might not be right for you.

lokilover
where did you say you guys lived again? I might know a doc who specializes in *our kind of stuff* who could help out.

> **chuckxavier**
> No sharing of personal info! I know I can't control what people do in PMs, but *please,* safety first. This is a forum for anonymous sharing and support, nothing more.

theneonthorn
this specific thing hasn't happened to me (not a mind reader) but I'm currently taking care of a friend who's had his power totally messed up. after some . . . trauma, he's had a hard time accessing his ability in the same way. so it's possible that your sister hitting her head threw something off with her ability and the way it interacts with yours?

> **thatsahumanperson**
> Except my sister isn't Unusual. Unless her ability just hasn't manifested yet, which . . . I suppose that's possible. Hmm.
>
> **theneonthorn**
> keep us posted, dude. I'm still trying to figure out what to do with my friend so let me know if you find anything that works.

SEPTEMBER 3RD, 2016

No matter how fast I ran, I couldn't get away. I've had nightmares like that before—where you run and run and run, you can feel your legs pumping away and still: nothing. It's *torture*. It's not even the thing chasing you—which, in this case, was a giant snake—that's the truly scary part. It's the feeling of not having control over your body. That dark dread that sits in the bottom of your stomach as you push your legs through invisible molasses, thinking that if you just shove a little harder, dig your heels in deeper, you'll be able to get free of the weight around you and make a clean escape. But that never happens.

Last night I was running—running, running, running—but then it was like something clicked on. Or off. A sharp smell in the air, like lightning in the distance or an imminent snowfall. And then suddenly I was aware of where I was. Standing in an endless black expanse, impossibly lit, just enough so that I could see the giant snake with red eyes and horrible, growing fangs barreling toward me.

When I woke up, I saw there were scratches all up and down my legs. Like I was clawing at them to stop the ground from swallowing me whole.

LATER

Well jesus jumping christ, that could have gone a hell of a lot better.

I should back up. I decided, in all my infinite wisdom, to try and talk to my family about the narcolepsy and the bad, *crazy vivid* dreams and the fact that maybe they're now turning into night terrors and, well, let's just say I was right to be worried about them overreacting.

It all started at dinner.

"When's your wrist supposed to be better?" Aaron asked, his nose wrinkling at his plate.

"Oh hush," my mom chastised, sitting down at our small kitchen table, setting a plate of soggy green beans in the center.

"Six weeks," I said. "Ish."

"Ugh." Aaron groaned. "But, I mean, you can still cook for us though, right? Like, you can figure out how to chop one-handed?"

"I mean, I hope so," I said. "I want to be able to go back to work."

"Our cooking isn't *that* bad, Aaron," my dad said, beans floating through the air to land on his plate. He caught me staring wistfully at the display of telekinesis and winked.

"Yeah," I said, trying to sound encouraging, "I think you did a great job seasoning these." I gestured to the green beans, which *were* well-seasoned, but horribly cooked. I don't know why my parents insist on boiling things like they're stuck in the fifties and haven't discovered roasting or pan searing and—

Never mind. This is off-topic.

"What exactly are you going to do when we don't live together anymore, Aaron?" I teased lightly. "Unless you were planning on taking your dorky little sister with you when you move out."

"I can pay the rent if you do all the cooking," he said, tossing me a smarmy smile.

"Is that your way of saying that you're going to make money and I'm not?"

"That's my way of saying that computer scientists make a decent living."

"They do. But you're not a computer scientist."

"Children," my mother chastised just as Aaron was sticking out his tongue.

I didn't take his ribbing particularly seriously. Family dinner is my safe zone—in non-sprained-wrist times, it's the thing I control, the thing I *excel* at. I feel less out of place, less like I have to hide, when I'm the one who controls the food, who's responsible for everyone sitting down and relaxing. As we've gotten older, it hasn't been a daily occurrence, but we always make time on Fridays for Shabbat. Having both grown up in fairly religious Jewish households, our parents still go to temple a few times a year, but stopped making us go once we'd had our bar and bat mitzvahs. None of us is particularly devout (and I know my mom has a particularly complicated relationship with her faith because of her visions, though she's never talked to *me* about it), but we all agree that Shabbat dinner can't be missed. I haven't thought about my own faith in a long time, but the ritual of making a meal, sharing it with my family, and proving that I have value, is sacred to me.

"Besides, you never know what career Rose might end up in," my mom said, before turning to my dad.

"Honey, Aaron is about to grab the salt and spill it everywhere, would you just pass it?" she said, exasperated, before turning back to me. "I should have listened to you about the chicken, Rose. I saw your comment about the beans and just assumed I'd gotten the whole meal right."

My dad floated the salt over to Aaron, who rolled his eyes before tossing it back into the air, my dad catching it with his telekinesis before it dropped onto the floor, both of them laughing.

"Oh honestly, how are you *still* getting salt everywhere," my mom said, as I tried to keep up with the whiplash of her taking a dig at my career and complimenting my cooking knowledge in a single breath, only pausing to predict her son's behavior.

"It's like you always say, Mom." Aaron laughed. "Your visions are never perfect."

I just wish my parents could remember that they approve of my cooking, even when I do it outside of their kitchen. I have a good, steady job that has opportunity for growth and all they think about is the late nights, the cutthroat competition, the drug use . . . my mom read *Kitchen Confidential* once and assumes that's the life I'm getting into. She's not wrong—I'm definitely nervous to play in the big leagues—but I wish she would trust me a little more. And it's not like I expect Aaron to come rushing to my defense, but he isn't exactly helping when he talks about how illustrious a computer science career is, even if he doesn't mean it as a dig against me and even if it doesn't sting as much in this setting.

Except . . . my dad was telekinetically cutting up his chicken while eating green beans with his hands, as my mom talked about her day at work—how she was able to be in a patient's room seconds before they would have fallen, saving them from a concussion. My dad smiled, and pride shone in Aaron's eyes, like he could read how relieved and proud my mom was.

I just wanted to be a part of that. That's my brilliant explanation for what happened next.

"Do we have a history of narcolepsy in our family?" I asked, because, remember, I'm an idiot.

I was met with three sets of silverware scraping to a stop and three blank stares before my dad said: "I don't think we do. Why are you asking?"

I saw my mom's eyes narrow in that knowing mom (and knowing psychic) way and Aaron cocked his head like something was clicking into place. OR like he was reading my thoughts, despite all his promises.

"What's wrong?" my mom asked.

"I've been having some . . . sleeping problems," I said vaguely.

"A cup of chamomile and some melatonin usually does the trick for me," my dad said, completely oblivious. I'm so grateful that my dad is just plain old telekinetic. I don't know if my mom and Aaron were using their powers in that moment, but I think their abilities have just given them heightened perception across the board. Especially with my mom, I've never been able to get away with *anything*. I'm honestly surprised, and a little proud, that I've been able to keep what's been going on with me a secret this whole time. And I'm really wishing that I had kept on that path instead of opening my big mouth.

"Uh, no," I said, "I'm not having a hard time getting to sleep, I'm . . ."

I swallowed, my dad now joining the cadre of narrowed eyes. Suddenly, I felt like I was sitting in front of a council of judges—three Atypicals prepared to bestow their verdict on the puny, normal human.

In for a penny, in for a pound, I thought.

"So . . . I'm pretty sure I have narcolepsy."

My mom's fork clattered against her plate as she dropped it and brought her hands up, leaning her elbows on the table and collapsing her head forward into her hands.

"I thought we'd gotten away with it," she mumbled into her palms.

"What?" Aaron and I both asked.

"How long has this been going on, Rose?" my dad asked.

"Um, I don't know, a few weeks," I said absentmindedly, still confused by what my mom had said.

"A few *weeks*?" my mom exclaimed, bringing her head out of her hands to stare me down. "Why didn't you tell us?"

"I don't understand," I said, trying not to let their reaction rile me up. "What did you think you'd gotten away with?"

Then my parents shared the kind of look that only parents can share. The look that says a million things in a single second that only they understand.

"You've been doing so well, Rose," my dad said after a few tense moments.

"Meaning . . ."

"Meaning," my mom chimed in, "I know I give you a hard time about your choice of career, but it's only because I love you. I don't want to see you burnt out before you're thirty."

"No, no, that's not what this is." I shook my head, feeling, for a moment, like I understood what was going on.

(I did not.)

"I promise you, I'm not falling asleep because of the restaurant. I don't feel more tired during the day or anything, I've just . . . passed out a few times—"

My dad groaned at that, a guttural sound of pain and concern I'd never heard from him before. The furrow in my mom's brow got deeper and I was about to launch into more words of comfort—the sleep studies that I was thinking about doing, the fact that the doctor at urgent care didn't seem overly worried, all the reading I had done online—when Aaron spoke up for the first time in a few minutes.

"*Oh,*" he breathed. "I get what's going on."

"What?" I asked.

"You guys think it's finally happened," he said, looking at our parents instead of at me, which was *incredibly* annoying.

"Oh my *god,* will someone just please tell me why everyone has a look on their face like the dog died."

"We've never had a dog," my dad said, pointlessly.

"Dad!"

"This sounds like the manifestation of your ability." My mom sighed, sounding way more exasperated than I would have expected at her claiming that I all of a sudden have SUPERPOWERS.

"Excuse me?" I said once I got my breath back.

"Remember Aaron's headaches?" my dad asked. "He had them for months before the voices started."

"Boy, out of the context of this family, that makes me sound *real* weird," Aaron quipped.

My spine was tingling and I was getting that dizzy feeling again, like maybe I was going to pass out, except it usually happened faster than this, so maybe I wasn't about to have a narcoleptic fit, maybe I was just panicking.

Here's the thing: I don't panic. I never panic. I didn't panic when I graduated high school with no plan, I didn't panic the first time Chef gave me a dressing-down in front of the whole kitchen staff for not cutting on a bias, I didn't panic when a total stranger in a run-down urgent care told me that I probably have a lifelong disease that's going to affect my every waking moment. Pun intended.

But I was panicking at the kitchen table. At least, I think that's what it was. My vision was blurry, my chest was tight, and it felt like there was cotton stuffed in my ears. Like I was underwater. But I was awake and upright, staying conscious against all odds, trying to focus on my mom's voice as she told me that she had been thinking that the Atypical gene had skipped me, that they'd gotten lucky and wouldn't have to worry about their only other child having a hard time in life, always struggling with being different. But her words weren't making sense to me, nothing anyone was saying was making sense because I can't be Atypical, I'm nineteen, it's too late, and what would my ability even be? The power to sleep whenever and wherever I want?

We didn't get a chance to discuss theories because I threw down my napkin on the table and bolted out of there. And now I'm here, hiding in my room, trying to figure out why I was having an anxiety attack ten minutes ago.

I'm not sure that this whole dream journal thing is really helping the . . . the *whatever* that's going on, but it does seem to be calming me down a little. There's something hypnotically soothing about writing out everything that just happened. Like dreams, the act of forcing it into an understandable shape feels like some kind of physical processing, helping me uncover the root of what's freaking me out about this whole thing.

I'm scared they're right. Growing up with a psychic mother and telekinetic father, I couldn't wait for the day that my power would appear. It was like waiting for Gandalf to show up in the Shire, knowing that you have a glorious destiny and amazing adventures ahead and all you have to do is get to that day when it all kicks off. It was one of the things that Aaron and I bonded over most. We'd spend hours playing make-believe, assigning each other abilities and acting them out like the great heroes we assumed they'd make us into. Him, pretending to be a pyrokinetic, a electropath—something big and bombastic like him. Me, wishing that I could fly. Up, up, and away from everything.

But then I grew up and both my imagination and Aaron both felt like distant childhood friends. I went through high school, and puberty, all the while devouring every fantasy novel and movie that I could, and slowly realized that maybe I was wrong. Maybe there were no exciting quests or Chosen One status waiting for me or for Aaron.

And then Aaron *did* get chosen and I was *so* jealous, the envy chewing up my insides, driving my obsession for cooking to new heights, making me so focused on trying to be exceptional at *something* even if it meant I didn't belong anywhere. But watching Aaron go through the realities of being a mind reader . . . how hard it is, how grating, how *lonely* . . . it made it harder to be jealous.

My parents are scared. They don't want me to be Atypical. They don't want me to be *special*.

The thing that I always wanted finally happened and I can't be excited. I can't even be relieved that maybe, finally, I got chosen.

All I feel is dread.

SEPTEMBER 4TH, 2016

"Don't take an umbrella today."

Those were the first words that my mom spoke to me this morning. No "Hello" or "Good morning" or "How are you feeling, do you think you have an Atypical ability yet?" Just . . . "Don't take an umbrella."

I looked at the sky, gray and heavy and *definitely* a sign that rain was on its way, but I left my umbrella in the front hall closet. Without argument, I heeded my mother's vision, hoping at least this one wouldn't lead to another injury, and tried not to let the annoyance show on my face as I nodded at my mom and left for the restaurant.

The weather matched my mood as I made my way to Milton. It rumbled, dark and oppressive above me, the heavy feeling of an impending storm hanging in the air. And, sure enough, the moment I got off the bus—the stop *several* blocks away from the restaurant—the sky opened and unleashed holy hell on me.

"Yep, that feels right." I laughed humorlessly to no one, taking the opportunity of an empty sidewalk to let out a guttural moan of frustration that I would *love* to aim at my mom if I had any kind of spine.

"Hey Rose!" Madison said, her bright white teeth nearly blinding me as I stepped out of the horrible rain and into the restaurant. I've never understood how Madison keeps up her relentlessly cheery expression, but I guess that's why she's front of house and I'm not.

"Hey, Madison. Sorry, back door is jammed again," I said. Kitchen staff aren't really supposed to come through the front, especially kitchen staff who are as soaked to the bone as I was, but our door is a tricky bastard that no amount of WD-40 seems able to fix. Given that the place wasn't even open yet, I figured I was safe to dry off in the front so Chef wouldn't yell at me for dragging dirty water through her kitchen.

I shook out my hair like a shaggy dog, wiggled my legs to get the excess water off my shoes, and then instantly regretted both of those decisions when I looked up through the tangled strands of my wet hair and saw that Madison wasn't alone.

“Oh my god,” I whispered, an involuntary reaction that felt punched from my gut.

“Uh, hey, wow, it’s you.”

That’s right. It’s me. Soaking wet Rose Atkinson. Unbelievably uncool. Staring right into the gorgeous face of BROKEN WRIST GIRL.

“Rose, this is Emily,” Madison said, completely oblivious to the desperate lesbian going through the most embarrassing moment of her entire life. “Emily, Rose.”

Emily. EmilyEmilyEmilyEmily—have you ever heard such a perfect name?

09-04-2016, morningwaffles, text post

OKAY BEFORE YOU YELL AT ME, an update to *somewhere a place for us* is coming tomorrow, I promise. I know some of you beautiful nutbars have new posts by me pushed to your notifications so I'm sorry for those of you who were hoping to read some good, good pining. *But,* I might have something even better: pining irl.

That's right, kids, cute urgent care diary-writing sprained-wrist fell-unconscious girl is *back.*

Here's what went down. One of my roommates at that college I go to that I'm not going to tell you the name of has a best friend . . . Jefferson (not her real name, obvi) who works at this super nice, old-school restaurant downtown. She's been really down lately—my roommate, not Jefferson—and she apparently loves the soup from this place so I thought I'd go down there and see if Jefferson would be willing to slip a girl some, you know?

And guess who was there? Guess who *works* there? In the *kitchen*? Making *food*? Like some sort of beautiful cooking angel??

Well, I'm not going to tell you her real name, of course. But I'll call her Daisy.

le sigh.

Daisy.

(I'm saying her real name in my head)

The mystery is solved!! And yes, she is as cute as I remembered. It was raining cats and dogs today and she came into the restaurant totally soaked. Which sucks—I hate when that happens, walking around in wet jeans is the *w o r s t*—but she just stood there right inside the doorway and did this full-body shake to get the water off and it was truly the most endearing thing I've ever seen. Especially when she noticed I was there and got totally red faced and stutter-y and stuck out her dripping hand when Jefferson introduced us.

We shook hands—her arm still in a brace and mine in a hard cast and ohmygod, it was a total 2005-P&P-meaningful-hand-touch kind of handshake. She was so gentle and wide-eyed—I've never had anyone treat me like that. Like I'm delicate, like I'm some kind of rare and beautiful creature that needs to be approached with reverence for fear of ruining something so perfect.

Okay, I realize I sound *e x t r e m e l y* up on myself, but I'm telling you, *that's* how she was looking at me. I laughed and made some quip about my cast and missing skateboarding and she blushed, for some reason, impossibly more, and then we were just kind of awkwardly grinning at each other, hearts in our eyes, like I live in the sappiest K-Drama ever. Jefferson legit *cleared her throat.* That's how obvious we were.

I know you all are on absolute tenterhooks now, wondering what's going to happen next, but I have to be across campus in ten minutes for my creative writing seminar, so I'm going to leave you hanging. Which, if you read my fic, you know is my modus operandi.

Laterz.

SEPTEMBER 5TH, 2016

Okay, so as I was writing the last entry, I fell asleep. Again. Which is now the *second* time I've quite literally swooned just thinking about how cute Emily is.

That's right, I actually know her name now! Her *full* name, which feels like a huge leap in the right direction.

"Emily Rodriguez," she said, smiling, and I almost started to feel dizzy again just at that. We'd just been standing there, kind of staring at each other, before Madison legit cleared her throat like a bad rom-com sidekick and threw us back into actual human being "we should probably introduce ourselves" mode.

Look, meeting new people, getting to know them . . . it's not what I'd call my strong suit. Unless they rollerblade or have strong opinions about sous-vide-ing, I usually don't have much to say to other people. And other people my age? Terrifying. The only reason I feel remotely secure in talking to Madison is because I've known her for six months and also she's the Energizer Bunny of good feelings and smiles, so she makes it pretty easy.

But standing there in front of Emily, seeing her cheeks dimple as she smiled, her brown eyes lighting up, I went a bit jelly-legged. So I opted for the safe choice: ignoring Emily completely and talking only to Madison like an asshat.

"I'm just here to pick up my paycheck," I said, looking over Emily's shoulder at Madison's bright, blond-haired head.

"Oh, right," she said, her eyes darting between me and Emily. I could feel a blush rising on my cheeks and everything in my body was screaming for it to stop. I don't usually blush in front of girls, I am not, in my nature, a blusher, but there's something about Emily. Something about how warm her smile is, how she asked me what I was writing, the small giggle she gave when we locked eyes and gestured to our shared wrist injuries. It drew me in in a way that no one ever has. For once, I actually want to listen to my irritating mother and turn my focus onto a *person*, not one of my obsessive hobbies.

"I'll just go back and grab it for you," Madison chirped. "I've got to grab Emily's soup anyway."

"Oh no, you really don't—" I started, but it was too late. Her long, blond hair whipping behind her, Madison zipped through the dining room and disappeared through the kitchen doors, leaving me staring at the back of her head, the only sound the steady drip-drip-drip of water falling off the edge of my raincoat.

Don't take an umbrella. My mother's visions have a sick sense of humor. There had to have been a way to get the same result without me being *soaking wet the entire time.*

"Rose, was it?" Emily's lilting voice, like music to my ears, broke the awkward tension and I refocused on her face. It was almost too much to look at at first. Her skin is a deep, warm brown like her eyes, and she was smiling enough to show that she has two perfect dimples in her cheeks.

"Uh yeah," I said, my voice gravelly and hollow, like I had just spent hours shouting. I made a jerky motion with my body before stopping still completely, once I realized that I'd been going to shake her hand. Again.

"This is a pretty weird coincidence, right?" She laughed, but it sounded more nervous than I would have expected. I finally blinked, the fact that I'd been staring blankly at her for the past forty seconds dawning at me, and saw a new tightness in her smile.

"I'm not following you or anything," I rushed to say, because apparently my brain and my mouth are no longer talking to one another.

"What?" Emily's eyes widened.

"I just mean," I said, my voice gaining back its usual strength much slower than I would have liked, "this really is just a coincidence. I know the odds of this are, like, really small, but I promise, I'm not following you or anything. I *work* here. So, maybe, *you're* the one who's following me. Yeah, I mean, that would be more likely, why else would you be here picking up soup?"

Oh my GOD, just writing this stuff down is mind-numbingly embarrassing. I think I embarrassed Emily too, because she started to blush furiously. I wish I had had more of my wits about me to fully appreciate how hot she looked when she was flustered.

But don't worry! There were even MORE opportunities for things to be awkward, because Madison came back with both our things, which means we left at the same time, which means we both were trying to navigate opening the door with casts and, in Emily's case, an armful of soup for her friend because she's a perfect person.

"Here—" I said, moving into her space. I was close enough now to see the light freckles dotted along the bridge of her nose and to discover that she smells like vanilla. She stepped back, taking her enticing freckles and cupcake scent with her and giving me room to open the door for her.

"Thanks," she said. "I guess . . . I'll see you."

Her foot stepped forward onto the sidewalk and under the awning that hangs in front of Milton's front door. Doing her best to maneuver around the cast and the soup in her arm, she extended her umbrella in front of her and I watched her grimace as she braced herself to step into the torrential rain.

And that was when it clicked. *Don't take an umbrella.*

"Wait!" I called, stepping outside after her. The door swung closed behind me as she turned around, confusion written all over her face.

"Um," I said, raising my voice a little to be heard over the rain. "I don't have an umbrella. Obviously," I added, gesturing to my still-soaked form. "Any chance you could walk me to the bus stop?" I tried to put on my best rakish smile, the one that Aaron's used on so many girls that I'm hoping is genetic but that I've never figured out how to deploy.

The confusion on Emily's face transformed into something like curiosity and soon a small smile was mirroring my own.

"Sure," she said after what felt like a thousand years. I could feel my smile grow bigger as she extended her arm, just slightly, in a silent invitation.

We walked in an awkward three-legged-race kind of gait—moving side by side, drifting over the wet pavement under the same small umbrella, but still complete strangers, afraid to get too close, even if looping arms would have made it easier to stay in lockstep.

I thought I should say something—say thank you again, ask her if she was taking the bus too or if she drove here, if she's now going way out of her way to help me—but the smack-smack-smack of the rainfall on the tight vinyl above us gave me the perfect excuse to stay silent. I focused in on her cast instead. With how close I was, I could see that it was covered in doodles and signatures, the hallmark of a person with dozens of friends. While that's a completely foreign experience to me—having people like you and seek out your company—I could understand why so many people gravitated toward Emily. Even standing shoulder to shoulder with her, I wanted to get closer, to lean in as much as I possibly could until her face was the only thing in my field of vision.

"How's, uh, college going?" I asked finally, wincing at the triteness of the question.

"It's going okay," she said. "I'm just a sophomore so, you know, not too much crazy pressure yet."

"Oh right," I said again and COME ON ROSE YOU HAVE OTHER WORDS IN YOUR VOCABULARY, SHE'S A WRITER AND YOU'RE SPEAKING IN MONOSYLLABLES *god* I'm such an idiot.

Thankfully, I was saved from further humiliation by the fact that we arrived at the bus stop.

"This is me," I said, jerking my head to the stop. "Thanks for the escort."

"No problem." She smiled and my legs turned to jelly. "It's kind of weird, right?"

"What do you mean?" My heart stopped in that moment. I knew I hadn't made the best first—or second—impression, but it seemed unnecessarily harsh to call me weird.

"Running into each other again," she explained. "Of all the gin joints . . ."

I gave her a blank look. What did gin have to do with this?

"*Casablanca*?"

"What?"

"Oh my god, have you never seen *Casablanca*?" She laughed, like bells.

"I'm not really much of a movie person," I said, too embarrassed to add that the movies I *do* watch are exclusively ones with sword fights or magic.

"Okay, I get that," she said, smiling and nodding her head. My stomach swooped. "But *Casablanca* is a *classic*. You don't have to be a movie person to get into *Casablanca*."

"All right, I trust you," I teased, feeling on surer footing. It felt like the beginning of a volley—the kind of conversational fencing that is as close as I get to a comfort zone with other people.

"So you'll watch it?" she asked, her eyes wide in hope. Out of the corner of my eye, I could see my bus approaching the stop, hear the hiss of the doors opening. And in Emily's eyes, I saw an opening, her hope maybe being about something more than just getting a random stranger to watch a movie you liked. I was running out of time but even I wasn't too clueless to see the perfect opportunity that had been laid out in front of me.

So in that moment, with rain pounding on the umbrella above us, I did something I have never, in my nineteen years of existing on this planet, done before.

I asked someone out on a date.

And against all odds—

community/TheUnusuals post by n/thatsahumanperson

Hey folks—so the situation with my sister has kind of escalated. We both still live with my parents (keep your comments about the computer nerd living in his parents' basement, I've heard it all before and I should think that you guys, of all people, should understand that I'm not your standard college dropout) and we were having dinner the other night when she dropped kind of a weird bomb on us.

Apparently she's been having these fits where she falls asleep—doesn't matter where or when, sometimes she'll just drop unconscious. She's claiming that it's narcolepsy, which definitely makes a lot of sense if we were, you know, a normal family. I've mentioned this on this sub before, but everyone in my family is ~~Atypical~~ Unusual—well, at least my parents and I are. My younger sister is past the age where we'd expect her to get her ability. At least, so we thought.

Anyway, this is just a long-winded way of saying that I think you were right, n/theneonthorn—I think my sister probably *is* ~~Atypical~~ Unusual. But has anyone heard anything about an ability that makes you lose consciousness? Or is it possible for her to actually have narcolepsy *and* have an ability? Any insight/informed guesses/thoughts you guys have would really ease my mind. I don't know why, but I've got a really weird feeling about all of this.

ETA: Couple of terminology edits—thanks n/chuckxavier for the reminder.

theneonthorn
told ya. let us know what power she's got—sounds like it's gonna be a cool one.

> **thatsahumanperson**
> By the way, how're things going with your friend? Is he better?
> **theneonthorn**
> his power isn't back yet, but he seems to be doing okay. we're having a good time trying to figure it out at least.

chuckxavier

I've got some advice in a sec, but first things first—remember we don't use the A-word on this forum.

lokilover

Can I ask why not? With how open everyone is on this forum about stuff, I don't see the big deal.

chuckxavier

This site is pretty searchable—Unusuals is a term that can apply to a lot of different things and doesn't have the same official associations.

lokilover

I still don't see the big deal. Half the people on this sub don't believe that any of this is real.

chuckxavier

But it *is* real and there are people out there who know that and I would rather they didn't track us all down and experiment on us.

franklinsteinsmonster

whaaaaaaa wait does that like actually happen?

iwannabelieve

ooh, hey, new person! welcome!

onmyown

Don't listen to Chuck, he's being overly cautious. We adhere so strictly to anonymity here because this is the *internet* and people get doxxed and harassed all the time. It's no different from what every other group on here does.

onmyown

How has it been going with reading her thoughts? Have you still been hitting that wall?

thatsahumanperson

Honestly, I haven't been trying that hard. Things kind of blew up in my house when she told us about the narcolepsy, so I've mostly been keeping to myself to avoid the family drama.

onmyown

Smart. Well, keep us posted. That sounded like a bit of a head-scratcher to begin with, and especially now with all this new info. FWIW, it's totally possible for her to have an ability and a normal human ailment. I've got telekinesis and an autoimmune thing, so it happens. At least in my case, it ended up being kind of a blessing in disguise.

franklinsteinsmonster
the autoimmune thing?
onmyown
Nah, the telekinesis. My other thing sometimes makes it hard to move, so being able to get water from the couch is *chef's kiss.*
franklinsteinsmonster
that. is. so. cool.

chuckxavier
Have you observed her at all as she's been sleeping? It might be worth watching her and seeing what you notice. This sounds like it might be astral projection. If she's especially limp when unconscious, if her eyes roll back in her head, and if she's really difficult to wake up, that would be my guess.

thatsahumanperson
Dude, no way, I'm not gonna watch my sister sleep, that's way too creepy.
chuckxavier
I don't see how you expect to figure it out otherwise. Careful observation and study is the only way to be really certain of something.
thatsahumanperson
Yeah, I guess. I'll look into the astral projection thing. Thanks.

LATER

I'm not even sure I can find the words. Or, even if I could, I'm not sure I can physically write them. I feel like something has crawled into my brain and made a home there. Like something is lingering just over my shoulder, breathing on my neck, but when I turn to look, it disappears just out of sight, back into the shadows.

I'm shaking, I can barely write. I'm just sitting on a bench in some square in . . . Cambridge? Maybe? I don't know, nothing looks familiar, but I just had to get off the bus. I woke up screaming, flailing in the hard plastic seat of the bus, opening my eyes to see everyone around me staring at me like I was some kind of dangerous, wild thing.

I should start over. My thoughts are a mess. I was just on the bus. Writing in this journal. On my way from the restaurant to the doctor—my *actual* doctor—for a checkup and then: lights out.

I was at home in my bed. Feeling safe and warm and like nothing in the world could ever hurt me. No work, no kids in the house . . . just me, able to linger in between the dreamworld and real life for as long as I wanted.

A chill passed over me. There was a light scraping sound running along the hallway outside my bedroom. The floorboard in the doorway creaked and my entire body tensed in a false rigor mortis. Except I couldn't open my eyes. I could feel someone—some*thing* moving closer, breathing, their heavy footfalls making my stomach drop in dread.

I tried to open my eyes, to *move*, but I was stuck. Wide awake but paralyzed. The bed sagged under a new weight as something moved above me, crowding me, hovering over me, pushing down onto me. I finally was able to open my eyes but seeing the figure close up did nothing to make them clearer. But I knew, I *knew*, that this was it. This was the end of me and I tried to surge up, run away, push my body into action, but large rough hands circled around my throat, squeezing squeezing squeezing—

And that was when I woke up screaming bloody murder. I even

woke up the person in front of me who had been sleeping soundly and I must have scared her so much by yelling in her ear, because I could see tears on her face once my eyes adjusted to the waking world. I looked around me and saw wide, scared eyes staring at me, everyone trying to press themselves into the seats and walls of the bus to get as far away from me as physically possible. So I got up, shouted something at the driver, who opened the door to let me out, and now I'm here, sitting on a bench, trying to get my breath back.

I don't know that I've ever had a dream like that before. It felt *so* real. Like I really was at home in bed, waking slowly from sleep, then waking very suddenly as something—some*one*—came into my room and began to suffocate me. I felt so helpless. I thought I was going to die. Then, when I woke up, I thought that maybe I had hurt someone. I've checked my arms and legs and neck for scratches, but everything seems to be normal. Whatever that means now.

I don't think I have a handle on this anymore. Are my parents right? Is this an Atypical ability manifesting? There's a pit in my stomach at the thought. What if I'm like my mom—a precognate—and I've somehow seen a vision of something that's going to happen to me?

But . . . now that I've written it all out . . . I mean, kids in the house? What am I talking about? I'm not sure I was . . . *me* in the dream. Is that normal? Maybe that's something I should ask my doctor about, when I do finally actually go to see her. Or maybe I can go to Readit like Aaron seems to do with every single problem he has and see if anyone on there has any ideas.

Also, our floorboards don't creak. At least the ones in my bedroom don't. Reading what I wrote and doing my best to remember that dream, I don't think it *was* my bedroom. Which would make sense, if it wasn't me to begin with. I already feel like half a person sometimes, or *two* people—making myself as palatable to my extraordinary family as I can, while trying to be true to the person I want to be . . . and now I'm not even me in my own dreams? How is that fair?

Oh. Also. I fell asleep before finishing my last entry in here. It hardly seems as important now, but . . .

Emily said yes.

SEPTEMBER 10TH, 2016

I wish I could go back in time to seventeen-year-old Rose, who wanted her mom to pay more attention to her, who was jealous of all the focused love Aaron was getting after his mind reading started and tell her that she's wrong, having all of Mom's attention is actually a terrible thing and she should enjoy her peace while she can.

"Mom, really, I'm fine," I said in my best soothing voice as I dried the dishes she'd strong-armed me into helping her with. I thought that having a wrist brace would get me out of household chores but, according to her, "Drying doesn't get the brace wet, and you only really need to move one of your arms." So there I was.

"Are you still randomly losing consciousness?"

"Yes, but—"

"Then you're not fine."

"What power do you think I have exactly?" I asked as she handed me another plate. "You know that narcolepsy is, like, a totally normal human ailment. I mean, sure, it's rare, but it's not . . . atypical." I winced at my own dumb, unintentional pun.

"Rose, do you think I'm an idiot?" She turned off the faucet and turned to me, leaning her hip against the counter and crossing her arms across her chest.

"What?"

"I know that you falling asleep randomly is not all that's going on." She lifted one of her eyebrows in the "I know what you did and if you admit it now, your punishment won't be as harsh" look that she's spent our entire childhoods perfecting.

"What?" I asked again, except this time the hair on the back of my neck pricked in the way it always does whenever my mom either a) has a vision or b) has caught me out.

"The other night, you fell asleep on the couch and it's clear you were dreaming. Vividly," she added significantly.

"Okay . . ." I said, focusing on putting the dried plates back into the cabinet, rather than take the risk of continuing to make eye contact with a woman who is literally psychic.

"Most people don't try to physically run away while they dream," she said. "It was like you were a puppet who'd had their strings cut. Limp but fighting."

"You don't have to make it sound so creepy," I muttered.

"It *was* creepy!" she said, not making me feel better about this situation at all. I knew exactly what she was talking about. I'd fallen asleep watching TV—it had felt like a natural dozing off more than dropping into a dream—and I'd had the same nightmare about being chased by a snake that I've been having.

"I'm just worried about you," she said softly and that was when I realized I hadn't said anything in a few minutes, lost in my own memories about the recurring nightmare.

"If it's really going to make you feel better, I can go to the AM, get checked out."

"I don't think that's necessary," she said shortly, turning the sink back on and picking up the sponge.

And just like that, I've disappointed again. My intended olive branch was actually a hot poker. Despite the fact that everyone in my family had spent time at the Atypical Monitors, my mom has always had some strange grudge against them. I thought about arguing, about forcing her to explain exactly *what* was so bad about them, but that's not what I do. Even when I don't want to, I have to step back, to let the superhumans have their way, try and be a daughter my parents could be proud of.

I feel a little bit like my life is falling apart around me right now—not able to work, no school, no friends, worrying my family and unable to stay conscious for more than eight hours tops—so I'm trying to hold onto the fact that *I have a date.* Basically for the first time ever. I've hung out with girls before, kissed a few of them, but I've never done the whole "ask someone formally out on a date and then go on said date with the full understanding that you both are aware this is a romantic outing and the stakes are very high as a result" thing and I have no idea where to start.

(And no, I am NOT thinking about the fact that the only reason I asked a girl out was because MY MOTHER HAD A PSYCHIC VISION thankyouverymuch.)

Emily and I exchanged numbers right before I got onto the bus—*no,* don't think about that bus ride, that dream, just focus on having a cute girl's number programmed into your phone—and when I finally shook off that whole weird day, I realized that she had texted me to ask when I was free.

Already, I was failing at this. I had asked *her* out and she had to be the one to follow up with me!! Humiliating.

CLEARLY, I need help. So I turned to the one person I feel like I can trust on romantic matters: my dad.

Again: *humiliating.*

I guess, maybe, it would have been less embarrassing to ask Aaron but 1) I don't want him to feel like he can lord anything over me and 2) he's never had a relationship in his life and that's with the benefit of being a mind reader, so how much can he really know? So I swallowed my pride.

"Hey, Dad?" I asked, coming into the living last night as he read on the couch.

"Yeah, Rose?"

My dad is the only person in my family who always, *always* calls me Rose. My mom throws out a ton of pet names for Aaron and me both—sweetie, honey, kid, pumpkin, hey you—and Aaron has been calling me Rosie since he was old enough to talk, but my dad only ever calls me Rose. It always makes me feel more grown-up, like we're on the same level.

"What do you do on dates?" I did *not* feel grown-up when I blurted that question out. My dad hadn't looked up from his book (one of those bland crime thriller political drama things with a strong-jawed white man in silhouette on the cover) when I came into the room but the moment I asked that, he put his bookmark in, set the book down on his lap, and looked up at me.

"Excuse me?" he asked, taking his reading glasses off. I could see the ghost of a smile on his face and decided to just push through before he could tease me too badly.

"I just mean . . ." I started, "like, when you ask someone out, and they say yes, what's the next thing you're supposed to do?"

His mouth twitched in amusement.

"I know what's *next,* obviously," I rushed to add. "You find a time and then you meet up and . . ."

I trailed off, hoping that he would forgo poking fun and head straight for the fatherly advice.

"Rose," he said, in a tone of voice that I knew meant he *wasn't* going to breeze past the good-natured ribbing portion of this conversation, "do you have a date?"

"Yes," I said loftily, as if having a date was something that happened to me all the time.

"With whom?" he asked, matching my formal tone.

"A lovely young woman named Emily Rodriguez." I sniffed haughtily.

"Well, that's very exciting." He was nodding his head, his toothless smile coiled so tightly like he feared opening his mouth would lead to a laugh breaking out. For a few seconds, we just stayed there, looking at each other and nodding solemnly, him seated on the couch and me standing above him, hyperaware of my stiff posture.

"Ugh, just tell me what to do!" I moaned finally, collapsing down on the couch next to him. At that, his smile *did* burst open, wide and bright, his head tipping back in a warm, hearty laugh.

"Stop, I'm serious." I groaned, hitting his arm lightly as he laughed. But soon I was giggling too, never immune to the infectious nature of my dad's joy.

"I'm really proud of you, Rose," he said, smiling wide at me.

"Ew, why?" I asked, blushing furiously. Even though I knew, deep down, that he was proud of me—more accepting of jumping right into the workforce than my mom was—I hadn't heard it so directly in a while.

"You put yourself out there! Asked someone out! That's no easy thing and, from what I understand, your generation barely ever takes that step." He punctuated each of his sentences with a flourish of his hand and I shook my head at how ridiculous he continues to be despite the fact that he is well into his sixties. Actually, I'm sure he'd hate that characterization. He's sixty-two, which he'd say is the new fifty-five.

My parents waited a *long* time to have children. They got married pretty young, in their early twenties, but because they were both Atypical, they knew the risks of combining their DNA. Neither of them have had much trouble throughout the years with their abilities—my dad can just choose *not* to move things with his mind and my mom can keep her visions to herself. Which she usually does, actually, never wanting to influence me or Aaron too much, even when we would beg as children to have her tell us our fortunes. The various tips and aggressive pushes she's given me recently are a bit out of the norm, like the path I'm on isn't quite right and she's trying to steer me back on track.

Even though being Atypical hasn't put too much of a wrench in either of *their* lives, I think they feared that, with their powers combined or whatever, they'd have a kid that could spit fire or fly or something.

And my parents' worst fear came true: Aaron suffered because of something that was fundamental to his nature. The AM helped him learn to control his power, which helped the headaches he'd been experiencing, but they never went away completely. I know there are still sometimes when Aaron reads minds too much or not enough and gets a migraine that puts him out of commission for hours. But over the years, things have gotten back to normal. Or as normal as they ever were in the Atkinson household. Aaron started to bond with our parents over the weird intricacies of having an Atypical ability, while I graduated high school and stayed the same boring, human Rose I always had been. I find it hard to complain though, when I have a wonderful, healthy, loving family, who will stand by me and help me no matter what, even with their own disappointment. It's why I try so hard not to rock the boat more than I do by existing, which is why I'm still KICKING MYSELF over telling them about the narcolepsy.

Which brings me to now. Trying to get back to the usual "Rose is normal and has normal problems" by asking my sixty-two-year-old contractor father, who likes basic white-man thriller books and thinks medium salsa is too spicy, for lesbian dating advice.

"My generation dates all the time," I rebutted, poking his leg with my foot and leaning back onto the armrest of the couch. "In high school, it seemed like that's all *anyone* did."

"Not you," he pointed out. He meant it totally innocently, but hearing it still stung a little bit, reminding me how I've always felt a little different from the people around me in the wrong ways.

"And people in your generation may date," he continued, "but I'd be hard-pressed to find another teenager today who actually asked someone out in person."

"How do you know I did it in person?" I asked.

"A father always knows." He tapped the side of his head and winked.

"Try again." I rolled my eyes. "Did Mom see something?"

"If she did, she hasn't said anything to me." He shrugged and I knew he was telling the truth. Outside of important "need-to-know" stuff or the little things that don't matter, Mom's rare-vision-sharing policy extended to Dad too.

"But I know you, Rose. You don't seem to text very much, unless you can do it entirely in emojis. So it had to have been in person."

"Okay, yes," I admitted, "I asked her out in person."

"See?" He was victorious. "That is the classy move! I'd say you're ahead of the curve already."

"Okay, yeah, sure, but what do I do next?"

"Have you picked a date yet? A date for the date?" He chortled at his own . . . I hesitate to call it a joke.

"Yeah, she suggested Friday."

"Friday is a very good day for a date."

"I guess . . . I don't think it really matters," I said. "I'm not working right now and she's in college, so it's not like she has to get up early or anything—"

"Still, Friday is a classic. I know some people would argue for Saturday, because you have the whole day to relax and prepare, but Saturday is a good second-date day. You want the first date to be on a Friday, because you get the person fresh off their week."

"And that's a good thing?" I asked skeptically. I don't know anyone who is "fresh" after a full work or school week.

"Absolutely," he said, nodding vigorously. "The Saturday version of a person is its whole own thing. Some people are incredibly active on the weekends, picking up a million hobbies. Some laze about all day and watch TV. Others sleep in so late they barely *have* a Saturday."

"If that's a shot at me, it's not appreciated," I said. "The restaurant business has terrible hours."

"All I'm saying is that Saturday is its own sacred thing."

"I don't know if Emily is Jewish, Dad," I said, before adding, "Don't tell Mom." Though I guess there's a chance she already knows.

"I think your mom will just be thrilled by you going on a date with *anyone*," he teased. "And you know the only thing we *really* care about is you being with someone who treats you well."

"Yeah, yeah, yeah . . ." I mumbled.

"But I don't mean actually sacred though, yes, that too," he added. "I just mean that you have to work up to sharing the intimacy of a Saturday. On Friday, there's no shortage of conversation points, with work or school still buzzing around in your head. *And*, if the date is going badly, you can very believably claim that you're tired and cut the night short."

"You've thought about this a *lot*," I said.

"Your mother and I had our first date on a Friday," he said, smiling at the memory.

"Yeah, and you met when you were, like, twelve—"

"Twenty, actually—"

"So when exactly did you have a need for this very weird and specific dating philosophy?" I tilted my head and squinted at him, and was surprised to see him blush, just a little.

"All right, so I have to be honest," he said and part of me got worried for a second. Was there some horrible infidelity in my parents' history that I was about to find out about in this very silly conversation?

"I did not originate this philosophy," he said and I relaxed. "It's something Aaron and I have discussed."

"Ugh, are you serious?" I groaned. "I come to you and I still end up getting dating advice from *Aaron*?"

"He has a lot of experience to draw on," he said, completely nonjudgmentally in the kind of way that only my dad has ever been able to achieve.

"That's exactly why I *don't* want his advice!" I said, throwing up my hands. "I think I could actually really like this girl and I really want there to be a second and third date."

"Then just be yourself, Rose," he said. "That's all you really need to do."

"That's even worse advice than Aaron's," I said.

"Okay, here's some practical advice, because I know you like steps you can follow." I nodded in agreement at that. "Don't do dinner and a movie unless you already know she's a film buff. You can't talk during a movie and it's too much of a dice roll to pick one out that you'll both like. Dinner is great, but make sure to tell her the restaurant first so there are no surprises, and don't get dessert at the restaurant."

"Why not?"

"You don't want to stay in one place the entire date, or it will feel just like getting a meal or coffee with a friend. If things are going well, go to a different bar and get a drink—"

"I'm nineteen," I reminded him.

"Oh right." He shook his head, like he was trying to clear it. "Ice cream then. Or frozen yogurt or whatever you kids are into. Get it to go and go for a walk."

"A walk?"

"Yeah, take her out to Cambridge or Boston Common and go on a nice walk after dinner. You can talk without having to stare at each other over a table in a restaurant, *plus* you can walk her home depending on the area you're in."

"Dad," I said, mock-scandalized, "are you suggesting I try to invite myself in?"

"Absolutely not, young lady." He pointed a finger at me. "I know you don't face the risk of getting pregnant, but STIs are very real—if overstigmatized—and I really think you should get to know someone before—"

"Oh my god, please stop," I begged, mortified.

"I just think it's the courteous thing to do," he said as we both ignored our red-hot faces. "If the night is going well, walking someone to their doorstep can be a lovely way to end the evening."

"Okay," I said, focusing on the bits of un-sex-related advice he'd given me. "Dinner, dessert, and a walk, I can do that."

And I'm actually feeling like I can. I've plotted the whole thing out and already texted Emily the name of the restaurant—a new place they were talking about in the kitchen of Milton that's trendy but not *too* trendy and nice but not *too* nice (I'm not making money right now, after all)—and have our route to a bakery and then the Common mapped out. I don't know where Emily lives yet, so I'll just have to wing that bit, but I'm feeling confident. Confident-ish. As confident as anyone with a sprained wrist can be when going on their first real date ever with a girl who *also* has a broken wrist and I keep thinking about how we hurt opposite arms so can still hold hands and *christ* I really should probably go to sleep now.

I just hope I dream of Emily.

community/TheUnusuals post by n/thatsahumanperson

Jumping into this sub with a slightly different set of questions today.

I went to sleep pretty late last night—got caught up trying to build a new website from scratch for my dad's business as a birthday present for him and, despite his best efforts, I know literally nothing about construction, so it wasn't as simple of a task as I expected. I dropped off pretty quickly, which isn't always the easiest for me. When I'm falling asleep, I'm not making as much of an effort to block out thoughts, so if anyone else in the house is awake, sometimes a stray thought will worm its way in and wake me up. I usually try to go to bed after everyone else, but last night was even later than usual.

I don't dream a whole lot. Or, well, I guess I probably do, because I think most people do every night, but I usually don't remember the dreams all that much. Last night was different.

I was in a huge, black expanse. No walls, ceiling, or floors, just endless, eerily lit void. I've had dreams in darkness before, a recurring nightmare where a snake is chasing me and I can't run fast enough to get away, but this felt different.

Nothing was chasing me. I was just standing, completely still, waiting for . . . something. I've never had such clarity of feeling before in a dream, outside of "run, oh god, run" and "please, let this be a dream and I'm not actually failing my junior year math final" but I just knew with absolute certainty that I was waiting for something. There was this strange, heavy breeze that kept moving across me, like it was trying to push me in one direction. But I couldn't move my feet, I don't think I was *supposed* to move my feet. And then, a light started to seep through a doorway, a doorway that wasn't there before and it was growing brighter and brighter, humming with light, and the door was going to come to me when, all of a sudden, there was this terrible screech and I heard my sister's voice say my name.

Then I woke up.

I know that there are some other Unusuals out there who had a similar experience to me when their telepathy first started. It's different for each person, of course, but for me, it started with just a low, constant humming whenever I was around other people. I thought I had tinnitus or another hearing/neurological issue, but then the humming started to take shape. Now, when I *do* turn on the thought reading (which I promise I don't do often, please don't get on me about this, Chuck), it's more like tuning a radio to the specific frequency of a thought train and then turning up the volume.

The sound in my dream reminded me so much of that early hum and then, that screech, like the first time I met another mind reader when I was at . . . well, you know. That Place that people like us go that we're not supposed to refer to by name on here in case they found this sub and shut it down for "safety" reasons. When I was there for my initial training/Unusual-onboarding, I met another telepath and when we were in the same room for the first time, I got that screeching feedback. It calmed down pretty quickly, but I won't ever forget that sound.

Then . . . my sister's voice. I can't make sense of it. I'm thinking maybe my sister is a mind reader like me, but . . . can mind readers share dreams? Or is this unrelated to her sleeping?

I just feel really lost. Anyone have *any* ideas?

iwannabelieve
damnnnnn, man, these just get better and better! I can't wait for the next installment—I hope we find out what's going on with the sister!

> **onmyown**
> Christ, dude, we don't want to ban anyone but c'mon, how did you even find this sub?
>
> **iwannabelieve**
> community/ZeroSleep!
>
> **chuckxavier**
> Crap. n/onmyown?
>
> **onmyown**
> Yeah, I'm on it.

onmyown
This might be a dumb question (I don't know your relationship to That Place) but why doesn't she just go there and find out for certain?

> **thatsahumanperson**
> I mean, my relationship with them is totally fine. My time there wasn't exactly . . . fun? But it was definitely helpful. I know folks have mixed feelings, but, as tough as it was, I don't think I'd be where I am today, have

the control I do, without spending time there. I think my sister hasn't thought about going because . . . what would she ask? I know that That Place helps Unusuals who are new to their abilities, but they don't exactly diagnose someone who hasn't actually shown any real evidence of having an ability. I'm not sure they'd know what to do with her.

chuckxavier

For anyone who might not take n/thatsahumanperson's comment about The Powers That Be shutting us down seriously, that *has* actually happened before. If it hadn't been for n/theneonthorn's backups, we would have lost this whole community.

onmyown

Oh, is that why we're *the* unusuals and not just community/Unusuals?

theneonthorn

yep. don't mess with TPTB.

tacotacotaco

Sorry for using the throwaway, there's some folks I wouldn't want finding out I post on here. I'm a telekinetic and, while I've never experienced what you're talking about, I totally have seen two . . . Unusuals (that's the term you use on here, right?) with the same ability clash before. I work with people like us and it really does sound like something is going on with your sister (I read through your other posts). I think you should suggest that she goes to the place that helps folks like us, if you live nearish one that is, which it sounds like you do. Worst-case scenario, she goes in for one appointment and they send her home.

thatsahumanperson

Yeah, I think you're right. I know that an actual research institution is probably the best place for her and when she first told us about the narcolepsy, I could hear her thinking about wanting to sign up for a sleep study, so it's not like she's averse to being poked and prodded a bit. But . . . I don't know. I think I'm just hesitant about having that conversation.

tacotacotaco

Because you think she might be offended?

thatsahumanperson

No, not offended, necessarily. She'd never admit it, but I think she was pretty disappointed when I turned out to have an ability. We both thought it skipped a generation and then . . . me. I think maybe she's just overwhelmed?

onmyown

I think n/tacotacotaco is right—and maybe you can talk to her and tell her you understand it's overwhelming, but you're there for her. Someone did that to me when I was first going through it, and it made all the difference in the world to just know that there was someone there for me.

thatsahumanperson

Yeah . . . these are all totally valid points and I know she probably *could* use someone right now . . . lord knows I really leaned on this sub when I was first going through it. I don't know what I would have done if I hadn't found you guys. Even after I was done with all the inpatient stuff and had a better grip on it all, this community was really a safe haven. It's a little weird that I've never actually met any of you—that I don't even know your names—but it's also easier to talk about stuff that way. My sister and I don't really have the kind of relationship where we talk about stuff. We're not exactly the heart-to-heart type. I don't know . . . maybe now is the time to start?

SEPTEMBER 16TH, 2016

I really have always been the weird little alien that doesn't quite fit into my family and tonight really clinched that.

I had just gotten home from my date with Emily—oh my god, my date with Emily! Okay, the family drama can wait, first the good stuff. I want to remember every moment and I feel like it almost got washed away by the maelstrom that sucked me under when I went downstairs the next morning. I'd had the *weirdest* dream and was still half asleep when I came into the kitchen and, well, my head is still a little all over the place. Clearly.

How do people do this? I remember in AP History, we had to do a project on, like, primary sources, and I read a bunch of personal diaries from ye olden times and how did people write so linearly? "I woke up and then this happened and now here's my entire conversation with my comrade and also every single dollar I spent on mead today." My brain doesn't work like that. It's always thinking of a hundred things overlapping at once, and then a hundred *more* things bubbling underneath all of that. I think that's why I like cooking. It's straightforward in the sense that it has a sequence and, especially in a professional kitchen like Milton, it can be downright militaristic in its precision, but it's also the perfect sport for the multitasking brain. You have to keep track of so many things at once—timings of what's on the stove, in the oven, what needs to be plated, making sure everything's seasoned properly, making sure everything is going to come out the perfect temperature. Working in a kitchen rewards my scattershot thinking and lightning-quick attention jumps.

Anyway. My dream.

I was back in that black, impossibly lit place. The floorless, endless void that sometimes has a doorway I still haven't been able to access. I woke up in the dream—I'm not sure how long I was there, but nothing was chasing me this time. I woke up and was just . . . there. Just standing. And there was this eerily beautiful hum, like siren song, like hearing a choir from very far away. The humming grew and suddenly I could move and I looked around and, off in the distance, there was a figure. Tall, wiry, pointy elbows. A figure I'd recognize anywhere. Even though I could turn my body to look at him, I still couldn't step my feet forward. So I called out his name, shouting "Aaron" and his head turned sharply my way, like it was a shock that I was there. Even though, thinking about it now, it wasn't a shock to me that *he* was there. It was like I woke up in the dream ready to find him. I was about to open my mouth again, call out louder, when I had a feeling like I was being kicked in the chest, and was sent hurtling backward through the black.

I landed, hard, on soft ground. Instinctually, I stood up and dusted myself off, even though . . . do dreams have dust? As I took in my new surroundings, I noticed that I was in a similarly infinite space as before, but not the bottomless black pit where there are so many things to run from. This was neutral, with light coming in from all sides, bright but not blinding. Like a blank canvas. I stayed there, able to move but walking nowhere, for what felt like hours and minutes. I remember having agency, feeling lucid, but I couldn't *do* anything, not even make myself fly like the lucid dreaming forums I've been reading say you can.

Eventually, I woke up. Totally unremarkable and utterly baffling.

Emily agreed.

"That is *so* strange," she said over her bibimbap, before biting into a perfect matchstick carrot. I still don't really understand what compelled me to tell her about my *dream* of all things, the universally agreed upon subject that no one ever wants to hear about, but I'll chalk it up to nerves. Thankfully, she seemed to be interested in my description of the blank canvas or, at least, was interested enough in *me* to pretend.

"I wish I could lucid dream," she said, her mouth quirking. Anytime I've seen that word in that context—a "mouth quirking"—I never understood what it meant. It always seemed like one of those made-up internet phrases to me. But over an hour spent eating Korean food, I began to understand. Whenever Emily finds something amusing, which it seems she often does, the corner of her mouth lifts and twists, like she's got a secret. On anyone else—anyone with a sharper voice or colder demeanor—I think I would feel made fun of, left out. On her . . . it was mesmerizing, like she was bringing me in on the joke.

"I had never done it before until a few weeks ago," I said. "So there's still hope for you." The quirk of her mouth bloomed into a full smile and my heart melted.

The whole dinner had been like that. Emily was vibrant and charming and easy with her smiles while I felt stiff and nervous. But every few minutes I would say something that would make her eyes light up, making my stomach swoop in turn.

"I know *exactly* what I would do," she said, all her teeth showing, perfect in their slight crookedness.

"What's that?" I leaned forward, putting my elbows on the table.

"*Fly*," she breathed, her eyes going wide, and I giggled. I am historically *not* a giggler.

"That's what all the forums say!" I laughed, too embarrassed to admit that's also what I would do if I could.

"What forums?"

"I've been checking out some lucid dreaming communities on Readit, trying to figure out how to . . . how to control it, I guess."

"Well, that's the whole point, right?"

"Yeah, seems to be." I nodded. "Everyone's got a different way of approaching it as far as I can tell, but apparently you can actually train yourself to start lucid dreaming."

"What, really?" She laughed. "That's nuts!"

"I know!" I laughed too. "Here I am just trying to figure out how to fly in the first place—which is a lot of people's go-tos and seems *completely* inaccessible to me—and some people are full-on going into meditative trances to learn how to control every second of their dreams."

"Okay, that sounds exhausting. Sleep is for resting, not . . . whatever that is."

"Ugh, it's true." I groaned. "I really do feel like I haven't gotten a good night's sleep since this whole thing started."

"Are you sure the lack of good sleep isn't because you've been sleeping in a cast? Because that's definitely been *my* issue."

"You know . . ." I said, "my whole lucid dreaming thing *did* start after I sprained my wrist. So if you start lucid dreaming too, maybe there's something going on at that urgent care."

"*Ooh*, like we both touched the same radioactive pens while filling out our intake forms and now we have *powers*." Her eyes were wide again as she fanned out her hands in mock drama, made even more endearing by the limited mobility of the hand in the cast, but instead of being able to fully revel in her goofiness, I felt a pit in my stomach at the mention of powers.

I took that moment to stuff a rice cake (crispy on the outside and chewy on the inside, I *have* to figure out how to do that) into my mouth and attempt a giggle around it.

Emily seemed to sense some degree of awkwardness—I get the impression she's one of those people who is good at social cues—and politely changed the subject.

"So Readit, huh?" she asked.

"Yeah." I shrugged one shoulder. "I haven't spent a lot of time on there or anything, but where else do you go for weird experiences?"

"Very fair," she said. "I'm more of a Mumblr and AO3 girl myself."

"Oh my god, please don't hate me, but I have no idea what that is," I said lightly, even though I totally meant it. Emily, with her casual tank top and jeans that still somehow looked so put together and cool, and her undercut, and her wing-tipped eyeliner that I've never in a million years been able to figure out, was *way* out of my league and I was convinced that the tiniest thing—the food I ordered, not liking her favorite websites—would be the nail in the coffin of my chance with her.

"Are you serious?" She laughed.

"Well, no, I know Mumblr," I rushed to explain. "I was on there for a hot second before getting more into Instagram."

"Ohhh, okay, so you were the cool photo art blog side of Mumblr."

"Photos, yes, but *definitely* not cool ones. Just recipes and stuff."

"Sounds pretty cool to me," Emily said and, again, that smile, like she had a secret I didn't mind her keeping.

"But, I *will* admit to never having heard of the other one," I said, feeling hot under her gaze.

"AO3?"

I nodded.

"It stands for Archive of Our Own. It's a fanfic site."

"You write fanfic?" I asked.

"Yeah . . ." She winced. "Is that the dorkiest thing you've ever heard?"

"No, not at all!" I blurted. "I think that's really cool!"

"You do?"

"Yeah!" I nodded enthusiastically, as if it would convince her more. "I mean, I don't know anything about it—I've never read any fanfic before—but you want to be a writer, right?"

"Yeah . . ." Her face softened, her smile turning into one I hadn't seen so far, one that felt like waking up naturally with the sunlight. "I do. You remembered that?"

"Of course," I said, and the wattage went up in her smile.

We just sat there for a second, smiling like total goofballs, both of us leaning closer and closer to stare at each other across the table. When I couldn't stand staring directly into the sunlight of her smile for a moment longer, I cleared my throat.

"Can fanfic be poetry?" I asked. "That's what you want to be, right? A poet?"

"I mean, yeah, that's the big dream." She rolled her eyes at herself. "But it's *kind of* a hard career path."

"Right . . . not a lot of professional, full-time poets these days, huh?"

"Not really." She laughed. "But fic is a good way to stretch my wings. I study mostly poetry and nonfiction prose in school, so it's nice to dip my toes into fiction from time to time. And yeah, sometimes poetry and fanfic overlap, but mostly I'm writing narratives."

"What do you write it for?" I asked. And then, realizing I had no idea what I was talking about: "Wait, that's how it works, right? You write *for* something? A fandom?"

"Yeah, that's how it works." She chuckled. "I write for the MCU—the Marvel Cinematic Universe."

"Oh yeah, my brother loves those movies!" I said. "I've seen bits and pieces of it before with him. It's fun!"

She laughed a big laugh.

"You don't have to say you like it, it's okay—"

"No, really! I'm more of a fantasy over superheroes person, but all the actors seemed good."

"Have you seen the Captain America movies?" she asked.

"I think so? Maybe the first one," I said, vaguely remembering Chris Evans in a WWII costume. "Is that the one about the two guys who are, like, childhood friends in love with each other and then one of them dies?"

"Yes, exactly!" Emily's entire body lit up, her hands coming in front of her to animate and punctuate every word. "That's exactly who I write about! Steve and Bucky. They are *so* in love."

"Wait, really? That's what your fic is about?"

"Yeah! Steve is Captain America, obviously, and Bucky is his best-friend-slash-soldier-slash-eventual-assassin—it's a long story. But it's, like, the most epic love story ever put to film. The angst of this normal person who's given all these powers and it makes him so different from the person who knows him best and then *that* person goes through the same thing but they're torn apart . . . ugh, the *pining* of it all!" She laughed big again and then collapsed back into her chair, shaking her head. "I can't believe you got that they were in love from one movie. *That's* how strong their chemistry is."

"And that's *me*," I joked. "I'm terrible at picking up signals."

Her mouth quirked again.

"I wouldn't say that," she said softly. A shiver rushed up and down my spine and I could feel the blush that I'd had on my face more or less since the moment we sat down growing. That was flirting, right? Even now, recounting it, it feels too good to be true.

"So how'd you get into the Readit thing?" she asked after a moment, when the air between us had become so thick with tension we were both feeling light-headed.

"Oh, uh . . ." I tried to clear the bright, shiny light that was blocking everything else out from my head. I'd never experienced that before—being so overwhelmed by someone's beauty, their . . . *them*-ness that concentrating on anything else felt impossible.

"I wouldn't say I'm *into* it," I answered finally, when my brain had come back online enough to register her question. "I've really only looked into the lucid dreams communities and even that because I wasn't sure where else to look."

"It would never have occurred to me to check *Readit* for something," she said, shaking her head. "Somehow I don't feel like I would be welcome there."

"Why's that?" I asked, taking a sip of my tea.

"I'm a pansexual Latina who spends her time writing slash fic and poetry." She laughed. "I'm not exactly Readit's main demo."

"Okay, fair, fair." I laughed, narrowly avoiding choking on my drink. "That's exactly what I thought too, if I'm honest. But my brother has met some good friends on there and yeah, he's a straight, cis guy, but I feel like the internet famously doesn't love Jewish people either, so . . ."

"That's a good point," she said. "Does your brother lucid dream too?"

"Uh . . . He's really into tech stuff," I said, soothed by the fact that I wasn't technically lying to Emily on our very first date. "Like, coding and all that."

"Ooh, very cool," she said. "Are you two close?"

"In age," I answered, my voice feeling more barbed coming out of my throat than I meant it to.

"Gotcha." She nodded sagely and I knew she was reading something in my tone that I hadn't fully intended to be there.

"Do you have siblings?" I asked, trying to change the subject and mostly failing.

"Two sisters," she said. "They're both older, already off in the real world." Her oldest sister, Maria, works in humanitarian aid and it was clear that Emily has been looking up at her with stars in her eyes since they were kids. The middle sister, Chelsea, was in law school and sounded sharp and funny. I found myself laughing more and more as Emily talked, imagining her as a young girl, getting into and out of trouble with two other girls with her smile.

The way Emily talked about them made me feel warm all over, and just slightly cold inside, as I looked at something that I felt close to having but couldn't quite grasp. When we found out what Aaron could do, what Atypical ability he'd gotten in the dice roll of genetics, there was a brief, tiny moment, when I liked the idea of Aaron being able to read my mind. It ended up being a lot weirder than I expected, but for one second, I thought that maybe if he could hear everything I was thinking, we could be effortlessly close like some other siblings seem.

But instead, when I got home from my date to find my family in some kind of weird argument, I couldn't look at Aaron and roll my eyes in a moment of sibling solidarity like I would if we lived in a TV show. I just stood in the doorway between the front hall and the living room, wondering what the hell was going on.

"I'm telling you, I left it right here," my dad said, pointing to the arm of the couch. "Are you *sure* you didn't move it?"

"Yes, I'm sure," Aaron said. "I haven't even been in here all day."

"We really should talk about that," my mom said. "I don't think it's good for you to be staring at that screen all day."

"Mom," Aaron said, "literally everyone stares at a screen all day. It's 2016."

"Can we focus please?" my dad said, sounding more exasperated than I'd heard him in a long time.

". . . what's going on?" I asked, practically tiptoeing into the room. I'd planned to tell my dad about the date right then (the end of which was *very* good) but the weird frustration rolling off of him in waves had squashed that plan.

"Your father has misplaced his book," my mom said, lovingly rolling her eyes, a talent that she seems to have perfected.

"Okay . . ." I said, confused. "Is this really a family summit situation?"

"It wasn't so much before you got here," Aaron said. "I was just passing through."

"Focus, *please*," my dad said again. "I put it right here"—he gestured sharply to the couch—"and now it's gone."

"Darling, did you look on the nightstand?" my mom asked.

"Of course I looked on the nightstand," he said.

"No you didn't." Aaron laughed, shaking his head.

"Don't go poking around in my head, Aaron," he said, jokingly pointing his finger at Aaron. The frustration that had been there seconds ago seems to have dissipated, his voice light and more like him.

"I'm not!" Aaron put up his hands in mock surrender. "It's not my fault the truth jumped out."

My dad threw a pillow at Aaron's head without lifting a finger and my mom snorted.

"It's not on the nightstand, I know it's not," my dad insisted, his tone taking a sharp turn back to annoyed.

It went on like that for a few more minutes, my dad refusing to look anywhere in the house because he was so certain where he'd left it and convinced that someone must have moved it and my mom gently suggesting different locations until she gave up to go to bed, leaving with a sarcastic comment about looking for it in a vision. All the while, Aaron just squinted at our parents, his eyes and mouth tight, without saying a word.

Writing it all out now, it doesn't seem that weird or bad but . . . I don't know, I just got such a *vibe* from everyone. Not a good vibe. Even with the moments of lightness, of my dad and Aaron goofing off like they always have, it felt charged.

Maybe we've all been living together too long, now transitioning into something more like roommates than parents and kids. Or maybe it's just me. Maybe I just don't understand the various ways that three Atypical people communicate, the way they're inherently connected. I know I'm inherently connected to them too, linked to them through blood and a lifetime of sharing a space, but it feels like I'm missing some fundamental part of what it means to be an Atkinson and nothing I do, no amount of Readit-searching or trashy-book-reading or future-worrying I do will ever be enough to bridge that gap.

09-16-2016, morningwaffles, text post

First off, thank you thank you *thank you* for all the wonderful comments y'all have been leaving on *somewhere a place for us*—your comments give me life, water my crops, et cetera, et cetera. I am THRILLED to tell you that I got a lot of writing done last weekend, so NO MORE DELAYS (she said, blindly confident despite the fact that midterms are looming on the horizon). So, for now at least, we'll go back to our regular schedule of posting new chapters on Sunday and, *hoo boy,* I think you guys are really gonna like tomorrow's installment. The angst of last week won't be . . . resolved, per se, but it will be . . . well, you'll see ;)

In non-angst news, my inbox is FULL of queries about the fair and lovely "Daisy." And, I think I left you all hanging last time when I described our latest encounter and then in the next post was like "lol I have a date now" but the important thing is: the date happened. And Reader, it was *good.*

She's a lot quieter than I expected. Last time I saw her, I assumed her initial shyness was just because we caught each other off guard and she was soaked from the rain. Because when I walked her to the bus stop, she seemed pretty dry and confident—I mean, she asked me out! Like, in person! That's a baller move.

So I was a bit surprised to find that she's a lot more reserved. Which is not a bad thing by *any means,* I'm just feeling a little self-conscious and nervous because I feel like I don't have a mode that *isn't* super talkative and giggly and overly enthusiastic. I seriously hope I didn't scare her off.

I don't *think* I did because, after dinner, she took me to this cool bakery and then for a walk around this big park that's in our city. And the way that it happened, it seemed like she *planned* it. SWOON. I can't remember the last time I went on a date where I felt . . . wooed. Maybe never. Okay, *definitely* never. And there was something about the walking that seemed to relax her, like not having to look at each other over a table weighed down with distracting food made it easier to talk.

Because here's the thing: Daisy *loves* food.

"I've just always been obsessed with it," she told me as we walked around a big pond in the middle of the park.

"Eating it or making it?" I asked. "Or both?"

"Definitely both."

She smiled. When she smiles, it's this lovely, hesitant thing. Like she doesn't really know if it's okay. Like every time she wants to smile, she has to dust it off first before bringing it out.

"There's something about getting something right," she said. "It's addictive. Food isn't something you can perfect all the way. You can master your technique, know all of the different ways of preparing something, learn every single dish but, at the end of the day, every time is going to be a little bit different. The ingredients will be just a little bit different than they were the last time because you've gotten them from a different grower, or the crop has changed in some minuscule way. Bringing out the flavors of an ingredient isn't the same each time you do it. That's what I love. You just keep doing something, over and over again, to try and get it right, knowing that each time you're starting with just a couple of bits of things that came from the ground or the ocean or the sky and you get to transform it into something else."

I genuinely didn't know what to say to that. Daisy hasn't even been to culinary school yet—she's saving up at the moment—but she thinks more about her craft and her work than 75 percent of the people I go to school with. It is . . . *unbearably* sexy. That level of dedication, of *focus . . .*

I want to go out with her again and have her turn that focus fully on me.

SEPTEMBER 18TH, 2016

I was wrong. I was so, so wrong.

I don't know why I was so resistant to the idea this whole time, that I could be Atypical. I think, deep down, I didn't even want to entertain the possibility, just in case it wasn't true. I'd made my peace with that never happening. I didn't want the old fantasy dangled in front of me.

Last night, I was back in high school. At first I thought I was just in the same old anxiety dream that's been cropping up ever since freshman year and, I was horrified to discover, did *not* go away when I had my diploma in hand. It's a standard dream: I'm late for class, I show up only to discover that we're giving class presentations about a book I've never read and I'm first up. I get up in front of the class, no notes, no knowledge of the book and then, you know, horrible sweat-inducing nightmare. Nothing earth-shattering.

So when I woke up inside Dream High School, I expected the beats of the story to follow the same path they always have. Except . . . I wasn't rushing down the hall to class. The hallway was *busy*, instead of the usual eerie emptiness of a school hallway five minutes after the bell has rung. This time, it was bustling, full of people I only vaguely recognized. Not the kind of recognition where you can place their name, or even remember their face, but the kind of knowing that prickles the back of your neck, speaks to something deep in your lizard brain.

And then: the humming. That faint inhuman chorus that I heard in the black space. A dream that now makes a lot more sense to me given what happened next.

Just as before, a familiar figure was in the distance, just down the hall, on the other side of a sea of people. My brother stood, not in the strange, still way he stood in the void space, but like he was himself, in school. Backpack slung over his shoulder, looking down at his phone, a slight smile on his face like he was texting one of his dumb high school friends he's since lost touch with or flirting with a new girl. I just watched him for a moment, as he slid his phone in his pocket and started to walk down the hallway. That was when I noticed the hallway was *different* than my usual Nightmare High School. It was wider, more spacious.

That was because it *wasn't* mine.

"Aaron!" I called out, like I somehow subconsciously knew I was in *his* high school. Like I wanted to ask him how he made the hallway wide.

He didn't respond—why would he have? Should he have? If it had been my dream? UGH okay I am getting *way* ahead of myself.

I called out. He didn't respond. So I started to walk toward him, but there were so many people and just the feeling of being back in high school with all those people who never liked me and never even *tried* to like me, I was starting to get overwhelmed, like this *was* the anxiety dream I always have, but with a different flavor, the crush of people creating the claustrophobia, not the narrow hallway, and all I wanted was for everyone around me to go away so I could talk to my brother, for them to just vanish into thin air and then—

They did.

Just like that, every single person in the hallway faded into wisps of vapor, immediately dissolving into the air like spun sugar. Like they were never there. Aaron and I were still a whole locker block of space apart but he stopped walking, looking down the hallway like he was seeing it for the first time. His brow furrowed, lightly confused, as if he sensed that something was off instead of seeing that a *whole hallway of students just disappeared.*

"Aaron!" I called out again, jogging toward him. ". . . Hi."

I didn't know what else to say. It felt like we were meeting each other in a place we were both surprised to see the other person, despite the fact that we went to the same high school and are sixteen months apart, so we passed each other in these halls all the time. But there was something wrong—we weren't supposed to be here.

I was partly correct. *One* of us wasn't supposed to be here.

". . . Rose?" His body was half-turned to me, his phone still in his hand. Something in his face flickered, like the image of him was glitching and for a moment I was looking at Aaron as I know him now, before I blinked and he went back to Aaron of a few years ago.

"Rose?" he asked again, his voice shaking.

Then, suddenly, everything around us shook and we were in the black void again, the air pressing in around us. There was a bright flash of light, like the sun exploding, and then we were in our living room.

Aaron, with no backpack, no phone, none of the youthful glow he'd had in the high school, looked frantically around the space. It definitely *was* our living room but, like the school hallway, there was something uncanny about it. Everything looked correct—the couch facing the fireplace, two armchairs on either side, my grandmother's old coffee table in the middle, photos on the mantel. But we weren't home.

"Rose, what—" Aaron was breathing heavily, spinning around in an attempt to understand his surroundings that made him look like a dog trying to see where the ball went.

"Where are we?" he asked, stopping his pivot to look at me, his expression like he was noticing for the first time that I was there.

"You—there's—we're—" I couldn't find the words. It felt like I was rebooting, my brain loading along with the environment, a computer trying to run a new program. That was how Aaron described it. Like he was getting the spinning rainbow wheel of death and then a rush of code all at once and then all the graphics coming into focus. I kind of get what he means—my dawning realization felt a bit like that—but I can't imagine how much worse it must have been for him. At least I already knew I was dreaming.

"You were dreaming." I breathed, the pieces finally clicking together in my head. "That's where we are. We're in your dream."

There was a long pause, completely silent. But the silence was *wrong*. If we had been in our living room, we would have heard the sounds of the street, birds chirping, the house creaking. People think they know what silence is, but dream silence—the silence manufactured by a sleeping brain—is a kind of pure quiet that is impossible to describe.

"What?"

"What were you dreaming about before you saw me?"

"Rose, I—I'm awake, I have to be awake. Why do I feel like I'm on drugs?"

"That's just what it feels like at first," I said, remembering the way my brain felt like Technicolor jelly the first time I lucid dreamed and how that feeling was impossible to imagine again the moment I woke up.

"What *what* feels like?" he asked. He was beginning to panic. His voice was doing the thing it did when our parents were away for the weekend and we broke an antique vase while playing "the floor is lava." I'd been convinced that we could glue the vase back together (I was wrong) and Aaron was convinced that we'd both be grounded for a year (we weren't).

"Lucid dreaming," I answered as calmly and authoritatively as possible.

"Rosie, what the *fuck* is going on?"

Before I could answer, the floor turned to lava.

And then I woke up.

I was surprised to find that it was already morning, the dream still ringing in my head, clear as a bell. I just lay there for a second, serenely turning the dream over in my mind, examining it, before the full weight of what had just happened hit me like a truck.

I bolted up in bed like I'd just been shot through with adrenaline and burst out of my room, only to find Aaron already marching down the hallway toward me.

"Uh . . . Rose?" he demanded.

"Yeah, so . . ."

"What . . ."

"That's never happened before . . ."

"Did you . . . ?"

"I think so? You remember . . . ?"

"Yeah . . . and then the floor . . ."

"Turned to lava. Yeah, that *definitely* has never happened before."

I have a lot of questions. But at least I have one answer: looks like I'm Atypical after all.

community/TheUnusuals post by n/thatsahumanperson

So . . . anyone ever heard of dreamdivers?

December 22nd, 2016

Dear Mark,

The one upside to being trapped in this hellhole: whatever they've got me hooked up to is letting me sleep, dreamlessly. You wouldn't know this, because I was always the one who was up first, the one who barely slept so that you could, choosing instead to keep an eye on the motel door, through the venetian blinds, out the windshield, wherever we were, to keep us safe. A lot of good that did. We were doomed from the beginning—manipulator versus mimic. It was always gonna go sour.

If you had been more awake this summer, or had stayed up to watch over me, you might have become privy to the nearly nightly terrors that jolt me from sleep. You might have watched me twitch and gasp awake, soaked in sweat. As it was, I always tried to make myself presentable before you woke up, hide the sweat and the circles under my eyes, thanking my lucky stars that we never had to share a bed, ~~even though I'd started to~~

Maybe this is the end of the road for me. There's so much I've done—some you know, most you don't—that should have been the thing that ended me. But it looks like Caleb did me in. Does he feel bad about beating me half to death? Or is he just happy that his boyfriend is safe?

I wouldn't have hurt Adam. I really mean that. Wadsworth doesn't seem to believe me though, and I guess she's reserved the only living part of her ice-cold heart for her sweet little nephew.

Sleep brings me peace—it's when I'm awake that I find myself in the nightmare.

09-22-2016, morningwaffles, text post

What do you do when you've had a great first date and you were pretty sure there was going to be a second—in fact, there was even a discussion *on* the first date about a second happening the following week and now that day is tomorrow and you'd talked about maybe seeing a movie so you've started looking up show times, but you're not sure it's even worth looking into because, despite that first date being really, *really* good, she hasn't texted you back in three days and you think you might be getting ghosted? Anyone have any advice?

SEPTEMBER 2?, 2016

I think I just spent two days sleeping. I don't remember much after . . . Sunday? Maybe? I know it's sometime in the middle of the week, I think, but everything has been so hazy. I've been awake for a few hours now—have eaten, washed my face because showering felt like too much work—and I already want to go back to sleep. But I promised myself, when I groggily got out of bed at 1 p.m. today, that I would try and write in here before I fell asleep again. That I would try and document everything that's happened the past few days. And *a lot* has happened.

After Aaron and I realized that we were IN THE SAME DREAM, we just sort of stood there in the hallway for a moment, staring blankly at each other. I had wanted to sit down, catch my breath, maybe have some coffee, and talk things through with him. Go over every detail of the dream and figure out if *he* had been dreaming about school before I got there, or if I had, or if we were somehow building something separately together. But Aaron put a wrench in that very civilized plan.

"Mom!" he shouted, his eyes not moving from my face. "Dad!"

Traitor.

Fifteen minutes later, we were all gathered around the kitchen table, sipping our coffee, our parents silently processing everything we'd just told them.

"Anyone want to say something?" I blurted, the veneer of calm freaking me out. "Chime in about what the hell is going on?"

"This explains the narcolepsy at least" was all my dad had to say.

"I knew this wasn't a 'run-of-the-mill' sleep disorder," my mom said, shaking her head. "It never is."

"Except you *didn't* know," I pointed out. "You didn't have a vision about me being Atypical, Aaron wasn't able to read it in my thoughts . . . so let's not pretend like I'm the only one here who didn't know what was going on. I *still* don't know what's going on."

"Don't be mad at me for not foreseeing this," my mom said. "You know I don't choose when or about what to have my visions."

"I'm not—" I sighed, stifling my outburst like always, before starting again. "I'm not *mad* at anyone, I just . . . I want to understand. What do we think is wrong with me?"

"There's nothing *wrong* with you, Rose," my dad said, reaching his hand across the table to pat my arm. "You're Atypical. That's a beautiful thing."

My dad was smiling softly at me, genuine warmth and excitement glittering in his eyes. Finally, I was part of the club, joining him in the specialness of being different, being *magic*. But out of the corner of my eye, I saw both my mom's and Aaron's expressions tighten around the mouth and eyes. Telekinesis has always been a fun, magical thing for Dad, but my mom and brother have a different relationship to their Atypical abilities. My dad has a gift, they have burdens. I wonder which mine will be.

"All right, what do we *know*?" Aaron asked after a moment. "You're sleeping a lot and you were in my dream. And we were able to talk to each other, but I was definitely still asleep. Are you a mind reader too?"

"She's a dreamdiver." My dad smiled and the word sent a shiver up my spine.

"A dreamdiver." I breathed. "What is that?"

"Exactly what it sounds like," my mom said. "You can go inside people's dreams."

"I think you were in my dream the other night too," Aaron said suddenly.

"What?" Goose bumps broke out all along my arms.

"You called out my name."

The empty space. Aaron standing still, the hum, the need to call out to him.

This was real. This was happening. I was in my brother's *dreams*.

"Oh my god . . ." I breathed.

"You remember too," he said, not a question.

"Yeah . . . yeah, I do."

That admission set off a whole other round of questioning—what was the first strange dream I had, where was I, had I seen either of my parents in any of the dreams. That was when the pieces really started to click together.

The snake chasing me, a recurring nightmare of Aaron's that I didn't realize he still had.

The nightmare I had on the bus and the stranger's scared face, like my screaming had woken *her* up from a bad dream. It had. I'd been screaming *because* of her bad dream.

The urgent care, with Emily, those two men I thought I recognized. I *did* recognize them, from a movie though, not real life. Was Emily asleep too? Was I inside her head while she was awake?

The further I tried to think back, the harder it became to remember when this all started.

"How do you even know about this?" I asked, one of the least important questions out of the millions running around my head, but the safest one. "Do you know other dreamdivers?"

"The AM told me about them," my dad said. "There was one there at the same time I was—I never met them, but they were the talk of the program. It's an unusual ability."

"Great . . ." I muttered. Looks like I won't even be fitting in among the weirdos.

I guess I'll find out for sure—it's already decided that I'm going to be shipped off to the AM. Tomorrow. The moment the place was mentioned, everyone decided that that was the next best logical step.

"Are we sure that's necessary?" I asked, fear crawling up my throat. "Can't we just play things out at home for a little bit? Maybe it's just a phase."

"Rose, you've been sleeping in more and more the past few weeks," my mom said softly. "I'd be more inclined to let it slide if we could say for certain that it was just typical teenage exhaustion, but now this . . . your ability seems to be escalating. You need to get help."

"I'm not sick," I argued.

"It's just like getting a yearly physical, Rose," my mom said. " Just a little bit more thorough. You'll just go and get checked out, stay for a bit to make sure everything's all right."

"By the end of it, you'll have such a good grasp on your ability, you won't need to worry about it getting in the way of your life," my dad added, rather foolishly optimistic in my opinion. This didn't feel like learning how to rollerblade, like I could just dedicate two solid weeks to it and have it figured out.

"It's true," my mom said, clearly sensing my skepticism. "You know I'm not the AM's biggest cheerleader, but there really is no better way to learn about your ability."

That was that. Aaron was uncharacteristically silent throughout the entire conversation about the AM, despite being the person who had been there most recently. So when we both happened to be in the kitchen again a few hours later, I bit the bullet and decided to just ask him directly.

I had been stress baking soufflé—which had *not* been going well, folding egg whites one-handed was difficult—when he came in and stuck his head in the fridge, scrounging for a midafternoon snack.

"Wait an hour and you can have some chocolate soufflé," I said. He closed the fridge and frowned at me.

"That's . . ." he started, searching for the right word, "nice of you."

I shrugged like it was no big deal, even if I knew he was right to be surprised by my offer to feed him.

"You feeling okay?" he joked.

"Obviously not," I grumbled, incapable of joining him in what felt like well-intended ribbing.

"Right," he said sheepishly. "Sorry."

"No, I'm sorry." I sighed. "I'm not trying to be a jerk. It's just . . . this is a *lot*."

"Yeah," he said, hoisting himself up onto the counter to watch me struggle with my spatula. "It's not always going to be too much to handle though. You'll get used to it."

"I don't know that I want to get used to it," I muttered, the bus stranger's nightmare ringing in my head. The realization that that was someone's real nightmare, a nightmare that felt inspired by reality—*based* in it—has stuck in my brain like gum on a shoe.

Aaron just sat there silently for a few moments. I don't know if he was reading my thoughts or just getting a vibe from me, but he was obviously staying because he knew I had something else to say.

"So, what's it—" I stopped myself, trying to find the right words and also wondering if I wanted to ask the question in the first place, or if it would be showing my hand too much.

"What's what . . . ?" Aaron squinted his eyes at me.

"*Stop* reading my thoughts," I snapped. He reeled back, blinking, like the idea hadn't even occurred to him.

"Rosie, I'm not—"

"Yes, you are, I know you, I know that face—"

"What face?"

"Your faraway-look face," I said.

"You mean the face I have when I'm thinking?" he asked.

"Oh, maybe that's why I didn't recognize it," I quipped.

"Hardy-har-har," he said, deadpan. I poured the fluffy chocolate and egg white mixture into a soufflé dish.

"So . . . what's *what* like?" he asked again as I put the dish in the oven. I didn't answer right away, taking my time to position the soufflé dish just so in its water bath, checking that the tin foil around the edge was high enough to support the rise. I closed the oven door, straightened up, wiped my hands on my apron, but I didn't turn to look at him, instead choosing to stare straight ahead at the counter, his folded figure on top of it just in the corner of my periphery.

"What's the AM like?" My voice was quiet and I could feel my throat tighten around the words. I hated this. I hated not knowing something, I hated *Aaron* specifically knowing more about it than me, I hated having to ask him, having to show my cards, admit that I was vulnerable. I braced for impact, for him to poke fun at me, or roll his eyes. Be the Aaron I've known since I was thirteen, even though in this moment I desperately needed him to be the Aaron I knew when I was ten.

"It's . . . kind of boring, to be honest," Aaron said, surprising me by being neither. I looked at him then, saw the lines around his frown, his hunched shoulders, and could see, briefly, the person that Aaron the grown-up was going to be.

"Boring?"

"Yeah," he said, nodding. "It's just a big hospital. And, yeah, it's a hospital filled with people who have magical powers, but other than that, it's pretty standard."

"Oh, yeah, other than that." I rolled my eyes.

"I'm serious, Rosie," he said earnestly. "Whatever you're imagining, I bet it's not half as bad. I was even—"

"What?" I prodded, when he didn't say more.

"I was gonna suggest you go even before all this," he said, avoiding my eyes.

"What? Why?"

"I promise you, I'm not reading your thoughts regularly or anything," he started and I tensed, "but I noticed that something was . . . off."

"Off?"

"Your thoughts felt different. Dad's thoughts do too though, like there's a . . . fog around them . . ." Aaron trailed off, staring distantly at nothing, before shaking his head and continuing, "I started to think it was me. That's why I didn't end up saying anything."

"Are you okay?" I asked, uncertain. We were in unusual territory here, skating dangerously close to sincere vulnerability.

"Yeah, I'm fine," he said, waving off my concern with a lazy hand. "I think I'm just out of practice. Though, seems like I was right about something going on with you."

"Seems like," I echoed, not knowing what to say to any of that. We sat in silence for a few moments before Aaron inhaled deeply and changed the subject back to the AM.

"You're gonna get evaluated and head-shrunk and spend a lot of time waiting for doctors just like in the normal world. And then you'll be back here before you know it."

I'm not sure I believe it.

community/TheUnusuals post by n/thatsahumanperson

I think I should probably apologize for writing that last post, not giving any context or further information, and then not reading any of the comments or PMs that people sent me. Thanks to everyone who dropped into my in-box with advice and concern. It's a weird comfort right now to know that there's this whole community of people looking out for me. You guys really helped me through when I first started hearing voices and it's looking like you're going to help me through adjusting to my sister's ability.

Yep, turns out my sister *is* an Unusual. A dreamdiver, as I alluded to. Meaning, she can go into people's dreams. *My* dream, specifically, the other night. It was . . . freaky. Like, even more freaky than hearing people's thoughts on the reg. There was this feeling, like there was another presence there. I don't believe in ghosts, but it's sort of what I imagine sensing a ghost would be like. Even before I saw her, there was something *off* about the dream. I don't know. Maybe I'm putting that feeling on top of reality now that I know what I know.

When she *did* arrive though, all sharp-edged and clear-voiced, everything in the dream changed. Then we both woke up and rushed out into the hallway to confirm . . . yep, we'd both just been in the same dream.

I don't really have a question this time, I guess. I more just wanted to update everyone on what was going on and say . . . thanks being here for me. She's going to That Place tomorrow, so hopefully she'll figure out how to control it pretty easily and we can skip over any embarrassing dream visits.

chuckxavier

Glad you figured it out and that your sister is getting checked out. I've heard of dreamdivers, but I think they're pretty rare, so it's good that she's getting the help she needs.

> **onmyown**
>
> Ditto. I've heard of them, never met one, but I've heard that things can get pretty gnarly, so good that she's getting ahead of it.

thatsahumanperson

Yeah, that's what our parents said too—that dreamdivers are rare. But what do you mean "gnarly"? Is it dangerous?

onmyown

Not physically, I don't think. Just some folks on this sub a few years back—before your time—talking about a friend of theirs who stopped spending a lot of time in the waking world. Guess the dreamworld is pretty sweet.

thatsahumanperson

Gotcha. Based on my sister's reaction to having the ability, I don't think her liking it *too* much is going to be a problem.

franklinsteinsmonster

COOOOOOOOOOOL.

lokilover

congrats, man. having a dreamdiver in the family is very, very cool. you should invite your sister to this sub—I'd love to get to know her.

thatsahumanperson

If I think she'd get something out of it, I'll invite her, but she's probably the least online person her age I've ever met. Also . . . not loving the vibe you're sending out n/lokilover.

lokilover

meant no disrespect. I just think her power sounds incredible.

iwannabelieve

Can I ask, why no ghosts? I would think with the special powers thing, anything supernatural would be fair game. But are they against the rules of the world?

thatsahumanperson

I mean, yeah, they're literally against the rules of the world as in like . . . the laws of physics? I get that a lot of us can do things that defy laws of the natural world, but death feels like one of those rules that no Unusual, no matter their ability, could break.

theneonthorn

almost ten years of this sub and I swear, this exact type of person never stops coming.

onmyown

OH my god, dude, for the last time, THIS IS NOT AN RP. I can't tell if you're just dense or an actual Unusual and just an epic troll. But FWIW, I actually *do* believe in ghosts. I haven't seen any proof yet, but I think there's still a lot about the world that we don't understand.

iwannabelieve

hey, no offense meant from me. I'm just out here tryna have a good time.

onmyown

Yeah, well the rest of us are just trying to live our lives. This isn't a game to us.

SEPTEMBER 23RD, 2016

I still can't quite believe that I'm here. The AM. The belly of the beast. That sounds more dramatic than I mean it—Aaron was right, it's not actually *that* scary. Though walking in was pretty intimidating. There's this huge, two- or three-story lobby—an atrium that slants down into the reception area, making it feel as if the sky is coming down on you the farther you go into the building. Like a visual cue saying: "Turn back, you're going to be swallowed whole by this whale if you take another step." But there I was, walking straight into the thing's damn mouth. Just like the dream rules I'm beginning to get a tentative hold on: no turning back.

But actually, space-age-y entrance aside, it's really just like a nice hospital. After going to the enormous circular front desk and talking to a super cute receptionist with an amazing 'fro and a cool name that I'm now forgetting (Maggie? something? why do pretty girls make my brain dumb?), I was led into a windowless room. Okay, that sounds really bad, but there was a little water feature in the corner and a cushy couch and soft lighting. It was kinda like being in a spa, tbqh.

And then that whole vibe was broken when a bespectacled sentient beanpole walked into the room.

"Hello, Ms. Atkinson. I'm Agent Green," he said, closing the door behind him and coming to stand in front of me. I stood up, partly so I could actually see his face—he was *tall*-tall—and partly because it seemed like the thing to do. He smiled down at me, the expression creating friendly wrinkles in his face, even if it didn't feel like the smile completely reached his eyes.

"Yes, I think we spoke on the phone, hello," I said, sounding like a complete ninny. There was something about his stiff suit and practiced smile that made me feel like I had to be the most formal version of myself. He wasn't at all what I had expected. The guy I'd given my preliminary interview to over the phone this morning—my mom hovering over my shoulder the whole time—sounded like he was trying to be the cool camp counselor. The guy who sat in front of me in that weird little spa room looked like he'd gotten his suit in the early 2000s and his haircut in the '80s.

"Do you need anything, Ms. Atkinson?" he asked, his eyebrows scrunching down into what I think he thought was a compassionate expression, but just really came across as confused. "Water?" He gestured to a cooler on the other side of the room, half stepping in that direction like he was ready to get me a glass the moment I said yes.

"No, I'm fine," I said through a dry mouth. It was starting to dawn on me that I was in a totally unknown place, with a totally unknown person, for a somewhat unknown period of time, and no way to contact the outside world. Cute reception girl had taken my phone, "protocol," she said, and I hadn't seen any landlines as I was walked through the halls. I'm just glad I was able to text Emily and tell her I was dealing with some family drama before going off the grid. GOD, I hope she'll go out with me again once I'm out.

"And you can call me Rose," I added.

"Wonderful." He smiled again, tightly, but his voice was warm and the ice in my stomach started to thaw. I felt myself smiling back, just a little. "Then you can call me Owen. Why don't we sit."

Silently, I sat back down on the couch that felt like it had been sat in maybe three times. The fabric was soft but the cushions stiff and unyielding. Agent Green—Owen—sat down in the chair opposite and crossed his legs.

He opened a thin folder on his lap and looked down at it. "Now, I know you went through everything on the phone, but do you have any questions?"

"Um . . ." Did I have questions? I had a *million* questions—what would I be asked to do? Would they give me medicine to stop the dreaming? Would they teach me how to dream? Were there other dreamdivers here? "What happens first?"

"Well, once I'm done with all your intake forms, we'll take you over to our medical wing, where you'll get a quick physical, and then we'll show you to your room, where you can get settled in before dinner. You won't be doing much this weekend—just meeting our other patients, getting to know our counselors. Then on Monday you'll start with some individual- and group-therapy sessions and then you'll start doing workshops to help learn control."

The mention of group therapy brought up an awful, stomach-rattling fear that I'd had the moment I'd woken up from sharing Aaron's dream. I'd spent so much of today thinking about when Aaron went to the AM—how hard it had been when he first started hearing thoughts and how hard it still was after. He seems to have pretty good control of his ability now, and it's like he's forgotten how . . . downright *awful* he was when it started happening. I certainly didn't want to go into some random stranger's dream and make them feel self-conscious about their innermost thoughts. But Owen assured me I'd be given my own room for extra privacy.

My "own room" is a bit of a strong phrase. It feels like somewhere between a hostel and a crappy dorm room: bed, nightstand with a lamp, a tiny bathroom separated by a thin, sliding door. I was allowed to bring my own stuff—clothes, toiletries, books . . . but no phone or computer. I brought a few cookbooks I'd been wanting to read all the way through and my battered copy of *Kitchen Confidential*, but *god* I am going to be so bored here without a kitchen to cook in or reruns to watch mindlessly. I get to call my family every day, but apparently they like to limit "outside contact" in order to keep us focused on our growth, or whatever bullshit borderline-cult-ish thing Owen said.

They let me keep my journal at least. Owen was so excited when I asked him about it—saying "wonderful" for the hundredth time since I'd met him and asking to see it.

"Oh, I don't want to read it," he'd rushed to say when I looked at him funny. "I just think it's wonderful that you've been keeping a dream journal. Our doctors here often ask dreamdivers to do just that, so you're ahead of the curve!"

He gave me a genuine smile then, brighter than any of the tight, practiced smiles that he'd given me as we'd gone through a questionnaire asking everything from what my "upper reach limit" of dreamdiving was (wouldn't even begin to know how to answer that given I barely understand the question in the first place) to what my body temperature is when I'm asleep and normally dreaming versus dreamdiving (literally . . . how would I know that?).

So I showed him this journal, already scuffed around the edges. His eyes lit up and for a brief, horrifying second, I thought he might actually *clap*.

"That's wonderful, Rose," he repeated. He looked so . . . *proud* of me, like I was already doing a great job. I get why they have that guy do the intake.

But now that I'm alone again, in this strange windowless cinder-block room, I'm starting to feel nervous again. Not fear-nerves—Aaron was right, this place is *weird* but it's not that scary. Instead, I feel like it's the first night of sleepaway camp and tomorrow I'm going to meet the rest of my cabin. Except, this time, the rest of my cabin are people who have supernatural abilities and I might accidentally pass out and go inside of their subconscious minds. So. You know. Not your usual summer camp.

SEPTEMBER 26TH, 2016

The weird, alt-summer-camp feeling I had the first night was driven home today by my first group therapy session.

The entire weekend went by with little activity—as anticipated, I got a big wire cap put on my head, got a tiny bit poked and prodded, waited in an itchy hospital gown for an hour for a doctor to come take my temperature and leave, like that's not something I could have done myself, and just generally slept. A *lot.* And, of course, I dreamed.

Dreaming feels different now. It feels like something clicked, like I've figured out the shape and dimensions of the dreamworld, even if I haven't nailed down all the rules. Every dream I have now seems to be lucid. More often than not, I'm waking up in that blank void, a comfortable place now, and I just know. I know I'm dreaming. And I know I'm in my own head too. There's a soft, warm edge around it. I don't always know where the edge *is,* the doorway that has sometimes appeared in that space hasn't materialized, but each time I'm in that emptiness I try to find it. With my hands reaching out and feeling for a seam, with my mind trying to control what's around me, with my eyes trying to perceive something that's barely there. I haven't cracked it yet, but I have the feeling that if I keep going back, eventually I'll be able to find the seam and open the door.

I'm not entirely sure if I've dreamdived at all since being here. As Owen promised, they've kept me away from other patients. My room is on a long hallway full of doors that I'm assuming lead to other, similar rooms. I've heard barely a peep from either side and have yet to see anyone else when I venture down the hallway, so I think I have the whole place to myself, not just my own room. I wonder if they've shuffled everyone into one corner of the building so that I have this place to myself or if there just aren't many inpatients at the moment. I should have asked Owen on Friday when he gave me the tour.

"There are two basic types of programs we run here," he'd said, walking me past the cafeteria right off the main lobby. "We have inpatients, such as yourself"—he smiled at me when he said it, like we were in on a secret together—"and outpatients. You'll eventually be an outpatient, coming here for annual checkups and to continue group therapy if you'd like."

"Oh yeah," I said, "I think Aaron did that for a while. I don't know why he stopped."

"It's not required. Of course," he added, "some people find group therapy most fulfilling, others prefer the one-on-one approach. We have someone we can recommend if you'd like to continue your own therapy once we leave."

"Is therapy really that important?" I asked skeptically. "I mean, it's the annual physicals and stuff that really count, right?"

"Therapy is *vital*," Owen said solemnly. "You have to keep your emotional and mental well-being maintained in the same way you do your physical body."

"My brother doesn't do therapy, and it seems like he's got his ability pretty under control," I said, having a hard time with the basic premise of either Aaron or me sitting still in a room and telling someone our feelings for an hour.

"Maybe he found an effective way to take care of his own interior life," Owen suggested. I tried not to scoff. "Meditation, or communities, even journaling," he added with a small smile in my direction, "can all be ways we actively participate in our own mental health. But that doesn't mean your brother couldn't benefit from therapy in the future—it's an ongoing process, not a one-and-done sort of thing."

I just nodded at that and Owen seemed satisfied. The entire tour he talked like he was reading from a brochure but a brochure he really *believed*. I don't know what I expected from an AM employee, but I'm not sure Owen Green was it.

In fact, nothing about this place is really what I expected. Other than a few typically matter-of-fact and therefore a bit cold doctors, everyone has been really nice and not scary. The whole complex is enormous and winding—a mix of old, turn-of-the-century ivy-covered stone and modern glass and steel. Like Bag End slammed into a modern art museum. So far, I think I've seen a tiny portion—just my room, the cafeteria, and a few labs—but just in those areas alone, I feel like I'm looking at millions of dollars' worth of facilities. Everything is state-of-the-art. Except the food. The food could definitely use some improvement.

I don't know *how* my family is paying for this. And now I'm feeling really guilty because I never even thought to ask. My family isn't struggling, but we're not *rich*. I'm not sure I really know where the AM gets its money from—the government? Its patients? Do they have an Atypical stashed away somewhere who's spinning yarn into gold? Whatever they're doing seems to be working—they seem to have a lot of people coming back to take advantage of the programs. My group therapy is *mostly* people who come in once a week. I can't say I understand it.

"Everyone, we've got a new face joining us today," the therapist, Dr. Loving, started. "This is Rose," she continued and before I knew what I was doing, my hand had lifted in an awkward wave, made somehow infinitely more awkward by the chorus of "Hi, Rose" that came from the rest of the group. It really did feel like we were kids away from home for the first time, getting ready to dive into icebreaker exercises. Except, we weren't all kids and, according to Dr. Loving when she greeted me, most of the folks sitting there had been in group for a little while.

"Why don't we go around and introduce ourselves," Dr. Loving continued and I braced for the "name, grade, and a fun fact about you!" rundown. I wasn't that far off.

"We can start with first names and your personal pronouns," she said, "and, if you're comfortable, you can share your ability as well. "I'll start: I'm Dr. Loving, she/her, and while I don't have an ability, I've been working with Atypicals for fifteen years."

Dr. Loving felt like the exact type of person you would want for a therapist, a perfect blend of confidence and cool. She's a tall Black woman with trendy square glasses and a better fashion sense than I've ever seen in a doctor, which makes her feel younger than she probably is, like she's one of us. And then she talks in that warm, assured voice she has, and you're instantly pulled into a sense of security and vulnerability.

So we went around the table and all introduced ourselves. There was Sharon, a middle-aged Asian American woman with superspeed that seemed to bleed into her *very* high-energy personality; Marco, a thirtysomething shapeshifter who changed his appearance so often throughout the session, I never got a grip on what he *actually* looks like. Then there was Ralphy, a young teenager with pale white skin and a shock of red hair who spoke softly, and refused to share what their ability was.

Two young, brunette women introduced themselves as a unit, Cam speaking while Cat, who's Deaf, signed. Cam can make force fields and Cat can walk through walls—everything about them seemed predestined to click and watching them talk throughout the sessions was . . . hard. I've never had that kind of connection with anyone and couldn't comprehend how they so easily understood each other. It wasn't just that Cam was interpreting Cat—I don't know any ASL, but Cat definitely makes her voice known simply by the way she expresses herself—it was the way they looked at each other, the way they both giggled at jokes that the rest of us didn't understand.

Eventually, it was my turn, and I'd been so distracted by learning everyone's ability (and wondering what Ralphy's could be) I didn't even have time to be nervous.

"I'm Rose," I said, sticking my hands between my legs and the chair to stop myself from giving another awkward wave. "And, um, I can dreamdive?"

It came out like a question, like I wasn't sure of my ability or I was asking for some sign that I'd done that right. Dr. Loving smiled and gave a tiny, encouraging nod as if my question was looking for an answer and not just a result of having never done this kind of thing before.

"Thank you, Rose," Dr. Loving said, bringing the group's attention back to her. But not before I could notice everyone's expressions—a mix of surprise and awe and curiosity.

Thankfully, Dr. Loving launched into the sharing portion of group therapy. I wasn't expected to say much beyond my name in the first session and I could definitely feel my eyes getting heavy at some points, the sweet lull of sleep wanting to take me away, but I was able to fend it off. It helped that the discussion going on was fairly engaging.

It wasn't quite the support group for superheroes that someone might expect from a therapy session with a bunch of Atypicals—it was far more . . . normal. Sharon can't seem to sit still—her hyperspeed manifesting in her emotional life, as Dr. Loving put it—Cat and Cam have bonded over the fact that Cat is the only one who can breach Cam's force field, and Marco has a hard time being truly vulnerable with people because he can always mold himself into someone else. Ralphy remained a mystery.

But it's interesting—everyone clearly sees themselves as capital-A Atypical. Like it's just as big a part of their identity as their race, their gender, their job. It affects how they relate to one another, to people who aren't Atypicals, people who know their secret and people who don't. Their abilities directly reflect the way they think about themselves and their place in the world.

And there I was, sitting silently and just thinking about the fact that all of them were living with their abilities existing, in that moment. I barely knew who I was before all this happened—always trying to balance fitting into my family with how I wanted to spend my own life—and now I'm even more unsure.

community/TheUnusuals post by n/thatsahumanperson

My sister is still at That Place, so things have been pretty quiet in the house. Not that she's loud but, before her ability started, her *thoughts* were definitely loud, even if she didn't voice most of them. It's not that I miss her thoughts—I hadn't really been listening that much anyway—it's just . . . well, it's been easier to notice stuff with her gone. Like what's going on with my dad.

I mentioned a while back that his thoughts had been behind a fog and I wasn't sure if there was something going on with my ability. When everything went down with my sister, I kind of forgot about it, chalking up the weirdness with her thoughts to the fact that her ability was coming into being. But that doesn't explain my dad's thoughts being altered too . . . unless there's some kind of interference? I mean, we now have four Unusuals in the same household—could we all just be screwing up each other's abilities? I haven't talked to either of my parents about them having issues with their powers, but maybe I should.

I bring all this up because it happened again with my dad. He was out in the yard, just standing there. When I asked him what he was up to, he kind of just shook his head and mumbled something about gardening, but I felt that same weird fogginess when I tried to look into his head. It dissipated pretty quick but it's still got me wigging out.

Anyway. Just thought y'all might want an update.

chuckxavier
Definitely keep us posted—the interference theory is an interesting one.
tacotacotaco
Maybe it's time for a full family checkup where your sister is? Might be worth getting everyone looked at to make sure it's all okay.

> **thatsahumanperson**
> My mom *really* doesn't like it there. She'll go once a year for her physical, but that's it. But . . . you may be right. Maybe I can convince my dad to go get checked out.

OCTOBER 3RD, 2016

Okay, so, *bit* of a setback.

I had group therapy again today and I guess I've gotten too confident about not falling asleep randomly anymore because I really let my guard down. I was sitting there, half-listening to Marco talk about how he'd introduced himself to a girl with a different face and it turned out he now really likes that girl and has to figure out how to reintroduce himself with his *real* face so that he can genuinely date her as himself, and then I fell asleep.

I wonder now if it's because I was so emotionally exhausted from the previous ten minutes. I had unloaded way more than I was planning to, even saying some things that I hadn't even realized I'd been feeling. That's the point of therapy I guess.

It all started with a simple question.

"How has your time at the AM been so far, Rose?" Dr. Loving asked, and five pairs of eyes swiveled to stare at me.

"Oh, um," I started, even though she'd warned me that I'd be asked to share this go around. "It's been fine."

Even as I said that, I was sure that it wouldn't be enough. Dr. Loving was good at gently poking someone until they cracked open like a piñata—she'd been doing it pretty effectively in our one-on-one sessions and I braced for impact.

"Is there anything new you've discovered about yourself? About your ability?"

Those five pairs of eyes somehow stared *harder*.

"Um, not really," I admitted. "I mean, I've been sleeping a little bit less, which is good. So I guess I have more control? But nothing has really changed."

"Do you *feel* like you have more control?" Dr. Loving asked, and I was a little confused. She'd asked that question plenty in our private therapy—where exactly was this getting us?

"Not really," I answered, the same answer I've been giving her this whole time. "I don't feel that different, to be honest. I'm just . . . conscious more of the time."

A few light chuckles came from the rest of the group, but they weren't laughing *at* me. It was the kind of dry laugh that you give when you *get* it.

"Like, if anything," I continued, "this has just been further proof that I have the least cool ability ever."

"What are you talking about?" Cat signed, Cam interpreting for her. "You can *go into people's dreams.*"

I didn't need Cam to interpret that emphasis—the movement of Cat's hands made it clear that she thought my ability was pretty freakin' cool.

This is what had terrified me about the idea of group therapy. I don't like people commenting on my life, especially people I don't know. At least in this case, it seemed to be positive, even if Cat calling my ability cool while she was sitting there in a leather jacket that made her look effortless and amazing made me feel like a huge fraud and disappointment by *not* actually being cool.

"Yeah, I know," I said, watching the flurry of Cam's hands instead of looking at Cat directly in the eye, too intimidated by the fact that she seems to be able to look at someone head-on without flinching, a skill I've always wanted but have no idea how to acquire. "But it's really not that cool. People's dreams are mostly boring and stressful and besides, it's not like I've been diving much while here."

"You haven't?" Sharon asked.

"Not yet," I said, shrugging like it wasn't a big deal, even though it felt like something inside my brain was itching. It's been over a week since I was in someone's dream, the AM having made good on their promise to keep me isolated from other people at night. They've been running tests on me while I sleep, putting that cap on me to measure brainwaves and monitoring my vitals or whatever, but they manage to keep their distance. It's been good to get a full night's rest without any big black voids or trips to high school, even if it means the one interesting thing about me has been taken away before I even have time to explore it.

"Not yet, so you're going to?" Sharon asked.

"I don't know, I assume they'll have me do it," I said. "But I'm not sure what good that'll do. I don't really know what I'm here to learn. It's not like dreamdiving is an ability that can help people or even help me. The rest of my family all got these cheat codes for life, and I'm stuck with . . . this."

"What do you mean 'stuck'?" Dr. Loving followed up quickly and calmly, but I should have known that I'd just thrown out chum for the sharks. And for some reason, I couldn't avoid tossing out more.

"I mean," I sighed, "my mom gets to see the future and, yeah, she doesn't let it completely dictate her life, but she does use it when it's important. And my dad is a telekinetic who works as a contractor! He's so much faster and cheaper because he doesn't need half the equipment that the regular guys need, or the amount of people, because he can just use his brain to help him lift stuff."

"He's out in the open?" Marco blurted, his eyes wide in horror.

"No, no, not at all." I rushed to clarify. There was one thing that had been abundantly clear from my scant interactions with other Atypicals so far: everyone was terrified of getting caught. But it's not like we're in a comic book and we have to hide from the government or else—we're all here, sitting at the AM, talking about the ins and outs of our abilities. Who do we have to hide from?

Other people is the answer.

"He still has a crew and equipment and stuff, especially for the bigger jobs," I explained, "but just not as much as a regular person would need. And he still acts like he's actually lifting whatever or that there's more crew people on a job than there actually are, but then he just uses his telekinesis. He does personal construction—houses and stuff—so he can usually manage most of a job on his own. Besides, most people don't know anything about construction. They're not surprised when my dad does something super fast because no one knows how long something should take."

"That's kind of brilliant," Cam said, Cat nodding beside her.

"Yeah, it's cool," I agreed. "And that's what I mean—my dad has built his entire career around his telekinesis. It makes him better at his job. Safer. I don't think there's a job out there where being able to walk into people's dreams is a benefit. If there is, it's *definitely* not working in a kitchen."

"What about your brother?" Dr. Loving asked.

"What about him?"

"He's telepathic, right?" Marco asked.

"Yeah, he's telepathic." I sighed. "And, okay, maybe it doesn't help with *his* job—"

"What does he do?" Sharon asked.

"Well, he's figuring it out right now," I said. "He wants to go back and finish his degree eventually, but right now he's just working freelance doing tech stuff. He wants to do computer science."

"So what's his cheat code?" Cat asked.

"I mean, he can *read minds*," I said. "That's the biggest cheat code there is!"

"What do you mean by that?" Dr. Loving asked.

"Like, he never has to worry about not understanding someone or saying the wrong thing or wondering if someone likes him because he always knows."

"Do you think that's easy for him?" Dr. Loving asked. "Do you think he views it as a cheat code?"

"I mean, I don't know," I mumbled. Dr. Loving stared me down, lifting one eyebrow in a gentle challenge and I sighed dramatically.

"Okay, no, he doesn't," I admitted. "I know it's hard for him. Things are a bit better now, but when his ability first started up, it was really, really awful. And not just for him, for *all* of us."

Now that I'd started to talk about Aaron, it all came pouring out, rising up in my throat like a tide before spilling out over the rest of the group.

"He couldn't stop the voices, couldn't turn the volume down like he can now," I went on. "So he was just reading our minds all the time, and it seemed like the only way he could get it out was by saying it all back to us, telling us what we were thinking at any given moment. And I couldn't take it, couldn't stand having him reflecting all of that junk back on me, so we started fighting about it and it was just . . . there was no way I could ever win that fight. Not with Aaron in my head, using the most fleeting unkind thoughts as weapons against me. I never hated him, I never *could* hate him, but that—that invasion, that violation—was something that I didn't know how to handle so I just made myself smaller and quieter in the hopes that he wouldn't be able to find me and now I don't know how to be loud anymore."

I wasn't sure I even knew I felt that way until I said it out loud to a bunch of strangers. I looked up, expecting to see six shocked faces, but was met instead with expressions of understanding. No judgment, just a few nods like they knew exactly where I was coming from. For that moment, I belonged.

That didn't last.

I hardly even remember what the dream was about now, which is a bit strange. It was flashes of different scenes from a life that wasn't mine—eating dinner with two adults I'd never seen before, walking through an unfamiliar college campus, a thin figure in a black hoodie standing in a lobby that was familiar in a way I couldn't put my finger on. Sometimes my dreams—or other people's dreams—are disjointed and confusing. In fact, they often are, but I've never gotten such clear, distinct, *real* flashes in quick succession.

I woke up suddenly, jarringly, my legs flailing for a moment against the plastic chair and linoleum floor, like I was trying to find solid ground beneath my feet. Every head swiveled to look at me, as if they'd just been watching me sleep, unperturbed, even though they know I CAN GO INTO PEOPLE'S DREAMS.

But there was one face that stood out against all the others. Ralphy, small and freckle-faced, was looking at me wide-eyed, like they knew exactly what had just happened. Where I had just been. And that was when I realized I *had* been in someone else's head, someone's *waking* head, and knew exactly whose.

"You're psychic," I breathed, before I could think it through. I knew, in my bones, that I was right, and then Ralphy's face fell. Their mouth grew tight, their chin wobbling, and then they *bolted*. Sneakers screeching on the floor, their chair clattering to its side as they ran off faster than I would have ever expected, almost as if *they* were the one in the group with super speed. And all I could do was sit there and watch them go, as my stomach dropped with the horror of what I'd just done. I wanted to run after them—apologize for opening my stupid mouth—but Dr. Loving ended group early, going to clean up *my* mess. I knew that if I went with her, I would just somehow end up making it worse.

Tonight we "kick up the sleep trials" as Owen put it. He tried to make it sound fun, like I'm leveling up or something, but my stomach is in knots. I don't want to violate anyone's privacy, don't want to get trapped in a nightmare, don't want to see something or hear something I shouldn't. I've just gotten my own dreaming under control, can recognize all the edges of it and know what it feels like to stick a toe outside those bounds. It's boring, sitting in that black space, but it's safe. What happens when I step through?

community/TheUnusuals post by n/thatsahumanperson

It happened again. There was that fog around my dad's thoughts and this time, I tried to go deeper, tried to actively read his mind to see if I could figure out what the fog was or where it was coming from. I got nowhere. Every time I found a thought of his, I would try to follow it down, see where it connected to other ones, but it would disappear into the fog before I could get a really good grip. That alone was freaking me out, but it was nothing compared to what happened next.

My dad doesn't remember where my sister is. He was just sitting in the living room today, reading the same book that he couldn't find the other day, and when I walked past he looked up and asked, "Where's your sister? I'm going to the grocery store later and want to see if she'd be up for cooking that salmon that she makes."

I thought he was joking for a second—I don't know what kind of joke he would have been making, but you know how dads are. They find shit funny that no one else does. So I brushed it off, saying, "I don't think she gets to use their kitchens while under observation, Dad. I think we'll just have to keep fending for ourselves." But instead of trying to joke about how he's such a great cook and could totally pull off the complicated dishes that my sister does (he's not and he couldn't), he put his book on his lap and looked up at me, his bushy eyebrows scrunched together.

"What do you mean?" he asked. "Use whose kitchen?"

I stared at him for a second, waiting for him to let go of whatever bit he was trying to do, but he just stared right back at me.

He didn't remember. My sister has been gone for over a week and it was like . . . it was like that hadn't been happening for my dad at all. Once I reminded him that she was at the AM, getting help for her dreamdiving, he nodded a bunch, like he was trying to listen to something really far away and then gave this, like, hollow laugh before walking upstairs to get his wallet (which—that's weird too! normally he would just use his telekinesis to bring it down and it's like he forgot about that too) and then going to the grocery store. That's where he is now and . . . I don't know, I feel like I should have gone with him?

I'm scared, you guys. I'm going to talk to him and my mom about him getting looked at, but . . . I'm scared.

OCTOBER 7TH, 2016

I did it. I found the seam and stepped through that invisible door and what greeted me on the other side was better than I could have imagined.

Something happened last night, something broke wide open and let a cool, sharp breeze into my head, throwing everything into perfect focus, bringing it all into the light. That doesn't make any sense as a metaphor—how could wind shed light on something? And yet, it makes perfect sense to me as a thought, even writing it down in the harsh light of day. That's the world I'm dealing with now—the world I live in. Wind can be made of light, light can make sound, sound can be tasted on the tip of your tongue. I'm Dorothy, the tornado has pulled me up out of drab black-and-white and dropped me in a Technicolor world that has rules I can't even begin to understand.

I walked into someone's dream and it was . . . it was like that blank canvas at first, like it is when I dream myself now, but then the canvas started to come to life. The AM volunteer—a younger doctor I think—started to dream about a plane, for some reason. Initially, it was just a boring old plane—cramped seats, stale air, too many people. But then I remembered how I got rid of all the other high schoolers in Aaron's dream, how I had a thought and they just vanished.

I half expected the simple act of remembering I did that to send all the plane people away. But apparently things are a little bit more complicated based on the person. And I started to *feel* that. There was something familiar about Aaron's dream. Not just the high school setting, or the fact that he was there, but the feeling of his dreamworld felt like a place I'd been before. Maybe it's because we're genetically related, maybe it's because he's Atypical too and this doctor wasn't.

It took me a few more minutes—seconds, an hour, who knows, time moves very differently in the dreamworld—to clear the plane, but I did it, watching each individual person disappear in front of my eyes. For some of them it took longer—if I let my concentration slip, they wouldn't disappear or they'd fade away unbearably slowly. I didn't see the doctor himself anywhere, but that had been the case for most of these tests. I guess that's part of why this guy volunteered—apparently he rarely dreams about himself and rarely has nightmares. People's brains are *wild.*

There was something slightly morbid about watching random strangers disintegrate into nothing, knowing that I was the cause. I had to keep reminding myself that they weren't real. Well, maybe they were real people in real life—images of people the doctor actually knows instead of truly random dream conjurations—but they weren't real here. *Nothing* in dreamworld is real, which should be scary, but it's incredible. There's no consequence. I asked the doctor if he'd felt anything when I vanished all the plane people and then the plane and he just said, "Oh, I was dreaming about a plane?" because he didn't remember a single thing about his own dream.

Once everyone was gone, I walked up and down the aisle, running my hand along the tops of the seats. They had the sensation of fabric, but not the cheap, scratchy kind you get on actual planes. Instead, it felt like the fibers were made of delicate spiderwebs, light and soft, but somehow not dissolving underneath my fingertips. When I looked out one of the tiny, rounded windows, I saw that the outside looked like cotton candy too. Big, puffy clouds lit by a beautiful orange-pink sunset. I wanted to see it up close. That was when I realized, I *could.*

I focused on my feet like the doctors had taught me. "Always find your solid ground first," they said, citing the experiences of dreamdivers they'd worked with in the past, always couching every piece of advice in the understanding that "every dreamdiver is unique. What works for one might not work for you." I guess that's why they have me fill out all these evaluations, to see what works.

The ground thing *does* work for me, and worked beautifully with the plane. I felt the carpet beneath my feet, the rumble of the engine as the plane moved through the sky, and concentrated on it all disappearing. It didn't go right away, so I grabbed onto the back of a fluffy seat, closed my eyes, and imagined the seat being a cloud instead. And then it was.

I was still on solid ground. Not physically, there was no pressure against my feet, no texture, but I knew I wasn't going to plummet to the ground thousands of feet below. I was floating amongst those pink and fluffy clouds, nothing but air under my feet. Nothing but the dusky sky around me.

A light wind blew across my face, warm and smelling of flowers. The wind had shape and texture, somehow carrying light on its wings, so that a glow pirouetted through the air, twisting the clouds into swirls so fluffy and full they looked good enough to eat. It felt like the most natural thing to walk over to one of them, my feet sinking and bouncing into the perfectly buoyant air as I went, and reach out my hand. Instead of pushing my arm through vapor—the way it would have worked if I had been, somehow, touching a *real* cloud—my hand met with the swirl, solid and soft. My fingers wrapped around it, grasping the bit of cloud and bringing it to my face. It shaped itself into a cartoonish version of a cloud and it *tasted* like a cartoon cloud. Like ice cream and cotton candy and every bit of animated food you see in movies as a kid that you wished were real.

I was eating a cloud, simply because I wanted to.

I burst out laughing, in sheer, unfettered joy, and flung myself backward onto the cloud. It caught me in its fluffy embrace, caving perfectly to mold to my body while still supporting me. I spent hours like that, bouncing among the clouds like trampolines, swimming into them to be enveloped in their warmth, flying through them, feeling lighter than air and brighter than the sun that still had not set, keeping my world in perfect pink-washed happiness.

And then I woke up. Not suddenly, not jarringly, but peacefully and slowly. I eased out of sleep at first and then all at once I was completely awake, without any kind of lingering grogginess. I lay there for a moment, in my strange windowless hospital room, and felt more at peace than I ever have.

I think I'm going to like this dreamdiving thing.

LATER

I'm writing this from my own bedroom, having completed my time at the AM and come back home. It's weird, being back. Even though I was only gone for a couple weeks, I feel like I was just getting started. Yeah, maybe group therapy wasn't for me, but as weird as the sleep trials were at first, they were really starting to work. After last night with the airplane, I feel like something has cracked open and now there's this whole new aspect of my life, my ability, that I get to explore. I cannot *wait* to sleep in my own bed tonight, but part of me is a little sad that I won't be training anymore. I want to get *good* at this.

Though according to Ralphy, I do have more training in my future.

As I was finishing up my final pieces of paperwork with Mags, the cute receptionist, Ralphy passed by the front desk.

"Oh, hey," I said awkwardly and they gave me what I assume was an attempted smile, but came out to be more of a grimace.

"Hi," they croaked.

"Here for . . ." I trailed off, realizing that I had no idea what to guess—there was no group today—and thinking that maybe it was rude to inquire about why someone would be visiting a medical facility.

"You checking out?" they asked, skipping over my half question and gesturing broadly at Mags, who had her head in my file but who was very obviously listening to our conversation.

"Yep," I said. They just nodded and stood there for a moment, chewing on their lip, their hands stuck in their pockets like they were wrestling with something

"Look, I'm really sorry for—" I started to blurt out, but they jumped in before I could finish my awkward, would-never-have-been-enough-to-make-up-for-it apology.

"You'll be back here," they said, avoiding my eyes.

"Oh, I've actually been assigned to an outside therapist—apparently Dr. Loving thinks it might be more helpful for me," I explained.

"I don't mean for group," they clarified.

"Then what do you mean?" I asked, trying to smile through the question, even though knots had started to form in my stomach at their tone.

"You'll be back here." And with that, Ralphy turned on their heel, leaving me wondering what the hell that was all about and why it gave me a distinct chill down my spine.

But I didn't have much time to think on it, or to go chasing after them, because I heard someone call my name.

"Dad!" I exclaimed when I turned around and saw my father of all people walking down the hallway toward me.

"Hey, Rose," he said, a big smile on his face. "I'm here to pick you up."

"What were you doing?" I asked, pointing toward the hallway behind him. The entrance was on the opposite side of the lobby and, as far as I knew, the hallway he'd just come from only led deeper into the AM.

"Oh, just wandering around." He shrugged. "It's been a while since I've walked around this place—they've really gussied it up."

"Do you approve of the work?" I joked.

"They could have done a smoother job on joining the additions to the older parts of the building . . ." he mused, looking pointedly around him, "but it's pretty decent. Stamp of approval granted."

I laughed, looping my arm through his and walking us out of the gargantuan main atrium. We went home and I made my parents' favorite salmon dish for dinner, feeling alive and awake and like part of my family in a way I never have before.

community/TheUnusuals post by n/thatsahumanperson

For those of you that have been wanting an update on my dad and his thoughts, I'll write more soon, but . . . we have an answer now, I guess. For why his thoughts have been behind a strange fog, why I've had such a hard time getting to them. I can't say more right now—it doesn't feel like my story to tell, or maybe it is, I don't know, it affects all of us, how could it not—and I'm not sure when I *will* be able to talk about it. Or how.

I'm okay. For whatever that's worth. Like with my sister and her dream-diving, my inability to read my dad's thoughts has more to do with what's going on in his head, not mine.

I *wish* it was me that had the problem.

chuckxavier
Without a drop of sarcasm or pedantry: I'm here if you want to talk about any of this stuff. No judgment, no preaching about safe and respectful mind reading practices. It sounds like you're going through something hard and I'm sorry for that. I want to do what I can.

onmyown
Ditto. I hope everything is okay but if it's not, we're here.

tacotacotaco
They're both right—we're a family and we're here for you when your IRL family is the source of stress. Whatever you need.

thatsahumanperson
Thanks, all. That means a lot. We're telling my sister this morning—she's the only one who doesn't know yet and I'm hoping that maybe this'll be the thing that brings us closer together but . . . yeah. It really helps to know that, whatever happens, you're here.

OCTOBER 8TH, 2016

Things keep falling apart just when I think they might finally, *finally* be coming together.

When we were kids, Aaron and I had a hamster, Mr. Wiggles. Mr. Wiggles was very small and very cute and very, very dumb. We would put food in a corner of his cage and it would take him, like, forty minutes to find it. But, like all hamsters, Mr. Wiggles really loved his hamster wheel. He would spend *hours* on that thing. Honestly, I'm shocked it didn't kill him. No animal should move that constantly, and this is coming from someone who tried to spend all of sixth grade on her rollerblades.

Round and round he would go, his tiny little feet pumping as hard as they possibly could. But it was so weird—sometimes he wouldn't scurry along, moving the hamster wheel in a consistent motion. Sometimes, he would push in these short and fast bursts, his paws working furiously for a few seconds until he screeched to a halt. It was like he was trying to escape. Like he was expecting the bursts of running to propel him forward past the curve of the wheel. But it never did. And if he went too fast, stopped too suddenly, sometimes he would get thrown off the wheel.

That's how I feel. Like any ground I gain is hard-won through intense running, before I'm flung from my path completely.

And what . . . what a completely and absolutely useless metaphor that is. Here I am talking about hamster wheels and ground I've gained like I have ANY control over what's happening at all, like these things aren't just happening TO me, like anything I do makes one tiny jot of goddamned difference.

Everything is falling to pieces around me and I feel like I have no other choice but to fall to pieces with it.

There's a reason that my dad came and picked me up from the AM yesterday. While I was doing my . . . my exit interview, or whatever, he was getting checked on. Because while I was gone these past two weeks, things started to go very, very wrong.

When I came down to the kitchen this morning—at the shock-

December 26th, 2016

Dear Mark,

I'm still mad at you, you know.

You reached in, without me knowing, and you took my power away. You did it without meaning to, which frustrates and comforts me in equal measure. You didn't mean to hurt me. You also didn't mean to change my life so completely, and you did it effortlessly. Thoughtlessly.

We were on a collision course from the start, but I never thought our abilities colliding would mean that I'd have my ability shunted back to some deep, dark place where I couldn't access it. I think that was worse than this. Yeah, I'm still handcuffed to a bed, spending Christmas with slowly healing ribs, but at least I know it's the drugs making my power feel far away. After what happened with you, it's like I was pushed underwater. Do you know what that feels like? To have a fundamental part of you pushed down to somewhere you can't reach?

Of course you do. That's exactly what got us into that mess in the first place. <u>This</u> place fucked you up so bad that you had to work for months to get your ability back. You were hitting against that wall so hard you broke all the way through and broke me too.

I know I'm partly to blame too. I <u>do</u> know that. But you never came by to check in on me. After we got back, ~~you just left me~~

I can't stay mad at you, that's the problem. ~~Well, no, the real problem—~~

I wish I could be mad at you. I think that'd be easier.

II

FOG

11-01-2016, morningwaffles, text post

Winter is really coming in like a lion this year, earlier than it has any right to. I was not built for the cold climate, but I love this city in the snow. I grew up down in the Southwest, where the days are scorching and the nights are freezing and nothing ever changes very much. The days get longer, get shorter, shrink and stretch with the turn of the earth, but there's always warm clay beneath your feet, soaking up the sunshine in the day and letting it off when the evening comes. There are always bugs buzzing, creatures scurrying, wind blowing literal tumbleweeds across your driveway. Even the stars feel loud in their shine.

Now, here I am, in the middle of a college campus, in a big city, a direct diagonal shot northeast from my home, and I'm amazed by the hush of quiet. With each new snowfall, the city feels made anew. It feels like just yesterday I was making my way through a summer storm to get soup for my roommate, running into a rain-soaked girl with a sprained wrist, who didn't smile easily, making me want to earn her smiles even more.

That girl is now curled up on my bed, fast asleep, while snow falls gently outside, blanketing everything in beautiful white quiet.

Okay, *yes,* I've been holding out on you all. A lot has happened in the past whirlwind of a month and I've been keeping my personal life close to my heart like the precious thing it is, but I'm just so over-the-moon *happy* that I need to shout about it to *someone* and all my irl friends are really sick of hearing about it. So, here I am, shouting about it to all of you.

Yes, things have been going well with "Daisy." Like, really, *really* well. We're still in the getting-to-know-you phase of things, but I really like who I'm getting to know. She's still quiet a lot of the time, and doesn't smile easily, but she's got this razor-sharp wit that comes out of nowhere and this deep, deep curiosity that lights up her eyes whenever she gets a whiff of something she doesn't know about. This doesn't feel like something that's light or casual. Which would scare me except . . . I'm just excited. Like I've woken up to a massive snowfall and my surroundings are no longer familiar but all the more interesting because of that.

Anyway, that's enough poetical writing about weather and girls for one day. Maybe if y'all are nice about this post, I'll share a teeny-tiny portion of poetry. But for now, I'm going to go curl up with my girlfriend and take a nap.

NOVEMBER 1ST, 2016

This afternoon I went rollerblading.

I'm not even sure what I had been dreaming about before I realized I was dreaming. The act of recalling a lucid dream is a bit like trying to perfectly pinpoint your earliest memory. I don't know when I arrived at consciousness in my life, couldn't mark the year, the moment when I started forming the long-term memories that have built upon one another to make me the person I am. We don't remember the moment of our birth, just like we don't remember the instant we slip from waking into sleep.

I woke up spinning inside my dream. Spinning without my muscles tensing, spinning without getting nauseous. Spinning with uncomplicated joy. Then I realized I was dreaming. I spun faster, sticking out my arms, the speed just fast enough to feel exhilarating, to make the wind whip through my hair, but not fast enough to make my neck ache.

And then, suddenly, there was that second waking. That sharp, cool wind that blows to tell me I'm walking somewhere else. That I'm in someone else's head. I opened my eyes, stopped spinning, to see Emily, beautiful, free, lovely Emily, spinning and spinning. I grabbed her hand and we spun together.

That was when I realized—we were *flying*. Finally, finally flying. Not just on solid ground among the clouds, not hurtling through a dark and terrifying nightmare, not floating bodiless through the woods, but flying of my own volition, in my own control. I gripped Emily's hand tighter and stopped us spinning, propelled us higher and higher. We floated up into the air, breathless with joy, and Emily's beauty was almost too bright to look at.

She was wearing a necklace I've never seen before, a gold conch shell that glittered against her skin, and her smile made *me* feel more beautiful. Like I didn't have to pretend with her, like I could be fully me and it would be okay. I reached out, wanting to make the conch shell glitter even more, make the sparkles light up her eyes, but it grew too big under my touch, the dreamworld screeching against my own head as I tried to control it, the shell starting to weigh us down.

I woke up too soon. Too suddenly. Before I could fix it, there was a click of a door opening and shutting somewhere, like it was inside of me and outside of me and before I could figure out which it really was, my body was twitching, my hands grasping around someone else's. When I opened my eyes, I saw Emily blearily rubbing her eyes, the ghost of a smile on her face, not as big as the one she had in her dream, but, impossibly, with the same amount of joy lining her face. I blinked and looked around her dorm, reacquainting myself with the waking world and the fact that I was in Emily's dorm and her roommate, Mary, was walking through the door. She and Emily exchanged some vague words about schedules before Mary had disappeared into the bathroom and Emily turned her soft smile onto me.

"Hey there, sleepyhead."

"Hey," I croaked, feeling a heady mix of self-consciousness at falling asleep and self-assured confidence that going back to the dreamland we'd been sharing would be far preferable to being awake.

"How are you feeling?" she asked, and it was so kind, so full of compassion that I wanted to run away as fast as my stubby legs could take me. It had been like this in the past month we'd been dating—I try my best to charm Emily, to be someone she could like and then, inevitably, something gets in the way and she *still* treats me like a beautiful thing. On our fourth date, a few weeks after I got out of the AM, a few weeks after . . . *everything*, we were taking a walk around the Common again, holding hands, more at ease with each other than we'd been the first time we took that walk, but still with the jittery nervousness of people who had only kissed a few times, and I fell asleep. Apparently it was pretty spooky—I started to stumble and thankfully Emily had caught me just in time to sort of . . . spin me onto a park bench we were walking past. I was only out for a minute or so I guess, because when I woke up, her face was pale and clammy and her phone was clutched in her hand, emergency services up but not yet dialed.

So that's how I told the girl I'm dating I have . . . drumroll . . . narcolepsy! Yeah, I lied. Kind of. I *do* still fall asleep randomly, obviously, so it's not a lie as much as it is not . . . the whole truth. And it's not like I've made a habit of going into her dreams—this was only the second time I'd ended up in her dreams and both times it was something sweet and innocuous. I'm not spying. If there was something genuinely revealing in them, I'd force myself to wake up. I know I would.

~~I wish I could just wake up from this whole~~

Never mind.

Stupid pen. All my pencils are in my work locker, because now that my wrist is healed I'm spending as much time as I possibly can there, just observing and helping where I can, even though I'm not officially back because they can't have someone on the line who might fall asleep at any moment, but it's the best way for me to ensure that between sleeping, work, and Emily, I don't have to—

Anyway. I'm home now. Just like my parents want. For me to be spending more time at home. And it's not that I don't want that too it's that . . .

Well, what am I supposed to do? How am I supposed to just go about normal life, just pretend like we're back in July and I'm sleeping great and my dad is healthy and Aaron is being his annoying self instead of weirdly doting and considerate and my mom is demanding the best from everyone instead of skulking around the house with fear in her eyes?

It's the worst when I come home to an empty house. Like I did tonight. I opened the door, put my keys on the front hall table, and heard the clink of metal on wood echo through the house. I didn't call out—wasn't sure if I actually wanted anyone to know that I was home, didn't know what I would possibly say to any of them to fix things. I'm not even sure what's broken, I just know *something* is.

Since that horrible morning around the breakfast table, we've all been circling around one another like one wrong move will send something shattering. We've been polite and courteous and quiet and measured and that's not the family I know AT ALL. That's been *my* job, to make myself smaller so they could all be larger than life. And just when finally, *finally* I was starting to feel like I belong, like I was going to come back from the AM and understand exactly what it was like to be an Atypical Atkinson, slot in right next to Mom, Dad, and Aaron as one of *them,* take up space, *belong,* our entire family dynamic gets shifted off its axis. My entire *world* gets shifted off its axis.

I haven't stopped falling since that morning and I don't know what's going to happen when I hit the ground. I will do *anything* to not find out.

NOVEMBER 3RD, 2016

I'll admit to being pretty skeptical about this whole therapy thing—even though I liked talking to Dr. Loving, I wasn't exactly thrilled at the prospect of making it part of my routine. But I guess I have . . . stuff I need to talk about. And Dr. Bright, a therapist the AM had referred me to but who didn't seem to actually work for them, was pretty good at getting me to talk. Even if I don't always tell her the truth.

Again though: a half-truth. A lie of omission. Same thing as telling Emily that I have narcolepsy when in fact I have a superpower. Not telling Dr. Bright about my dad is just like that. It's not relevant to what we're doing anyway. She was assigned to me by the AM; I'm supposed to be continuing the work I did with them. Meditating, talking about the particulars of my ability, all of which I've found to be surprisingly easy to do with her. She's a petite Asian American woman with a hard mouth but warm eyes, like she wants to be soft and vulnerable, but is always watching what she says. I can relate. At least she has the excuse of being a therapist.

Everything she's told me about dreamdivers—that they can occupy other people's minds, even when they're awake, that some of them can build entire dreams, entire *worlds*, whole cloth, that some don't even go into others' dreams at all, but places of their own making—she says like it's completely normal. And I guess maybe it is for her. She's probably got dozens of clients like me, has been working with Atypicals for her whole career, maybe she's even Atypical herself.

I want that, what she describes. I want to be able to control this thing perfectly, to not have sleep be this weird prison where it just happens whenever it happens and then I'm *stuck*. I want to be able to get out of this city and to go to culinary school and to not have to worry about money or my future or my family—

I want to be able to have a girlfriend without panicking about whether I'm lying to her. Making up a story to explain why I was gone when I was at the AM was awkward enough and now I'm just . . .

constantly wondering when I'm going to slip up and reveal something and give her a reason to call me crazy and delete my number. I'm really starting to like her—I feel comfortable falling asleep around her, I *love* the feeling of her dreams, even when I send them spinning out of my control, and I love the way she kisses and how she laughs and how her hands are always moving, but I don't see a future for us if she doesn't know, like, the biggest, most important thing about me.

"What do your patients do usually?" I asked Dr. Bright when the topic came up.

"That's not a choice anyone can make for you, Rose," Dr. Bright said. "Most of the people I know choose to only tell those closest to them—their immediate family, best friends, spouses, partners. It's true that the AM doesn't want Aypicals to go around broadcasting it—"

"Yeah, they made that very clear." I snorted, thinking of the brochure that Owen had handed me during our exit interview called *Your Ability and You!* which detailed all the ways to make up excuses for the weird things that might happen around Atypicals and how best to hide different types of powers. Not the most encouraging piece of material I've ever read.

"But it's your decision to make," Dr. Bright said, the warmth of her voice making my shoulders relax a little. "I would suggest caution. Not everyone reacts well and it is a very personal thing to share. Make sure you trust the person first. But other than that, it's really up to you."

"Okay." I nodded, considering. "I don't think I'll tell her just yet but, I don't know, I really feel like we could be something and this isn't a part of my life I'm willing to hide from a serious girlfriend."

"See?" Dr. Bright smiled and that time it felt real. "You already know your boundaries. Trust your instincts."

Dr. Bright was full of those things: "trust the process," "trust your instincts," "listen to what your body is telling you," et cetera, et cetera. I want to be annoyed by those platitudes, but they don't *feel* like platitudes when she says them, somehow. She seems to really have the whole therapist role nailed—even when the session was over, she rose in this calm and fluid manner that I'd noticed she did every movement with—like even her own physical actions could be a way to soothe a patient.

"Call me if you have any concerns," she said as she gently ushered me to her door, and then something happened that I don't think is supposed to happen when you're in a therapist's office midsession—the door opened before we could get there.

A man, about ten years older than me, maybe, walked through, mouth already open like he was about to say something, before Dr. Bright jumped in with a—

"Mark!" She sounded genuinely surprised and the quick change in tone gave me the weirdest whiplash. She sounded . . . *human*. Not the perfect therapist that she'd been in the few hours I'd spent with her over the past month. "What are you doing here?"

"I was in the neighborhood, thought I'd stop by," the man—Mark, I guess—said, looking between Dr. Bright and me. "Sorry, I didn't realize you had a patient."

"We just finished up, actually," Dr. Bright told him before turning to me. "I'll see you in two weeks?"

She said it like a question, back to the polite, neutral doctor, but her eyes were apologizing for the intrusion, the tightness around her mouth telling me that she didn't like surprises. I could relate.

"Sure thing." I nodded and I could feel a small smile lift the corners of my mouth, somewhat pleased at the fact that, maybe, my therapist's life was sometimes as chaotic as my own. "Thanks, Dr. Bright."

"Bye, Rose," she said as I stepped through the doorway into the reception area. I gave another nod and smile as she closed the door behind me, a beat of silence before I could hear low voices as she and the man talked.

I wonder who he was—a boyfriend? Husband? I didn't notice a ring on Dr. Bright's finger as I watched her hands sit in her lap throughout my session, but that's not necessarily an indication. But thinking back on it . . . I only saw him for all of a minute, but Mark had the same high cheekbones and warm brown eyes as Dr. Bright . . . a brother maybe? I wonder if *he* knows about Atypicals, if Dr. Bright shares that part of her life, the fact that she works with people who can do remarkable things. I wonder if her whole family knows, if they talk about it. If they talk about everything.

I really expected to talk to my family about this stuff. To come back from the AM and get to partake in all the conversations I assume they have about the wonders of being Atypical. Maybe they've never had those conversations, maybe I'm not missing out on anything at all, but it feels like I probably would be getting inducted into some kind of family Atypical club if it weren't for the bomb the AM dropped on my dad and, therefore, the rest of us.

If I'm not going to talk about being Atypical with them, if it's not going to be something I tell the girl I'm dating, if I can't actually belong anywhere, I may as well belong to dreams.

NOVEMBER 10TH, 2016

I hate this I hate this I hate this I HATE THIS.

I feel like I'm thirteen again, storming up the stairs after having a fight with my mom, except this time I'm basically a fully grown adult, lingering "-teen" attached to my age completely irrelevant when I have a job and a girlfriend (maybe?) and the problems of someone much, *much* older than me.

"Nice of you to come home in time for dinner," my mom said as I walked into the kitchen, not even turning around from her position at the counter. She was putting dishes in the sink, and I could see the remnants of a meal packed away in open Tupperware. Message received. Loud and clear.

"Things ran late at the restaurant," I said. Why didn't I just say *sorry*? Do the usual routine: apologize, sneak whatever food I could, and run upstairs to watch Netflix?

Snap. She put a lid on one of the leftovers containers.

"Have they let you get back on the line yet?"

Snap. Another lid.

"Not yet," I said. "Chef is worried about me falling asleep while manning the deep fryer."

"A valid concern," she grumbled under her breath.

Snap.

She stacked the three containers on top of one another and turned to put them in the fridge, her leg going up at the same time to close the dishwasher. The silent language of my mother—always moving, efficient and exacting, ice positively radiating off of her shoulder.

"I've been doing better," I said. Tiptoeing across the ice. Crouching down so that I can more evenly distribute my weight. Sliding over to her across the chilly expanse, all the while hoping that the ice beneath me wouldn't crack and send me plummeting into the freezing depths.

"I'm glad to hear it," she said, closing the fridge and turning to me. "Did you eat?"

"Yeah, I'm good," I lied. Chef doesn't like us eating on shift and

I missed family meal so . . . yep, still hungry. I'm hoping in fifteen minutes or so my mom will be locked away in her own room and I can sneak back down into the kitchen for a midnight snack.

God, tonight is really just full of kid clichés, huh? Guess I'm not as much of a grown-up as I'd like to think.

"I know your dad and brother would be glad to hear it too," she said after a moment where the two of us just stood on opposite sides of the kitchen, in an awkward standoff.

"What?"

"That you're doing well," she continued. "They worry. We all do. Especially since you're hardly around these days to tell us you're okay."

"I'm not the one you should be worried about," I mumbled. It struck me as pretty rich that my mom was just now taking issue with me not being around all the time, now that I'm Atypical, now that my dad is sick. Instead of pushing that feeling down, putting it into kneading some dough later, I just let it bubble up.

"And who exactly do you think we should be worried about?" she asked.

"I'm not the one who's sick," I pointed out, instantly regretting addressing the nine-hundred-pound gorilla that had been sitting in the corner of every family conversation for the past six weeks.

"Worrying is not an exclusive thing, Rose," she said as I reached to get a water glass, keeping my hands busy so I didn't have to talk directly to her face. "I've been a mother for twenty years and a psychic for far longer than that—worrying is my expertise."

"Bully for you," I muttered.

Snap.

I let the cabinet door swing closed, moving to the fridge to fill the glass I'd pulled down.

Ice. Ice spreading across the room, cracking beneath my feet.

"Must not be hereditary," she went on, "seeing as you don't seem to be concerned about anything at all. I'm glad nothing fazes you, honey, but a little care for your family, especially given the past few months, would not go amiss."

I wanted to say, "If you're the professional worrier, why should I bother?" but I knew the ice would crack completely if I pushed back.

"Things faze me," I said instead, taking a sip of water.

"I just want to know what's going on in that head of yours," she said, her voice calm and completely unnerving.

"What do you mean?"

"You've barely been at home since you got back from the AM, you're sleeping all the time—"

"I have supernatural narcolepsy!" My voice rose so much faster than I had wanted, my mom's few words like a knife straight between my ribs, stabbing a response out of me. I know. I *know* I haven't been around, but I'd just been hoping that no one was noticing, as usual.

"I understand that you're still learning how to control it," she said, "but we could help with that! You've barely told us anything about your ability, about your time at the AM and we want to help. We're worried about you!"

There it was. Wasn't that what I had wanted? To talk to them, be a part of the Atypical Family Atkinson? But "we're *worried* about you"—is there a single more condescending phrase in the English language than that one?

"I'm fine!" I said. "I'm in therapy and I'm doing my AM-mandated meditations, being the good Atypical, and I'm going to work and I'm dating a girl—who I really think you would actually like by the way," I added when I saw my mom ready to jump in with some probably snarky comment. Okay, so I haven't dated the nicest girls in the past, but I also haven't brought any home since junior year of high school because of the disastrous dinner where Phoebe, a girl in my class, had interrupted everyone throughout dinner and then absconded with my mom's favorite teakettle—a weird ritual that Phoebe had, it turns out, done to everyone she dated.

I got the kettle back but . . . still.

"I'm sure I will," my mom said, offering me an olive branch.

I didn't want to take it. I wanted to shout more at her, ask why she was demanding things of me when *I'm* hurting too. I wanted to ask why she didn't know about Dad before, if she did know and just didn't do anything. I wanted to demand that she tell me exactly what to do because I have no idea.

But I didn't say any of that. I just nodded, agreeing to the truce that she'd presented to me.

And then I turned and hightailed it out of the kitchen and up here as fast as I could, like the coward that I am.

LATER

I recognized the smell before I recognized the place. I guess I really *never* recognized the place, not really, just the *feeling* of the place. A school is a school. They all have the same essence of chalk, linoleum, fluorescents, anxious minds, and nervous, hopeful hearts. It didn't matter that I had never been in this particular school. The hallway, echoey and poorly lit, felt exactly like the hallway I'd walked for four years of my life.

I walked like a ghost, like I was hypnotized, down the hall to an open doorway, a light rectangular cutout in the otherwise blank and unremarkable walls. I could hear voices—a singular voice—distant and watery.

When I turned into the room, I saw a classroom. Or, a semblance of one. Dreams aren't exacting or particularly detail-oriented, I've found. I couldn't tell you a single thing about the other faces in the room—or even if they *had* faces and weren't just blank dream mannequins. But there was only one figure I cared about, the person my eye was immediately drawn to, the moment I entered the classroom.

It was my mom. A younger version of her—my age, maybe, or no, must have been even younger than that, a stiff school uniform hanging off her body. She had her head buried in her notebook on her desk, her dark bangs falling into her eyes, when the teacher called on her.

"What?" There was pure terror on her face, her eyes wide, skin white as a sheet, sweat immediately forming on her brow, making her hair stick to her forehead.

"Weren't you paying attention?" The teacher's voice was, quite literally, like nails on a chalkboard.

"Oh, I-I—" my mom stuttered, her hands starting to shake, her damp palms crinkling the pages of her notebook.

Then suddenly I was behind her. I hadn't moved, not consciously, but that happens sometimes—a dreamworld is so strong it makes the decisions for me. I could see over her shoulder now, see what she had written in her notebook and found . . . it was the same thing that was written on the board. A mathematic formula that I'm not sure was even real, but that Dream Mom had solved already. If she knew the answer, why was she panicking?

"Still too slow to keep up, I see." The teacher sneered and I wanted to punch him in his stupid face.

"No, I-I—" she stuttered again. I've never heard my mom stutter. Is this something that happened a lot when she was younger? Was this a typical high school stress dream (and *god*, great to know those never go away) or was it based in a real memory?

The kids in her class laughed and laughed and soon the teacher was laughing too and I could feel the red hot humiliation, the suffocating shame, radiating off of my mom. It tasted like pennies and dirt and anger rose up in me.

"Rose?" My mom had turned around in her chair, looking up at me with big, scared, teenager eyes. Did she know that I was here? Or was this just her subconscious speaking to me through the dream?

"Rose, you have to help me," she pleaded. "You have to make them go away."

I did try. But I couldn't move, was stuck to the floor behind my mom's desk, couldn't wave away all the people. I tried finding the seams along the corner of the dream with my mind, pull down the classroom so I could build something else, but it was welded shut.

"Rose," she insisted, "*do* something."

"I'm trying—"

"Try harder—"

"Am I never going to be good enough?" I snapped suddenly.

"Do something!" she shouted.

"Why didn't you!" I screamed back and all the other people vanished in an instant, blown away by the power of my shout. My mom's face flickered, the dream version of her morphing in front of me, changing in size and age as my frustration just kept pouring out of me.

"Why didn't you see anything about him?" I said. "Why couldn't you help him!"

"You know that's not how it works," she mumbled, looking smaller and smaller in the chair. "I don't get to choose what I see, when I see it—"

"Then what's the point?!" I shouted. "If you can't see the future in time to change it, then what's the point!"

"There *is* no point," she cried. "We have these abilities just because we do. It doesn't make us better or more equipped for the hard things in life—"

"Maybe when you don't *try*," I said. "But there *are* Atypicals who use their powers to get things done. Who use them to make their lives better—"

"Well, good for them." She finally stood from her seat, growing taller and older in front of my eyes. "But that's not the hand that I was dealt. Your father gets to have the fun ability, gets to use it for work, to make you and Aaron laugh when you were babies, to pour us another glass of wine when we're already all comfortable on the couch." Her voice cracked, and I could see the sob rising up physically through her body. "But my visions don't work like that. It has *always* been a curse. To know what's going to happen before it happens, but randomly, without reason or purpose, to be haunted by every stray thought or errant anxiety because you wonder if *that* was a vision, if you're somehow manifesting these things, making the future fold out in front of you in horrible inevitability—"

She stopped. At first I didn't know why but then I realized—*I* stopped her. Her mouth snapped shut because I didn't want to know this. Didn't want to know that my mom's magical ability was like *this*. I didn't want to look down the barrel of my own future, be forced to think about a version of my life where my dreamdiving isn't just an unwieldy nuisance, isn't an interesting new part of my life I get to explore, isn't a place for me to belong or be useful, but is instead something that plagues every moment.

I tried to relax, to concentrate on just being in the dreamworld, not controlling it. I tried to feel my feet on solid ground, focus on rolling my toes one by one and my hold loosened, my mom's jaw relaxing.

"I won't apologize for not having the answers to everything, Rose," she finished. "I *wish* I had known, I wish that there was something I could have done. But we know *now*. And you running around as much as possible, avoiding this family like we're a chore you don't want to do, will not fix this."

"Nothing will," I snapped. "So what's the fucking point?"

Before I could hear her reply, I was pushed back from the dream, sent hurtling through the nether realm and back into the black void.

I don't know what to think. I woke up feeling . . . relieved? Less heavy than I felt when I went to sleep. Like saying all those things, hearing my own roaring voice in my mom's dream, hot air pushing down the walls of her carefully constructed classroom, lifted a weight from my chest. But a big part of me is terrified that Dream Mom was somehow my real mom, and she'll remember all of this in the morning.

I think I understand her a little better now, at least. Always struggling to be taken seriously when everything is stacked up against her. People overlook her at work because she's a nurse, not a doctor, and people are dumb and cruel and think that nurses aren't as important even though they do, like, 90 percent of the work. And then in the Atypical community, she's shunned because she's a psychic and for some reason, in a group of people who can, like, READ MINDS, and TIME TRAVEL and shit, being psychic is too hard to grasp!?!?

Watching her sitting there, in the middle of a high school classroom, panicking over the fact that she had the right answer but just couldn't, for the life of her, figure out how to articulate it, was like seeing her for the first time. It wasn't just that I was seeing her when she was just a few years younger than me—or, at least, her mind's eye of what she looked like as a high schooler—but it was also feeling every emotion that she did. It was pouring out of Dream Teen Mom like shockwaves, bowling me over with its strength.

I didn't go about it the right way, but I *did* get rid of my mom's nightmare. I replaced it with me shouting at her, but maybe . . . maybe I could do it right next time. And maybe letting out my feelings in the dreamworld is healthier than letting them bubble up inside me. Maybe I can help my family dream more peacefully and their dreams can help me in return. I think my mom is wrong—I think there *is* a point to these abilities. And I'm going to find out what it is.

NOVEMBER 16TH, 2016

The monster breathes. It steps forward out of the darkness, heavy footfalls rattling the black expanse.

It's awake.

LATER

I can't do this. I really, really cannot do this.

I was in the kitchen, going through all of our cookbooks with a notepad and pen in one hand and Post-its in the other, ready to tackle the choosing and strategizing portion of the Thanksgiving recipes. My mom encouraged me to invite Emily for Thanksgiving, seeing as her family is all the way in Arizona. I'm not sure if it's a ploy to get me to spend more time with the family or to make up for the fight we had in her dream. She didn't give any indication that she remembered the dream at all but I still . . . I worry. The next day, after I had gotten some distance from it, I realized how not great that was. Yes, I should be more honest with my family, but making their nightmares worse is probably not the best way to achieve that.

I had more or less lost myself in the intricacies of the pros and cons of different turkey brining methods when my dad came in. He moved silently around the kitchen for a moment before going to the fridge and pouring himself a glass of water, peering over the books I'd laid out on the counter as he went.

"Doing Thanksgiving prep already?" he asked and I nodded and gave a vague hum. My body had immediately tensed when he walked in, clenching even further when I saw him looking at what I was doing, bracing for a conversation I didn't want to have.

I was so afraid he was going to say something about how he'd have to sit out on the helping this year because he might accidentally chop off his hand or put sugar in something when it was supposed to be salt or how we better make most of this Thanksgiving because we don't know how many he'll have left, or some other casual-sounding but actually really sad comment. That would be so like my dad, to make a joke of his disease, to pretend like it's no big deal while simultaneously trying to be honest with me about something that was hard.

But none of that came. Instead, he just nodded and said, "Good, good, as long as you've got your pecan pumpkin pie in there, that's my only request," before turning and leaving the kitchen.

I *wanted* him to ask for more, for me to get a chance to get words around the lump that forms in my throat every time I see him now. I wanted the chance to tell him that I wasn't ignoring him, that the reason I nodded and hummed instead of saying actual words was that it's just so hard to speak the moment I hear his voice.

I know it's unfair, but I need him to be the brave one. Because I don't think I have it in me.

community/TheUnusuals post by n/thatsahumanperson

I always knew on some level how strange and scary it must be for people when I—or anyone else—reads their thoughts, but I have a better appreciation now for the emotional toll of being on the other side of that dynamic.

My sister has walked into my dreams a few times, but it's always been pretty innocuous. That is, the dreams that she's seen and the interactions we've had have been pretty innocuous—mostly just boring anxiety dreams or brief conversations where we just remark on how strange it is that we can both exist in my subconscious and have a conversation.

That's the piece of this that we haven't totally figured out—I remember the conversations we have in my dreams. I've asked my parents if they remember Rose appearing in their dreams—well, I asked my mom anyway. I don't want to put pressure on my dad about anything, especially something like his dreams, which most perfectly healthy people don't remember anyway. But my mom said that she doesn't have any recollection of Rose appearing in her dreams, that she assumed the dream that I had where Rose and I spoke—the dream that sent Rose to That Place—was the one time that Rose had gone dreamdiving in the house. And I *guess* it's possible that Rose has only been walking in my dreams, but I find that extremely unlikely.

Anyway, I usually remember when she's there, when she walks into my head. I think it *might* be because I'm telepathic—she's walking in my subconscious and forming memories herself about that experience and I'm simultaneously reading her mind.

I think I had a dream last night that she was in, but I didn't see or talk to her so I'm not sure. And when I ran into her in the kitchen this afternoon, she acted like everything was totally normal, giving me absolutely no indication that she'd been in my head. That's the other thing, I was in the kitchen just grabbing water at, like, three o'clock in the afternoon, and my sister was grabbing *breakfast*. She's been sleeping *so* much the past week or so and I don't think it's because of the narcolepsy. Unlike before That Place, I'm not finding her randomly passed out on the couch or at the kitchen table. She's just been up in her room, completely unconscious for these enormous stretches of time. Everyone in my family is pretty sympathetic to it—I think we all remember how hard it was when our abilities first manifested. I, for one, barely left my room for a month and communicated with my family almost entirely over text while they sat downstairs, just out of reach. But it's something I want to keep an eye on. Then again, I'm not my sister's keeper—she's an adult, she can take care of herself.

But this dream . . . okay, so, probably unsurprisingly, it was about my dad. And, without going into details, this was *definitely* a nightmare. It wasn't like there was some big monster or horrifying imagery . . . it was just that, well, I'm scared. Obviously. Fucking terrified. And that manifested itself in one of those dreams where you're really trying to do something, and it's urgent, you know in your bones that if you aren't able to do this thing, and *fast,* something will drag you away by its claws and eviscerate your insides? No? Just me? So, yeah, it was one of those dreams. My dad was there and I couldn't help him, no matter what I did, I couldn't go fast enough and then, suddenly, I was at Fenway Park.

Just like that. Blinding, dire terror instantly transformed to the smell of peanuts and the crack of a bat hitting a ball, sending the crowd into a roaring cheer.

My dad used to take the whole family to Fenway during the summer. Someone he works with has season tickets and he would give my dad a few whenever my dad would offer to cover a shift for him. None of us are huge baseball fans—or team sports in general—but we would love sitting out in the hot, humid air, us with the rare soda that we weren't usually allowed to have, my mom and dad with the beers that they only ever seem to drink in the summertime, just enjoying the intensity of the fans and the sound of the announcer ringing through the stadium. That was where I was—suddenly ten years old, my eight-year-old sister sitting next to me, my young, healthy parents handing us some popcorn to share. Like night and day—a nightmare one second, a beautiful memory in a dream the next.

I think it *must* have been my sister. It had to have been. But even when she was with me at the baseball stadium, it was kid-her, not current-her, and she didn't seem to think that she was in a dream. I don't think *I* realized I was in a dream.

Maybe I'm being paranoid. Maybe my brain did me a solid and pulled me out of the festering pit of anxiety I was sinking into and dropped me into something peaceful and sweet. But there's just this feeling I have, in the back of my skull, that I wasn't alone there.

onmyown

Have you thought about confronting your sister about it? Asking her if she went into your dream? Changed it? Wait, *can* she change dreams?

thatsahumanperson

I'm not sure, tbh. We haven't talked about the ins and outs of her power very much. I was hoping to, when she got back from the hospital, because I think her power is really interesting and cool and, I don't know, I guess I was hoping we'd have an easier time connecting after finding out that we were *both* Unusual, but we never got the chance. My dad was diagnosed the same day that she finished the program, and since being home, she's mostly been hanging out with her new girlfriend (? not sure what their status is), going to work, and sleeping. Lately, mostly sleeping. So we haven't had a chance to talk about how it all works. The first dream she visited of mine, I think she did make all the other people in the dream vanish? Or maybe that was me? Or the dream itself? She wasn't aware of what she could do yet, so I don't think, if it *was* her, that she was consciously trying to control it. Ugh. I guess I could just ask, but . . . that's never been easy for me.

tacotacotaco

From everything you've written about your sister, it sounds like it's not easy for her either. Eventually one of you has to take the leap.

NOVEMBER 18TH, 2016

I think I figured it out. This whole dreamdiving thing.

I've been trying more to fall asleep on command and instantly dreamdive and that really clicked when I went into Aaron's dream the other night. He was having a nightmare, a nightmare I *really* don't want to talk about, and there's honestly no point in writing it down because, trust me, I am NOT going to have a hard time remembering it, but the important thing is that I *changed it.* The *right* way.

I was watching Aaron struggle, fight against the fog that overwhelmed him, and I just wanted it to *stop,* but I couldn't grab hold of the fog to change it. I tried to swat it away with my hands and it was like the whole dream glitched, the picture flickering, like the connection was bad. I knew I was close to succeeding, could feel the fog fighting back, so I gathered as much air in my lungs as I could, breathing in deeply, inflating like a balloon, my lungs impossibly full, and then blew out, pushing the fog apart and away and sending both Aaron and me hurtling through the dark.

Then, all at once, I was eight years old, in a memory, and the dreamworld that had molded around us felt like the old times. It made my heart feel warmer and more at peace than it has in months.

And it hasn't stopped there. I've been going into dreams for most of the past few days and it's *extraordinary.* I keep unlocking new levels of this ability and with each one comes a new rush of adrenaline, a renewed feeling of belonging and *rightness.* I think I've even been in my family's waking subconscious, a thorny and unpredictable place that I seem unable to control, sometimes staticky and hard to see, like when I went into Emily's head in the urgent care. But otherwise, I'm able to make a dreamworld in my own vision—the fluffy, cotton-candy clouds of the dream with the airplane I went into at the AM; the sunny bright skies above Fenway Park; a stretching, red-orange canyon that I can skate over like a weightless bird; tall, ancient trees that branch above my head, blanketing my entire field of vision in shimmering leaves.

I'm fully through the looking glass now, not in Kansas anymore, whatever you want to call it. There's a whole wide world out there, changeable and unpredictable, vast and beautiful, and it's all mine. I can even travel back to that strange little void space, which now has a door I can always open, if I get overwhelmed. That's the inside of my own head, I think, a blank canvas for me to build on. But without the materials of someone else's dreams, the canvas stays blank, like trying to cook a dish without ingredients. I want to eventually figure out how to dive deep into my own head, like Dr. Bright has said some people do, but she ghosted me this week for a "family emergency" so I'm on my own.

I never knew it could be like *this.* That sleeping could be so much better than waking life. Emily has been doing a Shakespeare unit in one of her classes this semester and has been analyzing the "to be or not to be" speech and, I'll be honest, I didn't get most of what she was talking about except "to sleep, perchance to dream." Hamlet wanted to sink into dreams, except the long sleep he was contemplating doesn't come with a guarantee of dreaming. We don't dream when we're dead. But there is no "perchance" when it comes to me, because when I sleep, I know I'll dream. I know I'll dream and it will be better than being awake and turning over life's big questions in monologue. Maybe if Hamlet could dreamdive, he wouldn't have worried so much.

NOVEMBER 24TH, 2016

I have always operated under the belief that good food makes everything better—it comforts people, brings them together, gives me a purpose, a role in my family—and I'm happy to say that, while that belief was battered and bruised today, it came out on the other side of Thanksgiving still intact.

To say that I was nervous about Emily coming is a HUGE understatement. I was completely fucking terrified. I'm not sure I would have even invited her if I hadn't dived into a dream she had about missing her family. I know having dinner with your girlfriend's family isn't the same, but I wanted to give her *something* to make her feel better. It's not like I could just say, "hey, I went into your brain the other day while we were napping and saw you making food with your sisters—yams and tamales and some kind of wild rice that I would definitely ask the recipe for if I could tell you about this stuff—and I could *feel* the longing that sits in your chest because along with diving into dreams and witnessing them, I also sometimes feel them very very deeply, hope that doesn't freak you out, anyway, how can I help?"

I know Dr. Bright has said that I should tell Emily whenever I want—that there's no rule book to follow—but I'm not ready. I'm just starting to get used to dreamdiving myself, without having to deal with yet another person's opinion on it. And I know that if I tell Emily about the dreamdiving, I'll tell her about my dad too and I'm . . . I'm definitely not ready for *that* conversation.

Neither is anyone in my family.

"All right, so does everyone understand the plan?" my mom asked this morning as she, my dad, and Aaron stood around the kitchen island drinking coffee while *I* scrambled to stuff and get the turkey in the oven.

"Mom, we're having someone over for dinner, not pulling a heist," Aaron said, and I could hear the eye roll even though my head was halfway inside a dead bird.

"It's been a long time since we had anyone over," my mom pointed out.

"Yeah, but it's not like we forgot how to be—Dad!"

My head snapped up at Aaron's shout to see my Dad reaching out to grab Aaron's coffee cup out of the air and taking a sip.

"What?" My dad shrugged, a smile on his face. "I thought you were done."

"You could just make more coffee," Aaron said.

"Yeah, but this is more fun." My dad winked and Aaron shook his head, but couldn't keep the smile off his face.

"See, this is exactly what I mean," my mom said, sounding exasperated. "You can't go levitating coffee mugs when Emily is here."

"Yeah, and you can't steal my stuff," Aaron said, snatching the mug out of our dad's hands.

"No, you can still do that, just don't use your powers to do it." My mom smiled at my dad, who burst out laughing, before turning on her heel to go upstairs.

"Oh, and Emily's going to be early!" she called back from the stairs.

"Shit," I mumbled, looking at the state of myself. Getting together a dozen dishes *and* looking cute all in the span of, like, six hours is the hardest thing I have ever pulled off.

But I think I did pull it off—Emily *was* early and when I opened the door, she took in my nice pants and knit sweater and smiled, color blooming on her cheeks. We went through all the extremely awkward introductions that were made a lot less awkward by Emily being her unbelievably charismatic self and making everyone comfortable. Which of course was immediately undercut by Aaron jumping in, totally unprompted, with:

"Don't worry, no intense traditions or weird fetishization of colonizers in this house," he said lightly. "And no football. This is strictly a food holiday for us, especially with this one around."

He gave me an affectionate push on the shoulder—something he has literally never done in his life—and smiled, completely oblivious to the way that Emily had gone still, her eyes widening. Like she was caught out—like she had *just* been thinking about the real, dirty history of this holiday and worrying how this white family might celebrate it. After a second, Aaron caught on to her expression and froze too. YEP, guess she *had* been thinking that and Aaron somehow decided it would be a good idea to respond to her thoughts five seconds after she stepped through the door.

"I just mean," he started, stumbling, "that's something *I* think a lot about. Don't know if you do too."

I winced at the awkward cover, but Emily relaxed.

"Oh yeah, totally," she said, nodding and pushing her cropped hair behind her ear in a nervous tic I've grown to love. "I mean, it's hard to find *any* American holiday that doesn't have some truly problematic roots, but at least this one has great food."

"Speaking of!" I jumped in, taking Emily's hand. "Let me show you what I've been cooking up."

I pulled her into the kitchen and we seemed to be over the first—and I had hoped, only—Atypical slipup. Emily helped me finish out the dishes (by which I mean, she put marshmallows on top of the yams, the only assignment I'll cede control over when it comes to Thanksgiving) while my mom asked about her poetry. And it was different than when she interrogates me about my work or my future—my mom seemed genuinely interested and supportive of a less traditional career. Jealousy and happiness fought it out inside of me the entire time I was plating things, but eventually gratitude that my mom was making an effort won out. A Thanksgiving miracle.

Another miracle? The fact that Emily didn't catch on to the weirdness of my family when MY DAD LEVITATED THE FREAKIN' PEPPER MILL ACROSS THE TABLE.

Aaron noticed it before anyone else did—I wonder if he could read something in my dad's thoughts that gave him a heads-up he was about to use his telekinesis. The pepper mill started floating on the table before spinning toward the other end where my dad was casually eating like nothing was strange. Aaron snatched it out of the air just as Emily looked up. Her eyes narrowed but there's no way she saw anything. There's no way. She would have said something if she saw a pepper mill move on its own, right?

"Here you go, Dad," Aaron said pointedly. My dad looked up at Aaron's outstretched hand and immediately paled, realizing what he'd done. He silently took the pepper mill, with his actual hand, and my mom jumped in with a funny story about work that took up enough oxygen in the room to cover up what had just happened.

I'm not mad at him. I'm really not. He explained everything after Emily left—

"I forgot, Rose," he said, sadness in his eyes. "I completely forgot that she didn't know. I wasn't thinking, I'm so sorry—"

"Dad, really, it's fine," I assured him. "It's not your fault. And I don't think Emily saw anything, so we're all good."

"Not that your brother's outburst was much help either," my mom muttered.

"I was nervous!" Aaron said, "I didn't mean to listen but her anxieties jumped out!"

"Guys, really, it's okay," I said, placating everyone as I got up to get another piece of pie. "Emily had a good time and nothing terrible happened."

And that's true—the whole dinner actually went really well. It was the after-dinner conversation that's left me with a slightly sour taste in my mouth. My family *loved* Emily. After the finger-pointing portion was over, they went on and on about how interesting she was, how clever, how charismatic. All the things that unaccomplished, laser-focused, friendless Rose is not. I think my mother would have adopted Emily on the spot and by the end of dinner, Emily and Aaron were halfway to having their own inside jokes.

I know that Emily puts her whole heart into everything she does, I've seen it—her intense commitment to school, her writing, her friends, her family—but it stings that being loved by my family came so easily to her. It's not her fault. I'm not even sure it's my family's fault. I've never screamed at them, "Pay attention to ME!" and so they haven't. They're just doing what they've always done—eating my food, being themselves, and tolerating my existence.

11-25-2016, morningwaffles, text post

I know you all have been *very* eager to hear how Thanksgiving with the girlfriend's family went and . . . drumroll please . . . I think it went well! We ate a lot of food and laughed and Daisy's family was super warm and welcoming and nice. I avoided making a complete ass of myself and even managed to go a whole three hours without talking about how I write porn about fictional characters (you know, THAT conversation that all of us have with the people in our lives eventually) though I actually think her mom might have thought that was cool? I thought Daisy's mom was cool, so maybe I'm just projecting hopefully.

Her whole family was cool, honestly. Really relaxed and at home with one another in a way that reminded me of my family, which made my homesickness even worse, but also soothed it in a strange way. But Daisy was . . . really quiet the whole dinner. It was like our first few dates honestly, like she was trying to hide parts of herself. Maybe she was nervous about me and her family clicking or maybe she was just exhausted from cooking all day. But part of me wonders if the Daisy I met on our first date is the person she is around her family all the time.

There *was* one kind of weird moment right at the beginning of the evening though. Not to be *totally* tinhat, but I think there might be a chance that her brother found this blog? If so . . . uh, hi? I guess? Daisy said he was really good with computers and I got a distinct "protective older brother" vibe, which was *so* not what I expected from what Daisy had told me, so maybe he tracked me down online. Right when I got there, he said this stuff about not celebrating the colonizing aspect of Thanksgiving, which is, like, exactly what my last blog post was about? So I don't know if we're just similar people thinking about similar stuff or if he read that post and was trying to make me feel comfortable. But, whatever, that really was the only odd thing of the whole dinner. Yeah. That was definitely all.

Anywho, that's the life update. I'm going back home in ten days for the holiday break, so Daisy and I won't see each other for a little while. But this felt like a really big step and I'm . . . hopeful. I think we might really be something.

DECEMBER 16TH, 2016

The monster has teeth. It's stepped out from the shadows, made itself known and snapped its jaws at the one person who doesn't deserve its ire.

It all started this morning when my dad actually *yelled* at me.

Part of me is relieved, honestly. That my dad cares enough to yell. That he feels well enough to. Because the possibility looms heavy over our house like a fog—the possibility that I'm going to wake up one day and the person in our house, wearing my dad's clothes, is someone different. My dad but not quite. My dad but further away, already in a place we can't reach him.

But today he really felt like himself. Like he was the same person who gave me the biggest lecture when I snuck in after midnight one night in sophomore year, bloodied and bruised from an ill-advised middle-of-the-night solo rollerblading outing.

Everything devolved after Thanksgiving. I think we were all surprised by how . . . nice? It was? To just have a family meal and not think about Atypical stuff or diseases or visions or anything else for a whole day. But when I went to sleep that night, exhausted from a straight day and a half of cooking and the stress of introducing Emily to my family, I stayed asleep. For two days.

They're used to it by now—me going to sleep for large chunks at a time. But it's been freaking them out, I guess. They called my doctors at the AM, who didn't seem overly concerned. My body processes energy and calories differently when I'm dreamdiving, so they said as long as I'm not getting dehydrated or undernourished, I should be fine. That was cold comfort to my family, but good enough for me. I told everyone I would be more diligent about eating and drinking but that I was totally fine.

I lied.

I haven't fallen asleep without meaning to in . . . a while. When I woke up briefly Friday morning and thought about going downstairs and spending the day eating leftovers with my family, it all seemed so . . . dull. Despite the fun of Thanksgiving, reheated turkey and post-holiday lethargy weren't exactly tempting, especially when I knew I could be riding a dragon and eating what Turkish delight actually *should* taste like, in the way that it's described in The Chronicles of Narnia, something good enough to betray your family to the White Witch for, instead of the gummy, gelatinous sugar rush it is in real life.

So I shut my eyes again. I was thinking I would just dip in, serve myself a delightful feast with food and drink that doesn't even *exist* on the regular plane of existence, and then wake myself up and join my family for some real and boring dinner. But time moves differently in the dreamworld and, in all my learning about how to perfectly execute the dreamdiving, I haven't *quite* figured out the translation of Dream Time to Real Time and, well, one thing led to another in my dreamfeast and the silverware starting singing, like a scene from *Beauty and the Beast* and THEN my ten-year-old neighbor fell asleep and he's got this absolutely wicked imagination where he dreams about these really fun and goofy quests in magical lands, so I got caught up in that for a bit and then Aaron was dreaming about computer code (the *nerd*) and I got to jump into a *Matrix*-style thriller and then I was feeling antsy and I flew for a while but then I realized that a few hours had probably passed and I woke myself up and it was twenty-six hours later.

I didn't think anyone in my family would understand all of that though, so I kept it to myself, pretending like I'd just made a mistake. Slipped up. That seemed to appease them for the time being but . . .

Okay, so. That's happened a few more times. Since Thanksgiving. And with my family's seeming lack of concern about me sleeping two entire days away, I figured, what's the harm? Well, this morning, I was ambushed by my dad in the kitchen.

"Look who's joined the land of living," he said. I looked over to the kitchen table, to see him staring at his cup of coffee, a newspaper open under his elbows sitting on the table. He was definitely speaking to me—Aaron and my mom were nowhere to be seen—but he wasn't looking at me.

"It's . . ." I looked toward the microwave clock. "Eight thirty. Aaron sleeps in later than that almost daily. I assume that's where he is right now," I added for good measure.

"Yes, but Aaron was actually awake for some of yesterday, which can't be said for every member of this household."

I recognized that tone of voice. There's always so much talk about "I'm not angry, I'm just disappointed" being mom-speak, but our mom just comes right out and tells us when she's mad. It's my dad who will sound disapproving and let down, in just the right way to make you feel like the worst person in the world.

"Oh," I said, unsure if there was any right thing I could say in this moment that would let me off the hook. I was also, legitimately, a little surprised. I'd thought it was Wednesday morning—the last thing I remember being sometime midday on Tuesday—but glancing at the sports section of the newspaper that was on the counter told me it's currently Thursday.

"Oh?" my dad asked, finally looking up at me, his eyes wide. I turned to pour myself a cup of coffee. "Is that all you have to say for yourself?"

"I'm sorry, Dad," I said, not really sounding it. "I'm not going to apologize for a *medical condition* I have."

I really thought I'd had him there. He, more than anyone else, should understand that different expectations and accommodations need to be made for people like us that have something we're battling against. And maybe he *would* have given me a break if that was what was going on. But, like always, he saw through my bullshit.

"You're not falling asleep at the drop of a hat anymore," he said, clearing his throat. "You're *choosing* it. We know you are. You're choosing to sleep through everything, to spend all your time in that other place."

I hadn't expected that. He said it so coldly, clinically, and my mind instantly jumped to interventions that I'd seen on TV shows. But Aaron and my mom weren't there, there was no banner hung over the kitchen table, just me and my dad and slightly burnt coffee, staring each other down.

"And why shouldn't I?" I asked.

"Because that's now how this is supposed to work, Rose," he said.

"Don't tell me how my *own* ability works," I said, taking a step toward him. "I know what I'm doing. I have *perfect* control over it—"

He scoffed, closing the newspaper.

"It's true!" I insisted. "I can do whatever I want in there!"

"Maybe you don't need better control over your ability itself," he said, "but over how you *use* your ability."

"What is that supposed to mean?"

He sighed and stood up, coming to stand directly in front of me, his most serious Dad face on.

"I think it'd be good for you to do another stay at the AM," he said.

"What??" I yelped.

"Rose—"

"No, no," I shouted, shaking my head. "I don't need to go back there!"

Why, oh why, did I *shout* at him? What kind of unrepentant monster shouts at their sick father when all he's trying to do is *help*?

"Rose, I really think it's for the best!" he said, stern but not matching my volume. How do I do that? How do I conquer the skill of speaking strongly, assertively, without my voice rising in level and pitch, without it feeling like my words are barbed wire pouring out of my mouth and wrapping around the limbs of the people I'm directing them to? In the dreamworld I never have this problem. I shout and scream, with joy and with fear, I laugh loudly and without shame, and the sound is carried up on that soft breeze that's always there, made of light and music, keeping everything in balance. Even me. Why can't real life be like that? Why can't real life feel like a place where your voice is always at the right volume, always perfectly poised to be heard in exactly the way that you want?

"No one else does!" I said. "Aaron is god knows where, there's no way he cares about this, and Mom *hates* the AM—"

"You know they don't appreciate people with your mother's ability—" My dad sighed, a wrinkle forming in between his eyebrows as he pleaded with me.

"Exactly, so what do they know!" I yelled. "I don't *need* them—"

"I don't understand," my dad said, blinking at me. "Did something happen in your first round? Something you haven't told us about?"

"Oh, you mean, besides feeling like a freak among freaks?" I spat. "Besides falling asleep in the middle of therapy or going walking inside someone's head during group and having people think less of you because you're not the perfect Atypical in perfect control?"

"Rose," he started, so soothing and gentle, "people there understand better than anyone how difficult it is to control an ability, especially when it's new. They know what they're doing—"

"No, they don't!" I shouted. "They don't know how to fix you!"

He didn't have any rebuttal to that. I'm not sure what I would have wanted to hear, or how I expected him to react. I know I *wasn't* expecting him to look . . . defeated. He had an answer for everything—for every reason I didn't want to go, for what I should do on my first date with Emily, for how I should approach Chef about a promotion. My dad *always* had the answer. And he let Aaron and me get away with stuff, would goof around with me, encourage risky flambé experiments, but he *always* knew where to draw the line. He called us on our bullshit.

I just wanted him to call me on my bullshit. I wanted him to say, "Actually, you're wrong, you need to go back to the AM, to trust them, because they're working on a fix for me. They've got it all figured out." But he didn't say that at all.

"Rose," he said softly, "I know it's frustrating, dealing with me like this—"

"What?" I asked. "What are you talking about?"

"I'd understand if you were all at the end of your patience," he said. "I know I am. Not being able to work very much anymore, forgetting conversations we've had—"

"Dad, no one is frustrated with you," I interrupted. "That's—how could you think that?"

The sadness on his face turned to confusion.

"Then why have you been avoiding me?"

"What?" My question barely came out, getting caught in my throat in shock.

"I assumed that's why you weren't around," he explained. "You don't want to watch your old man fade away."

"Dad, don't talk like that," I pleaded. "You're not fading away. I know that you sometimes forget where your book is or why you went into a room, but that happens to all of us sometimes!"

I was trying to make it sound like no big deal at all, like it was the most casual problem in the world, but I could feel the tears forming in my eyes. Why do I always cry right when I don't *want* to?

"I know it's going to get worse," I continued, gritting the words out and quickly moving on to the next thought, "but you're not—I mean, you're doing great. And we're going to be here whatever happens. If it gets worse, then we'll be here. And it won't be frustrating for us."

"If it gets worse?" he asked, his face completely collapsed. "Rose, it already has."

I wanted to ask what he meant but I couldn't get the words out. How much had I missed?

"You've slept through a lot of things, Rose," he said, answering the question I was too afraid to ask.

A tear escaped my eye, rolling down my cheek. I didn't want to wipe it away, didn't want to bring attention to it, but I didn't think there was any way my dad didn't notice. But he didn't make any moves to comfort me, to bring me into a hug like he would have normally. Instead he just said:

"Please go to the AM, Rose. For me."

And he grabbed his coffee cup and walked out of the kitchen.

I should have told him yes, okay, fine, I'll do whatever will make him happy, whatever will make him smile and tease me again. I should have immediately apologized for yelling. I should have told him I love him.

I should have told him about the dream I'd walked in last week, the one where he was back there, sitting in a doctor's office, waiting, waiting, waiting, so filled with dread and hopelessness that they were almost physically manifested Dream Things. I was trapped in that dream with him, so scared to have the doctor come in, scared he never would, filled with a terrible anticipation of what was next and also the deep certainty that the AM couldn't help. I should have told him that I tried everything—for what felt like hours—to change his dream, bring him to Fenway or to one of the spy novels he loves so much, but I *couldn't*. There was a fog around every part of his dream, around every part of *him*, and I couldn't get a solid hold on anything.

But I didn't say any of that to him. So I guess I'll be going back to the AM.

Ralphy said I'd be back. Guess I should have listened.

community/TheUnusuals* post by *n/thatsahumanperson

I've been trying to take n/tacotacotaco's advice and actually *talk* to my sister but literally *all she is doing* is sleeping. Granted, we've all kind of been running around to get ready for the holidays and I'm in a crunch for my current work project (I think I, fingers crossed, FINALLY have this remote freelancer thing worked out), but I think she's sleeping for practically days at a time, only waking up to eat and have water. I don't even know how she can handle it physically—she's always been a pretty active person, she loves Rollerblading and cooking and was even starting to get into yoga this past summer, and now she's spending most of her hours every day catatonic in her bed.

Does anyone know of *any* dreamdivers that have had this problem? What the hell do I do?

tacotacotaco

You know, a lot of people do the program a few times—there's no shame in your sister returning to That Place to get additional help. All that sleeping definitely . . . does not sound healthy.

thatsahumanperson

Yeah, I know. She only did two weeks there—I did a *lot* more and I don't think I would have come out the other side with nearly as much control as I did if I had only done two weeks. I think I need to talk to my parents.

franklinsteinsmonster

So there are, like, levels and stuff? A bunch of different ways you can do a program?

tacotacotaco

Yep, there are literally "tiers." Each tier is for different intensity of ability or stage of control—the higher the tier number, the more rigorous the program.

thatsahumanperson

Right. I did tier 2—was there for eight weeks. A lot of individual talk therapy, group therapy, training my ability, medical check-ins, etc. It kind of felt like what I imagine army boot camp would be like, just without the toxic masculinity and trumped-up patriotism.

franklinsteinsmonster
Like the beginning bit of *Mulan* where they're all training.
thatsahumanperson
Ha, yeah, exactly. Except you're surrounded by a bunch of people who can do things like make fire and move objects with their mind.
franklinsteinsmonster
That Place (which still no one will tell me the actual name of!!!!!) sounds like *the coolest.*

JANUARY 3RD, 2017

Looks like I won't be doing any group. Talk therapy is still really important, I guess, because I've got, like, four therapy sessions every single day, but they won't be putting me with any other Atypicals. At all. Owen explained it to me when I got here yesterday, sitting me down in the same room we'd met in the first time—that windowless, spa-like room, with soft lighting and squishy pillows. It made me feel a little less freaked out about being back to be sitting in a familiar room, looking at a familiar face. That feeling didn't really last once he started talking though.

"So, Rose," he started, his voice gentle, "tell me what's going on."

"Um . . ." I swallowed. "Didn't Dr. Bright fill you in? I thought I was supposed to do everything through her now, so we had a session last week—"

"Yes, yes, she did," he said. "And her notes, as always, were extremely thorough." He smiled a bit at that, like he admired good note-taking.

"But I want to hear it from you." He leaned forward, his elbows on his knees, his eyes warm and inviting behind his wire-frame glasses.

"Oh, well, um," I fumbled, not sure where to begin. I decided it was best to just . . . rip off the Band-Aid. "I've been sleeping . . . a *lot*."

"Define 'a lot,'" he said.

"Like . . . most days?" His mouth twisted, in disappointment or sadness, I couldn't tell. "I haven't been—I mean, it hasn't been random. Not really."

"You mean, you haven't been falling asleep without meaning to?" he asked and that's when I noticed that he didn't have any kind of notebook open, no pen taking notes on my file. It's like he was asking because he cared.

"Yeah," I said. "Yeah, I've been choosing it."

"And you've been dreamdiving?" he asked.

"Yeah." I nodded, feeling embarrassed by the answer. But why should I be? That was what they had taught me to do—all I'd focused on my first time here was controlling my ability enough to mitigate the narcoleptic symptoms and I'd *done* that. But I didn't say that to Agent Green, instead asking a question that had been bothering me since my last appointment with Dr. Bright, the one that had confirmed that I needed to come back here.

"Dr. Bright didn't think it was a good idea for me to come back here," I told him. "She agreed that I need help, but she didn't seem to like the idea of me doing another program at the AM."

"What did she suggest instead?" Owen asked, leaning back in his chair. His normally open face shuttered a bit, turning into a carefully neutral mask. That was the second time mentioning Dr. Bright had caused some sort of reaction. I still don't really understand what her relationship to the AM is, but I'm getting curious.

"More frequent therapy sessions," I said. "More diligence on my part—meditating more, journaling again."

"You haven't been journaling?" he asked, looking like a kicked puppy. It almost made me want to reach into my bag and show him that I'd brought this notebook. But I didn't want him to see how few pages I'd used since he last laid eyes on it.

"Not as much," I said. "It was always meant to help me track stuff so I could control things better. I don't know why I would have to keep it up now that I'm where I'm at."

"It's not just about your ability, Rose," he said. "Dr. Loving said that it was helping you process a lot of different things in your life—she seemed to think it was very beneficial to you, based on what you told her about it during your last stay. I would imagine there are still things worth writing down, especially with what's happening with your father—"

"So what's the plan this time around?" I asked bluntly. I like Owen, but I was not ready to have *that* conversation with him. He seemed to understand that, letting me steer the conversation away from the difficult things.

"Well, similar to before," he said, opening up my file for the first time. He didn't seem to actually read it, instead scanning his eyes over it like he just needed something to do. "You'll do therapy, physical checkups, dreamdiving sessions, but no group—"

"Thank god," I mumbled.

"I hear it wasn't your favorite last time," he said, giving me a small smile.

"Yeah, not really my thing," I admitted.

"That's perfectly okay," he said. "We're not focused on how your ability interacts with other people anyway. In fact, at first, we're going to ask you not to dreamdive at all. And, ideally, not even dream. Get your body used to normal sleep again."

"How exactly is *that* going to happen?" I asked. After that horrible fight with my dad, I wanted to show him that I could fix myself without coming here. I wanted to make things better with him. But anytime I fell asleep, I just couldn't *not* dreamdive. And every time I would get swept up in the wonders of the dreamworld and not notice the time passing and . . . well. Here I am. I wasn't sure I even *could* sleep without dreaming anymore.

"You'll be put in a room that's specially treated to . . . limit Atypical abilities," he said, hesitating slightly. "And given sleeping pills that should help you sleep without diving.

"I know, I know, it sounds scary," he added, seeing my face. "But I promise you, it won't hurt you at all. And you'll most likely only be in that room for the first week."

"And then what?" I asked.

"And then we'll put you in the same room you stayed in the first time you were here," he said, before softening his voice and leaning forward again. "Rose, we don't want to take your ability away from you, or make you feel bad for using it—"

"Really? Because it feels like that's exactly what I'm here for—"

"We just want you to use it safely," he said, unfazed by my combativeness. "Your ability is a part of you, a beautiful part, but you can't sleep your whole life away."

"You get that from Dr. Bright?" I scoffed, and he flinched, which was a bit surprising. I hadn't meant that as an insult.

"Yes, well, Joan is a very smart woman," he said and I immediately clocked the first-name usage. There's a story there and if I were allowed to walk in anyone's dreams right now, I bet I could find out.

But for now, I'm in the "detox" phase of things, I guess.

I had my first dreamless sleep last night and it was . . . fine. I was able to sleep and I didn't dreamdive. I even woke up at a reasonable hour.

Maybe this won't be so hard after all.

January 3rd, 2017

Dear Mark,

Finally the truth. Dr. B. and Sam brought me here—not you. I knew it. You wouldn't betray me, not like that.

In other revelations, Wadsworth definitely does think I'm a criminal.

Attempted kidnapping, actual kidnapping, breaking into a private facility, stalking, harassment, credit card fraud, and "oh yes, you haven't paid your taxes in, well, ever." Her smile feels like it could rebreak my ribs.

That was the list she rattled off. She's smart and knows way more than she should, but seems like the body that's buried in the Santa Monica Mountains is still buried. Murder—accessory to murder, I should say ~~who am I kidding I know the truth of what I~~—has stayed off my rap sheet. Though now that I've written it down within the halls of the AM, maybe it won't stay a secret. I don't know. I probably shouldn't be writing so many letters to you while high on morphine.

I never told you any of that. About Isaiah and the Unusuals and what we did. What I did. ~~I'm trying to~~

I think you would have liked Neon.

I like Neon. I loved Neon. Indah too. Marley, in his own way, but I never really saw him like that. Like something I wanted to get closer to, to touch. But Neon and Indah . . . enough distance from that time and a whole lot of what your therapist sister would call "self-reflection" has made me accept the stark truth, that I have, in fact, been in love before. And I so thoroughly ruined it. I keep ruining things. ~~And I'll just keep~~ I'm hard to understand, hard to love, hard to forgive. Everything in my life has been so fucking hard.

I think you'd roll your eyes at that. I know that Neon would have. She'd roll her eyes and call me an emo white boy before lighting a cigarette. I've been thinking about her so much the past few months. I understand her better now, understand why she was so upset when I used her power to do what I did. I sure as shit didn't relish you using my power and I like you. I'm not sure Neon *ever liked me. Not really. Not honestly. Not without me making her.*

But I've been thinking about her, and how she'd hate this place. How she'd want to burn the whole thing down.

I still don't know if Isaiah was Atypical. Whatever he was, he was dangerous. I'm glad he's in the ground. And, somehow, despite absolutely everything, I really don't want to join him.

JANUARY 7TH, 2017

I feel like I want to crawl out of my own skin.

It's now been five days since I last dreamdived. I slept quite a bit the first two days I was here—it was weird to go to bed at a normal hour and sleep without dreaming, but I'll admit, it was actually kind of nice. To fall asleep slowly and then, in the blink of an eye, be awake and have it be the next day. With the help of the sleeping pills they've given me, my body has readjusted to a regular schedule. Now I'm just . . . a normal person again. They're going to start letting me dive again soon, but for now, I'm just going from doctor's appointment to therapy to doctor's appointment to yoga to therapy to meals to yoga on a constant loop. It's simultaneously kind of relaxing and *completely mind-numbing*.

So. I've started wandering around the facility.

It's ENORMOUS. I didn't realize how enormous until I started to explore it, finding it far twistier and more confusing to navigate than I would have expected from the big, open-air lobby.

It's half a dozen stories, a big steel-and-glass monstrosity, with these strange little elements of old-school New England, like the stone floors and musty library smell. I wasn't able to access large swaths of the building—private rooms and most of the medical wing—but as I wandered down a hallway on the sixth floor, I saw there were also a bunch of private offices and conference rooms, most unoccupied as the doctors and such went about their day. As I passed one open doorway, I heard a familiar voice.

"Rose!"

Mags, the cute receptionist, came bounding out of a room that, from looking over her shoulder, seemed to be some kind of employee lounge. She had that big, beautiful smile on her face, but she also looked deeply, deeply confused.

"What are you doing up here?" she asked.

"Just wandering around," I said, shrugging. "I had some free time and nothing to do so . . ."

"So you've decided to go exploring where you shouldn't?" She folded her arms across her chest and fixed me with a stare that reminded me of my mom. Which . . . seeing that face on a girl I think is cute? Full body shudder.

"No—what—I wasn't—I'm not *snooping* or anything," I rushed to explain and Mags laughed.

"I'm totally messing with you!" she said. "I mean, yeah, patients aren't *really* supposed to be up here unless they've got an appointment, but it's not like it's forbidden or anything."

"Really? Because it honestly feels like I'm Belle and a talking candelabra is going to pop out from around a corner and tell me to never go into the west wing."

She laughed again.

"Yeah, that's very fair." She chuckled. "Come on, let's keep walking."

And so we did. Mags walked me around the rest of the floor, and back down to my room, telling me about the AM all the while. I think she meant it when she said it was okay for me to be up there, but I also think she walked with me to keep an eye on me, make sure I wasn't sticking my nose where it didn't belong. Because as it turns out, the AM has a lot of things going on that not even employees know about.

"Experiments?" I asked as Mags finished telling me about all the different things they did in this building. "What do you mean by experiments?"

"I mean, I'm not a scientist," she said lightly. "But I think it's mostly building off of the research they're already doing with patients. We know a lot about Atypicals—a lot more than we did even a decade ago—but we're still so secret to everyone, you know?"

I nodded.

"So regular, state-sponsored experiments are hard to pull off," she continued. "But we *need* to focus on Atypical healthcare. A lot of problems can be handled by regular doctors—broken bones for instance," she added, looking knowingly at me.

"Right." I blushed, looking down at my arm. You would never know that anything had ever been wrong with it.

"But for anything that intertwines with an Atypical ability . . . like, take a shapeshifter, for instance."

"You get a lot of those around here?" I asked, thinking of Marco.

"A fair few," she said simply, like that's not *extremely fucking cool.*

"If a shapeshifter gets a broken bone, that's something a regular doctor isn't going to be able to handle."

"Because a shapeshifter could affect their own bones?" I asked.

"A really in-control and powerful one could, absolutely," she said. "It's all about the way a person's ability affects their biology and vice versa. It's all intertwined and most of modern medicine has been focused on non-Atypical humans so it just kind of . . . ignores that."

"So an Atypical could need different treatment than a non-Atypical for the same thing . . ." I thought aloud.

"Exactly," she said. "After all, your unplanned trips into unconsciousness needed to be addressed differently than they would be in a non-Atypical patient."

"Oh yeah, I guess that's true," I said. We had arrived back at the patient dormitories and Mags had started her "oh look, what a convenient surprise" routine that was clearly meant to get me back in my room, but I was barely listening, my mind moving a million miles a minute.

What if the AM hadn't explored things fully with my dad's diagnosis? As far as our parents told us, the doctors had just said, "Hey, dude, you've got Alzheimer's, it sucks, and the telekinesis *might* make it worse, but we don't know why, you've got somewhere between two and ten years, good luck bro," but how much did they really consider how his ability factors into it? Is it just that it might make things worse? Could it make things *better*? I mean, if they've got rooms here that suppress Atypical abilities, surely they can untangle someone's power from a disease that's killing them. Right?

JANUARY 9TH, 2017

I've just finished moving all my stuff from the intense cinder-block Atypical-ability-dampening room to another, slightly more airy cinder-block room. Despite what Owen had said, I'm not in exactly the same room as I was the first time, but they're all basically identical, so it shouldn't really matter. Except I'm all the way at the end of the hall, right next to the stairwell, in the weird, old, stone part of the building and . . .

OKAY I'M A LITTLE SCARED. Ugh.

I get scared talking to girls, or before math tests, or when Chef comes into the kitchen with steam coming out of her ears, but I don't usually get scared by "spooky" stuff. A musty, windowless room in some corner of some old hospital would maybe freak a lot of people out but it shouldn't bother me.

Except, I'm going dreamdiving for the first time in a week tonight and I don't know what to expect. We're starting actual trials tomorrow, like we did the first time, where I'll put myself to sleep in the presence of doctors and try to walk into their heads. I think they're going to be waking me up every couple of minutes, training me to understand how long five minutes in the real world feels in the dream time. That was what Owen had said.

"They've done this with a lot of other dreamdivers?" I asked after he explained the scope of the tests, leading me down and around the halls of the medical wing, where all the sleep test rooms are. This is how we've done most of our talks the past few days—I sit still with Dr. Loving in therapy and walk circles around the facility with Owen. I find walking around with Owen a *lot* more productive.

"Yep," he said, sounding almost proud. "Believe it or not, you're not the first person who has had such a good time in the dreamworld that you haven't wanted to spend any time in the real world."

I looked up at him to see that he was smiling, lightly teasing me.

"Ha, yeah," I chuckled. "I guess that's not too surprising."

"I should think not," he said. "I mean, goodness, if I had the ability to go into dreams . . . it sounds wonderful."

"Not super on-message with the whole 'giving a girl addicted to dreamdiving a pep talk' thing," I teased back.

"Oh, gosh, of course," Owen rushed to say. "I didn't mean—"

"It's okay," I said. "I get it. I really do."

We walked in silence for a while, my shoulder practically brushing his elbow, that's how tall he is. Or how short I am, I guess.

"It won't be any different than the tests you did the last time you were here," he continued eventually, "not really. This past week has been all about reminding you what it's like to sleep dreamlessly, so your body recognizes healthy, normal sleep."

"My body was already getting healthy, normal sleep," I said. "Granted, it was getting a lot *more* of that than it should have—"

"It's true, your body is still able to get the necessary rest when you're dreamdiving," Owen said, "but we don't yet know much about dreamdiving's effect on the brain."

"What do you mean?" I asked.

"That's probably a question best left for the doctors," he said.

Hence: scared. Spooky stone hallways and creepy lab tests . . . nothing at the AM has felt like a horror show, but I worry that the slasher version of it might somehow creep its way into my dreams. I don't really know who else is around in the facility at the moment, and who might be reachable to me in my sleep, so it's possible I'll just be stuck in my own head with my own thoughts. And I know that I can create new ones, that if things start to turn to a nightmare, I can turn every killer clown into a funny one (though, to be honest, all clowns are terrifying), but I'm feeling . . . rusty. Seven days and nights is not enough to forget how to do something—I didn't roller skate for all of freshman year and hopped back no problem in sophomore—but dreamdiving is tumultuous and unexpected at the best of times. That's one of the things I love about it, but I . . . I'm scared of what might be waiting for me there. What might have been neglected the past week that's just waiting in the shadows for me.

And I worry even thinking about the possibility of a nightmare has sealed it into certainty.

I'm gasping for air, clawing at the ground, the smell of dirt and rot pressing in on my nose, my mouth, the earth clinging to me, squeezing in and around me, pushing me down

down

down

down into the ground.

I breathe, blood filling my mouth, there's the smell of burnt hair, sharp

metal

lightning

Electricity, electric shocks sending hairs standing on their ends, the current pulling me up and turning me inside outout*out*.

The smell of burnt hair.

Electricity.

Electric hair, electric blue.

Neon.

Bright.

The smell of flowers.

The perfume of her hair.

JANUARY 10TH, 2017

I don't remember writing that. I know I must have. It's my handwriting, looking like I'm guessing it would if I were a few sheets to the wind. I can barely read the words, but it was clearly about a dream I was having. A dream that feels like it's still right behind my eyelids and like it's already very, very far away. I don't remember the details, barely remember a single image, but I can still smell flowers. A woman's perfume. My skin feels sensitive, like I've touched charged metal and gotten a shock.

So it turned out that I was right to be afraid. First time dream-diving in a week and I'm instantly dropped into a nightmare. I just didn't expect it to be someone *else's* nightmare. I don't remember seeing anyone, can't recall anything about the point of view, but I know I wasn't me. I couldn't control *anything*, couldn't get myself out or change the dream from the inside. And none of those feelings were even remotely mine. Fear so real and visceral it tastes like rusted metal on your tongue, guilt so all-consuming I didn't even have to breathe it in for it to crawl down my throat and choke me.

And then . . . peace. A burst of blue neon electricity that transformed into warm yellow sunlight, the smell and texture of flowers and skin . . . calm and *rightness*. Like I was right where I was supposed to be. I've never been in a dream quite so abstract before, quite so abrasive, with so many conflicting feelings that lie on top of one another, none of them getting enough room to breathe.

Whoever's head I was in last night has some *serious* stuff they need to work out.

Warm sunlight.

Flowers.

The perfume of her hair.

The flowers on her arm, pink and blooming.

Her eyes, smiling and warm.

I'm so safe here. In the cornfields.

His smile. His *laugh*.

So warm. So safe. The cornstalks grow higher, they bend and bow, growing spikes from their ears, razor blades amidst the corn.

His laugh is as strong as a razor.

Her disappointment.

His teeth.

January 12th, 2017

Dear Mark,

The dreamless sleeping has stopped. The last bit of hospitality that the AM showed me has been taken away. I guess I'm healing up pretty well—I've even started taking supervised "walks," by which I mean thirty minutes where I get to circle my hospital room, handcuffed to an IV while a bunch of AM lackeys watch me through the window. It's nice to not feel like I've been put together with floss and Scotch tape anymore, but the drugs were . . . not bad.

I used to dream about my parents a lot. Not really dreaming at all for weeks, thanks to those wonderful sedatives, made me think about how long it's been since I dreamt about Them or anything related to Nebraska and my life there at all. It feels so goddamned far away, like another life. So does LA, but that I do still dream about. Ever since they stopped giving me the feel-good pills, I've been dreaming constantly throughout the night, frantically and almost painfully, and so often about that former life and the friends I had in it.

Last night I dreamt about you. ~~Which isn't new~~ About running to find you, here, just down the hall from where I am now. You were in pain, screaming in pain, and I couldn't run to you fast enough. I couldn't save you. A nightmare based on something that never happened. Because I did save you. I did.

I need you to save me now, Mark. Could you do that? Could you save me?

It's cold and I am asleep. I've been asleep for so long.

A bright burst of electricity.

Stone walls, icy and dripping, like a long-forgotten city. I walk closer to the walls, press my hand to their face, feeling the cool moisture transfer to my hand.

When I pull my arm back, my hand is covered in blood. I'm screaming—or no, someone else is screaming. They're screaming *for* me, and now I am screaming, not knowing where they are, not knowing who else might be looking for them.

I run.

JANUARY 12TH, 2017

Again. Again and again, I've been having these weird, scattered, staticky dreams, impressions of dreams, memories, *something*, nothing at all, bright and burning and then dissolved from my hands before I can feel their shape.

I've been waking up in the middle of the night, turning over bleary-eyed and still half asleep to write these barely remembered sensations. Then I fall back asleep, usually having more dreams, walking normally throughout the dreamworld, traveling to minds far and wide, familiar and unfamiliar. But nothing else is quite as interesting, as attention-grabbing as those initial dreams, the ones that happen right after I drop off, when I'm in my most vulnerable state. They're frightening, unsettling, but also . . . exciting. Untethered. Raw. But no matter what I do, I can't get back there. I've tried finding the seams, felt along every edge of my void for something familiar and unnamable but . . . nothing.

Last night, this last dream, bleeding walls and electric shocks, was finally different. It was as confusing and nauseating as all the others, like I'm running down a staircase in the dark and keep missing a step, but there was something tangible last night. A man. Two men, actually. One of them was the dreamer, I think. As I ran, I saw his reflection blur in the dark glass windows along a long, dark hallway. Dark hair, sunken cheeks, skinny, strung-out frame. He—I, we—ran and ran and ran until we got to a window that was lit up, a hospital bed with a different man in it, a man that looked impossibly familiar to me, so familiar I'm not sure if it was the feeling of the dreamer who I was with or a feeling of my own. Then I woke up.

I don't know why I care so much about figuring it out. It feels like maybe whoever's head I'm walking into has answers to questions I haven't even thought to ask yet. There's something about the dreams themselves, the frenetic nature, the fact that I'm never really able to catch hold, that makes me think there's something hinky going on. Maybe there's another dreamdiver around and we're like two radios set across from each other, our frequencies clashing. Or maybe the AM is experimenting on me somehow. I should ask Owen.

Oh my god, *Owen*. In a complete photo-negative of the first dream I dived into—or, rather, was yanked into and then spat out of—the last place I went walking was, I'm fairly certain, Owen Green's head. I didn't stay for long, too jarred by being in the dream of someone I knew but not *that* well and the fact that DR. BRIGHT of all people was there!!!

I was right in noticing the way that Dr. Bright and Owen have both reacted when the other one is mentioned . . . there really IS a history there. The dream was simple, an apartment living room, sunbathed and homey, with Owen and Dr. Bright wandering around comfortably, going about their day, watering plants and smiling at each other. Like they were in love. Owen just looked like Owen, though it was a bit weird to see him in something other than a suit and tie (I guess he's a chinos/cable-knit sweater kind of guy in the comfort of his own home) but Dr. Bright was *glowing*. She looked like herself in the sense that there were no big changes and, listen, she might be an older woman, but I know an attractive lady when I see one, so it's not like she wasn't already going to look beautiful in Owen's head but this was . . .

I want to be in love like that someday. God, I haven't talked to Emily in weeks—not since she went back to Arizona for the holidays. Before she left, we exchanged Hanukkah/Christmas/general-secular-end-of-the-year gifts and I've been living off the memory of her smile when she opened the box I handed her and saw the gold shell necklace nestled in tissue paper. It was a risk, I know, but I didn't get her a conch shell specifically, but something more generic, something that would remind her of the necklace she had in her dream without tipping my hand.

"How did . . ." she whispered, pulling it out of the box. "My abuela has a shell necklace, kind of like this one. She—she still lives in Mexico, so I don't see her much, but whenever I do, she's always wearing her shell necklace." She held the necklace in her palm, like it was a delicate, sacred thing.

"Really?" I said, making myself sound more surprised than I was and slotting away the answer to the question I'd had since that dream. "It just reminded me of you."

Her eyes went glossy and she kissed me and for a moment my ability felt like a good thing. Like *just* a good thing.

We were going to spend New Year's Eve together, with the lit mag friends that she's been wanting to introduce me to, but by the time she came back to Boston, I had already called her and told her I had to deal with some family stuff, keeping it vague but being as honest as I could about how serious it was. She was so sweet about it and all I wanted to do was kiss her at midnight but instead I spent the night packing for the AM, then watching the ball drop with my family, my eyes darting between the enormous Times Square clock and my dad as I panicked about the steady march of time and how there's nothing I can do about it.

I don't know where things with Emily are going to be when I go back tomorrow. I don't know where things with my family are going to be. Where things with *myself* are going to be. I don't know what I want. I want to feel the kind of love that Owen felt for Dr. Bright in his dream, I want to find the mysterious dreamer who has been grabbing hold of my brain every night for the past week, I want to go back to work and have Chef see that I have a good palate and excellent knife skills, I want to talk to Aaron about what it's like to be inside other people's heads, I want to ask my mom if she forgives me, if she still loves me, I want to quit literally everything else—Emily, my job, my *life*—and spend the next ten years sitting next to my dad at a baseball game or hearing him talk about the terrible pulp novel he's reading.

I want to sleep. I want to dive. Maybe not as much as before—I forgot the way that real fresh air tastes—but knowing that I could have all those things I want, and more, in that dreamworld makes it a lot harder to stay away. Does it matter if it's not real?

JANUARY 13TH, 2017

The last thing I expected to do when leaving the AM was make a friend.

No, wait, correction: the last thing I expected to do when leaving the AM was run into someone from *inside the dreamworld*.

It went like this.

Most of the day was pretty much the same as last time—final checkups, far more paperwork than makes sense for a two-week program, and a final therapy session. I'm happy to say that Dr. Loving was pretty pleased with my progress. I've started to . . . I think "open up" is the official term.

I still haven't talked about my dad though. I know she knows. But I just . . . I wouldn't know where to even begin. Dr. Loving wants me to continue with Dr. Bright, which I'm game for (especially since I'm weirdly invested in finding out what happened between Dr. Bright and Owen) so I guess maybe I could continue on the track of actually being honest about my feelings, except I'd have to explain everything to Dr. Bright. But where do I begin that conversation?

And maybe I *don't* need to talk about that stuff! Maybe I'm processing it just fine! Dr. Loving didn't seem to think I needed more work.

"But don't be afraid to come back here if things get hard again," she continued. "This is an ongoing process. As you explore your ability more, learn to live with it in a healthy way, your relationship to it will change, and that relationship will need constant tending."

"You mean I might slip again," I said.

"It's not slipping," she said, shaking her head, her curls bouncing. "There's no reaching perfection. Just living and learning to thrive. 'Slipping' implies failure, but you can't fail at being you."

"Right." I nodded like I understood but I'm not sure I do. But I think that's started to change with what happened *after* therapy.

As I was walking from Dr. Loving's office to the main desk to finish my release forms, I took a wrong turn and ended up in some weird back hallway I'd never been in before. There was basically nothing in it—just a door that looked like it led to a broom closet and two bathrooms that looked FOR REAL haunted. The whole hallway did—it had these old stone and vaulted ceilings that Mags had pointed out the other day, talking about how the AM had been here for a long time but had only built the main complex a few decades back, integrating it into the old, stone halls of the original nineteenth-century building. Except this hallway didn't have that blend of old and new: it was *all* that old stuff. Like they just kind of forgot to build in this part. I walked all the way to the end, where it led to a locked stairwell—an old emergency exit I assume—and when I turned around to walk back, I got the strongest swell of déjà vu.

I was practically dizzy with it, the light around me feeling like it was flickering, the world tilting slightly. I stumbled, throwing my arm out to the stone wall, catching myself so I didn't fall over. The wooziness subsided as I focused on the feeling of the cold stone beneath my palm. When I pulled back my hand, I half expected to see it covered in blood.

My dream. This was the hallway from my dream. The same stone walls, the same length and shape. The same *feeling*. But the dream hallway had had so many more doors and . . . interior windows. Windows like the hallway was lined with hospital rooms.

I turned around to try the door to the stairwell again, thinking there might be hallways above or below that looked the same, wondering if it's possible there was someone there whose head I had visited. Someone who had been dreaming wild and beautiful and terrible things. Someone who had a head I wanted a closer look at.

But no dice.

Except.

Then.

The checkout desk.

It's a Friday today, which seems to be the standard checkout day. The lobby was pretty busy, with Mags flitting from person to person, handing out paperwork, intaking and releasing. When I approached the large, round desk, she whirled over.

"Hey girl, you all ready to go?" She placed a file between my arms, set a pen on top of it, and zoomed away. I chuckled and opened the file, looking it all over perfunctorily before signing where I needed to and closing it again. I looked up to hand it back to Mags to see her, somehow, on the other side of the lobby, intaking yet another person.

Before I could call out to her or grab the file and walk over, a man stepped to the other side of the front desk. In any other circumstance, I wouldn't have noticed this generic white guy in a black hoodie but it was *him*. *The* man. The one from my dream. *His* dream.

He was a bit taller than I remember, maybe a bit shorter than Aaron but somehow even skinnier. But where Aaron always looked annoyingly at home in his body, in a way I've never felt, this guy made his skinniness look *wrong*. Like he'd been deprived of food and sleep for far longer than he should have been.

I couldn't help it. Before I knew what was happening, I was walking around the circular desk to stand in front of him. And that was all I did for a moment—just stand. Like, three feet away from him, staring at him, like a total weirdo.

"Um . . . can I help you?" he asked, lifting an eyebrow at me. His voice was gruff and dry, like he hadn't used it in a while, or he'd used it too much.

"You're him," I breathed.

I *really* wish I had opened with something else because a) very creepy way to introduce yourself to someone and b) his eyes instantly went wide with fear.

"What? What do you mean?"

"Sorry, I'm Rose," I said, sticking out my hand in an offer to shake. GOD it was almost as bad as when I tried to introduce myself to Emily. I mean, I guess this man *was* the man of my dreams. Hardy-har-har.

"Oh." He blinked, looking at my outstretched hand. "Um."

He reached his arm out slowly, before grabbing my hand in a shake, slow and hesitant.

"Nice to meet you?" he said.

"Yeah, sorry," I said, trying to laugh it off. "I know that was the weirdest way to introduce yourself to someone."

"I've had weirder," he said. The corner of his mouth twitched in a smile and he angled his body toward me so he could look directly at me, eyes glittering as they roamed over my face, like he was memorizing it.

"Oh, I'm, um . . ." I blushed under his suddenly SUPER intense stare.

"I'm not hitting on you," I blurted, blushing even deeper. The horrible anxiety in my gut was somewhat abated by the fact that my bluntness shocked a laugh out of him, short and harsh-sounding, but not mean.

"God, I should hope not," he said. "What are you, fifteen?"

"I'm nineteen," I said, annoyed. "Just because I'm short doesn't mean I'm young."

"Didn't say it did," he said, putting up his hands. "You just look young, that's all."

"Oh."

"So, Rose, why are we talking?" he asked casually, like the answer was not actually that important.

"Right, sorry." I winced. "You're a patient here."

Something in his face twitched and he looked around, like he was worried someone would overhear us.

"In a manner of speaking," he said. "Was, at least. I've sprung the coop."

"You're leaving too?" I asked.

"Mm-hm."

He didn't give me any more info than that, narrowing his eyes at me like he was waiting for me to say some code word that would reveal to him that I was a safe person to give information to. That was when *I* started to feel watched too, like everything around us had become hushed and still while turning its focus onto us. I broke eye contact with him to look around, only to see the lobby exactly as it had been for the past five minutes—busy and bustling. I turned my focus back to the man, to find him still staring at me appraisingly, barely moving, like he was ready for me to either soothe or stab him.

"I'm a dreamdiver," I said, deciding that blunt and straightforward was going to be easiest with the man whose head was anything but. "And I'm pretty sure I've been in *your* dreams the past week."

I saw him clench his jaw, like he was getting ready to snap. I jumped back in before he could.

"I think you know something about this place," I said. "And I . . . I'd like to know what you know. If you'd be willing to tell me."

He stared at me for a long moment, tilting his head like if he got the right angle in staring at me, he'd be able to discern if I could be trusted. That was what it felt like—someone sizing up an enemy to figure out their potential usefulness.

Then, suddenly, he turned to the desk, grabbing a piece of paper and a pen, scribbling something down before handing it to me.

"My phone number," he said. "Now's maybe not the best time and place to get into it. Text me."

And with that, he stalked off without another word.

"Wait," I called out, and he turned around, that eyebrow lifted again in a demand. There were a million questions running through my head—what happened to you? Why were you here? What was the dream about the old hallway about? What's your ability? But I went with the simplest.

"You didn't tell me your name."

He was silent for a moment, like he was considering the question and the answer he would give.

"Damien."

January 13th, 2017

Dear Mark,

I'm out and I'm . . .

This isn't what I wanted. None of this is what I wanted. And I always get what I want. That's the bargain that was made with me and the universe—I get everything, get to do anything I want, and in return, I don't get to keep anyone, don't get to belong. And now I have none of it.

Whatever that Caleb kid did to me wrecked something permanently. Maybe permanently. Probably.

I can't do it anymore. The thing that has made me me, has given me my life, and taken everything from me is gone.

Looks like everyone else finally got what they wanted for once. I'm powerless.

community/TheUnusuals post by n/thatsahumanperson

A bit of a lighter question for folks today—do you have a lot of friends who are Unusual?

Me . . . not so much. There's my family, of course—growing up with Unusual parents was its own unique thing and, I guess, maybe why I haven't sought out more people like me? Other than on here, of course. It's been a comfort to get to come here, to talk about my ability with people who are going through the same thing, like an extension of all the group therapy and programs I've done. But I've never brought that feeling, that sense of community, into my real life.

I totally could have. Anyone who's done a program at That Place (regardless of what division you're at) has probably met other people their age who are Unusual. After all, most of us get our abilities in our teens, and that's when most of us go through all the "you've got a superpower" starter kit stuff, usually with other people who are in the same boat. Have any of you taken those relationships—people you meet in group, that you do exercises with, whatever—and brought them into the real world?

I'm asking now because it never really occurred to me as a possibility when I was there. But my sister just came back from her second visit (thanks to all y'all who have been checking in—she's only been back a minute but seems to be doing a lot better) and already has a coffee planned with someone she met there. She was light on the details, but basically, I think she went into this person's dream and wanted to talk to them about it? Seems like kind of a strange basis for friendship, so I don't know.

So. Thoughts? Success stories, failures, horrible one-night stands with other Unusuals? I want to hear it all.

chuckxavier

When you say she was light on the details but you "think" she went into this person's dream . . . were you listening in on her thoughts?

thatsahumanperson

Not intentionally. She was telling me about it, that she was going to get coffee with them today because she met them at That Place and they seemed interesting? But—and I don't know how it works for you, Chuck—sometimes when someone is lying or being cagey about something, you don't need to actively read their thoughts to know.

chuckxavier

Okay, yeah, I know what you mean. Hence the no details.

thatsahumanperson

Right. If I had been listening I'd at least know what this person's deal is.

lokilover

unless your sister also doesn't know. she's taking on a pretty big risk meeting someone from That Place.

thatsahumanperson

She's spent four weeks there now, I don't think getting coffee with someone is going to put her in danger.

franklinsteinsmonster

I'm still pretty new to the whole . . . having a superpower thing, but y'all are the only other people like me I know. I don't know what That Place even is, but given that I live in bumfuck nowhere, I doubt that there's one near me. *god*, I can't wait to go to college.

tacotacotaco

Are you going in the fall?

franklinsteinsmonster

lol I WISH. I've still got another year and a half :(

theneonthorn

I've known a *lot* of Unusuals in my time, even though I've never found someone else with my specific ability. those communities have been really helpful at times but, in my experience, the more Unusuals thrown together, the more room for chaos and destruction.

franklinsteinsmonster

is that common? having an ability no one else has?

theneonthorn

not really.

onmyown

n/theneonthorn Holy shit dude, where have you been?? You haven't posted in here in like, three months, I thought you'd died.

theneonthorn

aw, come on, I'd never abandon my beautiful creation. I just took some unexpected breaks from normal life.

onmyown
I gotcha. Everything good in your world?
theneonthorn
not exactly. it almost never is. but, funnily enough, I actually have a coffee date myself, so things are looking up.

JANUARY 15TH, 2017

My sneaking suspicion that everything at the AM wasn't on the up-and-up has only grown since being there, so I *probably* should have been more hesitant to spend solo time with someone I met there, but I guess all my instincts were right: Damien had a *lot* to say about the AM and none of it was good.

"You were there for two months?" I asked, holding my coffee cup close to my face so the steam would warm my icy nose. After we'd gotten our coffee, Damien insisted on going to a park so we could "talk freely." I thought that was really weird at the time but by the end of the conversation, I understood why he was insistent about it.

Things are a lot worse than I thought.

"Yeah," he said, taking a sip of his coffee. "And I know that people spend that much time there voluntarily—"

"Wait, what do you mean?" I jumped in. "You *weren't* there voluntarily?"

"No" he said through his teeth, picking at the edge of his coffee cup with his bony fingers.

"Then how . . ." I started, not sure how to ask or even if I *should* ask. But Damien had said he wanted to talk freely, which to me meant that I could ask questions freely too.

Thankfully, Damien seemed to know what I was trying to get out and heaved a great sigh before telling me his whole story. His whole, COMPLETELY BUCKWILD story.

"I was attacked," he said.

"What?" Lemme tell you, I had NOT expected that particular hard turn in the conversation.

"By another Atypical."

"What?" I was louder this time, unable to keep my shock in, and Damien looked around like we were being watched and leaned in close to me, lowering his voice. At such a short distance, it was easy to see the deep bags under his eyes, his chapped lips, greasy hair—like he hadn't been caring for himself for weeks. Or, as I now suspect, no one had been caring *for* him at the AM.

"I . . . I got mixed up in some stuff," he said in a low voice. "A bunch of Atypicals who—things went sideways, that's the important bit. And it got out of hand, I got pummeled into the ground and the AM scooped me up."

"Wait, so"—I started trying to piece it together—"you didn't go to them yourself after you got hurt? I mean, isn't that what they're for?"

"I knew I couldn't trust them." He sneered. "I would never have gone to them for help. But I ended up there anyway."

"So, they just . . . took you? Like, grabbed you off the street?"

"I guess," he said. "All I know is, I was just going about my life, then I get assaulted out of the blue, then I woke up and it was two weeks later and I was handcuffed to a hospital bed in their basement."

"Holy shit," I whispered.

"And that was just the start," he said darkly. "Once I was awake again, they started doing experiments on me, testing my ability."

"What kind of experiments?" I asked, feeling sick to my stomach. "I mean, when I was there, they tested the limits of my ability too, but they never . . . I mean . . . did they hurt you?"

"Not . . ." I could see him searching around for the words and I wonder if he was looking at me—a nineteen-year-old stranger—and thinking that he should censor himself.

"They didn't physically hurt me," he said eventually. "But I don't know what would have happened if they had kept me longer, which I'm sure they would have if . . ."

He trailed off, his jaw clenching as he took another aggressive sip of his coffee.

"If what?"

"It's gone." He sighed and I stared at him until he continued. "My ability. It's gone."

It was cold, sitting out on a park bench in the middle of January, with nothing but a crooked wool hat my dad had knit with his telekinesis and a cup of rapidly cooling coffee to keep me warm, but in that moment, an even deeper chill ran through my body.

"What?"

"I used to have an Atypical ability and I don't anymore," he snarled. "I don't know if it's ever coming back."

"But that's not . . . that's not possible," I said. "Right? I mean, our abilities are part of us, they can't just be *taken away*."

"Sure they can," he said. "It's not easy, but it's happened before."

"How do you know that?" I asked.

"You pick up more than a few things when you're trapped in a basement with very little to entertain you for two months," he said. "Especially if that basement is occupied by a bunch of people who run a scientific research organization dedicated to this kind of stuff and they're not particularly careful about talking about said research around you."

"And they talked about how this has happened before?" I asked. "People losing their abilities?"

"Yep," he said. "I don't know about physical abilities, but anything based in the brain—abilities like yours or mine—can be affected by head trauma or neurological issues."

I thought about how I haven't seen my dad using his telekinesis very much since I'd been back and wondered if it was because it wasn't working that well anymore, somehow affected by the disease, or if he was forgetting he had it in the first place.

". . . and they say they don't know how to fix it, how to *cure* me, but I think that's a bunch of bull." I focused back in on Damien, who was in the middle of his story, speaking more and more bitterly.

"But why would they do that?" I asked. "I mean, if they had a way to help you, they'd use it, right? Isn't that the whole purpose of the AM?"

"You'd think, right?" he said. "That might be what's on the brochures but trust me, they do *not* have our best interests at heart."

"You say that like this isn't your first run-in with them," I said.

"Yeah, well, it isn't." But he didn't elaborate, instead looking back out over the park, stretching out his legs while he took another long sip of his coffee.

So I decided to take the reins and discovered that, incredibly enough, that wasn't the wildest part of Damien's story.

"Okay, so I feel like I should probably tell you about this dream that I saw," I said, hoping a change of conversation would help him open up. I was surprised at myself in the moment, that I just came right out with it like that, but there was something about talking to Damien that made being blunt feel easy. Maybe it was the fact that I'd been inside his head, that we had this shared experience, or maybe it was just that he had told me his whole situation at the AM without sugarcoating or beating around the bush.

"I assume it was of the nightmare variety?" he asked casually, stretching out even farther like he was trying to melt into the bench.

"Um, yeah." I winced. "Most of them were."

"*Most* of them?" His languid lounging position immediately tensed as he turned to me, throwing his arm over the back of the bench so he could face me head-on. "You went into *multiple* dreams?"

"I . . . I think so?" I said, a little surprised that he seemed bothered by this. It's not like he had been dreaming about anything really embarrassing.

"What do you mean you 'think'?" he asked.

"Well, I'm still not one hundred percent certain they were yours," I said. "You were only physically in the last dream—or at least, physically there in a way that I could see you. The rest of them . . . well, I think they were yours because they had the same . . . quality to them."

"What does that mean?"

"Dreams are like signatures, or someone's particular smell, or the way they walk," I explained. "Most people have unique ones but all the differences are really subtle."

"So how can you be sure that the 'quality' you were feeling was mine?" he asked.

"Well, your dreams felt different," I explained. "Usually when I go dreamdiving, I'm myself in other people's dreams, sometimes interacting with them, sometimes just standing off to the side and observing. But being in your dreams was like how it was when my ability first started."

"What was it like then?" he asked, seeming genuinely curious. It felt good—and weird—to talk to another Atypical about my ability, instead of a doctor who was writing everything down. With Damien, it just felt like sharing, without every single word being loaded with meaning that the other person is interpreting. Sharing in the way that I wanted to be sharing myself with Aaron—bonding over our abilities, something we haven't been able to achieve, too ready to go at each other's throats.

"It was like the dreams were happening *to* me," I said. "Like I was just inside the dream, experiencing it in the same way the dreamer was."

"So you were experiencing my dreams the way *I* was?"

"I think so. That's why it was so hard to tell whose dream it was—I only figured it out because the night before we met, you saw your reflection in the dream and then—"

"You recognized me the next day," he finished for me.

"Yeah."

"I was in the basement. Running." He turned his body back to face the park, his jaw tensing with each word. "That's the dream you're talking about right? I'm running through the AM to—to—"

His jaw tensed once more, like he was clamping down on whatever words he was trying to avoid saying out loud.

"To save someone," I finished, unaware up until that moment that that's what he was trying to do. "You were trying to rescue someone. That really *was* the AM's basement. That's why the hallway looked the same."

"What hallway?"

I explained about my exploring and finding a hallway I recognized from his dream, but without all the doors.

"Oh yeah." He nodded. "That must have been right above me."

"So, in the basement, they . . ." I wasn't even sure how to complete that sentence.

"They keep people prisoner."

"And you . . ."

"Yeah." He sighed. "That nightmare you saw . . . that was from the last time I was in that building. It was last summer. I broke in to save someone. Someone who had been trapped in there for a very long time."

"Where are they now?" I asked, imagining that poor man still trapped in the basement, looking hopeless and half-dead.

"Safe," he said, and it was clear that he wasn't going to give me any more than that.

"What— When— Does—" There were a million questions shooting through my brain but finally it settled on the one that would have the simplest answer. "How did you break in?"

"It was easy." He shrugged.

"*How?* I know it's not *actually* a prison—or, well, I guess it *is*," I realized, "but it's not like you can just walk in there—they've got security in the lobby."

"That kind of stuff isn't a problem for me," he said simply. "Or, at least, it wasn't."

"What do you mean?" And then the penny dropped. "Your ability . . . what was it?"

His jaw clenched, his mouth tightening. I now realize how careful he had been to avoid mentioning the specifics of his ability up until that point. How reluctant he was to say much about it.

"I was able to influence people," he said. "Make them . . . feel comfortable, if I wanted them to feel comfortable." The way he said it made it sound like there were a few other examples he could have given.

"Mind control?" I asked, feeling like I wanted to slide to the other end of the bench. But Damien just rolled his eyes.

"Definitely not," he said. "Several Atypical medical professionals have been *very* adamant about the fact that what I do is *not* mind control."

"Oh." I nodded, going for casual. "Cool."

"And, remember, I can't do it anymore anyway so . . . you're safe."

"That's not—"

He gave me a look.

"Okay, so yeah, I got a little freaked for a second, give me a break." It was my turn to roll my eyes. "I'm still new to this whole Atypical thing."

"Didn't you say your *whole family* was Atypical?" he asked.

"Yeah, they are, but I don't know . . ." I tried to find the right words to explain the difference. "It's always been so normal, my family having their abilities. I mean, we grew up with my dad moving things without lifting a finger and my mom predicting the future, so when Aaron started reading minds, it just felt like . . . of course. Of course this is my life. But it was always a secret—we don't talk about Atypical stuff with *anyone*. So the fact that I've now met dozens of people—total strangers, all of them—who are Atypical too, it's . . ."

"Yeah, I get it," Damien said. "I remember when I met my first group of Atypicals. It was . . . a lot to process."

"How old were you?" I asked. "Did you grow up with Atypicals?"

"No, I was about your age, actually, when I first started hanging out with people who were like me, but—" He stopped himself and narrowed his eyes at me. "Rose, why did you want to get coffee with me? It sounds like you've had plenty of opportunities over the past few months to hang out with other people like you, so were you just looking for an Atypical friend or do you . . ."

"Do I what?" I asked.

"I don't know." He put his coffee cup down on the bench and crossed his arms. "I was kind of hoping that you'd had some information about the AM. Something I could *use*."

"Use for what?"

"The woman in charge of the whole outfit, Wadsworth . . . I think she's holding out on me." He grimaced. "I think that she knows how to fix me and has set me loose so she can treat the world like her lab."

"I . . ." I had no idea what to say to that. "I don't have any information you can use," I admitted. "I was just . . . curious, I guess. About what I saw. About what the AM was really like."

"Did I satisfy your curiosity?" he asked dryly and I snorted.

"I wish," I said. "I just have more questions now."

"Yeah, you and me both," he grumbled.

"Do you think—I mean, if someone was—the thing is—"

"Rose, whatever weird invasive question you're gonna ask, just ask it." He sighed wearily. "I've answered every possible question about myself in the past two months."

"No, it's not that." I shook my head, like rattling my brain around would help it think better. "It's . . . my dad is sick."

There it was. The biggest weight in my life, the anvil that had fallen out of the sky four months ago to land on me like a cartoon coyote, dropped at this total stranger's feet. It felt . . . good. To just say it out loud, without consequence. One hour with Damien and I knew he wasn't the type of guy to say, "Oh god, I'm so sorry, do you want to talk about it?" He wasn't going to pry, he wasn't going to give me pity. I could just say it and have it out there, in the open, without having to pick it back up again.

"Sick how?" Damien asked and I felt relief flood my body. A simple, direct question, one asked without sad eyes staring at me.

"He's got Alzheimer's," I said, my throat desperately wanting to close around the word. "But that's what the AM said and if they can't be trusted . . . well, how do I know that they're telling the truth?"

"Look, I'm the last person to defend them," he said, "but why would they lie about that? Your dad's a telekinetic, right?"

I nodded.

"Right, so those are a dime a dozen," he continued. "Me, I'm unique, that's why they want to fuck with me. But your dad . . . they're not gonna bend over backward to experiment on a telekinetic."

"But what if they're just *wrong*?" I asked. "What if they were trying their best or whatever, but they didn't really take his power into consideration? Like, they said it might make things worse, but if that's true . . . I mean, if they took away your ability, maybe they can take away his too. Make him better."

"Yeah, maybe . . ." Damien said skeptically. "But would that be worth it? To give up his power?"

"Of course," I said. "Being alive is better than being telekinetic."

"I thought you could live a while with Alzheimer's," he said.

"Sure, yeah, you can," I said, "but ten years still isn't enough. And my parents aren't even sure that's how much time he has. The AM themselves said that they don't know for certain how or if his ability is going to affect things. I mean, it's a human disease and we're—"

"Not human?"

That hung in the air between us, so stark and heavy that it felt like I was in the dreamworld, like I could feel the words "not human" as a physical thing between us.

"No, I mean of course we're human," I rushed to say. "But we're unique. I mean, all humans are unique, but Atypicals even more so and there's stuff—I mean, you've said it yourself, everyone at the AM has said it—there's stuff we don't know—"

"Rose." He scooted closer to me on the bench, lowering his voice. "How serious are you about this?"

"What do you mean?" I asked, bringing my voice down to match his.

"Did they give you anything while you were at the AM? To control your power?"

"Uh, yeah." I nodded. "Sleeping pills. Which actually really helped."

"Oh, that's . . . that's good," he said, like he was expecting a different answer. "I'm glad they've figured some stuff out at least."

"What do you mean?"

"The AM has never seemed that interested in helping Atypicals," he said, his jaw tightening. "They're more interested in protecting themselves *against* Atypicals. Making themselves immune to Atypicals. Immune to their abilities. Dampening *our* powers to keep them safe."

"*What?* How?"

"I'm not totally sure how it works, but I've seen it in action, I know it *does* work." The tiniest of smiles was growing on his face and I noticed that it seemed kind of out of place, like it wasn't something he did very much. "If someone took it, you wouldn't be able to walk into their dreams, your brother wouldn't be able to read their mind—"

"And you think that's what they gave you to take your ability away?" I asked.

"Um, yeah, I think maybe it was." His eyes darted around, like he was nervous about someone overhearing us. "But think about what that could do for your dad. Isn't it worth a try?"

"You think I should have my dad ask the AM about it?"

"What? No—" His eyes went wide at the suggestion. "Definitely not."

"Why not? Surely if someone *volunteered* to be experimented on—"

"No one's supposed to know about it," he explained. "It's not really sanctioned by the rest of the organization. The head of the division, Wadsworth . . . it's her invention. And she doesn't want anyone else to have it."

"What is going *on* over there?" I said. "You're saying the director has, what, her own whole separate mad scientist thing going on?"

"That's not far off actually," he muttered.

"Wha—"

"Look, can you help me?" He scooted closer to me again, his eyes wide and pleading. He still looked so tired, like being out of the AM wasn't giving him any peace.

"What can *I* do?" I asked and I saw his shoulders relax.

"I'm not sure yet," he said, turning back to lean his back against the bench. "I need to . . . I need to do some thinking."

"Okay . . ."

"But you can't tell anyone about this," he said. "Not even your family. No one."

"Yeah, okay, sure," I said, starting to wonder exactly what I'd gotten myself into.

I guess that remains to be seen. Saying very little else, Damien got up from the bench, told me he'd text me, and then left. I walked home, hoping the cold air and long trek would help me clear my head. There were so many things about that conversation that were strange, that were hard to digest, that needed a lot more interrogation. But my brain was really stuck on one thing. Even though I denied that Atypicals weren't human, I'm not totally sure I believed it.

I don't always feel human. I don't always feel . . . here. In fact, sitting on that cold park bench with Damien was the most in my body, in the *world*, I'd felt in months. Talking to someone who understands—who knows what it's like to have an ability that makes other people uncomfortable, but that feels like the missing piece of who you are, who knows what it's like to feel utterly lost . . . it made me feel like I had my feet on solid ground.

I wish I could explain this to my family, explain how, despite the fact that we're now all bonded in our Atypical-ness, that I am one of them in the way I always wanted to be, I still don't feel like I belong. But before I could even broach the subject, maybe even tell them about my day, explain that the AM is not to be trusted in the way that they want, my parents jumped down my throat the moment I entered the kitchen.

"Where were you today, Rose?" my mom demanded. She was in her scrubs still, must have just gotten back from her shift, which is when I remembered that I was supposed to stay home today and help my dad with some house stuff that we weren't sure he could handle on his own.

"Shit," I mumbled.

"Shit indeed," my mom said, moving around the kitchen in an agitated storm, opening cabinets and pulling down cookware to make . . . something. Honestly, based on what she was grabbing, it felt like she was just taking things at random—I couldn't think of a single dish that would require all that stuff together, though now I definitely am thinking about what dish I could make with cottage cheese, long grain rice, seaweed, and pine nuts.

"I'm really, really sorry—"

"I don't need a babysitter," a voice said, and that was when I noticed my dad sitting at the kitchen table, his face buried behind a newspaper.

"Of course you don't." My mom sighed, stopping her whirlwind around the kitchen for a moment. "But Rose promised—"

"I'm so sorry, Dad," I said, hoping to see his face come out from behind the newspaper. It did not.

"Were you off sleeping somewhere?" my mom asked.

"What?" I said. "No."

"I know that you and Emily have been getting closer and that that might mean some bed-based activities—"

"Whoa—okay," I interrupted, blushing furiously. "Let's—"

"So if you were over at her dorm, wasting the afternoon in dreamland—"

"Mom, you *like* Emily," I pointed out, feeling prickly at the way she was making it sound like she was some kind of accomplice. Like I didn't rush over to see Emily the moment I got out of the AM, like I don't relish every single moment I spend awake with her.

"Yes, I do," she said. "I think she could be good for you, which is why I don't love the idea of you using her as another way to get your fix—"

And there it was. My mom wasn't concerned that Emily was an accomplice—she was worried *for* Emily. That I would be a negative force in my own girlfriend's life.

I thought I had gotten the monster under control, tamed it enough while I was in the AM, trusted that my family loved me enough to let some things go, but suddenly it roared up inside of me, remembering how my mom looked *proud* of Emily when she talked about her poetry at Thanksgiving and how I couldn't remember the last time she looked at me like that.

"My *fix*?" I yelled. "God, can't I get a break? I just spent two weeks in an *institution* because *you* weren't happy with the way I was using *my* power and now you're giving me crap about it?"

"Rose, it isn't healthy—"

"Have you seen me sleeping?" I demanded. "I've been so much better since I came back, which you would know if you ever asked about me!"

"Or maybe I would understand if you spent more time with us!" my mom shouted back, starting to pace again. "I know you've been doing better, which I why I thought that you'd actually *want* to spend time with us, with your family—"

"It's not that I don't want to spend time with you," I said. "I forgot about today—"

"But it's not just about today." My dad folded his newspaper down so he could look at me as he talked. "I don't care that you weren't here to help me fix the broiler—"

"I'll fix it tomorrow, I promise—"

"That's not the point, Rose, that's what I'm trying to say." He sighed. "The point is that you've been avoiding all of us for months. And we know that it's hard adjusting to an Atypical ability but we're here for you."

"I'm not—I'm adjusting *fine*." I sighed. "I just have other things going on in my life!"

"Things more important than your family?" my mom asked, coming to stand in front of me, her arms crossed.

"Why does it have to be either/or?!" I shouted. "Why can't I have a *life*? Isn't it my turn? I'm finally *one* of you and I—"

I didn't want to do this. I didn't want to be this thing that growls.

"You know what," I said, "never mind. I'm gonna go take a shower."

I turned on my heel and stomped upstairs, not even taking off my shoes in the hall, which is normally something my mom would yell at me for. When I got to the top of the stairs, I heard the creak of a door and saw Aaron stepping out of his room.

"Heard you and the 'rents fighting," he said, leaning against his doorframe.

"Come to gloat?" I snapped.

"What would I gloat about?" he asked, and it felt like he really didn't know. Like he was actually asking the question.

"Are you kidding me?" I said, opening my door and going inside, too tired to acknowledge the absurdity of what he was saying. But apparently, things weren't as obvious to Aaron as they were to me, and he left his stupid cool-guy doorframe lean and followed me into my room.

"Rosie, what's going on with you?"

"What do you mean, what's going on with me?" I snapped, throwing my bag and coat on the bed.

"I mean, why are you getting into fights with Mom and Dad and why do you look at me like I'm your worst enemy now?"

He was leaning on *my* doorframe now and I wanted to push him out and slam the door.

"Why am I being interrogated every time I come home?" I spat back.

"Look, we need you right now," he said, his voice softening. "With everything that's going on with Dad—"

"I know, Aaron," I snapped. "I *know*. But this has to do with Dad."

"Your coffee with some random Atypical has to do with Dad?" Aaron asked, his face scrunching up.

"Look, I can't talk about it—"

"What do you mean you can't talk about it!" Aaron shouted and I walked toward him, lowering my voice so we wouldn't attract Mom and Dad.

"Aaron," I said in a hushed voice, "did you ever get a weird vibe from the AM?"

"What?"

"When you were there, did you ever get a weird vibe?" I repeated.

"*Why?*" he asked, crossing his arms.

"Just . . . forget it." I sighed. "I have to take a shower."

"Rosie—"

"Bye, Aaron," I said, grabbing my robe and stomping down the hall to the bathroom.

I'm safely ensconced back in my room now, still in my robe, my hair wrapped in a towel, wondering if I skipped dinner entirely if my family would freak out. Probably. They'd assume I was sleeping which, yeah, sounds nice right now, but really I just want to hang out in here and text Damien. But it's probably not worth the fight I'd have with them—I should just go down and face the music, try to pretend like this afternoon never happened.

January 15th, 2017

Dear Mark,

I think I made a friend today.

Maybe I'm getting ahead of myself. It's not like my track record with "friends" is anything to boast about. But Rose is cool—she didn't judge me, didn't push me too hard on anything I was telling her . . . she just believed me. ~~It actually reminded me a bit of how you first—~~

I know you probably wouldn't believe this, but I actually do want to help her. I'm not sure I can, but I might as well try. What else do I have to do?

Should I feel bad about lying to her? I mean, it really was a lie of omission—I let her believe what she wanted to believe. That the reason that my power is gone is Wadsworth's serum, her self-administered vaccine. I wish. I wish Wadsworth had given it to me, that I was immune to you. ~~Even though I know it's not just your ability that I'm not~~

I just didn't think she'd have kept talking to me if I had told her the whole truth. Losing my power because I got beaten so badly by a seventeen-year-old who was just trying to protect his boyfriend . . . I know I fucked up. Trying to use Adam as leverage . . . I know it was wrong, okay? And I think not telling Rose the truth is wrong too, but I can't figure out why. It's not hurting her to not know. I can still try to help her without her knowing everything about me. I don't have my power, I can't manipulate her.

Fuck, this is hard. This is why I need to talk to you. I don't know how to be good. I think I could have learned from you. But I fucked that up too.

JANUARY 19TH, 2017

As much as I was relieved to be out of the AM, it was a bit weird being back in Dr. Bright's office. I feel like we'd barely gotten started at the whole "getting to know each other well enough for me to really actually tell her stuff" before I just went right back into the extreme level inpatient. But I really do want to do better. I want to *be* better. And I really wanted to try today with Dr. Bright. I wanted to answer her questions honestly and be vulnerable and maybe even tell her about my dad. And I think I did an . . . okay job. But I got a little sidetracked.

The conversation started normally enough with her wanting an update on my second go on the rehab merry-go-round.

"I take it your stay at the AM was helpful?" she asked, that carefully neutral mask perfectly situated on her face. I thought back to Owen's dream, the glowing, sunny version of Dr. Bright who smiled freely and wondered if that person was a figment of Owen's imagination or someone who truly existed.

"Yeah, it was." I nodded. "I think it was the right call, going back in."

"I'm glad to hear it," she said, giving me a warm smile that felt genuine but wasn't nearly as easy and natural as the one I'd seen in the dreamworld.

I meant that. Despite the fact that it hadn't been an exactly . . . relaxing stay, what with the first week of what felt like the worst kind of withdrawal and the second week of those twisty and unpredictable dreams, going back to the AM *had* been the right choice. I was feeling more grounded and centered, had been sleeping more normal hours, was even thinking about going back to Milton soon to see if they'd let me jump back into work, was planning on spending the whole weekend with Emily.

"Could you walk me through your time there?" Dr. Bright asked. "They haven't sent the file over to me yet."

"Didn't Agent Green call?" I asked. "He said he was going to fill you in."

"Ah. He did. I missed the call and didn't—" She cleared her throat before continuing. "I haven't had the time to call him back."

"Gotcha," I said, desperate to ask more. "I know that you weren't on board with me going back to the AM," I said, like it was my job to defend Owen. "But it did help. I think I needed that week of just no dreaming. It was really hard at first. Empty and lonely and I woke up with that itch under my skin but after the first few nights, I was waking up rested. And actually looking forward to my day. To being out in the world, talking to real people."

"That's wonderful, Rose," she said, and the way it sounded coming out of her mouth made me think of Owen. He says "wonderful" all the time. I wonder who picked it up from who. "And you're having an easier time getting up in the mornings? Staying awake?"

"Mostly," I said, thinking back to this morning, when I woke naturally, at a reasonable hour, for the first time in what felt like months. They had alarms at the AM that would wake me gently if I slept more than ten hours, and I'd been sleeping through my own alarms for weeks, ignoring the blaring sound when it would seep into the dreamworld by covering it up with music of my own creation. Which is pretty fucking cool if I do say so myself, but also completely baffling because I do not have a musical bone in my body.

"There were still times that I wanted to stay in the dreamworld. It's just so . . ." I tried to find the words. "Sometimes I think that learning to control it was the worst thing I could have done."

"Why do you say that?"

"I expected it to take forever," I said. "Gaining control, that is."

"You adjusted remarkably quickly," she said, sounding genuinely impressed.

"Do you think it's because I come from an Atypical family? That there's something in our DNA that makes us really good at this?"

I felt strange asking the question, like I was trying to suggest that my family was special or better, which I absolutely do not believe. I mean, I love my family and yeah, we're Atypical, but we're also just people. But Dr. Bright didn't seem to think it was a crazy question.

"Did your brother have an easy time learning his ability when it first started up?" she asked.

"I guess." I shrugged, annoyed that I was being asked to consider Aaron's duck-to-water ability to be good at everything. "It also only took him a couple months to get used to reading minds and learning how to lower and raise the volume on them. Though, he was at the AM for two whole months, so that might have made things easier."

"Does it bother you that you had an easier time than you expected?" she asked. The question surprised me. Aren't you supposed to be happy when you're good at something? When something is easy? I didn't know I was allowed to be anything other than satisfied with that.

"I don't know," I said honestly, still considering the question. "It bothers me how quickly I got sucked into it. In the beginning, I was so worried about going into people's dreams and learning stuff about them but now I want to do it. I understand Aaron a lot better now."

"How do you mean?"

"His telepathy. He *likes* hearing people's thoughts," I explained. "I didn't get that. I just thought it was really annoying to have a brother who could hear what I was thinking. And a little creepy. But it's not a voyeuristic thing for him. He tried to explain it to me once. That he wasn't listening to spy on people or to learn their deep dark secrets, but to understand them. He talks about how it's not just the thoughts themselves but the shapes of them—the patterns they make. He makes it sound like art or music. Something beautiful."

"And that's what dreams are like for you?" Dr. Bright asked, bringing me back to the present.

"Yeah." I sighed. "They *are* beautiful. I wish I could show them to you. To see what I see . . . it makes people make sense. I mean, dreams don't always make sense, obviously. A lot of the time it's just visual gibberish. Well, and sometimes actual gibberish. But once I got good at going into dreams, it was easier to find the truth."

"The truth?"

"People's true thoughts and feelings. Or, at least, some of them. Everything that lies underneath. Everything that people try to bury every day. You can't hide from those when you dream."

I don't think I did a good job explaining exactly what that's like—the feeling of *truly* understanding, truly connecting with someone when you're inside their head, while at the same time never getting a clear answer from the dreamworld. I tried to tell Dr. Bright about the dreamdiving I'd done in the past week—another nightmare of my mom's that this time I *was* able to change, a dream the other night when Aaron and I played in the snow, pelting each other with snowballs.

That was one of the dreams where Aaron was awake in the dream, reading my thoughts, making it so that we could communicate with each other inside the dream, like we did the very first time. And it was . . . good. The first time in a long time that I'd seen Aaron laugh, running around cackling maniacally as we both used the magic of the dreamworld to throw snowballs without actually lifting a finger, modeling the telekinesis that my dad has been using around us since we were kids.

The next morning there was fresh snowfall on the ground. We were both in the kitchen, looking out over the newly coated yard, and caught each other's eye. It felt like each of us was waiting for the other to make the suggestion that we go out into the cold and have a snowball fight for real, but in the cold light of the winter morning, I felt so old, so much older than I had been as Dream Me, and running out into the yard with my brother for some lighthearted fun felt completely impossible.

Dr. Bright listened patiently as I described these dreams, detailing how wonderful it felt to be inside them, controlling the world of my own making, the joint worlds that I make with my family.

"Did you ever read any fantasy novels when you were a kid?" I asked, trying to find another way to explain what diving feels like.

"Some," she said. "Why?"

"I read all the Narnia books growing up. Did you ever read those?"

"Yes, I did. Mar—my brother was a big fan."

I clocked that slip-up in the moment. I don't know why she would have been reluctant to say her brother's name, but it sounded like his name was Mark. The same guy who came in at the end of one of our first sessions! Presumably the same person who was responsible for the family emergency in the fall. I don't know why this feels like a mystery to be solved, but there's something about the whole thing that itches in the back of my brain. Whenever I think of Mark's face, which I only saw for about forty-five seconds, I feel like I've seen it before.

But because I couldn't put my finger on it enough to ask any specific questions, I just kept going.

"Right, okay, so you know the gist," I continued. "I loved them because that idea of climbing through a wardrobe and finding another world was just amazing. And then watching things like *Alice in Wonderland* or *The Wizard of Oz* . . . when you're a kid, you hope that there's some magical land out there for you to stumble into. And, as you grow up, you realize that there isn't. And I don't believe anyone who says they're fine with that, because it is crazy disappointing. But I found mine. An actual magical world. And I can access it whenever and anything is possible there but it's also completely safe because it's not real. But it feels real. And I can't give it up. I won't."

"No one is asking you to," Dr. Bright said soothingly, making me think that maybe all of that had come out a lot more passionately than I had intended. "As I said, we can't treat this like other, non-Atypical addictions. Your ability is part of you."

"Can we stop calling it an addiction?" I asked. I had just heard it SO much at this most recent AM stay. "It makes me feel like a failure or something."

"Rose, before you went into the AM, there were days when you were only awake for two or three hours. You were missing work, not talking to your family, or Emily—"

"I could have stopped it," I insisted. "I mean, I did stop it. Yeah, it helped to go to the AM, but I did the work."

"I know," she said, her eyes bright with earnestness. "You should be proud of yourself for getting help when you needed it. That's an extremely difficult thing to do. And Rose, you're not a failure. Addiction is not failure. Struggling is not failing. As long as we keep trying, we don't fail."

I swallowed, wanting *so* badly to believe that. I nodded, unable to find the right response.

"How are you feeling about other aspects of your life?" Dr. Bright asked after a moment. "Outside of the dreamdiving."

"Good. Fine," I said, unconvincingly. Dr. Bright fixed me with that powerful stare of hers and I cracked.

"I don't know." I sighed heavily. "Sometimes I wish I didn't straddle the two worlds, you know? That I could just pick: dreamworld or real world. And I don't know which I would pick, it changes day to day, but it's exhausting to jump back and forth."

"How do you mean?" she asked, her head tilting to the side.

"It's like I belong in both places and also don't belong in either.

And that's not a new feeling—being in an Atypical family and having to hide that, I always felt like I was living two lives. Hell, even being gay in a mostly straight world feels like that sometimes. But this is different from all that."

"In what way?"

"It feels more concrete. It's literally two different worlds. The way I relate to people now is completely different. I can bring information from the dreamworld into my real life if I want, but then there are times when I don't want the other person to know that I know something. Especially if it's someone who doesn't know what I am."

"Have you told Emily yet?"

"No. I'm going to. I really, really am. I just keep chickening out. And I hate it! I don't want to be this cowardly person anymore. But it's just so much harder than I thought it would be. And we've been dating seriously for nearly three months now and I know I have to tell her but the longer I wait, the more guilty I feel and the less I want to tell her so I keep putting it off and it just goes round and round."

"Do you worry she'll react badly?"

"I have no idea how she'll react, that's the problem." I laughed joylessly. "I told her I have a form of narcolepsy, which was already weird enough—"

"Thousands of people have narcolepsy. It's not weird—"

"I know, I know, I gave her the whole spiel. And she took it in stride, like she does with everything, but telling her that, actually, I have a completely fake-sounding, fantasy-novel condition might be a hard pill to swallow. I don't know that'd she'd believe me. I wouldn't believe me if I hadn't grown up in this world."

"And what if she does believe you?" she asked.

"Then I worry that she'll call me a freak," I said. "That she'll break up with me."

"How would you feel if that happened?"

"Completely devastated," I admitted, afraid to say the full truth but saying it anyway. "I think—I think if I let myself, I could fall in love with her pretty quickly."

"If you let yourself?"

"I've been trying to keep a bit of mental distance because, well, I'm scared," I said, exhausted already by this degree of vulnerability. "If I let myself fall head over heels and then tell her and she rejects me, I don't know what I'd do. The stakes feel really high. Like this is a huge thing that I could so easily mess up."

"How do you think you're going to mess it up?" she asked.

"By telling her or not telling her. There's no good answer. I tell her, she might freak and leave. I don't tell her and we get serious, I have to hide who I am forever. I want an option C."

"What do you think option C would be?"

"To stop dreamdiving," I said, the words leaving a terrible taste on my tongue.

"But you said yourself you don't think that's possible."

"That's what I thought at first but the AM, the pills they gave me . . . they worked really well. Totally dreamless sleep."

"And that could be a long-term solution? I thought those drugs were only for detox."

"I guess they've tweaked the formula, because they said they were basically like normal sleeping pills now. I could take them regularly."

"Is that what you want to do?" she asked.

"I don't know," I said honestly. "Maybe sometimes . . . . sometimes when it gets to be a bit too much. But not every night, I don't think. I want to . . . I want to find a safe and healthy way to do it. To dream-dive."

"Then you do whatever is going to help you find that balance," Dr. Bright said, like it was easy. "As long as it's within the bounds of what your doctor said was safe for you to do. And if there are any problems or you want to reevaluate, you should call them right away."

There it was—that strange contradiction I'd noticed in Dr. Bright. She was pro-medication when it helped, clearly very scientifically-minded, always wanted me to check with medical doctors about anything and everything, but didn't seem to really like the AM. That was when the thought occurred to me: maybe the AM weren't the only other people who could help.

"Are there other Atypical doctors?" I probed, as casually as I could manage. "You know, outside of the AM? My family has always gone there for Atypical-related stuff and to a normal doctor for everything else. Do you know of anyone who does both?"

"Not currently," she said, bursting the tiny bubble inside of me that had started to grow. "But if you're not happy with your AM physician, I'm sure you could ask Agent Green—"

"No, no, it's not that," I said, waving my hand in a dismissal. "My doctor is fine. It's—"

And there it was. My perfect moment to tell her about my dad. About how I wanted him to see a different doctor, one who understood about Alzheimer's and being Atypical and could find a solution to the fact that maybe one was affecting the other and he had different options than someone who *wasn't* Atypical.

But instead, I went a different direction entirely.

"You used to work there, right?"

"Yes." The perfect, neutral face was back. Somehow even more neutral than before.

"Did you ever get the feeling that . . . something weird was going on?" I asked, trying to match her neutrality.

"What do you mean?" Her eyes narrowed.

"Something shady." I shrugged a single shoulder like this was the most casual conversation in the world.

"Rose," she said, suddenly sounding very serious as she leaned forward on her elbows. "Did something happen while you were there?"

"No, no, nothing happened," I rushed to explain, wondering what can of worms I had just opened. "Not to me, anyway. I was dream-diving and I found myself in another patient's dreams and it was, I don't know, it wasn't good. At first I thought it was just a nightmare but then when I was leaving, he was checking out at the same time. I recognized him from his dream. And I introduced myself, because if there's any place where you can go up to someone and say, 'Hey, I was in your dream last night, can I ask you some questions about it,' it's at the AM."

"What did he say?" she asked urgently.

"He was freaked. He said he didn't want to talk there but we exchanged numbers and I—well, I'm getting coffee with him tomorrow," I said. Not technically a lie, even if it made it sound like Damien and I were meeting for the first time. It's not that I think Dr. Bright is untrustworthy, but I'm still figuring out Damien for myself. I don't need her hovering over this whole thing in the way Aaron is.

"Are you sure you should be meeting with this person?" she asked, confirming my fears.

"Yeah, it'll be fine," I said and she nodded, like she was considering her next words carefully. I jumped in before she could ask more questions about Damien.

"You never saw anything suspicious there?" I pressed. "At the AM?"

"I can't talk about my time there—it's all completely confidential. But you've had a good experience. The most important thing is to find physicians that you trust. As long as you feel you're making progress, that's what matters."

"Yeah, I guess. Well, anyway, I'll see this guy tomorrow and see what he says. I definitely don't want to go to an organization that's doing something unethical. Plus, it's nice to make new Atypical friends."

"That's very true. It's important to have a community of people you feel you can be yourself with."

"Maybe if he needs more help, I could introduce you guys?" It might be a hard sell to Damien, but she's right, a community of support is something I think *both* of us want. "It seemed like the AM . . . wasn't really helping him."

"My door is always open."

JANUARY 24TH, 2017

For the first time in a long time, real life has become slightly more interesting than the dreamworld.

I've been spending more time at Emily's dorm, not even napping, but playing board games and making out and watching Marvel movies so that I can fully appreciate her fic. And it's been wonderful, I feel so at peace with her, so at home, but it's still an escape. It's its own kind of dreamdiving. Emily still doesn't know about my ability, about Atypicals at all, about my dad, so I'm never really . . . *me* with her. Not in the way I can be with Damien.

We've gotten coffee every day since our first meet-up and Aaron got SO weird about it so quickly, wanting to come along and meet Damien himself, in a super annoying and uncharacteristic big brother play, so I've been going straight from Emily's to coffee in the hopes that Aaron will just STOP asking about it. But I'm worried that he's going to read things in my thoughts because, as I said, things with Damien have been even more fascinating than what the dreamworld can conjure up.

And today was very, *very* interesting.

Damien and I were sitting on what has become *our* bench, in a nearly empty and freezing cold park, sipping coffee and talking about his ability. He was explaining how it worked to me—how it wasn't mind control at all, but that his wants were so strong that they would go into other people, make them want the same thing. I know that my dreamdiving has its downsides but the way Damien talked about his power made my issues pale in comparison.

"So I never really know what anyone wants," he said sadly. "Or if anyone actually cares about me for *me*."

"Sheesh, that's so rough." I winced.

"Yeah . . ." He nodded. "It's just—people have always assumed I'm a bad person because I influence people, but it's not my fault, you know? I can't control what my ability does."

"I know what you mean," I said. "And it's like people with good control just forget what it's like to not have control. My brother used to read our minds without asking all the time and now he gets annoyed when I go into his dreams. It's totally unfair."

"Exactly," he agreed. "And just because we have abilities that affect other people's minds, doesn't mean that we're worse than other Atypicals with more straightforward abilities. I had this friend once—Blaze—he was a pyrokinetic, and his power was totally out of control, he was *constantly* burning stuff, but the rest of our friends just felt bad for him, because he couldn't control it."

"Well, it sounds like it wasn't his fault," I pointed out.

"That's exactly my point," he said. "It's not *my* fault either."

Something in the back of my brain itched at that. I understood what Damien was saying, that just because we have powers that can embarrass people or invade privacy, we're unfairly maligned. But I also don't know that we can say it's not our fault. It's not our fault that we have the powers we do, but the way we use them is up to us. I think.

I didn't say any of that though, because I was distracted by Damien telling me more about his friend Blaze. And guess what? Blaze had ALSO been kidnapped, ten years ago, but by a totally different group, one Damien doesn't even know the name of. And all the experimenting they did on him made his pyrokinesis go totally wild.

"And I would bet my last dollar that the AM has seen stuff like that before," he explained. "And they'd be idiots not to be coming up with a solution for it. I mean, the destruction that someone could cause, not to mention, it's hard to keep Atypicals a secret if there are a bunch that are out of control. So, my theory is that the immunity drug could be tweaked to make an Atypical immune to their *own* ability. Basically like a suppressant."

"But they kind of already have that, don't they?" I said. "I mean, they gave me these powerful sleeping pills that basically knocked me out so completely, I couldn't dreamdive. And we *both* were put in rooms meant to dampen our abilities."

"Yeah, not like I needed it," he muttered bitterly.

"So why wouldn't they be able to do something like that for your friend?" I asked.

"I mean, the fact that last I heard he was in an AM facility in California, still spontaneously combusting every five minutes, would suggest that they have *not* come up with a solution," he said dryly. "I think each ability is, you know, its own beautiful snowflake." He rolled his eyes. "And maybe they haven't figured out what to do for kinetics. Pyrokinetics, telekinetics . . ."

"Right . . ." I mumbled. Damien gave me a meaningful look, like he was waiting for me to speak. When I didn't, he sighed heavily and continued.

"I'm just saying that the AM is a totally corrupt organization and they might actually have all the pieces to put together a solution for your dad and they haven't because—"

"Because they're a totally corrupt organization?" I echoed skeptically.

"Look, Rose, I know you've had a good experience—" he started, leaning toward me.

"No, I get it," I said. "And I actually . . . I actually might have an idea."

"Oh really?" He looked impressed and I preened a little.

"Just give me a few days," I said cryptically. "I need to talk to someone first."

"Ooh, the intrigue," he said flatly.

"You're not the only one who gets to be all mysterious," I quipped and he laughed, the sound harsh and croaky as always. I smiled into my coffee cup, feeling like every laugh I got out of him was a little victory. Like the person I am, unfiltered, is funny and interesting.

"Do you miss it?" I asked suddenly.

"Miss what?"

"Your ability," I said. "I know I talk about maybe someday taking sleeping pills all the time so that I don't dreamdive anymore, but I think . . . I think I would be crushed if it was just taken away from me."

"Yeah," he said softly. He grimaced, squinting into the winter sun, as I sat patiently, waiting to see if he would say more.

"It's like a part of me is missing," he said. "Like everything is just a little . . . duller. A little blurrier."

"Everything back in black-and-white," I murmured.

"Hm?"

"I sometimes feel like I'm Dorothy and the dreamworld is Oz," I explained. "Technicolor and magical and surprising. If I didn't have the dreamworld, everything would be black-and-white forever."

"Dorothy, huh?" he said, sizing me up, one eyebrow rising.

I shrugged.

"Guess that makes me the Tin Man," he muttered, looking back out over the park. I thought about asking what he meant—if that meant he thinks he needs a heart, *why* he thinks that when he was so quick to care about me, about my dad, enough to try to help us—but I knew him well enough to read his body language. He didn't want to talk about whatever was going through his head.

"Okay, so, tell me more about all these Atypical friends you had," I asked, changing the subject.

And he did. He told me about living in LA with a bunch of Atypicals when he was my age, getting into trouble and having the time of his life. We laughed as he told me about the time they almost burned down a bar and I could picture the open road so perfectly as Damien described the road trips they would take. It was so refreshing to talk to someone who didn't follow the traditional path—who didn't go to college or have a regular job or a perfect family to live up to.

I genuinely don't know what Aaron is so worried about. For once, I have a friend who, yeah, might not be my age or have similar life experiences, but who *gets* me. What could be bad about that?

community/TheUnusuals post by n/thatsahumanperson

The family drama never seems to end and I'm posting again here today to ask you all, especially the mind readers among us, for advice.

So that Unusual that my sister got coffee with has turned into an actual friend of hers, which would be fine, except he's *ten years older* than her and seems, like, really obsessed with all things Unusual and with That Place. My sister is spending a lot of time hanging out with him and talking about all this stuff, apparently, and when I say a lot, I mean *a lot*. She's known the guy for two weeks and after their first coffee, she was going on about all this stuff to do with That Place and seemed kind of . . . manic? Things have calmed down in the past week or so but now it just feels like she's avoiding me because she doesn't want to talk about it again because I didn't react exactly as she wanted the first time. Then again, she could just be avoiding me because that's what she does now.

Before any of you jump to conclusions or have a chance to ask: I'm not worried about anything romantic between this guy and my sister. She's gay and very open about it, so that's not a concern. But to that point . . . if it's not some creep preying on her, then *what is he doing?* I don't know, I kind of want to tag along on her next hang with him and read his mind. But am I just being a crazy, overprotective brother?

chuckxavier
You know my feelings on using information from people's thoughts to manipulate or control them, but if you're genuinely concerned about your sister's safety, you should definitely step in. What's the point of having these abilities if we can't at least use them to protect the ones we love?

> **onmyown**
> For once, I completely agree with Chuck. Do whatever you need to do to protect your sister. Trust your gut.

theneonthorn
how do you know this guy is bad news if you've never met him?

thatsahumanperson

I mean, that's sort of the point—I think I should meet him and listen in, find out what he's really about.

theneonthorn

I'm just saying, give the guy the benefit of the doubt. everyone deserves a first chance.

JANUARY 31ST, 2017

"Promise me you won't get weird about this, but I want to try something."

Those were the words that Damien greeted me with when I sat down on our bench this morning.

"Hello to you too," I said, smiling into my coffee cup. I breathed in the smell of the grounds, that sharp, warm scent snapping me awake. Being around Damien was like that. He didn't pull punches in conversation—he was direct and unapologetic, in the way that I am in dreams; in the way I want to be in real life.

"I want to dreamdive with you."

"What?" I nearly choked on my coffee.

"I know you've already been in my dreams, but I don't remember," he said pragmatically, like this wasn't the weirdest conversation I'd ever had.

"I . . ." I searched for anything to say. "Even if you fall asleep knowing I'm going dreamdiving, that doesn't mean you'll remember. I don't think it works like that."

"Have you tried?" he asked, eyes wide.

"Um, yeah," I said, laughing awkwardly, "that's kind of the whole point of going to the AM. All the doctors I dreamdived into didn't remember anything about it on the other side."

"Oh." Damien settled back against the bench, looking disappointed. If possible, the bags under his eyes looked worse every single day—it felt like soon his entire face would be one weary bruise.

"Damien, what's—" I started, "I mean, why . . . why do you want to do this?"

He gave a big sigh, his chest puffing out against his ratty hoodie, and I couldn't help the tiny smile that crept onto my face. He is SO dramatic.

"You can change dreams, right?" he said.

"Yeah . . ."

He nodded, jaw clenching, refusing to make eye contact with me.

When he didn't say anything in response, I assumed he wanted me to keep going.

"I mean, it's not as simple as just going in there and waving my magic wand," I said, "but yeah, I can change things. It's . . . awesome."

I couldn't help the grin that broke out and was surprised to see Damien's expression mirror mine. His smile was . . . odd. All teeth, his lips tight, like he was imitating what he was seeing on my face, not *actually* smiling.

"It *sounds* awesome," he said, and I blushed at his approval. "And I want to see it in action."

"But if you don't remember, then what's the point?" I asked, my voice cracking unexpectedly on the thought. Damien, more perceptive than my doctors sometimes, noticed.

"What's going through your head, Dorothy?"

The nickname and the intense amount of focus he was giving me just made me blush harder.

"Just . . ." I sighed. "I realized that maybe that's what I'm doing with my dad."

It was easier to admit than I would have thought. Sitting on a cold park bench, talking to this odd, sharp-edged man who didn't seem to mind all that much that I'd dived into his head already, was asking me to do it again, and having him call me nicknames and look at me like he cared, felt like new, uncharted territory in a freeing way. Like I'd accessed some place between the real world and the dreamworld. It made it easier to be honest.

"What do you mean?"

"Avoiding him because I'm worried he's not going to remember the time we spend together," I said quietly. "Like . . . what's the point if he's going to forget? If he's going to fade away."

"The point is now," he said, like it was obvious. Maybe it is to everyone else. "The point is for you guys to have those moments together, in the present."

"Yeah." I nodded like I understood.

"You'll remember, Rose," he said, and something in his voice made me turn to look at him. He had an intense look in his eyes—something like fear—as he talked. "Even if they forget, *you'll* remember."

"They . . . ?"

"Never mind," he muttered. "Point is, you should be spending time with your dad. If I had had parents who loved me the way yours clearly love you—"

He stopped himself, clamping his mouth tight like he was physically trying to keep the words from coming out.

"Is there something you want me to see in your dreams?" I asked abruptly, trying to put the pieces together.

"What?" Damien's eyebrows scrunched. "No. Why would you think that?"

"If it doesn't matter if *you* remember, but it does that *I* do . . ."

"Oh," he said, catching up, "no, no—I just meant with your dad. I don't want to show you anything, it's not . . ." He sighed again. "Iwantyoutochangesomething."

He said it all like that—in a rush, one big exhale. Like he was embarrassed. I think I even noticed some color on his cheeks, which, wow, I really did NOT think Damien could blush.

"What?"

He sighed again, shuffling on the bench like he couldn't get comfortable.

"I want you to change something," he repeated, slower this time. "In my dream."

"Okay . . ." I said, still trying to figure out where this was going.

"I keep having this . . . this nightmare." He was steadfastly staring into the middle distance, his arms crossed over his chest like a plate of armor. "Ever since I left the AM, every single night and it's . . ."

At least I had an explanation for why he looked more and more worn every day.

"You want me to change it," I finished for him.

"Do you think you could do that?" His shoulders relaxed like even the possibility of it was a huge relief.

"I mean . . . I think so? But . . ."

"What?" He turned to me, slinging his arm over the back of the bench and leaning in.

"I don't know if it would change forever," I told him. "I don't know if what I do in the dreamworld . . . sticks."

"Do you want to find out?"

01-31-2017, morningwaffles, text post

Someone please hop in my in-box and tell me that my girlfriend hanging out with people other than me is actually completely normal, even if she didn't have many (or really, any) friends up until a few weeks ago and that her having a new friend she won't tell me much about is good actually! and she's definitely *not* cheating on me.

Because, like, I haven't talked to her outside of a few texts in three days and she was away for the first few weeks of this year and then was over all the time and extremely doting and wonderful and now I see her, like, once a week and I'm not saying that I'm panicking, but I'm panicking.

FEBRUARY 1ST, 2017

Damien's head is an absolute mess.

I know I should have told him I needed time to think about it, talked to Aaron or Dr. Bright or *anyone* about going inside the head of someone I'd known for two weeks, going over to his apartment, by myself, and immediately falling asleep, but if I'm totally honest, I jumped at the chance to dive into someone's head with their explicit permission. To use my ability to *help* someone, show myself—show everyone—that it wasn't just a compulsion I couldn't stop, but a powerful tool. The only reason I didn't dreamdive the moment he asked yesterday is, well, two people passed out on a park bench might draw some attention and Damien seemed reluctant to invite me back to his place.

I already knew where he lived—before one of our coffees, we'd stopped by his apartment to get his coat because "oh come on, Rose, it's not *that* cold" and then it turned out to, in fact, be that cold. Idiot. It wasn't far from our park, in a building that was a bit like Damien—totally unremarkable. Despite the proximity, Damien tried to brainstorm some other places we could go. But between my family and the fact that neither of us had an office (though I did wonder, briefly, if I should suggest going to Dr. Bright's, but she'd already agreed to come and meet Damien tomorrow, maybe see if she can help and I wanted to dreamdive *now*), Damien's place was the obvious choice.

"Let's do it tomorrow morning." He sighed. "I just need some time to clean the place up."

I was a little disappointed I'd have to wait, but I'm not exactly the neatest person in the world, so I understood. When I got there this morning though, I wondered what exactly he'd been cleaning up.

After Damien closed the door behind me, we just stood there, two steps into his apartment, not saying anything. He didn't invite me to sit or offer water or really do anything normal that a person would do when you're in their home but, then again, nothing about this was normal.

So I took the opportunity to look around the place. To call it a "home" may be too strong of a word. The furniture was nice—a lot nicer than I expected, honestly, based on the way Damien dresses—but there was nothing hung on the walls, no trendy throw rugs or comfy pillows, no TV, no knickknacks, no sense that anyone *lived* there. It was sparse as HELL. The sole non-furniture objects were a stack of dog-eared paperbacks by a chair near the window, the only blush of Damien's personality in the whole space. Something in my heart squeezed tightly.

"So, this is the place," he said finally, shuffling his feet and clearing his throat.

"It's nice," I said, feeling SUPREMELY awkward as I looked at Damien's haggard face, the circles under his eyes somehow even more pronounced. I wondered if he'd kept himself up all night in anticipation and was about to ask when—

"Right, let's get to it," he said, abruptly walking over to the couch, throwing himself onto it, and closing his eyes.

And that was that. The niceties were over and we were getting straight to the point. And that was where the straightforwardness ended.

The moment I dove into Damien's head, I knew something was wrong. Most dreams are fixed locations—a classroom, a magical land, a grocery store, outer space. Everything from the mundane to the fantastical, sometimes one location through the whole dream, sometimes rapidly changing. They usually have blurred edges—like a video game that hasn't fully rendered—but each location is at least *coherent*.

This was . . . not. More solid than the flashes of images and emotions I got from him when we were both at the AM, but no easier to grasp. It was a cornfield, long stalks stretching into the sky, but also the woods, spindly branches hanging over my head, scraping my skin, ocean water lapping at my feet. A patchwork of nature, not a beautifully constructed place crafted from imagination, but a jumble of memories and feelings clashing together to make an unnavigable maze.

"Damien?" I called out. Other than calling out Aaron's name in those first few dreams, I don't typically announce myself, instead choosing to familiarize myself with the materials in front of me. But I didn't know *what* to do with this.

There was a sound. A crunching of leaves, a wave breaking against the shore, the rustle of wind through cornstalks. I spun around, trying to find the source, only to discover that *everything* had vanished. I was suddenly in a motel room. This, at least, was comprehensible.

I started to wander around, looking for the seams of the world, looking for anything out of the ordinary that I could use to construct something that might comfort Damien. I wasn't sure what he wanted me to change—the dream so far had been frustrating but not a nightmare.

It was like just having that thought brought the nightmare along.

The ground shook, the motel bed falling through the floor before I'd taken more than a few steps. It became a grave, a pale hand clawing its way out, a tall man pulling himself up from underneath, crawling toward me with skeletal arms. I thought fast—the floor had swallowed up the bed, maybe it could open up and take this corpse away with it. I centered my feet, imagined the floor underneath the crawling man opening up and then it did, taking him into the black, but it just kept opening and soon I was falling too, down down down down—

I landed, hard, back in the cornfield. At least this time it was *just* a cornfield.

A blur ran past me, rustling the stalks.

"Damien?" I tried again. He didn't respond, but I saw his back disappear farther into the field and I chased him, my feet tramping down the cornstalks, following the path he had been carving out. That meant the tall stalks *could* be destroyed, pushed down by both of us. I focused on that reality of this dreamworld and soon the field was flattened, the cornstalks splayed like a meteor had hit them.

Damien reached his destination, a slim figure curled up in the fetal position on the ground. In a flash, I was next to him, watching him kneel down to look at the person—an Asian man, Damien's age I'd guess, sunken face and long hair. The man looked familiar, so it must have been the person he rescued from the AM last summer, the person he was trying to rescue in that dream. But he said that person was safe, so why still have nightmares about him?

And this *was* a nightmare. Damien was shaking the man by the shoulders, shouting at him to wake up.

He was dead.

"I'm sorry, I'm sorry, I'm so sorry." Damien was crying into the man's hair, whispering into his ear as he pulled him close. The body was limp, looking small and broken in Damien's arms, but still somehow *beautiful.* Like a handsome prince who had been cursed, Damien the knight who was too late. The two of them shook with Damien's sobs, the pain of loss cutting through the air like a wind sharp enough to make you bleed.

It was truly awful. And I felt completely unequipped to fix it. Nothing about any part of the dream had given me any indication of what would comfort Damien and I had no idea how to bring this guy back to life. I didn't ever create *people* in dreams. Wild animals, magical creatures, sure. The closest I've come is manifesting my family in a dream, but they're my *family.* I know them well enough to build a dream construct of them. I didn't even know this guy's name.

Two shadowy figures appeared then—two women, both incandescently beautiful. One tall and tan, one short and dark skinned, both like projections of people. See-through and wavy, not really *there.*

"Do you forgive yourself?" they asked in a ghostly chorus. Damien shuddered, pulling the man closer.

Suddenly, I knew what to do.

The man in Damien's arms opened his eyes, shocking Damien into still silence.

"I forgive you," he whispered.

Damien and I both gasped awake at the same moment.

We sat there, on the couch, getting our breath back, not looking at each other. I had *no* idea what to say. No idea if I'd helped. No idea if Damien was going to be mad at me for seeing something so personal.

"I—" I started, not sure what I was going to say, if I was going to apologize, if I was going to ask a question.

"You were there, weren't you?" Damien jumped in, his voice soft. "It worked?"

"Oh, uh . . ." I blinked. "Yeah. Yeah, I was there but . . . I don't know if it worked. I tried—I tried to change things."

He nodded, cleared his throat, rubbed his hands on his legs, and stood up.

"I've gotta—" He made a vague gesture toward the back of the apartment. I stood up too, unsure what he was trying to say.

"I'll see you tomorrow?" he asked, a pained look on his face.

Aha, he was kicking me out.

"Oh, yeah, okay," I said, moving toward the door.

"Cool." He moved farther away. "Cool."

It was silly to feel rejected, but that was what was coursing through my body in that moment. Panic and doubt that I had done the right thing, that I hadn't ruined the first friendship I'd made in years.

I put my hand on the doorknob.

"Rose?"

I turned to look at Damien, his hunched shoulders, his hands stuffed into his pockets, his pained face. I braced myself for an excuse for why he couldn't meet tomorrow after all, a chastisement.

"Thank you."

FEBRUARY 2ND, 2017

I don't know what I expected after yesterday, after going into Damien's head, but I hadn't anticipated that we would just ignore it completely. Today started the way every day starts since we had that first coffee; Damien and I texting each other. We've been talking about everything: our abilities and the AM, yes, but also our lives, sharing random YouTube videos and Spotify playlists back and forth, just . . . normal stuff. Damien likes to read too, has read all the fantasy novels I loved as a kid, so we talked about books when we ran out of people in the park to make up stories about. I haven't really read a book in what feels like years—it was nice to be reminded that it's something I used to love.

I really thought I was starting to make a friend. A real friend. Not someone I work with and kind of get along with, not someone I'm dating while hiding half of myself, not a family member I tiptoe around on the best of days and fully collide with on the worst. But someone who liked me for me, for the entire person I am, and who I could trust.

That all promptly went to shit this afternoon.

It all started when Damien turned up to our coffee hungover. At five in the afternoon.

"God, you look terrible," I said the moment he came into view. And he really did. I didn't think the bags under his eyes could get worse, that his hair could become *more* of a rat's nest, that his cheeks could get *more* sunken. I was feeling pretty bad about my so-called attempt at "help."

"Hello to you too," he grunted, though he honestly didn't seem that annoyed by my greeting. I was finding that if I just treated Damien like Aaron—like the irritating older brother who I actually loved—his shoulders relaxed and his barely-there smiles came more easily.

"Sorry," I said anyway. "Are you okay?"

"Yeah, I'm fine." He groaned. "Just a little hungover."

"It's five o'clock in the afternoon." I couldn't help the little laugh that escaped me.

"It was a rough morning," he said darkly, rubbing his eyes.

"Yikes, what happened?" I asked, my heart beating fast. Had I made the nightmares worse?

"What do you think happened, I drank half a bottle of bourbon, drunk dialed my—" He stopped himself, wincing and averting his eyes before taking a deep inhale and continuing. "Then I took a nap and a cold shower and now I'm here and I've got a headache so can we skip all the probing questions about the AM for today?"

Even though I was feeling like I was starting to get to know him, it was still easy to forget that Damien was like this. You could never ask him questions or talk to him like a normal person. But I *can* tease him like I tease Aaron, hold him at an arm's length and rib him instead of risking either of us ever admitting we care. That's a more comfortable lane for me to stay in anyway.

"Jeez, cool it on the attitude. Here—coffee." I handed him a cup, not as quite as hot as it should have been, given that I had been sitting in the cold for thirty minutes.

"God bless you." He sighed before taking a sip.

"So . . . drunk dialed an ex?" I guessed. He flinched, trying to pass it off as the coffee being too hot, but I knew I'd hit pay dirt.

"I've been there," I continued, faux-casual, even though I barely had.

"You're nineteen," he scoffed.

"Okay, so I've sugar-high-dialed an ex, it's basically the same thing."

"He's not an—" Damien started, sounding more uncertain than I'd ever heard him. "I mean, he's not—it was never like that."

"Ah, gotcha." I nodded sagely, clocking the pronoun Damien had used. I don't know that I'd pegged him as a fellow member of the queer family, given that he literally looks like a textbook example of "straight cis white man from 2010" but the way Damien's cheeks were reddening made me think this was more than a friend breakup. I thought of the way he'd been holding the man from the AM, the pain in that nightmare, and felt like I was starting to get the whole picture. "Not an ex-boyfriend, just an ex . . . something?"

"Yeah," he said. "Something."

He was looking down into his coffee cup like he wanted to drown in it.

"What happened with you guys?" I asked.

"What did I say about the probing questions?" He grimaced and took a sip of his coffee.

"Okay, okay, sheesh," I said, knowing that I was going to circle back to this.

"Are you sleeping all right?" I asked, tiptoeing toward the real conversation I wanted to have.

"Bit better." He nodded.

"No more nightmares?" I asked hopefully.

"I said better, not perfect."

"Right," I said. I'd take better. I actually *had* helped. And I was going to keep helping.

"Well, hopefully that'll change soon," I said meaningfully. I had been planning on telling Damien about inviting Dr. Bright to our coffee after the dreamdiving but then things turned so awkward and I didn't know how to broach the subject. But, more than ever now that I'd seen his glitched-out dreamscape, I wondered what the AM had done to Damien, if there would be any way to reverse it. And that wasn't my expertise.

"Yeah, what are we doing here?" he asked, looking around at the park that was distinctly not *our* park.

"There's someone I want to introduce you to," I said simply.

"Okay . . ."

"Someone who I think will be able to help." God, I was so stupid, feeling excited and accomplished and having put this together, finding an avenue we could explore that might get us more information.

"Look, if it's someone actually from the AM, you know I'm not interested," he said, fear building in his eyes.

"Of course it's not." I rolled my eyes, repeating the same sentiment I feel like I'd repeated over and over to Damien. "I'm on your side. I know you're worried they're going to snatch you again and I believe you."

"Oh." He blinked. "Thank you."

"Well, it is a bit easier to believe someone when you can see inside their head," I said, herding him back to the topic of yesterday.

"Yeah?" He snorted. "I wouldn't be too sure. You only got into a few dreams. That doesn't show you everything."

"Why, are you hiding something?" I teased and he flinched. I knew he was hiding something—the tall man crawling out of the grave was a pretty good indication that Damien had skeletons in his closet, no pun intended.

"Aren't we all hiding something?" he teased back. "I mean, can we ever really know another person?"

"Oh, don't be cute." I sighed.

"It's an honest question," he said. "How are things going with Emily?"

"Fine." I sniffed, taking a sip of my coffee, which was now completely cold.

"Have you told her yet?"

"That's none of your business," I said, even though Damien had been the only person I had talked to lately about my desire to tell Emily. But we'd mostly talked about it over text—any time I tried to talk about it out loud, the mere thought of telling her about my dreamdiving gave me a stomachache.

"So that's a no then," he said smugly. "Kinda proves my point."

"I don't know why I even told you about her in the first place."

"Because I'm the only Atypical you spend time with that you're not related to?" He grinned at me, a mockery of a true smile.

"God, yeah, that's true." I groaned. "But you said you know others. When are you going to introduce me?"

"I'm not exactly on speaking terms with them at the moment," he said darkly.

"Oh really?" I said, grabbing onto this clue. "Does that have something to do with the things you may or may not be trying to hide? Or your ex something?"

"I said leave it alone, all right?" he snapped, the comfortable teasing camaraderie gone in an instant. "What about this person who's gonna help me? They must know other Atypicals."

"Yeah, but there's a whole confidentiality thing." I shrugged.

"Wait, why are we meeting here?" Damien turned to me, his entire body language changing as he questioned me urgently. "Why this park? Who is this person?"

"She works just over there," I said, waving my hand toward Dr. Bright's building. "She *used* to work for the AM and I think she already knows the AM is not on the up-and-up and just needs some more concrete proof. You're the proof to really do something about it. So please stay, I hate to disappoint."

"Oh, I'm most definitely going to disappoint."

The way he said it, in that dry, affected way, made it sound like it could have been another self-deprecating joke, but his expression told me there was nothing funny about this. The moment Dr. Bright arrived, I understood why.

"Hey Dr. B.," Damien said before I could even introduce them.

"Damien." I had *never* heard that kind of tone from Dr. Bright before. She had stopped about ten feet away from us, her eyes wide with surprise as they darted back and forth between us.

"You two . . . know each other?" I asked, even though it was *very* obvious.

"Rose, how—" Dr. Bright started, before sighing and closing her eyes.

"Of course," she murmured to herself. "Damien is the mystery patient at the AM. And that's why you weren't aware of his power. Because he doesn't have it anymore. Isn't that right?"

She aimed that final question toward Damien, but it didn't sound like she was actually asking him. It sounded like she was rubbing it in his face.

"Wait, how did you know he doesn't have his power?" I asked.

Neither of them said anything. They just stood there, staring at each other, until Damien broke the silence.

"I should go," he said, starting to step back.

"I think that's a good idea," Dr. Bright said, not taking her eyes off of him.

"Wait, what?" I said, confused. "Damien, don't—"

"Thanks for trying, Rose." He sighed, looking at me sadly. "I hope you have a nice life."

"Damien—" I called after him, thrown by how quickly he had turned cold but he just . . . left. Turned his back on us and walked away.

"Dr. Bright—" I started but she jumped in before I could even form a question.

"I'm sorry, Rose," she said, "but I think you should go home."

"What?"

"I never should have—I need to—" I'd never seen Dr. Bright stumble over her words like this. I had absolutely no idea what to do or say so I just stood there, waiting for her to explain it all to me.

"Damien was a patient of mine," she said finally.

"Oh."

"And he . . ." She swallowed and took a step toward me, lowering her voice. "What exactly did he tell you?"

I scanned over her face, trying to figure out why she was asking, what answer she was looking for. Eventually, I decided that the fastest way to get the truth from her was to give her the truth myself.

"He said that the AM kidnaps and experiments on Atypicals," I said for a start.

She just nodded at that, not looking in the least bit surprised. That made me SO mad. Had Dr. Bright known that the whole time? That the AM was doing horrible, illegal stuff? When she'd been reluctant to talk about it with me and wasn't super enthusiastic about me going back, it seemed like maybe she just had a difference in philosophy. Or, honestly, since finding out about her and Owen, I thought maybe her distaste was just because she'd had a messy breakup or something.

But here she was, not even batting an eye at the information that the place I'd spent four whole weeks at was experimenting on innocent people. Suddenly, I didn't want to tell her a single thing more about what Damien and I had talked about.

"I'm sorry that you were dragged into this, Rose," Dr. Bright said.

"Dragged into what?"

"Damien is . . ." She sighed. "He's a troubled person. And I certainly was not expecting to see him today."

"So you're not going to listen to him?" I asked. "Help him?"

"Damien doesn't want my help," she said cryptically. "But I hope you won't hold this strange encounter against me. I'd still like to see you for your session next week."

"I . . ." I was surprised by that, that she just wanted to move forward like everything was totally normal, but continuing therapy with her might be the only way to dig into all of this more, so I just nodded and agreed.

Is Dr. Bright involved with all of this somehow? Was Damien lying to me? How, exactly, do they know each other? I had started today thinking that Dr. Bright and Damien might be able to put their information together and yield some answers but all I have are more questions.

FEBRUARY 3RD, 2017

Well, I have some answers now.

I'm still trying to piece everything together—both how I got to here and what I've been told. Because it doesn't feel . . .

I don't know. I get that the past six months have been . . . a lot and maybe I don't have the best judgment in the world at the moment, or ever, but what they told me about Damien doesn't feel *real*. God, I hope it's not real.

It all started this morning when I got a phone call from an unlisted number.

"Um . . . hello?" I answered.

"Is this Rose Atkinson?" a woman's voice said on the other end of the phone.

"Yes . . . ?"

"My name is Sam Barnes," she said, "and I heard that you had a run-in with Damien yesterday."

"Oh, um . . ." This had not been what I was expecting. "I'm sorry, who is this?"

"I'm like you," she said. "And Dr. Bright is a friend. I know that she told you Damien was troubled but I think—I think you deserve to know the whole truth. She made it sound like the two of you were friends."

"We are," I said, feeling weirdly defensive of a man I'd only known for a few weeks. But who the hell was this woman? Why did she think she could just call me up and act like we were already in the middle of a conversation?

"Then I think you need to know who he really is. What are you doing today?"

And that was how I ended up at a house somewhere on the outskirts of the city, talking to a whole bunch of strangers. Sam gave me an address and I got right on a bus.

Remember what I said about not having great judgment?

It all ended up being fine—Sam wasn't exactly the confident master spy that she seemed on the phone. Instead, she was anxious and awkward, looking away if I made eye contact with her for too long. But she seemed to be more comfortable around her friends, a group of Atypicals and Dr. Bright, who came with their own surprises.

That's right—Dr. Bright was there too. But that wasn't the most unexpected part.

Sam was happy to see me, nervously shaking my hand and offering to take my coat, which I declined, wanting the option to peace out of there if things got too weird or intense, and then I walked into the living room to see Dr. Bright sitting with a familiar man on Sam's couch.

"You know Dr. Bright, of course," Sam said, leading me into the living room. "And this is my boyfriend, Mark."

The man on the couch got up to shake my hand and I completely froze.

"Oh my god," I breathed, taking his hand automatically. "It's you."

"Uh, yeah." He laughed awkwardly and then his face lit up. "Oh, right, we bumped into each other that one time! In Joan's office—"

"Yes, this is my patient, Rose," Dr. Bright said, coming to stand next to Mark.

"I'm her little brother," Mark said, jerking his head toward Dr. Bright. "I don't make a habit of barging in on her sessions, don't worry."

So I was right. The man who had interrupted the end of my session *was* Dr. Bright's brother.

But that's not why I felt like I'd been hit by a truck.

The man from Damien's nightmares. The one who had been trapped in the basement, who had been lying, dead, in Damien's arms, was standing in front of me. His hair was cropped short, his face more filled in. He had been sickly and long-haired and supernaturally beautiful in Damien's dreams, so I hadn't put two and two together.

Damien had rescued Dr. Bright's brother from the AM.

Dr. Bright used to work at the AM.

Damien had nightmares about Mark dying.

Mark wasn't dead, Mark was safe and standing in front of me with his girlfriend.

What the hell had happened between these people?

Maybe I should have left right then. Part of me wishes I didn't know what I know now.

While I was busy having a total mental breakdown, the front door opened again and two teenage boys piled in. Everything turned even more chaotic as Dr. Bright chastised Sam for pulling this meeting together, when none of us knew what we were even doing here.

"Can someone please tell us what the hell is going on?" the taller of the two boys, Caleb, asked, interrupting the various arguing and introductions that were taking place.

"Damien is back," Mark said, speaking up for the first time in a few minutes. After our awkward handshake, he'd taken to pacing the room, a dark look on his face.

"But I mean, he's been back for, like, a few weeks though hasn't he?" the other boy, Adam, said. "I mean, he's been out?"

"But now he's back in our lives," Mark said, sounding bitter.

"No, he isn't," Sam said, brushing a hand down Mark's arm in a soothing gesture. "He's in Rose's life."

"I barely know the guy," I said, not sure where I was supposed to stand with these people or with Damien.

"Okay, seriously," Caleb interrupted, "just someone start from the beginning and explain why you all feel so worried."

"Caleb's an empath," Sam said, turning to me to explain. I nodded like I was keeping up. I barely know what that means—he can feel feelings, I guess? That must SUCK.

"Gee, thanks, Sam." Caleb rolled his eyes.

"It's okay, she's one of us," Sam said.

"Right, because we can always trust other Atypicals," Adam mumbled, and I had a LOT more questions about *that* comment but Dr. Bright spoke up before I could ask.

"Rose is a patient of mine," Dr. Bright explained calmly. "She met Damien and thought I might be able to help him. As you can imagine, the reunion did not go well."

"How do you even know Damien in the first place?" Caleb asked me.

I went for a simple "we met at the AM" hoping that would lead to the least number of awkward questions, but Adam immediately jumped in, asking me if I worked there. When I told him I was a patient, he and Caleb both looked confused.

"Why?" Caleb asked.

"Because I needed help . . . ?" I said, wondering why that was such a weird idea.

"The AM isn't all bad," Dr. Bright said to the boys.

"Oh, good, we're doing *this* again," Mark said, starting to pace again.

"She's right," I said, nodding toward Dr. Bright. "I was having a hard time balancing my ability and they helped. I dreamdive and—"

"What does that mean?" Adam asked.

"I can go into people's dreams," I explained, wondering how the term "dreamdive" wasn't clear enough. Both Caleb's and Adam's eyes grew wide at that.

"What?" Adam asked, smiling.

"That's a thing?" Caleb asked.

"Yes, it's a thing, and I was at the AM for it and I traveled into Damien's dream and saw a lot of weird and creepy stuff—"

"Well, it *was* the inside of Damien's head—" Sam scoffed.

"This was creepy stuff about the AM," I said and Sam looked embarrassed. "They did stuff to him. That's why I brought him to Dr. Bright. I found him as we were being discharged and I got the whole story about what happened to him and I thought it was important that she know. He never told me anything about how he used to be your patient or about any of you."

That wasn't a lie, was it? I mean, Damien didn't *tell* me about Mark, not really, even if I feel like I already knew a lot about the guy from a few dreams. But something in Mark's tightly wound posture told me he probably wasn't in a place to hear about Damien dreaming about his death.

"What *did* he tell you?" Mark demanded.

"He said he was brought to the AM because another Atypical attacked him—"

"Bullshit!" Adam cried. "He wasn't attacked, it was self-defense!"

The whole room went silent as every single person in it exchanged a series of significant looks. My head was spinning.

"I'm guessing you guys know something about this?" I asked eventually, stating the obvious.

"It was me," Caleb said quietly. "I'm the one who hurt him."

I took a long look at Caleb, trying to imagine it. He was young, yes, but broad-shouldered and bulky, someone who looks like he *definitely* plays sports and maybe also beats up nerds and stuffs them into lockers. But the way that he said it . . . it didn't seem like he was happy about the fact that he'd hurt someone.

"Why?" I asked.

"Because he threatened to kidnap me?" Adam said.

"*What?*"

"Why don't we all sit down," Dr. Bright said, putting on her best therapist voice.

So we did, and Dr. Bright explained the whole thing. Well, actually, *Mark* explained a lot of it.

"I'm a mimic," Mark started off.

"Okay . . ." I said, because it felt like he wanted a response.

"Have you ever met a mimic before?" he asked.

"No," I said. "I'm not even sure what that is, if I'm honest."

"I'm not surprised," he snorted. "The rarity of the thing is kind of the whole problem."

"What do you mean?"

"I can share people's powers," he explained. "That's my Atypical ability."

"Whoa." I breathed.

"Yeah."

"That's . . . cool," I tried, though I was having a hard time wrapping my brain around the logistics of it. "But what does that have to do with . . ."

"The AM *likes* rare abilities," he said, unknowingly echoing what Damien had told me.

Turns out, Mark *had* been kidnapped by the AM a few years back—that much was true, that the AM kidnaps Atypicals and experiments on them. He glossed over that whole part, his hand reaching to hold onto Sam's as he casually talked about years of experimentation before falling into a coma.

"And the coma is when the real trouble began." He chuckled darkly and I saw Dr. Bright wince. That was when Dr. Bright—who had been working at the AM—found out that it was holding her brother captive. She worked for years to try to get him out but couldn't find a way in.

"I recruited Damien to help," Dr. Bright explained. "With his ability . . . do you know what his ability is?"

"Um . . . yeah," I said, unsure if everyone knew that he didn't have it anymore.

"And you still hung out with him?" Adam asked, incredulous. "Even though you knew that he must have been manipulating you?"

"Oh, no, he wasn't—" I rushed to explain.

"He can't do it anymore," Mark interrupted. "His power is gone."

"How do you know?" Sam asked, her eyes narrowing.

"He called me," Mark said.

"What?" Dr. Bright asked. "When?"

"Yesterday." He sighed. "He was wasted. Going on and on about he'd never gotten drunk before but now it didn't matter because his ability is gone."

"That explains the late afternoon hangover . . ." I muttered, my suspicions confirmed. Mark was the reason that Damien had been drunk yesterday. But I still couldn't get a grip on what had happened between them.

"So, wait, Damien rescued you," I said, trying to get us back on track. "Why would he then try to kidnap Adam?"

"Damien is obsessed with—" Mark sighed again, gritted his teeth. "He wants to be immune to Atypicals. Immune to me."

"And you could help him with that?" I asked Adam. "Is that what your power does?'

"Oh, I'm not—" Adam started. "I'm not special like all you guys."

"Adam is like me," Dr. Bright said. "An average human with a lot of Atypical friends."

"But you and Caleb . . ." I trailed off, unsure how to phrase the question.

"Yeah?" Adam asked.

"You guys are together."

"Yeah, we are. Is that a problem?" I recognized that defensive tone immediately and realized that Adam thought I was asking a very different question than the one I was asking.

"Hey, chill, I'm gay too," I explained and he noticeably relaxed. "But . . . you're cool with it? Having an Atypical boyfriend?"

"Yeah," Adam said, seeming baffled by the question. "Yeah, of course, why wouldn't I be?"

"I don't know." I shrugged. "That's good to know though. Thanks."

"You're welcome?"

"I've been thinking about telling my girlfriend," I explained, "but I'm not sure how she's going to react."

"Gotcha." Adam nodded.

"Wait—" I shook my head to clear it, trying to stay focused. "Damien wanted to be immune to you because . . ."

"He didn't want to share his power with me," Mark said. I initially found that hard to believe—Damien let me use my power on him only a few weeks after meeting him. "Last time we tried to use our powers together, I kind of . . . broke him."

"Oh," I said, wanting to ask if that was why things shattered between them but not wanting to reveal that I knew more about Mark than I should. "That was after he rescued you from the AM?"

"Rescued," Sam muttered. "That's one way to put it."

"I don't understand," I said.

"He kind of . . . kidnapped me," Mark said.

"Oh."

"Yeah . . ." he continued, "he was supposed to bring me to my sister and to Sam, but he kind of . . . went rogue. Before . . . everything happened, he actually *wanted* to share his ability with me. He's never found anyone like him before and I guess . . . I guess he thought I was the next best thing."

I wanted to jump in, to explain that I don't think it was just about that, that Damien dreamt every night about losing Mark, that Mark had broken more than his ability. But hearing Mark talk about the road trip Damien had dragged him on, like he was bitter as hell, but also like he *missed* it, I decided it wasn't my place.

"So it wasn't Wadsworth's serum that took his power away," I said, trying to sift through everything Damien had told me and find the lies. "It was you."

Every face turned toward me in surprise. I guess I knew more than I was supposed to.

"He told you about Wadsworth?" Mark asked.

"Yeah." I nodded. "About how she handcuffed him to the bed, experimented on him, how *she's* immune to Atypicals . . . but he also told me that she was the one who took away his ability. Not that he *wanted* to be immune."

"That's why he tried to kidnap me," Adam piped up. "Wadsworth is my aunt."

"What?"

"He thought he could use me to get to her, but then Caleb . . ."

"I got overwhelmed," Caleb said, looking at his hands. "All the emotions . . . everyone's anger . . . *I'm* the reason his power is gone. I *beat* it out of him."

"*God*," I breathed, wincing.

"No one blames you, Caleb," Dr. Bright said soothingly. "You were protecting Adam. Who knows what Damien would have done."

"Damien had his ability back by then," Mark explained to me. "It took him a while, after our abilities collided, but he got it back. And he's *dangerous* with his ability. He used it to gaslight me for months, to manipulate my sister for *years*, put Adam in danger . . ."

"I had no idea," I said, thinking about the man crawling out of the ground and what else Damien had used his ability for.

"Yeah, he's good at making you believe he's a decent guy," Mark said darkly, looking down at his hands, and my stomach dropped. "Believe me."

"After everything you just told me, I definitely do," I said. And I did. The way Mark talked about Damien . . . I know he wasn't lying. He didn't hate Damien, that much was obvious. I don't think he had any reason to lie.

"I have to ask . . ." I started and everyone stiffened in preparation. "If Damien is really as dangerous as you guys say, why didn't the AM just . . . keep him? It doesn't seem like they have a problem with that kind of stuff."

Mark snorted in agreement while Dr. Bright jumped in with a theory.

"I think Wadsworth is hoping that Damien's ability will eventually come back. If she put him away or continued to experiment on him, he might not heal properly. But if he returns to his life and some semblance of normalcy . . ."

"He'll bounce back," Mark said.

"I think that's her hope," Dr. Bright said.

"But if his ability makes him dangerous, why would she want that?" I probed, filing away that Damien had said the same thing.

"I imagine she'd want to use it for something," Dr. Bright said.

"Make another drug. Like the immunity," Sam said grimly.

"Exactly," Dr. Bright agreed.

I sat there, taking it all in, trying to separate the lies from the truth, figure out who to trust. It seemed like Damien had been lying about the AM taking away his ability, but *not* the fact that Atypical immunity was possible. And the big takeaway from the whole night was clear: the AM could not be trusted.

I hate when my mom is right.

The rest of the details of the night are a bit of a blur—it feels like I've been over here living out my own fantasy novel and, for a moment, I stepped into a companion series with its own cast of characters and plot lines. I watched the personal drama unfold in front of me, trying to pick up on as many clues as possible, and understand who—if anyone—I could trust.

I don't really know where I've landed with how I feel about Dr. Bright. I don't think anything she told me was a lie, but she's absolutely still hiding things from me. And maybe from her friends and family too.

We did agree on one thing though: I need to find a new therapist.

FEBRUARY 4TH, 2017

I didn't really plan on going to see Damien, at least not yet. I had planned on calling Owen or Mags or Dr. Loving, go all Nancy Drew at the AM and try to uncover a little bit more of the truth so I could line up everything that everyone had said and compare them, find the real truth amidst all the hurt feelings and different perspectives.

But the recent snowfall had melted away, and it was a cold and bright day, sunny and clear enough to go rollerblading. And without thinking, I ended up at Damien's building.

Suspecting that Damien wouldn't buzz me in, I waited, changing into my sneakers and tossing my skates over my shoulder, until someone left the building to get through the locked front door and then I knocked. I immediately heard footsteps rush toward the door, which swung open as fast as light, revealing Damien, looking the worst I'd ever seen him. He was wearing jeans, a ratty black T-shirt, and no shoes, comfortable and vulnerable in his own space, and his eyes were lined with red like he'd been crying.

"Oh," he said. "It's you."

"Were you expecting someone else?" I asked, not waiting for an invitation and instead choosing to act braver than I felt, breezing past him to stand in his apartment.

"Please, come on in," he said dryly, closing the door behind me and coming to stand a few feet away.

Damien cleared his throat and I refocused on him. He was standing with his arms crossed and looked down at his feet as he spoke.

"I assume you're here to yell at me?" he asked, his voice even raspier than usual, like he'd been shouting.

"I—" Honestly, I had been, but he looked so beaten down already, it didn't really seem fair. "No, I'm not here to yell at you."

He looked up at that, eyes wide with surprise.

"I'm just trying to understand what the hell is going on, Damien," I said. And then I told him everything that Dr. Bright, Mark, and the rest had told me.

He winced every single time I said Mark's name.

"Mark—he's . . . he's your ex, isn't he?" I asked finally, choosing which elephant in the room to address first.

"Ex something," he scoffed, repeating my words from the other day. "Yeah."

"You guys . . ." I wasn't sure how to ask it. Knowing everything about Damien's ability that I knew now, I wasn't even sure what I wanted to ask. What I would be okay with knowing.

"It's not what you think," he said. "Nothing ever happened between us, it wasn't—it wasn't romantic or sexual or whatever it is you're thinking."

"I wasn't thinking anything," I lied, putting up my hands.

"I thought we were friends," he said. "I thought that we could be . . . I don't know, Butch Cassidy and the Sundance Kid."

"Didn't they die in a gunfight?" I asked. Emily loves that movie.

"Yeah, but they got out first," he said, smiling hungrily. "They got a second act in a world where those aren't handed out easily."

"You wanted Mark to be your second act?" I asked, still trying to understand what Damien wants, what Mark is to him. Did he kidnap him or had they been on the run together? Was it somehow both?

"Look, Rose, why are you here?" Damien sighed. "What do you want from me?"

"I just want to understand, I guess," I said. "I thought *we* were friends."

"Yeah, well, I don't have those."

"But you just said—"

"I'm not going to have any answers that you like," he said, moving into the kitchen.

"I'm not asking you to tell me what I want to hear, Damien," I called after him, unsure if I was allowed to follow. "I just want to know the truth."

He came back into the living room, a nearly empty bottle of bourbon in one hand and a half-filled glass in the other.

"Breaking into the booze again?" I asked sharply. "Was your afternoon hangover all but two days ago not a strong enough deterrent?"

"It's been a rough coupla days," he said gruffly.

"Yeah, tell me about it," I snapped.

"Oh please, you just arrived at this party," he said, setting the bottle on the coffee table and coming to stand in front of me again. He rubbed his forehead with his free hand, looking down at the ground, before lifting his eyes to look at me, his face pulled into a neutral mask.

"I don't think we should see each other anymore, Rose." He sighed before taking a big swig from his glass.

"What, are you . . . breaking up with me?" I asked, confused by the abrupt turn in the conversation.

"Don't tell me you came here today to say you're on my side," he scoffed. "I know how this particular movie ends and I don't really need to sit through the credits."

"I came here today because I wanted to give you the benefit of the doubt," I said. "Because I know I haven't known you for very long but I thought we were becoming good friends. I thought you understood me, I thought you could help—"

"Aha!" he hissed. "There it is, the real reason."

"What are you talking about?"

"It's not that you want to let me tell my side of the story," he said, his smile like barbed wire, "it's that you want to know which bits I've told you are true, right? You want to know if the AM really is withholding some kind of secret cure from your dad."

I swallowed, trying to match his stare-down as best I could. I recognized the look, knew how he felt. His eyes were unblinking, filled with rage, with a kind of pent-up energy that didn't exist anywhere else in his body, like he didn't know how to *be* angry. Like he wasn't used to getting into arguments where he didn't immediately get everything he wanted.

"Well?" I asked finally, doing the best I could to keep my voice steady. "Were you actually going to help me?"

"What do *you* think?" he said, his eyes a challenge.

"I think you're scared of the AM," I said and he didn't blink. "I think you're scared of Mark."

He flinched at that and I kept going.

"And I think that there are a lot of things we don't understand about being Atypical and that you and I are looking for some of the same answers—"

"You still think there's a way for the AM—*the AM*," he spat, "to help your dad?"

"You weren't lying about the immunity," I told him. "I know you weren't. Or about them experimenting on you, so if you think that they have all the pieces to help your friend Blaze, to help my dad then—"

"I *lied*, Rose! There's no Blaze, no research about kinetic suppressants," he yelled. "I needed another way into the AM so I manipulated you—"

"No." I shook my head. "You don't have your ability anymore, *that's* real—"

"You think I need to use my ability to manipulate you?" He laughed. "You're a sad, desperate girl who lives inside of dreams and would do anything to save her dad—you were the easiest mark in the world."

That knocked me back. I was completely speechless, tears forming at the corners of my eyes as I watched Damien pour himself more bourbon. They were all so right. He *is* the selfish, manipulative asshole they all said he was.

"So there's . . ." I said finally, my voice wobbling around the tears in my throat.

"Look," Damien started gently, a complete one-eighty from twenty seconds ago, "if there really was a cure for those things, I'm sure the AM would tell you. They'd want to shout it from the rooftops.

"And I'm . . ." He sighed. "I'm sorry about your dad. That—it sucks—"

"Screw you, Damien," I snapped. Without giving him another look, I turned around and wrenched his front door open, slamming it shut behind me.

So that's it then. What a wasted month it's been. I never should have gone back to the AM, never should have supported them, never should have trusted anyone connected to it. And now I've burned two whole weeks thinking that . . . well, it doesn't matter now.

There's nothing I can do to fix any of this.

February 4th, 2017

Dear Mark,

I saw you today. You know that, of course, but still it bears repeating. It deserves being written down. It is, quite literally, noteworthy. And you came to me. It was the last thing I expected. Especially after . . . well. The phone call. Not my strongest moment. But, in my defense, the past few months have been . . . unideal. Especially now, I thought I was making strides, I thought that maybe I could . . . I don't know, make an actual friend. Try a little bit of that normal life that people are going on about.

In retrospect, making my one friend a teenage girl and spending the rest of my time trying to figure out how to exact revenge on a government organization while simultaneously trying to get my ability back may not have been the best way to get to normal but we all make mistakes. I hadn't hurt Rose. Not yet. Not in the way she thinks.

I lied to her. She came over, twenty minutes after you left, if you can believe it. I ~~hoped~~ thought it was you. ~~I rushed to the door so fast~~ I don't know why. You made it pretty clear that you're never coming back.

She wanted to know if all that stuff that you told her was true. I didn't deny any of it, didn't even try to explain my side of things, even though that's what she was begging me to do. The damage was done. Despite what she said, there's no way she was going to give me a real chance to prove her wrong. I know what I sound like from the outside. My actions have always been an effective poison against me.

So I lied to her. I told her I manipulated her, that I made up everything I told her. It wasn't fair of me to give her false hope, even if it was based on something true. Maybe the AM really will make something that could help her dad, but I really do believe they'd already have told him if it was a possibility. But I had to tell Rose that it wasn't true. She wouldn't have stopped, she'd just keep burying herself deeper and deeper into the AM looking for something that might not exist and I . . . I needed to give her a concrete reason to write me off.

That was the right thing to do, right? I have no idea what the right thing to do was—that's what I had you for—but all I know is that there were no good choices.

A lot of things in my life have felt unfair but I know this one is. I had a clean slate—a real, true clean slate. No ability, no one coming after me . . . a chance to start over. I'm not saying that Rose and I would have become best buds but . . . I don't know. It felt like she maybe understood.

Then again, it felt like you understood. And you just told me, in no uncertain terms, that you don't. Or you don't want to. Whatever the truth of your feelings or your ability to forgive me, to give me a clean slate, to understand me and give me a second (okay, third, fourth, infinite) chance, you've made your choice. You don't want me around anymore. You've told me to leave.

I scorched the earth beneath us and you're salting the ground—that's what you said. I thought letting Rose go, pushing her away, was what you'd want me to do. Now I'm not so sure.

You were a good navigator, Mark. People really don't appreciate paper maps, but even now, with smart phones and satellite GPS and everything else, there are huge parts of this country that push you completely off the grid. People who drive around without an atlas in their backseat pocket are idiots—the last thing you want is to get stuck in the desert with no reception, seventy miles from the nearest gas station, with the sun going down.

But you loved looking at the paper maps and telling me where to go. On the best days, you would tell me to take a turn because you thought there might be a cool lake or forest just down that road and you missed the open air so much. Half the time, it'd turn out to be a mall parking lot. That's what I get for having a Rand McNally from 2003.

~~I bought new maps. I was hoping that we~~

It's back to the open road for me, I guess. You asked me to leave and, for once, I'm going to do what someone asks of me.

III

SMOKE

03-01-2017, morningwafffles, text post

Thanks for all the love you've been filling my in-box with the past few days! I was pretty nervous about posting this most recent chapter and it's been SUCH a relief to see it go over well.

A lot of you have been surprised by the twist I threw in there and some of you are mad at me. And I get it. I advertised the story as something that it didn't end up being. But I've removed the *Alternate Universe - Modern: No Powers* tag from AO3 so that new readers don't pick up a tin of tuna only to find out it's beans. For those of you that are already in deep (I mean, god, I've already written 80,000 words, I would understand if you didn't want to give up now—I hope you don't!), I *promise* you, all the rest of the tags that have been there since the beginning are true. There will still be a Happy Ending. I'm not interested in telling stories that don't have a happy ending.

Now, you might be wondering, why the sudden change? Why introduce Bucky being the Winter Soldier when the whole story hasn't been about that? Have I been planning this twist since the beginning? A question to which my response is just a very long laugh. You guys know I'm a pantser through and through. This is why I love writing fanfic and why my original work tends to be short-form poetry, emphasis on short. With someone else's words, I can wing it, see how the story organically develops and always have canon to fall back on (or, more often, viciously rip apart).

So, no, I didn't know that I was going to bring all the superhero stuff into it from the beginning. But you guys know I love angst (in my stories at least—in my real life . . . well, that's a post for another day. Actually that's a post for never and probably something I should talk about with a licensed professional instead) and I thought it might be interesting if we—and Steve—learned that Bucky had this big secret the whole time. Should he be pissed? Should he be relieved that he finally has an answer for why Bucky sometimes gets cagey and withdrawn? Does he choose to stay with him even after his understanding of his partner and, frankly, his entire perception of the world has completely shifted? Does he just accept the fact that Bucky has a whole network of former assassins and superpowered people in his life? Because I think it would be reasonable if he totally freaked out. I think it would be reasonable if he got mad and wanted to break things off because he'd just had his world thrown totally upside down and feels like he doesn't even *know* the person that he's been falling in love with. That's going to rattle anyone!!

Anyway. I'm not here to defend my own creative decisions as correct or better than where someone else might have taken the story but I just . . . I thought it would be interesting to explore. Trust me, I want them to end up happy together as much as you do, and I'm going to do my damnedest to get us there. I'm just not sure . . . how yet.

That's life though, right? You get thrown a curveball and you hope that you'll be able to catch it, but sometimes it just smacks you in the face. The most important thing is that you don't let it knock you out.

I don't even know what I'm talking about anymore. It has been a very stressful day/week/year and you guys don't need to hear about my personal drama. I'm going to go eat my weight in Ben & Jerry's and watch *Drag Race* and pretend like my world didn't get completely spun upside down last week.

MARCH 1ST, 2017

I wish I had kept this journal strictly about dreams and that I was writing in it now because today has been some awful dream and not real life. But I didn't and I'm not and it's not. This isn't a nightmare that I've stumbled onto, it isn't someone else's head that I'm trapped in. It's real life and it is total garbage.

I *knew* it. I mean, no, not really, I didn't KNOW know it, but I knew that it wasn't going to be *easy* to tell anyone about Atypicals and my dreamdiving and just . . . everything. But I also knew that it wasn't okay to keep dating Emily, get more serious with her, and NOT tell her about this stuff. I also just—I wanted to be myself with her! Like I hoped I could be with my family, like I was with Damien before he turned out to be a completely different person than I thought.

I'll admit, maybe I could have picked a better time and place to tell her. I should have taken her to the Common, re-created our first date, found a quiet spot where I could have told her privately, but she wouldn't feel trapped or ambushed, could instead focus on asking me questions, giving me the benefit of the doubt. I should have made her feel safe. I should have bought her coffee so she could tear at the corners of the cardboard sleeve like she loves doing whenever she's distracted or anxious.

But hindsight is twenty-twenty. And I'm an idiot who decided to tell her while we were half-naked in bed together, completely vulnerable. In *my* head, being vulnerable was a great thing! I wanted to be totally open, honest, accessible to her. I realize now that maybe *she* would not have wanted to be fully vulnerable for that conversation. Finding out that there are people in the world with magical abilities is maybe not a revelation you want to have when you don't have your clothes on.

"Hey," I started softly, brushing her hair back from her forehead as she lay in my arms. "I have something to tell you."

"Okay," she said, snuggling in closer to me. She had this beautiful, gentle smile on her face, open and hopeful. Thinking about it now, I wonder . . . did she think I was going to tell her I love her? That would be the natural thing to assume. We've been dating for the past six months and whenever we're together it feels really serious. Yeah, we've been seeing each other kind of sporadically because, well, my life is what it is, but we're exclusive and . . . yeah, I do love her. I think. I *want* to let myself love her. It's just . . . it feels like I don't have room in my heart or my brain to be that open, especially when Emily doesn't know the full, real me.

So even though it seemed like she was expecting some kind of declaration I figured, hey, if this goes well, we'll get to that! I still thought that it might go well! So I just barreled forward! Like a total idiot!

"I have . . ." I started. "I have a kind of big secret."

She leaned back, propping herself on her elbow so she could look straight into my face, her curls falling back over her forehead.

"Okay . . ." she said again, a small smile on her face, but I could hear the hesitation in her voice, could feel the pulse in her wrist, still draped over my stomach, pick up.

"I'm . . ." I hadn't planned this out at all, had only hazily imagined her big smile once she realized she was dating a superhuman. In that moment I was *really* wishing I had decided how I was going to explain Atypicals, even thinking that I should have talked to Aaron or my parents about it.

"So, there are these people," I said. "They're called Atypicals."

"Atypicals," she said, eyes narrowing.

"Yeah," I said. "And we're . . . well, it's a secret thing. Like, a whole secret group in humanity."

"What, like a secret coven of witches?" She smiled, her eyes going wide in mock-surprise.

"No, not really," I said, even though I knew she was making a joke. "It's not . . . organized, really. It's more like . . . okay, you know how a certain portion of the human population is gay?"

"And thank goodness for that," she said, smiling and then kissing me lightly on the cheek. I blushed and did my best to keep myself focused on the task at hand.

"Right." I chuckled. "This is kind of like that. It's a small portion but—"

"An awesome one?" she teased.

"Yeah," I said, nodding enthusiastically, relieved she was on board so far.

"Okay, so what are Atypicals?" she said.

"People with supernatural abilities," I said, diving straight in.

"What?" She laughed.

"Atypicals are people with supernatural abilities," I said. "Like telepathy and pyrokinesis and super speed. And I'm one of them. My whole family is Atypical, actually."

She went still for a second, face scrunched up, before bursting into laughter.

"Rose, what are you talking about?" she said, still smiling.

"I'm a dreamdiver," I explained. "And Aaron can read minds, my dad is telekinetic—" I tripped over the word but kept going. "—and my mom is psychic. It's not as accurate as you might think though—she gets these random visions but she still has to figure out what they mean. All our abilities come with, like, major terms and conditions."

"Rose . . ." Emily wasn't laughing anymore, her smile rapidly collapsing.

"I've never told anyone that before." I exhaled a huge sigh of relief, wrapping my arms tightly around Emily, so full of warmth and joy in that moment I barely knew what to do with it.

That didn't last long.

Emily's hands wrapped around my upper arms as she gently pushed me away, to look me in the eyes with a face lined with worry.

"Rose, what are you talking about?" she asked. "Are you . . . are you okay?"

"Yeah, I'm—" I leaned back to get a better look at her. Her eyebrows were tipped toward each other in a stressed V-shape, her eyes darting frantically around my face, like she was trying to take in an image she didn't understand.

"I'm *fine*, Em," I insisted. "I'm—I'm great, actually. I've wanted to tell you for so long—"

Suddenly, she was standing up, out of bed and putting on her clothes faster than I could blink, talking rapidly the whole time.

"Rose, I don't know what kind of weird prank you're pulling on me," she said, her cheeks growing red, "but you know how I feel about jokes meant to make other people feel stupid."

"Emily, I promise you, I'm not pulling a prank," I said as I followed suit, not because I necessarily wanted to get out of bed but because it felt weird to stay while she was clearly having a hard time processing this stuff.

"So you mean to tell me that there are, what, *superhumans* and no one knows about them?" she said, growing louder as she paced around her small dorm room. "How is that even possible?"

"It's not like *The Avengers* or anything," I explained. "There aren't superheroes or anything, at least not that I know of. Just people with—"

"With abilities," she finished.

"Yeah."

She scoffed, stopping in her pacing and setting her hands on her hips.

"I'm sorry, I just—" She sighed. "I know you're not messing with me, because this would be *such* a weird joke but . . . I mean, come on."

She looked me dead in the eye.

". . . what?" I asked.

"If you're not joking and you're . . . you know, feeling totally fine . . ."

"I'm one hundred percent fine and one hundred percent serious," I said. That made her sigh even more heavily.

"Okay," she said, crossing her arms. "Then prove it to me."

She was standing there, with crossed arms, an adorable small smile on her lips, challenging me to prove my abilities to her in the same way she challenged me to race her, both of us with casts, on our second date. I felt reckless and brave and like I couldn't possibly get hurt, not again, not with Emily by my side, so I did what I did then—without thinking, I barreled forward. By telling her every detail of every dream of hers that I'd been inside during the past three months. Like a COMPLETE buffoon.

And as I talked—telling her about the fic she was imagining the first day we met about Steve and Bucky in the woods after Bucky's fall (one of the few fics she let me read), the scary anxiety dreams she has about reading in front of her creative writing seminar, her sweet homesick dreams about making food with her abuela, the dreams that I haven't even let myself think about too much where we're both in our late twenties, in a warm, well-worn apartment, me making her dinner while she writes—her face started to fall. And fell and fell and fell.

"And remember Thanksgiving?" I continued, piling on information like an IDIOT. "The weird moment with my brother at the beginning? He accidentally read your mind."

She took a shaky inhale and I rushed to explain.

"It really was an accident, he's usually good at controlling it," I explained.

All the color had drained from her face, her arms uncrossed and hanging limply at her sides, making her look like a strange mannequin version of herself.

I eventually noticed that I had stopped talking and that she hadn't started. We'd been standing in silence for nearly a minute, just standing on opposite ends of her tiny room.

"Emily." I breathed, taking a small step toward her. She immediately backed up, her hands going up defensively in front of her, and my heart shattered.

"No," she said, shaking her head. "No, you—how—why—"

"Emily, I know that all sounded bad," I tried, even though I really hadn't known that until that very moment.

"Sounded bad?" she said. "You—you've been inside my *head*. Without my permission. Without me knowing. That's—"

She sounded so disgusted, so betrayed. We both just stood there, ten feet apart, crying and barely looking at each other.

"And your brother—oh my god—" Realization dawned on her face. "Your dad! I'm not crazy, at Thanksgiving, he really did move something with his *mind*."

"I'm so sorry." I sniffed. "I never meant to—I couldn't control it for so long and then I just—I wanted to feel closer to you—"

"*That's* why you were asking about my abuela, why you asked me to show you how to make pozole, because you *saw* me, with her, in my dream—"

"You seemed so sad after we woke up and I thought if you talked about her, if we cooked the food she taught you . . . I don't know, I thought it would make you miss her less. Or that it would feel good to share that with me—"

"It *did* feel good, Rose," she cried. "I *want* to share that kind of stuff with you. But it has to be *my choice*."

"I know—"

"I think you should leave," she said, crossing her arms again, closing herself off to me.

"Em," I whispered. "Please—"

"I just—I need some space, okay?"

"Okay." I nodded. I hadn't respected her boundaries up until now, so I had to get this right. "I'll call you tomorrow."

"Don't," she said.

"Oh."

"Rose, wait—"

I spun around, hope beating against my chest.

"Here." She stretched out her arm. "I think you should have this."

The shell necklace was sitting in her palm.

"After all," she said, "you basically pulled it out of a dream, right?"

"Em—"

"Just go."

So I took the necklace and I left. I got on the bus, my ears ringing, and walked into the house and up to my room like a zombie, not paying attention to any of the calls from the kitchen from my family asking if that was me.

GOD, I really was falling in love with Emily. And I had this idea in my head that I wasn't allowed to, not fully, until I told her the truth. But what a lie that was. My heart wasn't listening to my head and I fell just the same.

I can smell dinner from downstairs but I'm going straight to the dreamworld.

LATER

It's the middle of the night, but I want to put the dream I was just in in amber and hold it up to the light and look at it forever.

It was Aaron's dream, I knew that right away from the dusty, sun-soaked edges of it, the way the backyard smells in the summer. Warm, humid air mixed with the sawdust from my dad's personal projects that he would do in the shed he built on the other end the yard, projects he would sometimes let Aaron and me help with, never letting us use the saw, but giving us goggles and gloves just so we could pretend we were part of it. That's what Aaron's dreams—the non-nightmare ones—feel like, always, no matter what they're about.

Except this one *was* about building stuff with our dad. But Aaron was himself, as he is now, not little kid Aaron. He and my dad were in the yard, putting together what looked like a doghouse, which was eventually confirmed by the CUTEST dog in the world loping into the scene. I hung back, sitting on our back porch, just watching them laugh and smile. Aaron hadn't noticed I was here and I didn't want to disturb him. He was happy. My dad was happy.

I was so outside of it and I didn't know how I would possibly get in. Before I could get up and walk toward them, the dream changed and suddenly the porch was the edge of a cliff and Aaron and my dad were sitting on a cloud hanging over a broad canyon beneath us. It was breathtakingly beautiful, a thing out of my brain, of my own creation, unbelievably real and yet something *more* than real. Like being inside a magical world or a beautifully painted picture book. And Aaron and my dad paid absolutely no attention to it. They just kept laughing and smiling and working on the doghouse, the puppy running happy circles around them, kicking up the cloud into perfect wisps that went unappreciated.

I was sat atop my own, perfect kingdom, surveying its beauty, unable to bridge the gap between the edge of the canyon and the circumference of the cloud. A sad and lonely king with an infinite kingdom and no subjects.

Writing about it isn't like being in it. When I woke up I had such a sense of joy and peace, but now that I've written all that out . . . it wasn't as perfect as I thought. Maybe dreams aren't meant to be examined too closely.

MARCH 3RD, 2017

I just keep doing *everything* wrong. My family, Damien, Dr. Bright, Emily, *everything*.

I slept from about eight thirty last night until eleven this morning, with that small break in the middle of the night when I woke up from Aaron's dream, and for the first time in a long time, I actually woke up kind of groggy. I guess my body had become unused to sleeping for fifteen hours in the past two months. I was also hungry as *hell*, so my first stop was the kitchen, where I found Aaron on his laptop, typing frantically.

"Nice of you to show your face, Rosie," he said, not looking up from his computer.

"What are you doing down here?" I asked. Aaron normally worked on his desktop in his room. Something about RAM and gigabytes and blah blah blah. My computer was for memes, YouTube cooking videos, and Serious Eats.

"My computer's on the fritz, I'm picking up a part later today—I can drop you at work if you want," he added, looking up at me while holding the coffeepot, which I was sad to discover was empty.

"All the coffee's gone," he said.

"Yeah, thanks, that's really helpful," I said, going into the fridge for some juice instead.

"So . . . ride?" he asked, tapping away.

"Um, yeah, thanks," I said. "My shift doesn't start until four though."

"That's okay, the store is open until six."

I just nodded as I poured myself some OJ. Suddenly the typing stopped and I looked up to see Aaron staring at me intensely.

"What," I snapped.

"You were in my dream last night, weren't you?" he asked, like it had just occurred to him. Maybe it had.

"What?"

"Don't play dumb, Rosie, you're bad at it," he said, snapping his laptop shut.

“Thanks.” I rolled my eyes, even if there was a little part of me that was actually complimented by that weird backward insult.

“I thought we talked about this.” He sighed, sounding WAY too much like our dad in that moment.

“Look, can we just . . . not? Today? Please?” I tried to make it sound casual, like I was just over everything, totally cool and aloof, but my voice cracked on the last word and Aaron stood up, coming to stand on the other side of the kitchen counter from me.

“Are you okay?” he asked, leaning on the island to look right at me.

“What, you’ve decided you’re gonna be an older brother today?”

“Damn, Rose,” he said, leaning back. And yeah, that was harsh. Boy, do I wish it was the worst thing I had said to him in this conversation!

“Sorry,” I sighed, even though I didn’t really sound it. “I just—”

I took a deep breath and Aaron leaned back in, clearly understanding that this was actually serious.

“I told Emily,” I said finally.

“Oh,” he said. “About your ability?”

“Yeah.”

“And . . . ?” He winced, like he was bracing for impact. God, I hate when he’s right.

“Well, I don’t have a girlfriend anymore,” I snapped, turning back to the cabinets to try and throw some food together in an effort to distract myself. I wasn’t even hungry anymore, my empty stomach replaced with twisting knots.

“Oh jeez, Rosie, I’m so sorry,” he said and, to his credit, he sounded genuine. “What happened?”

“What do you mean, what happened?” I asked, cracking eggs against the counter and throwing them into a bowl. I didn’t particularly feel like eating scrambled eggs but I sure as hell felt like cracking and scrambling something.

“I told her that there’s a whole subset of humanity that can read minds and make fire out of nothing and, you know, she had a normal person’s reaction to that,” I explained.

“But she believed you?” he asked before murmuring to himself, “That was always my question, how you would even go about making someone believe you.”

“She believed me all right,” I said. “And you know how you get people to believe you? You give them proof.”

"Proof . . ." His eyes suddenly went wide. "Rosie, you didn't."

"What?"

"You went into her dreams?" he asked.

"What, you've never read a date's mind?" I asked and the guilty look told me my answer right away. "See? Don't act like you're better than me. How else was she going to realize I wasn't pulling a prank on her! Telling her about the dreams I'd been in seemed like the easiest and best way to help her understand!"

Aaron rocked back on his heels, his arms going up, hands waving in front of him.

"Wait, wait, wait," he said. "Dreams? Plural? And, wait, you *told* her what you saw? You didn't fall asleep and try to meet her in her head? Give her some advance warning?"

"I didn't think that would work!" I defended. "The only reason I'm able to talk to you in your dreams is because you're a telepath! No one else ever knows that I'm there. Telling her about the dreams I'd already been in was the only way."

"So it wasn't that she was freaked out about Atypicals," he said.

"I mean, I don't know, I guess she might have been, but she was a little busy being furious with me!"

"Yeah, I bet." He snorted.

"Oh, that's really helpful, thanks," I said. "I spent all of last night thinking about how the girl I love told me that I'd completely invaded her privacy before she *dumped* me, but please, be a smartass about this."

"I mean, I understand where she's coming from!" Aaron said.

"God, couldn't you just have said, 'Sorry, that sucks' and left it at that?" I yelled. "Why aren't you on my side in this, Aaron!"

"Because she's right!" he shouted back. "It *is* an invasion of privacy."

"How could you say that?" I asked. "*You* of all people should understand what it's like—what it's like to have this—this—this—freaking weird as hell look into people's brains!"

"Dreams are *really* private, Rosie," he said, like I didn't know.

"And thoughts aren't?"

"I can choose not to listen," he said.

"Is that really true?" I snapped.

"What?"

He rocked back on his heels as he asked it, like it was being punched out of him.

"I mean, can you really choose not to listen?" I repeated, taking a menacing step toward him. "All we have as evidence is your word, which . . ."

I wanted to take the words back the moment they left my mouth. I wanted to rewind back to the beginning of this whole conversation, to the beginning of this year, to the beginning of my life. But they just hung there, those weighty words, the implication of them ringing throughout the kitchen.

"You know what," Aaron started quietly after a moment. "You can take the bus to work."

He grabbed his laptop and I listened to his footsteps rush upstairs, his door open and close, and then I was alone, in the empty kitchen, the only sound the oil sizzling on the cooktop, still eggless. I turned off the burner, put the bowl of scrambled eggs in the fridge, and went outside to sit on the back porch, grabbing this notebook, which I'd set on the counter when I came in all but ten minutes ago, on my way out.

It's cold out here. March has come in like a lion. Emily loves that expression—she'll use it for anything. Other months, a good opening sentence of a book, a particular flavor in a dish I've cooked for her. To her, it just means something that's bold and undeniable, like she is. Like I'm not. For me, right now, it just means what it's always meant: that March in Massachusetts is fucking cold.

The monster that lurked in my dreams all those months ago hasn't stalked me in the dreamworld since my second visit to the AM. It followed me out and now it's got ahold of me in dreams and in life. Pretty soon the monster is going to be all that's left of me.

community/TheUnusuals post by n/thatsahumanperson

Have any of you ever told a non-Unusual about your ability? How did it go?

onmyown

Don't think we're not noticing that you're posing this question without any personal context, which is a bit weird for you. How badly did it go?

thatsahumanperson

Really, *really* badly. But it wasn't me. My sister finally told her girlfriend about the dreamdiving. As she put it, she "doesn't have a girlfriend anymore."

onmyown

Ouchhhhhhhhhh. That sucks. Is this the first person your sister has ever told?

chuckxavier

Is there any concern that your sister's girlfriend would tell the greater public? (ETA: *ex*-girlfriend)

thatsahumanperson

n/chuckxavier, I don't think so. She seems like a good kid and I don't think she'd want to do anything to hurt my sister. She also loves all things superheroes, so I feel like she knows the importance of keeping this kind of stuff secret, you know? n/onmyown, yeah. It's the first person really anyone in my family has told. I've never had a girlfriend I've been serious enough about that it's seemed worth it. And after seeing what my sister has gone through . . . god, I don't know how I'm going to do the whole wife and family thing—telling anyone seems *terrifying.*

theneonthorn

honestly, this is why I've never invested in building relationships with anyone who isn't either a) Unusual or b) knows about them. there's still always shit to deal with because a lot of Unusuals in one place can have some . . . bad side effects, but it's easier than trying to constantly get people on board with the idea.

thatsahumanperson

Yeah, that makes sense. I guess on some level I've always thought I would end up with another Unusual. I just haven't met all that many of them. And a lot of y'all know how weird even Unusuals can be about mind readers—it's not the easiest ability for people to digest.

theneonthorn

you're telling me. without going into details, my ability is . . . well, for a lot of people, it's even less likable than mind reading. I also haven't really ever had a successful relationship, platonic or romantic, so maybe don't take advice from me.

onmyown

Aw, come on, thorny! You've got us!

theneonthorn

yippee.

MARCH 5TH, 2017

In the month since I went to his apartment and we had our big fight (I seem to be getting into a LOT of those lately), I haven't heard a word from Damien. Our nearly constant texting in the few weeks we'd been friends went to total zero overnight and, even though I sometimes got the temptation to reach out, especially after everything with Emily, I never did. I was too proud to make the first move, especially when I knew that he would *never* take that leap himself. So when I got a text with nothing but a time and the name of a local diner, I assumed it was an emergency.

"Damien," I said as I slid into the booth across from him.

"Rose," he said, matching my tone, like we were two enemy spies meeting. That was a bit what it felt like, what with all the people who had warned me to stay away from him.

He didn't say anything else to me, instead flagging down a waitress to ask for two cups of coffee.

"What am I doing here, Damien?" I asked finally when the waitress had come back with mugs and Damien *still* hadn't said a word.

"Having coffee."

"Damien."

"They also have pretty good pie," he said. "I mean, I know you're picky—"

"I am picky," I said, "and I can give you the whole lecture about what makes the perfect pie crust, I always have it prepared—"

"Yippee."

"—or you could just tell me why you texted me."

He sighed.

"I'm leaving," he said after a moment.

"What? *You* invited *me* here, you can't just—"

"No." He cut me off. "I'm not leaving here, right now. I'm leaving *Boston.*"

"Oh," I said, a little surprised that this was reason enough for him to reach out after a month of radio silence and more than a bit confused.

"When will you be back?" I asked, feeling like it was my turn.

"I won't," he said and that was when I understood.

"Oh," I said again.

"Mark—" He cleared his throat, like Mark's name had gotten stuck there. "I've been asked to leave town, to leave everyone alone, and I—I'm going to do it."

"Why?"

"Because for once in my goddamn life, I want to do something right," he growled.

I didn't want to say "oh" again, so I said nothing.

"It's taken me a month, but I—there's nothing keeping me here," he said. "I don't know what I was waiting for, what I was holding onto, but I know it's finally . . . it's time."

"So . . . why did you ask me here?" I asked, still barely understanding what was happening.

"I wanted to say goodbye, I guess," he said, shrugging a single shoulder. That was the first moment I took a really good look at Damien since sitting down. He looked better than when I last saw him, though that wasn't a difficult metric to clear. His hair was clean, he was wearing a hoodie that actually looked like it had been purchased within the last year, and the bags under his eyes were . . . well, they were still there, but not *quite* as pronounced. Maybe my trip into his dreams had really helped.

"Do you *want* to leave?" I asked as I watched him rip a sugar packet and dump the whole thing into his coffee.

"What?"

"Do you actually want to go?" I asked again.

"I don't know what I want," he mumbled.

"Are you just going because you don't know what else to do?"

"I mean, what else *would* I do?" he scoffed, taking a sip of his coffee and wincing.

"Not run away," I suggested.

"I'm not running away," he said. "I've been asked to leave. Repeatedly. By several different people."

"But that's not fair," I said, shaking my head. "You can't just be run out of your home."

"I don't have a home," he mumbled, ripping another sugar packet and dumping it into his coffee. "And I'm dangerous."

"You don't have your ability anymore," I pointed out.

I watched Damien fold the now-empty sugar packet over and over and over again until he had a tiny little square. It reminded me of Emily, and my heart hurt.

"I had this argument with my dad a few months ago," I started, "about how I can't be expected to do the same as Aaron when he has total, perfect control over his ability. Perfect, perfect Aaron." Damien just kept folding.

"But that's totally unfair," I went on when Damien didn't immediately join the Aaron-pile-on, "and I mean, my dad should get that. He has Alzheimer's and it would be totally unfair to expect him to remember that we asked him to take out the garbage or whatever. I shouldn't be expected to sleep like a normal person. I shouldn't be expected to stop something that's just . . . in my nature."

"I don't think it's really the same," he said.

"Oh, suddenly you're the expert on this stuff?"

"I've been trying to learn," he said. "I've done a hell of a lot more therapy than you, that's for damn sure."

"So you're telling me that we're just . . . always responsible for what our abilities do to us?"

"What's going on with you?" he asked, his eyes narrowing at me. "You're acting . . . odd."

"What do you mean?" I snapped, probably proving his point.

"Come on." He stared at me in a way that made me think he'd be using his ability on me if he still had it. "I know we're not the best of friends, but I can tell that you're pissed about something. And it's not me leaving town."

I sighed, leaning back in the booth like putting physical distance between us would stop the questions. But he just kept staring.

"I told Emily," I said and he looked actually surprised. "And it went . . . bad."

"She was pissed that you'd been in her dreams, huh?" he said, and that immediately set me off.

"Yes!" I yelped. "How did you—"

"I've been around the block, remember?" he said. "I know what it's like to have someone hate you because of what you do with your ability."

My body relaxed slightly at that because I realized that this wasn't going to be the conversation I had with Aaron all over again. My brother was somehow under the impression that he was perfect and had never had a conflicted feeling about his ability. But Damien understood. He understood having that monster inside of you, and I didn't think he'd judge me for it.

I was wrong about that.

"It's just not fair," I said. "I was actually looking forward to sharing the dreamworld with her. I mean, I hadn't figured out the exact logistics yet, but I wanted to. And now we'll never have that. I might not have that with *anyone*."

"You don't know that," Damien said. "Just . . . next time you have a girlfriend, don't go into her dreams without permission. Or just *never* go into her dreams."

The thought of having another girlfriend—one who *isn't* Emily—made me feel queasy, but hearing that particular advice from Damien of all people really grated on me.

"I can't just not go into her dreams," I said. I'm still not sure I believe that that's a lie. "I'm not going to never sleep around my partner and when I sleep, I dreamdive. It's a pretty simple equation."

"But you've got pretty good control over it now, right?" he said. "So I'm sure you could work it out."

"Why does everyone assume it's so goddamned easy to do that? To just *not* do the thing my body *wants* to do."

"Look," he said, "all I'm saying is that it seems that going into the dreamworld is the source of all your problems. Maybe take it away."

"It's only the source of my problems because no one will ever give me a chance to explain that it's not . . . it's not a creepy thing!" I said, my face heating in an effort to get Damien to understand. He's the one person who's supposed to. "You said yourself that it's not our fault. It's like any other Atypical ability—I didn't get to choose it."

"But you *choose* to spend all that time in the dreamworld," he said.

"And you *choose* to be an asshole," I snapped. "At least my dumb, destructive choices never put anyone in danger."

"What, you think you've never hurt anyone?" he asked. "You think it didn't hurt your family that, after learning your dad is dying, you chose to spend two months in some other place entirely instead of spending time with them?"

"Fuck you."

I don't know why I didn't get up and leave in that moment, but I was stuck to that stupid vinyl booth, looking at Damien's stupid, sad face.

"I'm sorry."

"What?" I wasn't being glib when I asked that, I genuinely wasn't sure I'd heard him correctly, he spoke so quietly.

"I'm sorry," he repeated, only slightly louder. "That was way out of line."

"Oh," I said, picking at the corner of the paper place mat to avoid making eye contact. "No, you—you're right. I hate that you're right, but you're right."

"You—" I looked back up at him when he didn't continue. When we first met, Damien was so quick with his words, wielding them like knives, and now he seemed to stop after every other thought, uncertain how to complete them.

"Look, I don't know how many chances a person deserves to get, but Emily should have given you at least one."

He looked straight at me as he said it, like he really wanted me to know that he meant it. Looking back on it now, this was his way of saying goodbye. I wish I'd said something.

He pulled out a few crumpled bills from his pocket and threw them on the table, before getting up out of the booth, standing right at my shoulder for a second, and looming over me.

"You wanna know what I want, Dorothy?"

I looked up at him. Nodded. His jaw clenched.

"I want to not be me."

He brushed past me and I didn't turn around to watch him go. It had become painful to look at him, so I just listened for the sound of the bell in the doorway to chime to know. He was gone.

I'd had this idea of how my life would go and there's not a single part of it that's matching up to that idea. I'm not even sure why I went to meet Damien, what I'd been hoping for. I had barely known him—had barely even scratched the surface of who he really was—but he had made me feel comfortable, unselfconscious about the kind of Atypical I am. At least, he had until tonight.

I got a text from Sam today, asking if I wanted to come to a classic movie night at her house this week. I got it while on the bus to meet Damien and couldn't decide if I wanted to respond. I'd texted a little bit with her, and with Caleb, the empath, in the past month, but I wouldn't necessarily call them friends yet. I'd been too caught up in my feelings about Damien, some lingering sense of loyalty to him because he was my friend first. Because I wanted to give him a chance. Because *I* want to be given chances myself. But Sam and all the rest seem nice. Normal. Or, at least, as normal as a bunch of Atypicals caught up in the midst of conspiracy and trauma can be. A kind of normal that I could maybe be a part of.

I'm going to text her back. I'm going to text her back and try not to think about how a classic movie marathon is something Emily would love. Try to make new friends. Try to be normal for a little while.

MARCH 8TH, 2017

I stepped forward, bringing the edge of the void close to me, to feel the seams where my world ends and someone else's begins. I could feel a few different threads, one that was sharp and cold but not in an entirely bad way, like a rough wind that chaps your face but also makes you feel like you have more oxygen in your lungs, like you're more alive somehow. That was Sam, I knew it immediately.

I turned my head away from the sharp wind and smelled fresh cut grass and sunlight. Still cool, in the way any subconscious other than my own is, but softer, drawing me in. Caleb.

Turning once more and I found the final thread—smoky and pulled tight, a warm glow that gave off no heat emanating from the seam. Mark.

If I had just stopped at Sam and Caleb. If I hadn't gone into Mark's head, had remembered that he's a mimic, that he would *remember* . . . maybe it would have all been okay.

"Did you just . . ." Mark asked, eyes wide.

We'd woken up at the same time, just like I had with Damien, and Mark stared at me over Sam, still asleep on his lap. I hadn't meant to fall asleep, but Sam's comfortable couch, the hum of classic movies on the TV, the dark room, the seductive pull of other people's subconsciouses, was irresistible.

"I'm—I'm sorry," I whispered.

It hadn't been as bad as Damien's nightmare—not as viscerally violent or confusing, but what I had seen in Mark's head definitely *was* a nightmare. Pleading with his sister to fix him, while crying over the fact that he would be broken forever. The pain and self-loathing had been such a sharp edge I worried I'd wake up with physical cuts.

"Where's Joan?" he asked urgently, leaning over Sam to hiss at me.

"What?"

"Where's my sister?"

"Oh, I think she's still in the kitchen," I said. "With Adam maybe."

"So she wasn't . . ." He looked so, so afraid.

"No, no, no," I said, realizing what he was so panicked about.

"That wasn't her. Not really. It wasn't really Sam either." No one had heard his brokenhearted lament except for me.

"Right. Okay." He nodded his head and his shoulders went down in relief. But then he looked back at me, eyes narrowing. "Why me?"

"What?" I asked, unsure what he was asking.

"Why did you go into my dream?" he asked, jaw clenching.

"Oh, um," I stumbled, "I was—"

"You did it with everyone, didn't you?" Realization dawned on his face as he leaned back and away from me. "You know, I'd almost be impressed by that level of control if it wasn't so . . ."

He clenched his jaw, like he didn't want to finish that thought. I didn't know what to say, not when looking at an expression on Mark's face that I had seen on Emily's. Betrayal. He felt betrayed.

"I'm sorry," I whispered finally, knowing I had to repair this as fast as I could. "I—"

"Just—" He cut me off. Sighed. "You should go."

I have my answers now, at least. Somewhat. I had wanted to know if I could trust Mark and Sam and all the Atypicals that Damien had hurt, wanted to know if they were telling me the truth about Damien, if they were good people, and it turns out they're just *broken* people. Like Damien, like me. Except Damien and I just keep making the same mistakes over and over and over again and they at least seem to be *trying*. To be growing.

I also wanted to know if I could be normal. Have a normalish life. I can't even hang out with other Atypicals without royally screwing it up. I have my answer.

I'll never be normal. The monster that followed me out is stuck to me for good.

MARCH 20TH, 2017

Aaron and I sat on the cliff's edge, looking out over the watercolor expanse. An ocean of pink and purple starshine ebbed and flowed beneath us as a soft breeze fluttered our identical eyelashes, somehow more prominent in the dreamscape.

"This is really nice, Rosie," he said after a few seconds, a year, a hundred years.

"Have we been here before?" I asked, my voice echoing gently through the infinite abyss.

"I don't think this is a real place," he teased and I rolled my eyes, feeling lighter than air.

"I mean, together, in dreams. This all looks familiar. Have we been here?"

He looked away from me and back out across the broad ocean that, in the past few seconds, had transformed into a blanket covering the whole world.

"I don't think so," he said. "I think I'd remember."

"Do you remember all the times I come into your dreams?"

"I think this is *your* dream, Rosie," he said, turning his face back to me. "If you recognize this place, it must be yours."

"So you're reading my mind," I guessed.

"That's one option," he said and I didn't ask what the other options were.

We sat in silence, staring at each other, and I watched him transform from Aaron in the present to Aaron of the past, the knobby-kneed boy of ten who would catch fireflies for me in the summertime. As soon as the boy appeared, he was gone again, and I was looking back into the world-weary face of a young man untethered.

I know how he feels.

"I think I do," he said suddenly. "Remember, I mean. All the dreams."

"Oh." I didn't know what to say to that. Did I want him to remember? No one else ever does.

"Why don't we ever talk about it then?" I asked.

"I don't know," he said, his familiar shrug out of place in the fantastical Technicolor landscape. "We just don't talk like that."

"Do you ever wish we did?" I asked.

"Do you?"

"I . . ."

I wasn't sure how to answer that question. Showing Aaron my vulnerable underbelly has never been easy. But somehow, in a place that was so separate from reality but increasingly becoming *my* true reality, it wasn't as complicated.

"I do, sometimes, I guess," I said honestly. "I wouldn't really know where to begin but . . . I think I'd like to know you. More than I do."

"I know what you mean." He nodded, squinting into the bright purple sun, staring directly at it in the way you never can with the real sun, seeing its whole shape, its beautiful perfect roundness.

"I just don't . . . I don't know how to connect to people. It's like I forgot how."

"Is that why you dig into people's heads?" he asked, his voice turning sharp, the pinks and purples of the world turning bloodred in an instant.

"What?" I asked, turning to Aaron, who was transforming before my eyes, morphing into an unrecognizable monster.

"You've been here for too long, Rosie," said the demon wearing my brother's face. "Why did you come here?"

"I—"

"Why did you come here?" he asked again, his voice transforming into something familiar, and then he wasn't Aaron or some horrific monster, but Mark. A Mark made of stone, with cracks forming along the lines of his face as he pleaded with me.

"Why did you come here?" he asked, his voice choked with tears. "You don't belong."

More fissures formed on his face, around the corners of his desperate eyes, and darkness spilled out through the cracks like light, a blinding kind of darkness that spread over his entire body, spread into me, the world, flowing out over the cliff's edge like a waterfall. I was trapped under the weight of it, unable to move, unable to change it, and then—

I woke up in a cold sweat, gasping for air.

A nightmare. I'd just had an actual, honest-to-goodness normal-person nightmare. But I was still lucid dreaming, still thinking that I was diving, that I had wandered into Aaron's dream or he had wandered into mine but really . . . he was just a figment of my imagination in the same way Mark was.

I hadn't talked to Mark since the other week at Sam's. I'd texted a bit with Caleb still, and thanked Sam for having me over, passing pleasantries back and forth before the conversation dried up, but I was operating under the assumption that I would never see or speak to him again. After all, it's not like his sister was my therapist anymore.

I should probably get on with finding a new therapist.

APRIL 6TH, 2017

Another three weeks without roaming around people's dreams and I'm starting to wonder if I'm completely broken. It's not that I don't feel the dreamworld anymore, I do, I can sense the edges of it, can smell dust and sunlight and freshly cut grass and perfume on the sharp, cold air, the hallmarks of my family in slumber. But it just feels *right* out of reach. It reminds me of those anxiety dreams of Aaron's that I went into when this all first started, but in reverse. In those, he could never run fast enough to get away from the thing chasing him, his feet always being dragged down by molasses. This feels like I can never run fast enough to reach the edge, like it keeps moving, *just* beyond my grasp, every time I take a step.

I've been wondering if this is just what happens after you've had your ability for a while. If it just starts to even out, to dull, as your body gets used to it.

I hung out with Caleb and Adam today, hoping for a little bit of normalcy, hoping that I'd be able to glean some useful insight into what it's like to be an Atypical who has had their ability for over a year. Instead, we mostly ended up talking about how much it sucks to tell someone about your ability and, according to Adam, how much it sucks to be *told* about an ability. How it turns your entire world perspective upside down.

"I mean, it's a really jarring thing," he explained. "Like, I'm the biggest fantasy and sci-fi nerd there is—"

"Psh," Caleb scoffed. "I'm a *way* bigger Star Wars fan than you."

"It's not a competition," Adam said.

"It is when we do Star Wars trivia and I get more answers than you do," Caleb teased, and Adam pushed at him playfully, their momentary scuffle turning into a nauseatingly sweet kiss.

"Emily and I used to do trivia nights," I said sullenly, which sobered them up from their lovefest pretty quick.

"There's this coffee shop near her dorm that does trivia nights that we would go to every week," I continued. "There's one next week, so . . ."

"You should ask her to go!" Caleb suggested earnestly.

"Yeah, so . . . I actually already did?"

They both got very excited about that, asking me frantically what she'd said.

"She said yes but not . . . enthusiastically?" Emily and I had been texting a bit for the past few weeks. She got back from a spring break writer's retreat and said she'd had a lot of time to think about everything that happened and she was still really pissed but she wanted to maybe meet up again sometime before the end of her semester. A few days ago I texted her about trivia, thinking that would maybe be a good way to ease back into spending time with each other.

"I mean, a yes is still a yes, right?" Adam said, shrugging his shoulders, which were drowning in Caleb's letterman jacket. It was so strange seeing them, so . . . normal. Just two high school sweethearts, wearing each other's clothes, holding hands, and getting froyo with a friend like they were completely average people. Like one of them didn't have a supernatural ability and the other wasn't connected to a mysterious government organization meant to study them.

"Yeah." I sighed. "A yes is still a yes."

That was my hope. A second act, like Damien had said. I know that he wasn't the most reliable expert on who was deserving of second chances, but GOD I hope Emily gives me one. I feel like I'm running out of them everywhere else.

As we walked around Cambridge, eating our frozen yogurt on a surprisingly warm day, talking about romance and how stressful it was to be us, I *did* start to feel a little normal. Just normal enough that I came home feeling confident, which is how I walked directly into a serious conversation with Aaron.

I was just sitting in my room, minding my own business (by which I mean, going through every single item of clothing in my closet to try and find something cute to wear to trivia), when I heard a knock on my doorframe.

"What?" I barked, without looking at who it was, still half-inside my closet.

"Got a sec?"

I turned around to see Aaron standing in my doorway, looking . . . nervous.

"Uh, yeah," I said, stepping around the piles of clothes on my floor and flopping down to sit on my bed. "What's up?"

"I want to plan a trip for all of us this summer," he said, the words coming out in a rush like he was afraid if he didn't say it quickly he wouldn't say it at all.

"A trip?" I asked. Aaron took a few steps into my room to stand in front of me.

"It's been a long time since we had a family vacation, you know?" he said, eyes big. "And I was thinking it could be really nice to do something all together this summer. Maybe go camping like we used to."

"You think that's a good idea? With Dad, I mean . . ." I trailed off, letting the subtext stand on its own.

"It's not like we'll be dropping him somewhere in the woods to fend for himself," Aaron said. "We'll be with him the whole time. I think it could be really good for him. For all of us."

"Uh, yeah, sure," I said, pulling one leg up onto the bed to wrap my arm around it. I used to love our camping trips. But the idea of being stuck in a couple of tents for a week, unable to escape my family, really scared me. But I knew that if Aaron presented the idea to our parents—which it sounded like he hadn't yet—they'd insist on a family bonding camping trip.

And I know, in my heart of hearts, that I shouldn't hesitate to jump at this idea. That this is a good, important opportunity to make things better with my family, to connect with them after months and months of hiding inside of my own head.

"Okay, cool," Aaron said, nodding. "So, the thing is, I know money is tight right now. Because Dad isn't able to work at sites anymore and there's only so much admin he can do, and *you* haven't been able to work—"

"Give me a break, Aaron," I said, prickly, "it's been kind of a hard year."

"God, Rosie, why are you always like this now?" Aaron sighed, exasperated.

"What do you mean?" I asked, my stomach starting to twist into knots.

"You jump down my throat at *every* opportunity." He sighed again. "I feel like all we do is fight these days. We never used to do that."

"Yeah, well, it's easy to not fight when you never talk," I snapped, challenging him without thinking about it, without really *wanting* to. But he didn't pick up the gauntlet I'd thrown at his feet, instead collapsing on the bed next to me, still somehow so much taller than me even though we were sitting side by side. He leaned his elbows on his legs, examining his hands as he twisted them together.

"I'm not the person you think I am," he said softly, sending a chill down my spine. He had taken my line—*I* was the one who was supposed to convince him I was better, but here he was talking like he had to apologize to me.

"What do you mean?" I asked.

"You keep expecting the worst in me," he said. "Like I'm still that fifteen-year-old asshole who wouldn't take you to the movies with him and his friends."

"Yeah, well, it was always supposed to be the two of us," I said. "What's the point of having a sibling if you can't hang out, right?" I said it like it was a casual thing, like I was simply pointing out how things were supposed to be if we followed the script, but I knew he could see through it and understand that, somewhere along the way in him growing up and discovering his ability, he'd abandoned me.

"I needed to do my own thing for a while," he explained. "But I'm not that person anymore."

"So who are you?" I asked, twisting the tassels on the throw blanket under me into braids so that I didn't have to look at him. This was the most open and vulnerable conversation we'd had in what felt like years and I was terrified of moving too suddenly and breaking everything apart.

"I'm a guy who's just trying to do something nice for his family because it feels like everything's gone to shit?" he said and I looked up at that to see a soft smile on his face, one I didn't see very much anymore.

"Wanna help me?" he asked and I nodded.

"Good," he said, getting up with a heavy sigh. "I need money."

"Oh, so *that's* what this was all about," I said, rolling my eyes and feeling back on more certain territory. "And we almost just had a nice moment."

"We *did* have a nice moment, Rosie," he said, smiling. "So don't ruin it."

"How much?" I asked lightly.

"Not sure yet," he said. "I'm still looking up RV rental prices."

"Ooh, are we traveling in style?" I asked.

"I think a true road trip could be nice." He nodded, looking pleased with himself. "Just start saving."

I'm going to. I'm going to pick up more shifts and look up fun places to go and spend the summer with my family, doing my absolute best to be the person we all wish I could be. Second acts, right?

April 10th, 2017

Dear Mark,

You're never going to get this letter. You're never going to get any of the letters I've written to you. I guess I could mail them, when I'm somewhere far, far away, but I don't think . . . I don't think that would be fair.

I'm trying to learn. To be better, the way you wanted me to be. The way that so many people have wanted me to be.

I talked to Sam earlier. Not how I expected my day to go.

I wanted to come back. To see you again. Sam said that you were having a hard time and before I knew what I was doing, I was getting into my car and driving east. That has to mean something, right? That I wanted to come back? But I know you don't want me there. So I'm just sitting in my car, writing this letter that you'll never see. I don't even have most of the other letters anymore. The AM kept them, the ones that I wrote when I was there.

You know what Sam said to me on the phone today? Oh man, you would be so pissed at her. She called me worried about you. Wanting to know how it worked when you took over my power, like I had any fucking idea at all. She said she wants to "protect" you. I wish she could, but I don't think your girl there has that within her powers. Your sister couldn't, I couldn't, why would Sam be able to?

But that's not the fucking hilarious part, though her calling me behind your back to try and dig up dirt on you definitely gave me a little rush. I don't want bad things for you, Mark, but god, I hope that blows up in her face. I hope you see that she's not perfect either, that maybe no one is perfect and we should all just cut one another some slack.

Anyway, the crazy thing Sam said was, well, she said:

"We're in love with the same man. I think that's enough in common without calling us friends."

I bet you'd like to know what I said in response, huh? I don't know, maybe you wouldn't care. Maybe my answer doesn't make a difference to you. It doesn't matter anyway. I didn't have a response for her.

I've spent a lot of the past month wondering if leaving really was *the right thing to do. I wanted to respect your wishes, wanted to give you space, wanted to . . . I don't know, punish myself, I guess. I'm really lost, man. Maybe that's why Rose and I clicked so fast. Maybe that's why you and I clicked so fast. I mean, it's different, obviously. ~~The way I feel about you is something~~ I didn't hurt Rose as much as I hurt you.*

We're all just going to keep hurting one another, aren't we? Sam is gonna hurt you, and Rose is gonna hurt her family, and I'm gonna blow into some other town and break everything like I always do. I'm just a storm moving from coast to coast and I don't know when I'm gonna run out of steam.

Something has to break the cycle.

APRIL 11TH, 2017

BOY has it been a weird twenty-four hours.

First off, inviting Emily to do trivia night turned out to be a good instinct, even if it didn't turn out exactly like I'd been hoping. Things had been going well—I bought her a hot chocolate and the theme of the trivia tonight was nineteenth-century literature and she LOVES that stuff—but then an enormous wrench got thrown into our evening and now I'm worried that any potential good favor I'd built back up has been totally shattered.

It all started yesterday morning when Mark texted me to tell me that he'd told Sam about my dreamdiving excursion at movie night. He had initially promised that he would keep it to himself but . . . I guess that didn't last. I can't begrudge him that. It was *his* head I was invading, his and everyone else's, and he's allowed to be pissed about that for as long as he wants. He's allowed to tell anyone he'd like to, especially the other people who were there. I just wish I had been the one to tell Sam. It makes me feel like a terrible person that she had to hear it secondhand. At least Mark has promised not to tell Caleb and Adam. Then again, he made that promise while extremely drunk and Sam could tell them now, so who knows?

Yep! That's where my evening went!! With a random Atypical crashing my date with the girl who broke my heart and proceeding to get drunk while we sipped on our hot chocolate! Yikes!

Honestly, the whole thing just made me really sad. Emily too—once I explained everything to her, after we'd poured Mark onto my living room couch (oh yeah, I'll get to that), she looked totally sick at everything that had happened to him.

"They just imprisoned him for years for no reason?" she hissed as we stood in the kitchen, trying to avoid waking up Mark or my family who were all asleep upstairs.

"Yeah," I whispered. "I guess that's happened to a lot of Atypicals. I mean, it makes sense . . . that's what always happens in stories about people with supernatural abilities, right? They get kidnapped and experimented on."

"But that's *fiction*," she said. "Real life shouldn't be like that."

I just nodded, unable to disagree, but also unable to provide any evidence for life *not* being like that. I'll never understand how people don't instantly get why I like to spend so much time in the dreamworld.

"Rose," she whispered, "are you safe?"

"Yeah." I nodded again. "Yeah, I'm— My whole family has been going to the AM for years and, they're not good, obviously, but they're also . . ."

"They're the only ones who can help your dad," she finished.

"Not that they've been much help with him though," I said. "They just treat it like he was a normal human with Alzheimer's. Like there's nothing they can do."

"And you don't think that's true?" she asked. I peered at her through the darkness, her soft brown skin a beautiful beacon of warmth in the otherwise cold kitchen. She was looking at me like she used to—like she *cared*.

"I don't know what to think," I whispered. She reached across the kitchen table to grab my hand and I felt more tethered to the world than I had since last summer.

I didn't sleep at all the whole night. I was too scared to. Even though I've barely dived in the past few weeks, I was terrified that having Mark in the house would send me careening into his head or him into mine. So I'm now running on thirty-six hours of no sleep. Emily stayed up with me for a long time, before going back to her dorm, and I think we ended up in a good place. I actually feel . . . hopeful.

But the real reason I don't feel like sleeping is because of the conversation I just had with Mark while I made him eggs and bacon. There was plenty of awkwardness when he rolled off the couch and into the kitchen, *very* hungover and confused about where he was, but I poured him a cup of coffee in the biggest mug we owned and eventually we pushed through the uncomfortable small talk and apologies and I got to the bottom of why, exactly, Mark thought it had been a good idea to crash my date, get wasted, and sleep it off on my parents' couch instead of going back to Sam's or Dr. Bright's, both of which were ideas that were shot down immediately last night when Emily and I offered to bring him home.

"Ughhhhh," he groaned, putting his face flat on the kitchen counter. "I *didn't* think it was a good idea. I didn't think at all."

"Yeah, that was pretty obvious," I said, feeling a little smug. This whole catastrophe made me feel like Mark and I are probably on even footing now. Taking care of him and letting him stay the night feels like as good of an apology for going into his dreams as any. Thankfully, he agreed.

"You really didn't need to help me," he said after he'd had some eggs in him. "Especially after the way I treated you . . ."

"I get it," I said, shoveling eggs into my own mouth. "I would have reacted the exact same way, I think."

"Still, it's not cool. I remember when my ability first started—I mean, hell, even now, I make mistakes," he sighed. "*Plenty* of mistakes. And you're so young, your ability is still so new to you . . . I shouldn't have gotten so mad at you."

"It's really okay, Mark," I said. "I was an asshole. I knew what I was doing."

"Yeah, but I wasn't just being a dick to you because of the dream-diving thing," Mark grumbled.

"What do you mean?" I asked.

"It's Damien," he said. "I didn't trust that . . . that he didn't get to you somehow. That you weren't . . ."

"That I wasn't like him?" I guessed and Mark nodded.

"I don't know how much he told you about what happened between us but it was . . . I don't know." He sighed again. "I'm still messed up over it I think. And it was hard to trust someone who was friends with him."

"I get it." I nodded and took a bite out of a piece of bacon. "If it makes you feel any better, I also thought he was someone I could trust. I . . ."

I looked at Mark, wondering how honest I could be. His face had the pallor of the very hungover but was open and inviting so I took a dive and admitted something I hadn't before.

"I liked him," I said simply. It shouldn't have been such a big confession, but it was, and I knew Mark would understand that. "I really liked him."

He nodded. "Yeah . . . yeah, I really liked him too."

That seemed to be the big elephant in the room, because from there we were able to talk openly in a way we hadn't up to that point, and I finally was able to ask him about the AM. I didn't probe him about his time there specifically—I might be a curious person to a fault sometimes, but even I know when something is *private*-private—but I did ask him what he thought about the likelihood that the AM was hiding something that could help my dad.

"I mean, the AM could be hiding anything," he said. "But I don't know what motivation they'd have to keep a cure to dementia to themselves. That's something they could apply to humans too—I'm sure something like that would increase their government contracts tenfold."

"But what if my dad *is* the experiment?" I asked. "I mean, he was totally fine until September and then all of a sudden . . . he's sick? I know he goes to the AM for his checkups, so—"

"Look, I know that you want an easy fix for your family, I get that," he said. "And *trust* me, I'm the last person to defend the AM, but I'm not sure even they would do something like that."

"What about ability suppression?" I asked. "My dad is a telekinetic, his ability is based in the brain—what if that's somehow causing the disease? That's happened before, right? Someone's ability interacting with the rest of their biology in a destructive way?"

"I mean, yeah, I guess so . . ." He looked thoughtful for a moment. "I have heard about ability-specific suppressants being developed, but those are pretty controversial. The AM wants Atypicals who are powerful, not ones who can't use their powers, and most Atypicals don't like the idea of their abilities being taken away from them. They're a part of us."

"But you think the AM is developing it anyway?" I asked.

"I think they would be stupid not to," he said darkly.

We didn't have a chance to talk about it more because that was when my parents came in, completely baffled to see a total stranger eating breakfast at their kitchen counter at eight in the morning. But that's enough for me to go on—if the AM is developing something that could stop a power long enough to reverse or slow the effects of an illness, then I need to convince my dad to go back.

APRIL 13TH, 2017

When I walked into the kitchen, tea was making itself.

For a brief moment, I just sort of thought I'd wandered into a dream for the first time in weeks, despite the fact that I didn't remember ever falling asleep.

But it was just my dad was using his telekinesis to make breakfast.

"Someone's feeling good," I said, going for chipper. My dad turned around and shot me an unconvincing smile.

"Is that someone you?" he asked as a plate of muffins floated toward me.

"Did you go to the bakery today?" I asked, grabbing a muffin off the plate and watching it float back to place itself on the table in front of where my dad was sitting.

"Yep," he said.

It was really odd—the whole kitchen was bustling around him, buzzing with activity, like it was a normal morning from a year ago, but my dad seemed sullen. I sat down across from him, putting down my uneaten muffin.

"Dad, are you okay?" I asked.

"Have you been dreamdiving, Rose?" he asked bluntly. I blinked, trying to read in his face why he was asking, what I could have possibly done to make him want to ask.

The truth is, I hadn't. I told him as much. That I hadn't dived since Sam's house (though I didn't tell him the details of that particular evening), that I felt trapped in my own head.

"I miss it," I admitted.

"Why do you like it so much, Rose?" he asked, so soft and genuinely curious and fully focused on me and I wanted to cry.

"None of you have ever asked me that," I whispered. He didn't have anything to say to that, but I saw his hands tighten around the mug.

"It . . ." I started, trying to figure out how I could possibly articulate what it's like to be in a world in which anything and everything is possible and there are no consequences.

"It makes sense," I found myself saying.

"I know that sounds backward," I continued, "but it's true. There's something about the dreamworld that's . . . clear. Uncomplicated. Even though it's the most unpredictable place I've ever been, there's a comfort in it. A safety. It helps me understand you all better."

"What do you mean?" he asked.

"The dreams you all have, they're . . . I don't know, they're perfect distillations of who you are. You dream about big, broad canyons, so much that I've started to dream about them too. Mom always dreams about forests and oceans, and Aaron . . . Aaron dreams about real life in a way that feels even realer than *actual* life. Does that make sense?"

"I'm not sure," he said, huffing a laugh. "You know, your mom and I went to the Grand Canyon right before we had Aaron. I wonder if that's why I dream about it so much."

"It's a place that you and Aaron like a lot." I nodded.

"You know, Rose," he said, leaning forward a bit to catch my eyes, "we're *here*. We're not in there, in that dreamworld—"

"Aaron is," I said. "Not always, but I can talk to him in there. We can . . . share it, in a weird way."

"And when was the last time you talked to him? In the dreamworld?"

"Okay, yeah, I haven't lately," I admitted. "But I haven't been dreamdiving at *all* lately."

"We just miss you, Rose," he said, sounding sad. "I know you've got work and Emily and your friends, but even when you're here, you're . . . you're somewhere far away."

"I'm sorry," I whispered. "I'll do better, I promise."

He patted my hand, and I couldn't tell if it was a pat of appreciation, that he believed I would do better, or if it was a pat of consolation, knowing that I would try and try and continue to fail. But I needed him to understand. I needed him to understand that I wasn't distracted by the thought of the dreamworld, I was distracted by the thought of him getting better.

"Dad," I said after a moment, "can I ask you a question?"

"Of course, Rose."

"You're using your telekinesis today," I pointed out. "You haven't been using it very much but today . . ."

"It's hard to access sometimes," he said, confirming what I'd been thinking for months with a single shrug. "I think the . . . well, you know . . ."

I nodded.

"I think it might be messing with more than just my memory," he said. "But today, I woke up feeling okay. So I thought I'd take things out for a spin." He gave me a real smile then, looking out at the kitchen, which was now dutifully cleaning itself. I never understood how he was able to do that—to keep his focus so perfect that he could be controlling so many objects at once, making them move just so, all in different ways, all at the same time. What has that kind of effort done to him over the years?

"Would you give it up?" I asked. "The telekinesis, I mean. If it helped you?"

"What?" He looked at me with confused surprise.

"It's just . . . I've heard some stuff," I explained. "About how abilities can . . . well, they can hurt us sometimes. Atypicals, I mean."

"Our abilities are a fundamental part of our biology, Rose," he said calmly.

"I know that," I said. "But a lot of people—normal humans—have fundamental parts of their biology that hurt them, or make it hard to live—"

"What are you talking about?"

"Has the AM thought about how your power interacts with this disease?" I asked. "I mean, *really* thought about it, examined every single possibility?"

"Of course," he said. "Rose, they're doing everything they—"

And that was when he collapsed.

Without warning, my dad slid out of his chair and onto the floor, where he started to seize. I jumped up immediately, kneeling down next to him, yelling out for my mom, for Aaron, in a complete panic. What happened from there is a complete blur—they both came rushing down the stairs (thank GOD they were home), my mom calling the emergency number, Aaron moving our dad's body away from any furniture that could hurt him, while my shaking hands hovered above him, wondering how and if I could possibly help.

We're sitting in the AM now, waiting for them to finish running tests. I don't know how long we'll be here—how long *he'll* be here—or what any of this means. But whatever hope Mark might have given me the other day has been effectively soured by watching half a dozen doctors gather around my dad's pale form as he lay unconscious, unreachable, even to me.

IV

CANYON

05-10-2017, morningwaffles, text post

Hi, everyone. I'm sorry for being so absentee the past few weeks. Things have been . . . intense. But I'm done with my finals for the semester, I don't start my summer internship for another two weeks, so I thought I'd catch up on things here. And catch *you* up on what's been going on.

I'm still going to be posting Stucky fic from time to time, though now that *somewhere a place for us* is done, I might stick to drabbles. I even have some *super* earnest poetry from sophomore year of high school that I wrote about Destiel that I'm far enough away from now to find vaguely amusing and not just bone-chillingly mortifying. But it might be a while until I really dig into another chunky, multi-chapter fic.

Without going into too much detail, the past few months have been really tough. Things with my girlfriend got kind of intense and dramatic and then stuff with her family got intense and dramatic and I really want to be there for her right now. We have a lot of our own stuff to work through, and I'm not sure exactly where we're going to end up, but she's going through something that she shouldn't have to go through alone.

Some of you have been in my in-box wondering if my big blowout post about *somewhere a place for us* from a few months ago was about something more than just fic. Guess what? Y'all are right! It was. Turns out, Daisy had some pretty big secrets that she'd been keeping from me and I kind of let it bleed into my writing. There was . . . a lot I needed to process, and *no* I will not be talking about it here so don't even ask. It was such a huge, monumental, life-changing kind of thing that we actually broke up for a little bit. Or, I don't know, I think we're still broken up? It's really hard to say. I saw her two weeks ago and I'm seeing her again before my internship starts so . . . we'll see.

Anyway, thanks for all of you who have been rooting for us. It's so weird having so many strangers on the internet invested in my relationship—good weird! But weird. This community—the *whole* MCU community, not even just the people who I interact with on here—has been so important to me. Not just during this bonkers, wacky, upside-down year, but through the past eight years of my life. I've grown up with you guys and I can't wait to see what's next.

Wow, does it sound like I'm giving my Oscar speech or something? Or my own eulogy? Here's the tldr: you guys are the best. And I want to keep leaning on this community for everything in my life, but I've realized there are just some things that are best kept offline, and that includes my relationship with Daisy. Even though I've been using a fake name with her and, hello, none of you know who I am anyway, I've thought a lot about privacy and boundaries these past few months and . . . well, it's important to be responsible with other people's stories.

I'm here to tell my own stories, in my own way, on my own terms.

And I've got a lot to say.

MAY 19TH, 2017

It felt like time had been rewound, to two months ago, sitting in this same booth, across from Damien, watching him dump sugar packet after sugar packet into terrible, burnt diner coffee.

"What are you doing back here?" I asked, folding my arms in front of me in my best attempt to seem intimidating. I don't think it had the desired effect because he just smirked, his cheeks rising unevenly. At least they looked a little fuller than the last time I'd seen him, like he was actually eating for once.

"Believe it or not, I don't actually let a bunch of people who hate me dictate where I do or do not go," he said.

"Really? Because that's pretty much the opposite of what you said last time we were here," I said. "You seemed *very* adamant about doing what other people were telling you to do, even if it screwed over other people."

"Are you . . . mad at me?" he asked, having the gall to sound genuinely surprised.

"You've been gone for two months, Damien," I snapped. "A *lot* has happened."

"Yeah, no kidding." He snorted. "I got all the way to Wyoming."

"So why come back?" I asked again.

"I have some lingering business to attend to," he said.

"With Mark?" I asked, aiming to hit him where it hurt.

"No," Damien said adamantly. "None of that gang knows that I'm here and I'd like to keep it that way."

"Why?" I asked.

"Because I fucked up bad with them," Damien said simply. "I don't particularly want to repeat that pattern."

"Yeah, well, if it makes you feel better, I fucked up bad with them too," I said, ripping open a sugar packet. I didn't like sugar in my coffee but I wasn't sure how else to drink diner coffee that had been sitting around since the lunch rush when it was now an hour to closing.

"What, you try to kidnap one of them?" he asked dryly. "You *actually* kidnap another one?"

"No . . . ?" I said, unable to tell if he was joking or actually asking if I'd made the same mistakes he did.

"Then you didn't fuck up as badly as me," he said, mock-soothing.

"What'd you do?" he asked after a moment, a rapid series of blinks giving away how deeply interested he really was in the answer.

"I went for a dive," I said. "Several, actually."

"Without permission, I'm assuming?" he guessed. I nodded. "*Why*? Why would you even want to see their dreams?"

"I wanted to see who they really were," I explained. "After everything they told me about you . . . I don't know, even though you didn't deny any of it, it just felt like they were hiding something."

"You thought they were lying?" he laughed. "Those Eagle Scouts?"

"They lie a *lot* to each other," I said and I saw his eyes flash in glee for a second. "Or, at least, they hide things. Tell each other half-truths. I wasn't sure what to believe."

"That must get confusing," he said, before taking a sip of his coffee and wincing at how hot it was.

"What do you mean?"

"We lie to ourselves so much in dreams," he went on. "Our brains tell us stories about ourselves that aren't true; make monsters out of even the smallest fears. But that's half your reality. More than half sometimes. Where does the real reality begin and the animated fear end?"

"That's . . . surprisingly insightful, Damien," I said.

"I'm not as heartless as everyone thinks I am." He smiled wolfishly. Someone had clearly regained their confidence and I felt like I was looking into a kaleidoscope and seeing the person Damien was when he had his ability. I wasn't sure I liked this version as much as the broken man I'd met in January, the man who really understood what it was like to have a monster follow you out from inside your head.

"Did you get your ability back?" I asked and he blinked in surprise.

"What, no, why would you think that?" He sounded panicked.

"You just seem . . . different."

But I believed him, despite all my best instincts. Because there he was, sitting across from me after texting me out of the blue and asking to meet at the diner that somehow felt like ours despite the fact that we'd only been there once, understanding me better and faster than anyone I'd ever known.

I wanted to tell him everything—that I'd spent a terrifying four days pacing the hallways of the AM, not even caring that I maybe was walking above a basement full of people held against their will because all that mattered was that the AM was taking care of my dad. I wanted to tell him that those four days were for nothing; that we were sent home with a new medication, one to help him manage the seizures but do nothing else, and just told to wait and keep an eye on him, not leave him alone in his work shed around all those sharp objects or let him operate heavy machinery in case he had another seizure. That that was likely, that the seizures might happen more frequently, but it was just a symptom of the disease, that it didn't *necessarily* mean things were getting worse. That I'd lost all hope that I was going to have my dad at my eventual culinary school graduation. At my future wedding.

Instead, I found myself asking the question that had been begging to be asked since I'd first been in Damien's dreams, seen all those bits and pieces of his soul. The question I knew the answer to, but not the full truth of.

"You were in love with them, weren't you?"

"Who?" Damien's eyes were wide with fear—somehow deeper and more real than the fear in him when he talked about the AM.

"Mark."

"What?" His eyes widened impossibly farther.

"And Sam?"

"*What?*" Something in his fear broke and he shuddered. "God, no. Sam? No. Ugh," he added for good measure, shaking his head back and forth like he was trying to shake water out of his ears.

"But Mark . . . ?" I ventured.

"What makes you so sure?" He crossed his arms, narrowing his eyes at me. He also wasn't very good at being visually intimidating and it made me feel a little better.

"What do you think?" I said, fixing him with a blank stare. He blushed.

"Yeah, okay," he conceded. "Fair enough."

He shifted in his seat.

"It helped, you know," he mumbled. "What you did. It helped."

"Oh." I breathed, and then my face broke out into a smile. "I'm glad."

"What did you mean by 'them'?" he asked.

"There was something else I saw," I said. "A woman. Two women. Warm smile . . . flowers."

"Indah." He sighed, his eyes closing like he could smell the flowers suddenly. That was a look of love if I'd ever seen one.

"And the other woman . . ." I tried to remember the flashes of feeling from those early dreams. "Bright and blue . . ."

"Neon," he whispered, his voice growing hoarse.

"Ex-girlfriends?" I asked.

"Ex-somethings," he said annoyingly.

"Like Mark?"

"Yeah," he said after a moment, like admitting that out loud, even in a single word, was difficult.

"So you *were* in love with them?" I pushed.

Seeing his expression, like he was trying to put something indescribable into words, like he was in pain and always had been, I rephrased.

"You *are* in love with them?"

"No," he said, somewhat automatically. I raised an eyebrow.

"I don't know." He breathed. "Indah and Neon . . . I haven't seen them in ten years. They wouldn't even remember me."

"I'm sure they would," I said, trying to comfort him.

"Trust me, they wouldn't," he said darkly before exhaling loudly again.

"I guess . . . I don't really know what being in love means," he said. "But I've felt things for people . . . Indah and Neon and Mark . . . it's different from how I feel about other people. Even people like you."

"People like me?"

"Yeah," he said, shrugging one shoulder. "People that I like."

I found myself oddly flattered at that, especially when our eyes met and Damien gave me the tiniest smile, one that threw me for a complete loop for a moment before I realized that it was because I'd never seen a true, genuine smile from him.

"So what you're saying is you're not in love with me?" I said, deadpan, trying to cut the tension but unable to keep myself from smiling back.

"Don't be creepy, Dorothy." He chuckled, and his smile grew. I laughed exhaustedly and put my elbows on the table, leaning forward into his space.

"Damien, *why* are you back here?" I groaned. "Just tell me whatever it is you want to tell me and then we can be out of each other's lives for good." I had meant it as a joke, but it vanished Damien's smile immediately and I wanted to take it back.

"Is that what you want?" he asked. "Because I wasn't even planning on calling you when I first got back but then—"

"Wait, how long have you been back?" I asked.

"A month."

"A *month*?" I gaped. "What—why—what's going on?"

"I was getting to that," he said, lowering his voice like he was trying to use it to calm me down, which I found VERY annoying. "I came back because . . ."

He blew out a big breath—I had kind of missed his drama if I'm honest—and leaned back in the booth.

"I need some things from the AM," he said after a moment and I instantly snapped.

"No, no way—" I shook my head. "That's what you were trying to trick me into doing the very first time we met and I'm not having it—"

"I'm not asking you to go back into a program or make an appointment or anything," he said.

"What *are* you asking?"

"To break in with me."

I sat, shock-still for a second before a hollow laugh burst out of me.

"Oh, so just the *way* more illegal version of the already very sketchy thing you wanted me to do—"

"There's—" he started, putting up his hands to calm me down, before lowering his voice. "There's a new doc who just arrived in town."

"Okay . . ."

"Dr. Sharpe," he said, letting the name hang in the air.

"Is that supposed to mean something to me, or . . . ?"

"Not necessarily," he said. "But it means something to me."

That was when Damien explained the whole truth. The *real* truth this time. And FUCK I was so goddamned furious at first I wanted to stab him with a diner spoon.

"Wait . . . so you're telling me that your friend, Blaze, the pyrokinetic who got experimented on and had his power start to burn him alive from the inside out—that was a real story? That *really* happened?"

"Yes." He nodded and at least had the good sense to look sheepish about it.

"So you lied to me—"

"I didn't lie—"

"No, you lied to me about lying, which is somehow even more messed up—"

"I wanted to cut you out, Rose," he said, leaning forward, almost like he wanted to grab my hands. "I needed you to hate me. I just wanted you to have a good normal life and there was no way you were gonna have that if we were friends."

"Nice to see you've given up on that hope for me completely," I grumbled.

"You're missing the point of what I'm trying to tell you, Rose," he said. "You can yell at me all you want later—"

"Oh, I will—"

"But my friend Blaze *is* real, and he has been sick for the past ten years and I—after I got out of the AM, I got curious. About what happened to him. So I tracked him down. And like I told you, he's been in a facility out in LA but he was just brought *here*. To Boston. The lead doctor on his case—"

"Dr. Sharpe, I'm assuming?"

"See, I knew it was good to have you around." He smiled. "You're . . . *sharp*."

"Wow," I said dryly.

"I couldn't help it."

"Get to the point." I waved my hand in a "hurry up" gesture.

"She's working on a cure for Blaze," he said. "Something to suppress his power, make him able to live his life without constantly lighting himself on fire. I promise you: this is *real*."

I started to shake, and not just because the diner coffee may as well have been jet fuel. Damien told me all the details—Dr. Sharpe had been working on the serum in LA but had come to work at the AM in Boston because they could offer her more resources. And she was *close.* Close to making something that could turn off abilities in Atypicals who were hurt by their powers.

"But there's a catch," Damien said and I didn't even have the wherewithal to roll my eyes at this expected turn of events. There was always a catch with Damien but this was a chance—a *real* chance.

"I want to break Blaze out at the same time," he said. "And everyone else down in that basement. No one should be stuck down there."

He leaned closer, lowered his voice to a whisper.

"You in?"

I'm on the bus home now, and my mind is racing. I know it's a long shot, I know that this Dr. Sharpe might not have a cure, but, at the very least, I can help Damien's friend, and stop the AM from experimenting on him anymore. For once in my life, I can do something *right.*

LATER

I knew it. I KNEW IT. I knew that Aaron has been reading my thoughts ever since I came back from the AM the last time, because he was always a little too present whenever I was about to go off and do something stupid, like meet with Damien, and now it's confirmed.

I had been home all of two minutes when Aaron came storming into my room, slamming the door behind him, and launching into an argument like we'd already been having it.

"Are you serious?" Aaron asked, looming over me in his most imposing big brother stance. "Like, *really,* Rosie?"

"What? Aaron, what the hell—"

"Damien!" he snapped. "You said you were working the late shift—"

"I *was*—"

"And decided you'd cap it off with a midnight rendezvous with your favorite creep? I thought that guy was out of your life for good!"

"He was," I said. "He *is* but it's just—he knows a lot of stuff that we don't know, has had a lot more experience than us with Atypical illnesses and the AM and just everything weird that comes with being Atypical and I'm not going to ignore that stuff just because it's coming from an inconvenient source."

"An 'inconvenient source'?" he scoffed. "Come on, Rosie, you're smarter than this—"

"Don't patronize me—"

"He's a kidnapper and a liar by his own admission and now he wants you to break into a government facility with him?"

"Wow, so have you just given up the pretense of not listening in on my thoughts entirely?" I snapped.

"Rose, I'm *worried* about you—"

"No, stop!" I shouted. "Just stop!"

To his credit, he did. We stood there, in my bedroom, both panting with anger and scowling at each other.

"You don't get to just decide when you want to be an older brother," I growled. "You can't just do it whenever it's convenient for you."

"And you can't just decide what you believe is moral or immoral based on how much it's going to serve you," he snapped back.

"Get out." I stomped to my door and wrenched it open, not looking at Aaron. "Get. Out."

Even after I slammed the door on Aaron's exiting back, I willed myself not to think about anything related to Damien. It's only now, now that I can feel the edges of Aaron's unconscious sleep state, that I feel comfortable writing the rest of it down.

community/TheUnusuals post by n/thatsahumanperson

I just got into the worst kind of knock-down, drag-out fight with my sister. We've been swinging between approaching something like real, genuine connection and absolutely at each other's throats for the past month, maybe longer. Ever since she came back from That Place a second time . . . things were so bad in the fall when she was sleeping all the time, and it felt like I was dealing with my dad being sick all on my own, but now that she's doing better with the dreamdiving and is actually spending more time awake, it's somehow worse. It's like she's replaced her desire to stay in the dreamworld all the time with trying to solve some weird mystery with That Place that has nothing to do with her. She now has all of these Unusual friends—or, I don't know that she would even call them friends—and thinks that there's some kind of big answer to my dad's illness being kept from us and I'm *really* worried about her.

Not to mention, that guy that was in her life earlier this year—the one who turned out to be bad news *exactly* like I expected—is back in town and back in her life. That's part of what we were fighting about. I don't think she should be spending time with him, but she was all, "it'll be fine, he has an idea that could really help Dad," which I find incredibly suspicious.

I know this goes against a whole slew of sub rules, but if anyone has any *real,* concrete proof that That Place is doing something illegal, please PM me.

onmyown

I know this is going to make me sound like Chuck, but I *really* don't think this is a good idea. There's a reason that we don't mention That Place by name, that we don't use the real word for what we are on this sub. There are a lot of powerful people out there who would not want you digging up this information.

thatsahumanperson

I just want to keep my sister safe, man.

chuckxavier

Then you should try to stop her from whatever you think she's going to do.

franklinsteinsmonster
they haven't posted yet but I bet n/lokilover would have some stuff!

theneonthorn
they've been banned. turns out they weren't actually Unusual themselves—not the first creepy person to try to invade our space and I'm certain they won't be the last.

theneonthorn
you all know I have a personal no PM rule for myself, but I'll just say: every whisper you've heard about That Place is true.

tacotacotaco
I'm going to message you—I have some *positive* insight, actually, which I know puts me in the minority.

thatsahumanperson
I'll take it.

MAY 28TH, 2017

My hands are shaking as I write this. I can't believe I just did something so crazy, so reckless. *In real life.*

It wasn't a dream. It *feels* like a dream, like something I conjured out of thin air, but every inch of it was real. I'm still processing it, still trying to understand everything that happened, want to write it down so that I remember every moment, not because it was good, because it wasn't, but because it was important. I know something changed inside of me tonight, permanently, and that's worth making permanent note of.

It all started with a text from Damien.

> I'm going back there tonight. Dr. Sharpe has set up her lab and it'll just be a skeleton crew with the long weekend.

I wanted to pretend I didn't know what he was talking about, wanted to pretend that I was going to listen to Aaron and not do something incredibly stupid, that I wasn't still thinking about the idea of some magical cure being in the halls of the AM but I just couldn't.

So I went. And it *was* incredibly stupid.

I'm not even sure I could write down exactly what happened—or if it would be smart to. I mean . . . I just committed a crime. I'm not even sure how. Damien was confident, saying he'd done this before, but that had been with his ability. I didn't know *how* he planned to break in when he couldn't get everything he wanted.

It started with Damien picking me up outside our diner in a car that did not at all reflect his personality (a boring, tan sedan), parking it in the middle of nowhere, walking a mile to the facility, and then sneaking down to a service entrance Damien was sure would be easy to break into.

"This is your master plan?" I hissed. "Just . . . picking a lock?"

"This exit was totally clear when I broke Mark out. And that was a holiday weekend too, so it's the same guard rotation."

I tried not to pass out from nerves as Damien struggled to pick the lock.

"Haven't you done this before?"

"Not since I was thirteen," he muttered and then, to my enormous surprise, the door actually opened. We were in.

Walking around it in the middle of the night, with most of the personnel gone, felt like walking inside of a dream. I trailed behind Damien who, despite having spent less time conscious and wandering the halls of the AM than me, seemed to know it like the back of his hand. I realized that it's probably because he had studied the blueprints when he broke Mark out—he had done this before. But he had had his power then, and had gotten in and out with very little trouble.

This time it wasn't so simple.

We found Dr. Sharpe's office and spent fifteen frantic minutes rifling through her cabinets until we found what we needed—her notes on the serum. That had been the plan: we would take the notes, break out the Atypicals who were trapped, and then figure out how to get the serum to someone who could make a medicine to help both my dad and Blaze. The AM had backups to be sure, would certainly make their own serum and use it to help people, but we couldn't trust that they would do it. We had to take matters into our own hands.

So. Goddamn. Stupid.

As we were on our way out of the lab, the file clutched in my hand, still unopened—I was too terrified to look, even though I knew I might not understand it, I just feared opening that folder and seeing big letters saying THERE'S NO WAY TO HELP HIM, GIVE UP ALL HOPE. So I just clutched it in my hands as we ran as silently as possible down the hall, making our way down to the basement.

But then, we turned a corner, and Owen was suddenly ten feet in front of us. Some kind of veteran-break-in instinct kicked in for Damien and he immediately disappeared into some shadows while I stood frozen, a complete deer in the headlights.

Owen stopped in his tracks, a deer in the headlights all his own.

". . . Rose?"

"Owen!" I yelped, wondering if I could play this off somehow. "Agent—Agent Green, I mean."

"Director Green, actually," he mumbled. "What . . . what are you doing here?"

"*Director?*" Damien's voice hissed from the shadows and I tried not to react, instead repeating his question out loud as cover.

"Yes, it's . . . it's very recent," Owen said absentmindedly as he took a hesitant step toward me, like he was still trying to figure out if this was all a dream. I could relate.

"Rose . . ." he said. "You're not supposed to be here."

"I—I'm back," I said. "For another round of the program. And I think I must have started sleepwalking when I'm dreamdiving because I don't know how I got out here."

I tried to laugh it off, but Owen took another step closer to me, peering owlishly through his wire-framed glasses at me. My laugh wilted and shriveled under the weight of his disappointment.

"No, no, you're not," he said. "First of all, I'd know. I actually care about your progress, Rose."

"Owen—"

"And second of all, we don't have any programs running right now," he continued. "We're overhauling the organization, which has meant limiting the long-term services we offer for a while. Which brings me, again, to my question: what. are. you. doing. here."

"I . . ." I floundered, trying to come up with a plausible excuse for why I would be here, in the middle of the night, if I wasn't doing a program, and then Owen's eyes went down to the folder I was still holding.

"You're not here alone, are you?" he asked, though it didn't sound like a question.

"I just . . . I wanted some answers," I said, clutching the file tighter. "And what you're doing here, it's—it's not okay."

"I know." He sighed. I hadn't really expected the moral high ground to work, but it turned out that Owen Green is exactly the person I thought he was. He's pretty much the only one.

"But that still doesn't explain what you're doing here," he said.

"All those people you have in the basement," I said, digging into the righteous argument, "that's not okay. They deserve to be set free."

"I agree. And we're going to do that. But we have to do it *carefully.*"

"What do you mean 'we'?" I asked. "When—how—you're the *director* now? What happened to Wadsworth?"

"A lot has changed in the past month, Rose," he said. "Joan and

I—Dr. Bright—we've been working to stop what's been going on here, to take over, fix things, and we finally did it."

I just blinked, frozen in place, trying to process what he was telling me.

"We're going to make this place better, Rose," Owen went on, the belief shining out of his mouth so strongly for a moment I thought I could see it, that somehow I was in a dream.

"*How?*" I asked. "How could any place that experiments on people like this be a good thing?"

"It can't," he said simply. "That's why we're going to stop. Come back in a year—six months, even—and this tier will be gone. All these people will be safe and we'll be starting something new here."

"At least let us take Blaze," I pleaded. "I want to trust you, really I do, but he's Damien's friend—"

"Who's Blaze?" Owen asked, before doing a double take. "Wait, *Damien*—"

"The pyrokinetic," I went on, brushing past the fact that I'd just revealed who I was here with. But I hadn't heard any noise from the shadows behind me at this point, so I barreled forward. "The one who Dr. Sharpe is *experimenting* on."

"Rose, how do you—" He took a step back, genuine surprise on his face. He looked at me for a moment, like he didn't recognize me, before sighing heavily.

"Alex Chen." He took off his glasses and rubbed his eyes. "Dr. Sharpe isn't experimenting on him. I mean, she is—"

I scoffed.

"But she has his full consent," Owen insisted, putting his glasses back on. "Alex is very, very sick and Dr. Sharpe has been helping him."

"So you say—"

"We *all* are helping him. We're building a custom space, just for him, somewhere he can be safe while we figure out how to fix him, how to stop his pain. When he gets here next month, he's going to be coming into a state-of-the-art—"

"Wait, next month?" I asked. "Alex isn't here yet?"

"No." He shook his head, confused. "We don't have a reinforced space for him yet, he'd burn the whole building down."

"But Damien—"

Suddenly an alarm started blaring. We both spun around, looking for the source of the sound, and that was when I realized that Damien was gone. The shadows he had slunk into turned out to lead to an emergency exit stairway and he must have snuck down while Owen and I had been talking.

Owen looked between me and the shadows and he must have realized the same thing and that was when *I* realized he had known Damien was here all along.

"That must be Damien doing something incredibly foolish." He grumbled at the empty doorway before turning back to me. "Listen, if someone else finds you here, I don't know that I'll be able to explain your presence away—"

"I thought you were the director now," I hissed.

"Of this division, I am," he said. "There are still people I have to answer to."

"But Damien—"

"You need to get yourself out of here, let me worry about Damien."

Given that I had just discovered that Damien had lied to me AGAIN and I had fallen for it AGAIN, I barely hesitated to follow Owen's advice.

But just as I had turned on my heel, Owen called out to me.

"Rose!" I turned to look at him. He looked . . . so *sad*.

"That file you're holding . . ." He gestured to it. "It doesn't hold the answers you want. Not yet. We're working on it and, when we have something, I will tell you. We'll try whatever we can to help your father. You have my word."

Another alarm started to sound then, so Owen didn't say anything more, just nodded and waved me away with his hand. I ran.

I ran and ran and ran. I ran down the stairs and through the side exit and across the parking lot and into the woods surrounding the complex. I ran without looking back, in the vague direction of where we'd parked the car, but I had no idea if I was headed the right way. I just kept running.

Eventually I was running out of breath, realizing I was probably lost, and desperate to read the file all at once. I stopped in a clearing and tore it open.

Owen had been right. The notes were filled mostly with things I didn't understand, but Dr. Sharpe's personal notes were clear—she didn't have the cure. I couldn't tell if she was anywhere *close* to having the cure. I threw the file to the ground and wanted to *scream*, was about to let loose, let the AM security come and find me screaming bloody murder in the woods, when I heard a breathless voice say my name.

"Rose—"

I spun around to see Damien coming through the tree line, stopping when he was well inside the clearing, putting his hands on his knees and panting deeply.

"God, I'm out of shape," he mumbled before straightening up. "Christ, I'm glad you're okay—"

"You—" I growled, stepping toward him. "You lied to me! Again!"

I pushed him hard on the shoulders and he stumbled back, making no effort to resist me. It made me want to push him more, but I just paced around the clearing, afraid of what I might do if I let all my rage out at him. The energy in my balled-up fists traveled up my arms and flooded my eyes, transforming my kinetic anger into unwanted tears.

"Did you get the notes?" he asked, seemingly unfazed by my temper.

"Yes, I got the fucking notes," I snapped.

"Well?" he demanded. "What do they say?"

"Who cares, Damien!" I shouted. "You lied to me, tricked me, *again*, Blaze was never there—"

"Oh, come on, Rose, you knew what you were getting into," he said. "You know *everything* about me—"

I scoffed, thinking of his dreams that had felt real and still have no clear explanation, like the ones with dirt and decay and death.

"Okay, maybe not *everything*," he said. "But you had all the important information. You know exactly who I am and what this was. And you had your own reasons for doing it. We didn't need to be totally honest with each other about what those reasons were to work together."

I laughed hollowly, paced back to stand in front of him.

"No, you manipulated me, Damien," I said. "You might not have your ability anymore but you're an expert at this—"

"Fuck you—"

"That's your response to everything, isn't it!" I yelled. "Fuck everyone else because nothing is *ever* your fault." I laughed darkly. "God, I think I understand Mark a lot better now."

"Don't you dare talk about him," Damien snarled, stepping toward me.

"So what *were* your reasons, huh?" I asked. "Because it wasn't to get Blaze, who was *never* there, so what was it?"

"I wanted my own file, okay?" he snapped. "I wanted to know what they'd done to me, if there was any way to reverse it."

"Why not just *say* that?"

"Because you'd never have helped me!" he cried. "If it had just been about me, you would have told me to fuck off."

"You don't know that," I said. "I've been *trying*, Damien. Trying to be your friend, to give you a second chance. I wanted to help you!"

"But you turned on me the moment you found out the truth about me!"

"You pushed me away! Because that's what you do," I said. "No matter how many chances people give you, you just squander them. But it's *never* your fault, right? I try to give you another chance and it's somehow *my* fault for falling for it."

"You're Dorothy, right?" he sneered. "Always heading off to Oz, to the land of Technicolor magic? Well, I'm the tornado and you didn't get down into the basement fast enough this time."

"You might be the tornado, but I'm *not* Dorothy, I was wrong," I snarled. "I'm the—I'm the Cowardly Lion, I always have been and I've just been trying to find a way to be *brave*, to protect the people I love—"

"And you thought breaking into a government institution was the way to do that?" he said. "Don't act like you're so perfect. Just because you're off in your own little world doesn't mean that *you're* not responsible—"

"*I* know that, Damien!" I shouted. "That's what I'm trying to tell you."

Silence settled between us, heavy and sharp, as we stood glowering at each other, gasping for breath.

"Why did you come back, Damien?" I asked wearily. "It wasn't just to get your AM file—it can't have been *that* important."

"It *is* important," he growled. "They had *no* right—no right to hold that information from me, to keep me in the dark."

"I'm not saying they did," I said, trying to keep my head cool. "But is that really all you wanted?"

"What I wanted is *my* business," he grunted.

"Of course it is," I mumbled.

"Just—" He sighed, running his hands through his hair, the bags under his eyes creeping back in from the healthier version of him that I'd seen ten days ago. "Rose, don't be like me."

"What?" I asked, getting whiplash from the hard turn.

"I can't ever come back here, do you realize that?"

"Damien, despite how phenomenally stupid that was, we actually got away with it, Owen isn't—they're not going to come after us—"

"No, not—well, first of all, the AM can *always* come after you. Don't forget that for a second." He moved toward me like I couldn't break him apart with my kneading arm, like he still had the power to influence me. Like he wasn't scared. I didn't flinch and I knew that bothered him and in that moment I think I hated him.

"You have to protect yourself, Rose."

"Really?" I laughed, no joy inside of it. "You're telling me to *protect* myself after you invited me along on some light crime?"

"I didn't force you to be here," he spat, his eyes wild. "You came here all on your own."

"Because I thought it was important!" I shouted. "I thought that what you needed was going to help you, that it was going to help all the Atypicals that you say are locked up in that basement."

"I don't care about them!" he yelled back, but the tears running down his face made me think he was lying.

"How can you not?" I pushed.

"That's not why I wanted to get back in there and don't pretend it's the reason *you* came either," he snarled.

"What do you mean?"

"You wanted *that!*" he shouted, throwing his hand out to gesture at the file on the ground. "To get answers, just like me. To find something that can fix . . . *everything*."

"I'm not going to apologize for doing what I need to for the people I love," I spat, my mouth feeling like it was full of marbles, my knees hurting from running, my eyes stinging with tears.

"And how did that work out for you, huh?" Damien said, stepping toward me, like he believed himself more menacing than he actually was. "Do you feel fulfilled? Are you happy with this whole errand?"

"Why are you saying it like this was *my* idea?" I asked. "Damien, this was entirely *your* plan, I came along to help you—"

"To help yourself, more like."

"Okay, yes, I had my own reasons!" I shouted. "But, *god*, has no one ever done a kind thing for you?"

He opened his mouth, fire in his eyes, ready to rebut.

"That's a rhetorical question," I snapped. "I know the answer."

"Oh, you do?"

"Yes." I nodded. "The answer is yes, people *have* been kind to you."

He clenched his jaw.

"You might not want to admit it," I continued, "but you've had people who *care*. You *have* people who care."

"You?" He scoffed.

"To start."

He didn't seem to have anything to say to that, the wind letting out of his sails. He looked down at his feet, scuffing his shoes along the forest floor before tilting his head back up to look up through the trees to the night sky, squinting hard like he was trying to stop himself from crying.

Even now, going back over the whole thing in my head, I can't explain it, but that set me off. Watching Damien, the most casually cruel person I'd ever met, the only person who has made me feel even a little understood these past six months, this Tin Man who let me into his dreams, trying his best not to feel *anything* just . . . broke me. If he wasn't going to crumble, then I would, for the both of us.

I felt my knees hitting the dirt beneath me, my torso bending forward like I'd been snapped in half, folding in on myself involuntarily, as a sob was *pulled* out of me. Loudly, painfully, viscerally. Without a care of being heard or getting my hands dirty as I sank them into the mud and leaves, clutching at the earth like it was the only thing keeping me tethered to the ground, I cried. I cried in a way I didn't know my body could produce. I never expected to cry like that in my life. In a strange forest with a strange man, my strange self screaming into the ground while my body tried to purge the truth from its own reality.

"Rose . . ."

I heard his voice distantly, saw the shuffle of his feet in my periphery, blurry through my tear-filled eyes. Something in the back of my mind braced for impact, for empty soothing words, a hand on my shoulder. But nothing came. I sobbed and sobbed, the only moving thing in a still world.

When the storm finally subsided, leaving my body nauseated and dizzy with the effort, I wiped my eyes on the backs of my hands, the only clean parts of them, and looked up. Damien was sitting there, a few feet away from me, his arms around his tented knees, looking down into his lap like he was just . . . patiently waiting for me to finish.

I sniffed loudly and his head snapped up. We stared at each other, the tears in my eyes mirrored in his, a fraction of what I'd shed but sharper and shinier.

I sniffed again. I don't think either of us knew how to break the silence.

We sat there, for a long time I think, unmoving, three feet apart but unable to bridge the gap at all. I hated every second of that silence. I didn't want to commiserate anymore, didn't want to wallow in my own misery. It felt . . . well, not good, but like *something* to cry that hard, to let the emotion overtake me, violently pour itself out. An empty, anonymous forest now carries that splatter, but at least it's not inside of me anymore. I let the monster roam free.

"Fucking forests . . ." Damien muttered finally.

"What do you mean?" I asked, my voice a shadow of what it had been when I'd last spoken.

"Just . . . I've never had a good time in one," he said. "Only . . . turning points."

I thought it was odd, that he wasn't commenting on the breakdown I'd just had. He wasn't trying to comfort me or check in with me, but he also wasn't disgusted or afraid. He was just . . . there. I was appreciative of it in the moment, the lack of judgment, the lack of expectation that I would explain what I was feeling, but thinking back on it now . . . I don't know. There's not a wrong way to feel. But it's like something in Damien broke a long time ago and he's never been able to get his insides ticking again.

"What do you mean 'turning points'?" I asked, relieved to be turning the conversation to him and his problems.

"You can't go back, Rose. There's a certain point where you just . . . you can't ever go back. In the span of ten years, I've burned bridges on both coasts and now I—I have nowhere to go."

"There's a lot of country between Boston and LA, Damien."

"Yeah," he said quietly. "Yeah, I guess there is."

A warm breeze moved through the trees, carrying the true smell of a summer night on it, humid and tangy. I closed my eyes and longed to be anywhere else. I could hear Damien's shaky breathing next to me.

"This thing that you have," he whispered, "it will swallow you whole if you let it. *Trust* me."

I looked up at him to see tears rolling down his face.

"I won't let it," I said, not sure if I believed it. He nodded, but I could tell he wasn't sure if he believed it either.

"I'm never going to see you again, am I?" I asked, surprised by how even and calm my voice was.

"Would you want to?" he asked. It wasn't a dig or a passive-aggressive call for help, but one of those rare genuine questions. I decided it deserved a genuine answer.

"I don't know."

He nodded, like I'd just told him something eminently practical, and stood up.

"That's good," he said. "You'll know eventually. It'll wear off."

"What will?" I asked, taking his offered hand, letting him pull me to my feet.

"The doubt. It'll wear off and you'll realize the answer to that question is a very simple no."

"You don't have your ability, Damien," I pointed out. "You never have around me. I'm not being influenced by anything."

He gave a dark, hollow laugh.

"As far as we know," he said. "But maybe it's not my power. Maybe it's just . . . *me*."

"Damien—"

"My name is Robert, actually," he said abruptly. "You can call me Robert. I mean, you can call me whatever you want, it doesn't matter, because as soon as I get in that car, you won't be calling me *anything*."

"What do you *want* to be called?" I asked.

"I don't know." Another honest response. I had just gotten good at reading him, only for him to walk out of my life forever.

May 29th, 2017

Dear Mark,

I went back. To the AM.

I wish I could explain exactly why I did it. I told Rose it was because of Blaze, because I wanted to help her find a cure for her dad. And maybe it was partly because of that—I do want her to be happy, but I knew that Blaze wasn't there yet. I wouldn't have wanted to see him even if he had been. He wasn't there when I erased everyone's memory of me. I'm terrified to find out what he remembers.

But I never should have asked Rose to come. I'm not sure why I did.

Watching her break . . . I wanted to break too. I haven't done that in so long. Let everything out. From what I remember, it feels absolutely terrible in the moment but then . . . there's relief. There's feeling lighter. Feeling better. Is that how things are supposed to be? Are things supposed to get better with each passing year? Or is life just a slow descent into misery? Fast in my case, I guess.

It was so familiar, watching her sob into the forest floor. Like a recurring dream that you don't have for years and then one night, it grabs hold of you and you wake up with a familiar taste on your tongue. Except that is a dream I have—dreams of dirt graves and tall trees and people I love looking at me like I'm the worst thing to ever happen to them. And maybe I was. God, I hope I was the worst thing to happen to them. I hope I'm the worst thing to happen to Rose. I hope I'm the worst thing to happen to you. You all survived me, maybe a little rougher around the edges than you were before, but alive. Alive and ready to move on beyond me, without me.

I cried like that in a forest. Full body sobs, racking your body and carrying so much oxygen into your lungs you think you might either pass out or throw up. Rose didn't throw up, but I did. Moved just in time to not do it over Isaiah's grave.

I've never told anyone that before. That I broke down. Before I saw the Unusuals for the last time, I fell apart. I wonder now if some part of me, deep down, knew that I had already said goodbye *to them. That maybe that's why I didn't cry even one tear as I drove away from Los Angeles.*

I wanted to comfort her. Hug her. I can't remember the last time I hugged someone.

I don't want to be this person anymore. I told her that two months ago and I meant it then. I want to be someone else. I want to be someone who would have comforted Rose without hesitation. Who would have known exactly what to do, how to soothe her, what to say to make things better.

I want to be the person that would have known how to comfort you. How to take care of you. ~~How to love you~~.

I don't want to be me anymore. And maybe that's a choice I have.

LATER

I slept for a few hours before waking up from a nightmare of running through hallways, never finding an exit. I tiptoed downstairs to get water, grateful that the house was pretty much empty. Our parents were away for the long weekend, getting some much needed R&R for the both of them (probably one of the reasons I even considered joining Damien, the fear of my parents being away and something horrible happening to them while they were gone driving me to act without thinking), and Aaron had been fast asleep when I came home.

When I got downstairs, I discovered he wasn't asleep anymore. I didn't even make it to the kitchen, Aaron's voice from the living room stopping me in my tracks.

"Where the hell have you been?" he said, his voice quiet and unfeeling. A *very* bad sign. I decided not to pretend he didn't already know everything.

"Why don't you tell me?" I said.

"Rose," he started, clearly putting a lot of effort into keeping his voice calm, but the use of my actual name told me everything about his state of mind. "How could you be so stupid?"

"I had to try," I said, and that seemed to wake something in Aaron and he was up from the couch and pacing in the span of a blink.

"Look, I know that we've both been going through a lot with what's happening with Dad," he said frantically, "but breaking into the AM with a *known* criminal?! You really thought that was the best idea?"

"I don't see anyone trying anything else!" I shouted back, now that he'd broken the seal on the volume of our voices. "I had to try," I said again, and Aaron furiously shook his head.

"No, you—you wanted to do something reckless," he said. "The dreamworld has become too predictable for you, too boring, and you wanted to mix it up—"

"Oh come on, that's not fair—"

"It's completely fair!" he yelled. "That's all you've been doing the past six months. Just reckless thing after reckless thing—"

"I just—I wanted to be an active participant in my life!" I shouted, words Dr. Bright had said to me coming out of my mouth in an unconvincing parrot. "Isn't that what you all wanted? Isn't that what you and Mom and Dad have been pushing me to do for *months*?"

"Rose, you really think this is the best way to do that?" Aaron shouted back, his face lined with pain that made him look ten years older. "We meant—we meant for you to spend more time with Emily, bring her over for Shabbat, spend more time with *us*—"

"Because you've *so* clearly relished time with your little sister," I spat. "You know, I don't think it counts as really wanting quality time if you only want it when I'm in *crisis*."

"That's not fair." He took a step back, shaking his head.

"Oh, it isn't?" I continued, unable to stop the words pouring from my mouth, even though I could feel their sharp edges as they rose up my throat. "Sorry, could you remind me of all the times when you asked me to hang out because you wanted to spend time with me? When we really connected outside your *dreams*?"

"What are you—" He blinked. "I've *tried*, Rosie, but for the past few months—since the beginning of this year—you've just kept pushing me away! I'm sorry I wasn't there for you in high school. I'm sorry I was caught up in my own stupid bullshit all the time, but I'm *trying* now, and that has to be good for something."

"What exactly are you trying to do?" I asked. I wasn't trying to hurt him, to argue, I genuinely wanted to know, but I don't think I had any control over how my voice was rising and crashing against him and I saw him flinch.

"I'm trying to be your brother, Rosie." He sighed, his shoulders collapsing.

Aaron has always towered over me—him as tall and thin as I am short and stout, a visual representation of what opposites we are, even though we have the same unruly brown hair, the same dark brown eyes, the same pronounced eyebrows and strong hands, made slender and nimble by our respective passions. We're fun-house-mirror versions of each other, a bastardized set of twins. Always *one goddamn step* from clicking together completely.

"That's all I'm trying to do," he said. "And I'm sorry I've failed until now. But you need to meet me halfway."

"I *have* been meeting you halfway. Every time I've been in your dreams it's—" I choked around the words, tears gathering at the corners of my eyes. I turned around, putting my back to him and the living room and marching into the kitchen.

"Rosie, what are you—" I heard him say, feeling his lanky form following ten feet behind me.

"Right there," I said, pointing out the kitchen window into the dark yard. "You and me used to sit right out there and play pirates and help Dad with his little projects and we—we connected!"

"Yeah, we did!" he agreed. "But why—"

"I can go back there in the dreamworld!" I shouted. "I don't even participate, not always. Sometimes I just want to watch you and Dad, being together, laughing, and—"

A sob rose in my throat, making it hard to talk.

"I've been trying to connect, I *have*."

"That's not how to connect, Rosie," he said, softer than he had any right to be when we were supposed to be shouting at each other.

"Why *not*?" I yelled. "You get to read everyone's minds and you're telling me you don't use that to understand people better?"

"Clearly not!" he shouted, throwing up his hands. "Because you just said that I don't understand you and apparently I'm reading your mind all the time!"

He paced around, his arms waving like he was a frustrated, neglected marionette caught in a strong wind.

"I didn't say you were *good* at it," I snapped, that toxic feeling of being mean to someone I loved circling round and round in my chest, the strong and recognizable monster that I felt completely powerless to stop.

"For fuck's sake, Rosie." Aaron groaned, rubbing his eyes with the heel of his palms. It was so late. Early. The clock on the microwave glowed 5 a.m. I remember thinking that our parents were expected back in sevenish hours and in that moment, I wasn't sure if Aaron and I would still be standing there.

It's now a little after seven thirty in the morning. I've been lying in bed for an hour, willing myself to go to sleep. But I couldn't. Despite all the time I've spent sleeping in the past six months—the near perfection I achieved at falling asleep and waking myself up—it has been impossible this morning.

I was replaying every moment of the fight with Aaron in my head anyway, so I figured I should write it down.

"I just really don't understand you," he had said, shaking his head. "I don't understand how you could trust someone you barely know and help them *commit a crime*."

"Damien understands me," I argued and Aaron laughed darkly. "He does."

"Rose, he's a thirty-year-old man whose only friend seems to be a nineteen-year-old girl that he coerced into breaking into a government facility with him," Aaron said simply. "It doesn't matter if you feel understood by him, that's not real."

"He's twenty-nine," I rebutted, like that meant anything at all. I knew it was weird. I've known the whole time. I know that it's strange that Damien and I have been friends in the same way that I know I will never see him again.

That was when I started to cry again. Not just little tears, but another wave of enormous sobs. At that point, I'm not sure what I was even crying about. I thought I had cried about my dad, my life, in the woods, that I had gotten everything out, but there I was, sliding my back down the kitchen cabinets until I was sitting on the floor, because I just couldn't support my own body weight anymore.

"Rosie—" I heard Aaron whisper and then he was next to me on the floor, his long arms wrapped around me. I turned my face into his chest and cried into his sweatshirt, his hands rubbing my back like they would whenever I got sick when we were little. That just made me cry harder.

"I'm so sorry," he whispered into my ear. "I'm so sorry that things have been like this. But they're going to get better, I promise. I'm here now. I'm here now."

"There's nothing I can do," I sobbed. "There's nothing I can do for him and we're gonna lose him, Aaron. We're gonna lose him."

I felt Aaron take a shuddering breath in when I said that, and soon I could feel tears falling into my hair, Aaron's chin resting on the top of my head, as he held me close.

"I know," he cried. "I know. So please—I can't lose you too. Please."

He kept whispering and we both kept crying. It felt like a piece of me was coming back together while every single part of me was breaking apart.

"He's not . . . he's not a bad person," I said eventually, not wanting to talk more about our dad, instead focusing on defending my choices, like I needed to assure him that I was going to be okay. "He's got a lot of issues and he lied a lot to me, but I think he was lying a lot to himself too. I think he wants to try. I really do."

"That doesn't mean he's a safe person," Aaron said, still rubbing my back in strong, soothing strokes. "I mean, he clearly *isn't* a safe person. He put you in real danger, Rosie."

"I know." I nodded, swiping at my nose. "I know. And I'm not—I don't think I'm ever going to see him again."

Saying it out loud, letting those words ring in the kitchen, in the pale light of the morning that was just starting to bleed into the kitchen, sucking out the darkness, reminding me that I was human, that it was daytime, and that I was supposed to be awake soon, in the world, ready to be an active participant in my life, made the tears start all over again.

Aaron rubbed my back harder, shushing in time with the movement of his hand. Not in a patronizing way, not to get me to be quiet, but like he was trying to calm a spooked horse, like I was a wild, untamed thing that he had to treat with steady hands or I'd hurt him or myself. That made me cry harder.

"Rosie," he whispered. "You don't know that. You don't know that you'll never see him again. Maybe you will. It's gonna be okay."

"No, it's not that," I said after a moment, once I'd gotten just a tiny bit of my breath back. "I'm not crying because I'm going to *miss* him."

That wasn't entirely true. I think I *am* going to miss Damien. But I think Aaron knew that I was lying, just a little bit, to myself just as much as him, and he let it slide. That made me feel more understood and cared for than any of the physical affection or soothing words.

"It's—" I sobbed. "He's *alone*. He's so alone. And I know I won't see him again because I can't. He can't. If he's going to change, he has to move on completely."

"That doesn't seem healthy," Aaron said.

"Maybe it's not." I sniffed. "Maybe choosing to isolate himself and run away will mean that he'll never get better. Maybe it'll be just like before, like the people he loved before, when he was my age, that he can never go back to.

"*That's* what I'm scared of," I whispered. "He's left so much destruction in his path, hurt so many people so many times, and he doesn't seem to know how to stop and it all started when he was *my age*."

"I thought Damien's ability started when he was way younger," Aaron said, like that was the important thing.

"But the real trouble—all the really bad stuff he did, or, at least, the first round of really bad stuff, I guess—"

"Yeah, *really* not thrilled this is the person you've been spending most of your time with," he mumbled.

"That's when he was my age. And that's—that's—"

"That's not you, Rosie," Aaron said, finishing my sentence for me. "That's not you even one bit. From everything I know about him—"

"Everything you've read in my thoughts, you mean," I corrected.

"Can you just—" Aaron sighed. "Can we just agree to go easy on each other? At least for the rest of this conversation? Especially when it comes to our abilities. Because we've both fucked up. And we're going to *keep* fucking up. I mean, first off, we're human beings and we're you and me so . . . you know . . ."

"Fuckups."

"Right."

"You know that's not true, right?" I sat up, pulling myself out of the safety of his arms to look at him through my puffy eyes. "You're not a fuckup. Neither of us are."

He scoffed. Rude, but . . . fair.

"I mean, okay, yes, we are," I conceded. "But not because neither of us went to college or because we don't know what we're doing in our careers or because we both have failed to bring home a nice Jewish girl—"

That made him laugh and the sound was like the wind of shimmering light that ran through all the best dreams.

"But we're not fuckups at our abilities."

He raised an eyebrow.

"Okay, yes, *fine*." I groaned. "I've fucked up. So much. So, *so* much."

A sob started to rise in my throat and Aaron's arms tightened around me.

"No, you're right," he said solemnly. "There's a difference between making mistakes and being a bad person."

"And that's the difference between fucking up and being a fuckup?"

"I don't know. Maybe. We . . . we're learning," he added after a moment. "That's the important bit, I think. We just have to keep getting better. We have to try."

We have to try.

JUNE 2ND, 2017

My eyes feel so dry and puffy, my throat raw, from all the crying I've done lately, but finally, today, that outpouring of emotion led to something good.

Emily leaves for her summer internship next week and asked if she could see me before she went. I agreed immediately—we'd barely talked since texting about my dad when he was in the hospital and I couldn't tell if she had been giving me space out of respect for my need for family time, or if she was trying to avoid talking to me so she didn't have to do the hard part of ending things for good.

So when I met her in the Common today, I was sure that this was it—another nail in another coffin of my disastrous year. But, much to my surprise, she really just wanted to talk. To truly hash things out.

"I don't think I ever really got over the fact that you had looked into my head, seen all of those private pieces of me, and I had no idea," she explained.

"I know." I nodded. "And I'm so, *so* sorry. But I promise you, I would never do that again."

"That's not really what I'm worried about, Rose," she said. "I just . . ." She swallowed, looking out over the Common, and I could see a pinprick tear at the corner of her eye. "I'm not sure I even really know who you are, Rose."

It felt like a lance through the heart, even if I knew she was right.

"You *do* though—" I started weakly, but she shook her head.

"It's not like I expected to know *everything* about you right away, but . . ." She took another deep breath.

"I'm not sure it's possible to know a person completely," she continued after a moment. "And that's fine. That's life. And there are things that you don't know about me, things I'm not sure I'll ever share with anyone."

"I *want* you to share everything with me," I pleaded. "Everything you want to share."

"I know." She smiled softly and I couldn't tell if it was genuine or pitying. I hated that I couldn't read her expressions in that moment, like coming forward with my secret had pushed *her* into hiding somehow.

"But it's unrealistic to believe that we'll share *everything* with each other," she said. "Or even that we'll share all of the harder stuff right now. I mean, we've only known each other for eight months—"

"I know," I jumped in, "but I really, *really* like you. I don't care that it's only been eight months, the way I feel about you—"

"I know," she said, grabbing my hand and holding it in both of hers. "I know, I feel the same way."

"Then what are you trying to say?" I asked. "It sounds like you're . . ."

I didn't want to say it. Even though voicing it out loud wouldn't change the outcome, I didn't want to admit that I'd thought she was breaking up with me for good and I was *terrified* of that prospect.

"I'm . . ." She pulled away and I wanted so badly to reach my hand out and snatch hers back. But she was looking back over the park again, a clear signal that she needed thinking space.

"I don't really know what I'm trying to say." She sighed. "It's like . . . it's like if I had been dating you for eight months without knowing that you liked cooking."

"What do you mean?"

"I mean, cooking is pretty fundamental to who you are, right? It's your passion. It'd be like if this entire time I never mentioned poetry or fandom."

"Yeah," I said. "Yeah, I'd feel like I'd missed something huge."

"Exactly," she said. "I think I knew, on some level, that I was missing a big part of the picture. You were already hiding pieces of yourself, whether or not you meant to. I thought I could break through your shell, but I—I never expected *this*. I'm . . . I don't want you to feel like I'm freaked out because of what you can do . . ."

I could see her *wanting* to believe that, wanting to just take everything I'd told her in stride. But I let her off the hook.

"It's okay to be freaked," I told her. "I know it's . . . weird."

"It's *incredibly cool*," she said, a real Emily-grade smile blooming across her face for the first time in this entire conversation. "You have a *superpower*. You can go inside people's heads!"

"It doesn't creep you out?" I asked, even though I *definitely* didn't want an honest answer.

"It's . . . a lot," she admitted, being nicer to me than I think I deserved. "And I don't want you to—you can't use it to try and be the person you think I want. But it's still exciting. It's fantastic, it's—it's—it's—I mean, I wish *I* had an ability, but just knowing they exist . . . it's everything I've always dreamed of."

She winced.

"No pun intended."

There was a beat where we just looked at each other, wondering how the other was going to react, waiting for permission, and then Emily's mouth twitched at the corner and we both burst into laughter.

It felt so good. It felt like all the information I would ever need was in the melody of her joy and as long as I could harmonize, we would never need anything else.

But that didn't last. A relationship cannot be built on joy alone because life isn't like that. *I'm* not like that, and neither is Emily. She is more than her infectious laugh and bright, wide smile.

"I want you to know me," I breathed once we'd settled down. "I want to tell you all the hard stuff. I want to share all of it with you. I mean, just telling you—"

"I know." She nodded solemnly. "I know how big of a deal it must have been to tell me the truth. And this isn't just about you, I get that. But now that I know . . . it changes things."

"Does it have to?"

"Rose, it's one thing if you're sleeping through the day because of a medical condition, it's another if you're choosing to so that you can go into people's dreams."

"Yeah," I said quietly. "Yeah, I know. But I'm not doing that anymore. Not as much. And I'll never go into your dreams again. Not on purpose. I promise."

"It's not about that," she said. "Not really. It's that the person who is going to sleep so she can mold someone's dreams is a different person than the one I know."

"You're—you're right." I sighed, terrified at the admission. "It really *does* feel like I'm two different people sometimes—Dreamworld Rose and Real World Rose. And I don't know if it's always going to be like that or which person I want to be, but . . . you deserve to know who you're dating. That's, like, pretty baseline."

I tried to smile at her, let her know that I understood how much

I was asking of her—how much I had *been* asking of her—and she rewarded me with a small smile of her own.

"Look," she said, "I barely know who I am. I mean, we're technically still *teenagers*. We're not going to have it all figured out. But I want to try to get to know who you are now. Not every gory detail"—she smiled bigger and my heart lifted with the corners of her mouth—"but the truth of who you are. There's this enormous piece of your life that I knew nothing about and I . . . I *want* to know."

"You do?"

"Yeah." Her smile grew again and soon I was fully smiling back.

"Maybe we could start fresh?" I asked, feeling like I was reciting a line from one of the rom-coms that Emily loved. Her smile re-formed in a way that made me feel like that was exactly what she was thinking too.

"Yeah," she breathed. "I would like that."

She shuffled on the bench a bit, straightening up, squaring her shoulders, and clearing her throat. Then she stuck out her hand.

"Hi, I'm Emily Rodriguez, I'm a creative writing student, I spend all of my spare time writing about fictional characters kissing, I have two older sisters who I love but have always felt inferior to, and my greatest fear is that I'm going to live a life that is completely unremarkable."

She said it all in one breath, not looking at me, and I fell in love with her a little bit more.

I took her hand.

"I'm Rose Atkinson, aspiring chef." Her mouth twitched, but she lifted her eyebrow, like she was challenging me. I took a deep breath and dove in.

"I don't really know who I am," I said, the words catching in my throat. "Eight months ago I found out that I'm a little bit magic, which was much more of a surprise than it should have been, considering everyone in my family is a little bit magic. And I thought that it would make me closer to them, that I'd finally feel like I belong, but it's just made it harder to connect with anyone. So I've been going inside people's heads to try and understand who they are and I think I lost myself in the process."

I was gripping her hand tight in a handshake, my arm shaking either from effort or nerves. Emily adjusted her hand so she was just holding mine, and brought our joined hands down to her lap as I took a shuddering breath. When I first saw her in that urgent care, thinking that the hands on our non-injured arms were made for holding each other, I never would have expected that we'd end up here.

"And I'm worried it's too late," I said, one tear escaping from my eye and rolling down my cheek. "I'm afraid that if I don't figure out who I am right now, I'm going to lose you, I'm going to disappoint my mom, and I'm going to miss any chance I had at being friends with Aaron, which I think is maybe the only thing I've wanted for my whole life, even more than being a chef. I'm terrified that I'm going to lose my dad, a little bit, every single day, and never find myself, you know?"

"Yeah, I think I do." She nodded, the tears gathered in her eyes reflecting mine. "I don't know what it's like to lose someone that way, but all those fears . . . I *get* it. I'm so scared so much of the time. I'm scared I'm never going to be a good enough writer to make a living, but more than that I'm scared that my writing is never going to connect with anyone, that my family won't be proud of me. I worry that I'm going to be too focused on trying to have an extraordinary life that I'll miss out on all the beautiful, ordinary parts and it's even harder to focus on those things now because everything I thought I knew about how the world works kinda changed the other month when this magical girl told me that superpowers are real.

"I don't know who I am either," she whispered. "But I'm so afraid that there's really nothing remarkable about me at all and that there's nothing I can do to change that."

"You *are* remarkable," I said, and she scoffed. "No, I'm serious—I know that I've got this ability, but you—you're the most extraordinary person I've ever met. I didn't know that people like you—people who are kind and passionate and strong-willed and *good*—actually existed.

"You feel like a dream to me sometimes," I whispered, and Emily's eyes softened. "I wish I could show you exactly what I see when I look at you."

"I think I'd like to let you try," she said, squeezing my hand. "I'd like to see what you see."

I smiled, a giggle escaping through the remaining tears, and Emily laughed lightly back. Before I had a chance to think about it, I kissed her, quickly and just on the cheek. But it made her cheeks turn red, which made me feel warm and tingly. She laughed and blushed harder, burying her face in my shoulder.

So we sat there, her face turned into my neck, my arm around her shoulders, just enjoying each other's warmth. Enjoying the silence, now comfortable between us with so many secrets laid bare. I thought about how to let someone know you when you don't really know yourself. Maybe that's the point. Maybe no one knows who they are and we're all just trying to build the pieces of ourselves with the help of other people.

I don't know what the future holds for Emily and me. And I don't want to know. I don't want more cryptic hints from my mom, don't want to plan out the next year—five years, ten years—of our relationship. Or my life. I want to understand how Emily sees me. I want her to understand how I see her. And maybe we'll learn something about ourselves in the process.

community/TheUnusuals post by n/thatsahumanperson

Thanks to everyone who messaged me with their stories about That Place. Some of it was really harrowing to read but I heard from one of you that, at least in the division near me, things might be changing for the better. I really, really hope that's true.

And I think those of you who told me to stay away from inserting myself into that whole mess were right. I wasn't able to stop my sister, but she's okay, somehow, thankfully, against all odds. And I think . . . I think *we're* okay. But keeping things that way is going to take a lot of work. From both of us.

I feel like I've been doing the same thing with this community that she's been doing with her dreaming—using it as a personal diary, a place to come and dump all my thoughts and worries without actually sitting with them. And I don't think that's always a bad thing. You all have helped me so much since I got on here, and in this past year especially, and I think there's real usefulness in anonymous communities. I mean, it works for alcoholics and people addicted to drugs right? And that's basically what therapy is too, telling someone all your deepest, darkest secrets without the consequence of them being a person in your real life who might judge you. But all those things also encourage you to take what you learn *into* the real world, which is something this community has encouraged me to do and I just . . . I haven't been listening.

Because of the anonymity of this place, I've been pretending like I can say and do anything and there's no consequence. But there *has* been a consequence in that I'm not saying any of this stuff to the people who need to hear it. So I'm going to try to change.

Basically, the tldr is this: I think I'm going to be spending less time on here. I'm not leaving entirely—I really value this community and I'm happy to still be our resident web designer, but I can't let it be a substitute for in-life connection anymore. The connections I've made here, the support I've found, is as real as real life, and so important to me, but I need to find a balance. Human connection can exist outside of the internet and outside of people's thoughts. I think I forgot that for a while.

Stay strange, community/TheUnusuals. I'll see you around.

JUNE 16TH, 2017

Today is my twentieth birthday.

I decided to keep my feet firmly planted on the ground—no party, no big to-do. Emily was back in Arizona for the summer, with a promise that we'd make a point to talk every week. My parents were both working today, so I was going to make my own birthday cake. But as I was gathering together the ingredients, Aaron came into the kitchen, a determined look on his face.

"Come on," he said. "We're going for a drive."

Without thinking about it, I got into the car. We didn't speak, I didn't ask where we were going, just looked at the open road and all the lush, green trees that were in full summer bloom. Eventually, watching the roads pass, familiar landmarks entering the rearview, I realized where we were going.

There's a river, just outside of Boston, that we would go to when we were ki⬛⬛⬛⬛⬛⬛⬛⬛⬛⬛⬛⬛⬛⬛⬛⬛⬛⬛⬛⬛ we'd sit on
an old ⬛⬛⬛⬛⬛⬛⬛⬛⬛⬛⬛⬛⬛⬛⬛⬛⬛⬛⬛⬛⬛ whatever—
and pr⬛⬛⬛⬛⬛⬛⬛⬛⬛⬛⬛⬛⬛⬛⬛⬛⬛⬛⬛⬛t really, we
were j⬛⬛⬛⬛⬛⬛⬛⬛⬛⬛⬛⬛⬛⬛⬛⬛⬛⬛⬛water, and
enjoy ⬛⬛⬛⬛⬛⬛⬛⬛⬛⬛⬛⬛⬛⬛⬛⬛⬛⬛⬛⬛
Th⬛⬛⬛⬛⬛⬛⬛⬛⬛⬛⬛⬛⬛⬛⬛⬛⬛⬛⬛
"T⬛⬛⬛⬛⬛⬛⬛⬛⬛⬛⬛⬛⬛⬛⬛⬛⬛⬛:dge of the
bridge⬛⬛⬛⬛⬛⬛⬛⬛⬛⬛⬛⬛⬛⬛⬛⬛⬛⬛
"I ⬛⬛⬛⬛⬛⬛⬛⬛⬛⬛⬛⬛⬛⬛⬛⬛⬛⬛ick to grab
somet⬛⬛⬛⬛⬛⬛⬛⬛⬛⬛⬛⬛⬛⬛⬛⬛⬛a packet of
them.⬛⬛⬛⬛⬛⬛⬛⬛⬛⬛⬛⬛⬛⬛⬛⬛⬛
"Ye⬛⬛⬛⬛⬛⬛⬛⬛⬛⬛⬛⬛⬛⬛⬛⬛⬛
We⬛⬛⬛⬛⬛⬛⬛⬛⬛⬛⬛⬛⬛⬛⬛⬛⬛ing of what
he'd s⬛⬛⬛⬛⬛⬛⬛⬛⬛⬛⬛⬛⬛⬛⬛⬛t he'd read
my th⬛⬛⬛⬛⬛⬛⬛⬛⬛⬛⬛⬛⬛⬛⬛s onto him,
so not⬛⬛⬛⬛⬛⬛⬛⬛⬛⬛⬛⬛⬛⬛⬛at I had an
older ⬛⬛⬛⬛⬛⬛⬛⬛⬛⬛⬛⬛⬛

"Does it ever get lonely?" I asked. "Hearing people's thoughts but not having them hear yours?"

He didn't seem surprised by the question, but stopped to consider it for a moment, gnawing on a Twizzler stalk.

"Yeah, it does. But, I don't know, I guess I'm used to being lonely," he said. "Just being what we are—being Atypical—it's . . . it's kind of lonely."

"I know what you mean," I said. "I think that's why . . . I mean, I thought that the dreamworld was *it*, you know? I thought that that was what I was supposed to be doing. After all, why have this ability if I don't use it? Being this way has to have some, I don't know, some *meaning*."

"I don't think we have these abilities for any reason other than random genetic chance," he said, biting into another Twizzler.

"Yeah, I know, I know. But still—it felt like the right thing. It felt like that's where the answers were."

"I get that," he said. "I mean, I can read people's minds, I thought that was the answer to everything for a while."

"But doesn't it help you connect?" I asked. "I mean, despite the loneliness, surely it makes things make sense. Makes people make sense."

"Yeah, I guess sometimes it can," he said. "But people think a lot of stuff that they don't mean. That they don't believe. And people sure as hell *dream* that stuff. It's about your actions. At the end of the day, that's what matters."

"I guess."

"That's what makes you different from Damien, Rosie," he said, that faraway look on his face.

"Ugh." I groaned. "Stop reading my thoughts."

"Am I wrong?" he asked, turning his stare to me. "Isn't that what you're afraid of?"

"Yeah, can we not rehash the very intense heart-to-heart we had that night?" I asked.

"Of course." He chuckled. "Trust me, I don't exactly want to relive that either."

"Good." I took another bite of a Twizzler and sighed deeply.

"I'm scared of missing connections," I said. "Of missing my chance with someone."

"I thought you and Emily had worked everything out," he said and I sighed again.

"Yeah, we have. Or, at least, we're going to *keep* working everything out," I added, reminding myself that nothing was ever really complete, no relationship ever not in need of tending. My new therapist has been teaching me that.

"Then what is it?"

"What do you think?" I asked lightly, and Aaron nodded knowingly.

I don't think he even needed to read my thoughts to understand that I was talking about Dad. And I didn't need to go into his dreams to know that he felt the same. That we'd had our chances to really connect with our dad and we spent our teenage years being angsty and distant and then getting wrapped up in our own Atypical drama. And now the time was running out. We could do better now, but we'd never get back that time.

"Maybe it'll work, Rosie," Aaron said softly. "Maybe that Dr. Sharpe person will figure it out and we'll get more time with him."

"Yeah," I said. "Maybe."

We drove home with the windows down, the hot wind whipping through the car, chapping our faces, but feeling better for its realness than any breeze I could conjure in a dream.

JUNE 30TH, 2017

Tonight I dreamed of enormous trees. Their branches stretched over me, protecting me, their roots going deep into perfect, glistening, blue-green water. Salt and pine soaked my skin as I flew over the water, skimming the surface until I came to a clearing, every blade of grass perfect and green. I landed gently on a large tree root, flowers blossoming up from it, kissing me with their soft petals and sweet perfume.

I had been there before. This was a place that was familiar to me, deep in my bones familiar. Not because it was real, but because it belonged to someone who belonged to me.

"Rose!"

I turned around to see my mother looking at me in surprise, like she hadn't expected to find me here. Which . . . fair.

"Hey, Mom," I said, moving toward her. We hugged, something we'd only done in grief and fear in real life lately. But this was a hug of joy, of belonging. I can still feel it now, wrapping around me, an all-encompassing warmth.

"It's been a while since you've been here," she said, her smile brighter and freer than she's able to give in the real world.

She came to sit next to me on the tree root, the grass humming in perfect harmony under her bare feet as she walked.

"I . . . I haven't been in Dad's head at all," I told her, it being easier in here than anywhere else.

"Why not?" she asked, no judgment in her voice.

"It hasn't felt like the right time," I said. "I want to give him something nice, make sure he has good dreams, but I just . . . I wanted to fix it.

"I wanted to fix it so badly," I whispered, embarrassed. "And I couldn't."

"I know, sweetheart." My mom wrapped her arms around me, pulling me into her shoulder. I hugged her back, seeking answers in her arms.

"I'm not going to stop trying," I promised. "If there's a way to help him, I'm going to find it. And then I'm going to give him the best, most fantastical dreams I could ever make up."

"You can't wait, pumpkin," she whispered. "You can't wait for everything to be perfect to start."

She pulled back from me, putting her hands on my shoulders so she could look right at me.

"The future is just some faraway place, Rose," she said. "It's like this place."

Her eyes moved around, taking in her surroundings. I followed her gaze, trying to see my world—or *her* world, our world, whatever this shared dream was—through her eyes. The large, lush trees, with leaves as big as horses, branches that sparkled and bent of their own volition, reaching down to touch the ground like a kiss, the grass stretching up to meet them. Her mind, the landscape her subconscious conjured up as she slept, is rich and full and wonderfully imaginative. I could see colors I don't think exist in the real world, feel textures that are completely impossible to describe.

It was beautiful. So why'd she sound so sad when she spoke about it?

"It isn't *real*," she continued, answering my unvoiced question. "Just like the future, this place isn't real. The only importance it carries is what we give it."

I understood. But why wouldn't I want to live there, in that faraway place?

I asked her this, out loud this time.

"The dreamworld is Emerald City," I explained, all the conversations I'd had with Damien echoing in my head. "And life is the yellow brick road and I don't want to keep walking along that road, getting pelted with apples by cruel trees and running into dangerous witches when I could just be *there*."

"But remember what happened when they got to the Emerald City?" she asked.

"They got a dope makeover."

My mom laughed, the sound turning into pure music in the air, the melody winding its way into the roots of the great trees.

"Well, yes, that's true." She chuckled. "But they also found out the wizard was a fraud. It's all just a mirage in the distance that evaporates into smoke when you reach it, only to re-form even further down the line. The only thing that's real is the road beneath you."

She touched my cheek, like that simple gesture would keep me grounded, keep my feet firmly rooted on the path instead of racing toward a horizon I could never reach. I put my hand up to cover hers and then we, and the world around us, evaporated into smoke itself, just like that far-off, glittering city.

She didn't remember saying any of that to me, I don't think. When I asked her how she slept, my mom just kissed me on the cheek and said that she'd had the most wonderful dream.

"I don't remember a single thing," she said, "but I know it was peaceful." But she gave me a look like she knew that I had been part of that peace somehow. That we shared it. And that was enough.

July 2nd, 2017

Dear Mark,

It's been exactly a year since we met. Since I stood by your bed, waiting for you to wake up, waiting for my life to start, even though I didn't realize that at the time. I barely knew why I had agreed to help your sister—for some vague promise that she would find someone like me, a vague promise of a distant future where I'd be understood.

I lied to you before. In one of the letters you'll never read, I lied. I guess that means I was lying to myself, if I'm the only one reading them. I think I've been lying to myself for a really, really long time. About . . . well, about a lot of things.

But I lied to you. I said I didn't have anything to say when Sam accused me of being in love with you.

I didn't say anything to her. That much is true. But I did have something to say.

I was.

I am. Still.

In love with you, I mean.

I think that's what this feeling is. I barely know anything anymore—I don't know what feelings are real, what wants are worth giving space to, what parts of myself I should hate. Is it all of me? I think maybe I'm supposed to hate all of me.

But I don't hate you. That's the one thing I do know. What I feel for you, whatever it is, it's a physical ache. Sometimes when I'm on the road at night, the white lines flashing by in the glow of my headlights, hypnotizing me, I feel you in the seat next to me. If I keep looking straight ahead, if I ignore the empty shotgun seat in my periphery, I can imagine you fiddling with the radio dial, trying to find a good station as we go from nowhere to nowhere.

I would drive through a thousand nowheres, would never take my foot off the gas, if it meant keeping you next to me. I would tell you everything about me, answer all those questions you had that I was too scared to answer, reveal every mortifying detail of the childhood you were so curious about just to make you laugh, *remove every stitch that's sewn me up so you could look at the insides of all my scars and warm me with your pity.*

Loving you feels like drowning. God, how I love you.

And I think it's okay that you'll never know. I think I finally understand now, what it means to love someone, all the different ways you can love them. It isn't about me. It's about you. And you've made it very clear to me that I'm not what you want. And that's okay. It has to be okay. Loving you on my own has to be enough.

I want only wonderful things for you, Mark. And I'm sorry that couldn't be me.

I wish that could have been me.

JULY 3RD, 2017

I woke up with the sun this morning for no reason that I could explain.

I tiptoed down the stairs, careful not to wake anyone, the house still filled with a beautiful, heavy hush. I started to make myself a cup of tea, planning on standing at the window with my hands wrapped around the warm mug, and just enjoying the silence, when my phone buzzed.

It was a text from an unknown number, one I'd never received a text from before, but I knew immediately who it was.

Play him music that he loves, the text read. It'll help him remember.

My heart clenched when I read it, both at the idea that Damien had bothered to transfer my phone number to a new phone and was thinking about me enough to text me, and at what the text was telling me. Suddenly, I wanted so badly to sleep, to dreamdive into my dad's head, bring him music.

So I did.

There was fog at first. Deep and gray and heavier than before. But I was stronger now, I knew what to do, so I puffed up my chest and blew it all away. And then it was the canyon again, soaked in color and impossibly huge. My dad sat on the edge, looking out over the expanse, watching the clouds go by. I walked over to him, a Jim Croce song coming up from the ground with every footstep. Like with my mom, my dad seemed to know instantly that I was there. He looked up, smiling at me and humming along to the song.

"Rose!" he said, his smile enormous, as I crouched down to join him at the edge. "What are you doing here?"

"I just wanted to say hello," I said, smiling back.

"I was wondering when I was going to get a visit from you," he said jovially.

"What do you mean?"

"Your mom said she thinks she got a visit from you the other night," he explained. "I've never seen her look so at peace after waking up."

"See?" I said lightly. "Dreamdiving can be a beautiful thing."

"I never doubted that," he said. It was an old argument at this point, but the way we were having it here didn't feel dangerous or heated. We were just talking, with no consequence, enjoying the feeling of being here.

"Are you saying goodbye?" he asked eventually, after the color of the canyon had turned from pink to orange.

"What?" A momentary spike of panic brought a shadow over the world, and it was like my dad's subconscious self knew a panicked Rose meant panicked dreams because he instantly put his hand over mine and starting hushing me soothingly, like I was a little kid.

"No, no, not like that," he said softly. "I just meant . . . it seems like maybe you're not going to be diving into our heads quite as much."

"Oh." I breathed, relief filling me up. "Yeah, I guess so."

I hadn't thought about it, hadn't thought about my visit into my mom's dream the other night as some kind of goodbye tour, but he was right, I didn't want to be in their dreams anymore. I wanted to give them space. I told him as much.

"But I'm still going to dreamdive," I went on. "I'll just . . . create my own worlds. It's not quite as fun, but . . ."

"No, I understand." He nodded. "And I also understand why you want to spend so much time here. It's extraordinary."

We sat there, taking in the unimaginable world that we, somehow, had imagined. The canyon was deep without limits, light and shadow playing over it in mesmerizing shapes and movements, but it never gave me the feeling of being too deep. I was never worried I would fall into the abyss. Instead, looking out over it felt like understanding the beauty and simplicity of infinity.

"Maybe it's like this," he said.

"What?" I asked, my voice barely a sound on the breeze. But I knew he'd hear me all the same. This was our world, our rules.

The most perfect cloud floated above our heads.

"What comes after," he said, serenely staring at the cloud as it gently skated by.

The word "after" hung between us like a physical thing. And then it *was* a physical thing. The light in the air came together to form the word, shimmering and so much less threatening in appearance than in concept.

"I think that'd be nice," I said finally.

I don't know that I believe that completely. As enticing and mesmerizing and *beautiful* as the dreamworld can be, I'm stable enough now to admit how genuinely terrifying the unpredictability is. Even though I'm almost always aware I'm dreaming, almost always in control, there's something huge and yawning at the center of every person's dreaming landscape. The entirety of their existence, bottomless, lightless, unreachable to them and even to me. I didn't like to think of staring into that expanse forever.

"Rose?"

I turned to look at my dad. He looked younger, younger than even a few moments ago. Vibrant and full of life, his dimples deep, his eyes bright.

"Don't go," I whispered. Tears swelled at the corners of my eyes, as wet and real as they are in my waking life.

I'd never cried in a dream before. I'd had the feeling, but tears never came, not until now.

"I'll stay as long as I can. But let's just focus on right now. Let's wake up and make blueberry pancakes."

"But you won't remember this," I said, the tears starting to roll gently down my cheeks. "It'll just be like any other morning."

"No morning with you is ever like any other morning."

"What if we just stay in here," I said. "I can make us pancakes. I can make us *anything*."

As soon as the words were out of my mouth, a stack of pancakes, impossibly buoyant and fluffy, materialized next to my dad's elbow, nudging him gently.

"We can't." He gave me a sad smile. "You know we can't."

"Let me give you this. *Please*."

"But you were right, Rose. I won't remember this, not really. I'll wake up happy, but I won't know why." He smiled again, but this time it was just a practiced movement of his mouth, no warmth or feeling behind it.

"There are already so many things I'm not going to remember," he whispered, almost like he didn't want to say it out loud. Not to me. "I don't want to add too much to the list."

I wonder now if maybe it was easier for him to say that, to let me know that he's afraid, knowing that he wouldn't have to face me in the morning with the knowledge that he broke down in front of his daughter, just a little. Part of me thinks that I should ask him about it in the waking world, let him know that it's okay, that he can lean on me, that he doesn't have to pretend he's okay just because he's the parent. But maybe he *wants* to be the parent. To move forward as normally as possible. To pretend that nothing's changed.

But everything's changed.

"I'm sorry," I sobbed, the words barely getting out, my tears being carried away by the wind of light.

"Don't be sorry," he said, wiping my cheek with his thumb. "Just promise me you won't dream your life away."

"I promise."

We sat there for what felt like a few seconds, a few hours, a few lifetimes, his big, warm hand holding my face, tears gathering in his eyes, reflecting mine. The breeze swept over us, that impossible mix of cool air and warm light, somehow given shape and weight. No matter what my dad said, I wanted to stay in that moment forever, sheltered by his dreamworld and the frozen-time feeling I always have when dreamdiving, even if there's some conscious part of me aware of the fact that time *is* passing, rapidly, as I sleep.

After either another thousand lifetimes or instantly, my dad broke the silence.

"Promise me one more thing."

"Anything."

"Make your homemade orange butter for the pancakes?"

And I did. He ate every last bite.

July 3rd, 2017

Dear Rose,

I know you might not want to get a letter from me, seeing as I put you in danger just to get a file and some dumb letters I wrote that I have no intention of ever sending. But I think I might send this one. So, if you are reading this, I'm sorry. I'm sorry for putting you in danger and I'm sorry for not saying any of this in person.

I sent you a text just now. Though you wouldn't know it, I spent a lot of time crafting that text, wrote whole paragraphs out, deleted them, wrote more, deleted, and so on. I don't think I'm really suited for that style of communication, even though it was a lot easier with you. Though I guess there's an argument to be made (and some definitely would) that I'm not suited for <u>any</u> kind of communication.

I saw that you and Emily are working things out. Confession time: I read your girlfriend's blog. Oh yeah, your girlfriend has a blog—did you know that? I think I'm probably more tech savvy than you, which isn't saying much, because you have to be the least tech literate Gen Z-er I've ever met, but it surprises most people that I know what I'm doing. I guess my wardrobe is pretty "Mr. Robot" as you called it, but for some reason, people never assume that I spend much time on computers. But I'm actually pretty well-versed in the more hidden corners of the internet.

Just ask your brother who theneonthorn is. That's my last little surprise for you. The last bit of truth that no one knows.

I'm really happy for you. Genuinely. That's a new feeling for me, but I think it's one I could get used to.

I thought I knew your story, Rose. I thought I knew mine. But we only ever know pieces of people's stories and it can take years—a whole lifetime—to get the full thing.

I don't have a whole lifetime. You do. Don't dream it away.

But I think I might have a second act in me yet.

Love,

~~Robert Damien~~

Your Tin Man

ACKNOWLEDGMENTS

It's hard to know where to begin. My journey with the Atypical world started seven years ago with the tiniest seed of an idea born out of needing to put my own loneliness into words. I never could have expected that idea to bloom into three podcasts, three books, and, most important, an enormous, loving community of collaborators, listeners, and readers. I have so many people to thank for loving this world, for lifting it and me up, for making me less lonely. I'm going to do my best to thank as many of those people as I can here.

Firstly, to the incredible team at Tor Teen. To Devi Pillai, Fritz Foy, and Tom Doherty, for taking a chance on me and these books; to Isa Caban, Eileen Lawrence, Saraciea Fennell, Sarah Reidy, Lucille Rettino, and Anthony Parisi for coming up with the most inventive ways to find readers for this series, for putting on the best debut book tour I could have ever asked for, and for making me feel just as excited and celebrated when I was releasing my second book from a quarantined apartment; to Melanie Sanders, Steven Bucsok, and Kristin Temple for taking this story from a patchwork manuscript to a real and lovely book; to Victo Ngai, Sachin Teng, and Esther Kim for bringing my characters to vibrant life with the stunning covers that I get to look at each and every day.

To Ali Fisher, my brilliant editor who deserves an entire book of acknowledgments. I'll never be able to express the depth of my gratitude for you and your brain. You make me a better writer with each and every note, make me smile with the reactions and Easter eggs you leave in copyedits, and always lead me to be more thoughtful about the stories and messages I'm putting out into the world. You have an Atypical ability all your own, and that's the power to bring out the best in writers, to make them love their stories more, to challenge them with care and kindness, helping them grow. I feel absurdly lucky to have an editor who understands me, who knows what I'm trying to say better than I do, who will celebrate with me when my ships go canon and put *Hannibal* quotes in her notes. From the bottom of my heart, thank you.

To Matthew Elbonk, who knew there was a book in me before I was brave enough to voice the desire to write one. I'll never forget our first phone call—talking for an hour because we instantly connected, immediately resonating with the same kinds of stories. From putting the proposal for this trilogy together to helping me with my least favorite part (coming up with a title) to helping me navigate the wide world of publishing, it is the understatement of the century to say that I couldn't have done this without you. You're the best agent in the world, and I'm going to keep sending you my gay cowboy stories.

To my sensitivity readers, Ariane Resnick, Jon Reyes, and Melissa Vera—thank you so much for your thoughtfulness and perspective, and for helping me bring this set of characters to authentic life.

Writing Rose's—and Emily's and Aaron's and Damien's—story was a process of discovery unlike any other I've experienced. The things I learned about this story, these characters, myself, would not have happened without the music I listened to while building the dreamworld. So thank you to Animal Collective, Lady Gaga, Matt Duke, and Jónsi for the perfect music to get me into a dream-writing trance, and to Halsey, Julia Michaels, Ira Wolf, Sasha Sloan, Billie Eilish, FINNEAS, JP Saxe, and SYML for helping me find the dimensions of Rose and Damien's relationship.

The Atypicals wouldn't be what they are today without the amazing original cast and team that helped me bring them to life in the podcast: Julia Morizawa, Briggon Snow, Anna Lore, Charlie Ian, Alex Gallner, Ian McQuown, Andrew Nowak, Alex Marshall-Brown, Phillip Jordan, Alanna Fox, Mischa Stanton, and Evan Cunningham. Beyond being such wonderful collaborators, you've all become very dear friends, and that is the thing I am *most* grateful for.

To all of my friends. My Menaces, my New Year's Crew, FTH, all the amazing people I've met through podcasting and publishing who I've bonded with over drinks, brunches, convention tables, livestreams, video games, and one another's shows and books—thank you for inspiring me, for comforting me, for laughing with me. My world is infinitely better because you exist in it.

To my wacky and wonderful family, who are nothing at all like the Atkinsons, but superpowered in their own way: I wouldn't be who I am without you. Mom, Dad, Betsy, Don, my little OWL and

EAL—like Emily, all I've ever wanted is to be someone you can be proud of.

To B, for being the best partner I could ever ask for, like someone I dreamed up. The best thing that writing these stories ever brought me was you.

These books have been the realization of my oldest and most precious dream. I never expected to be a published author, never expected to be fortunate enough to connect with people through words I wrote. To all of you who have picked up a book, who have listened to the podcast, who have recommended either to a friend, who have written me about what the stories mean to you: thank you, thank you, thank you. From the folks who found this story in the earliest days to the newest pals screaming with me about Stucky on our Discord server, you have all enriched my life beyond measure.

We're all dreamdivers together, building a world in our imaginations that we share and morph however we choose. Thank you for your imaginations. Thank you for loving mine. While my time in the world of Atypicals is coming to a close, I'm not done telling stories, and I hope you're not done hearing them. I hope our shared imagination will always be a place we can all belong together.

Thank you. Stay strange.